THE MIDNIGHT LOCK

Also by Jeffery Deaver

NOVELS

The Colter Shaw Series

The Final Twist
The Goodbye Man
The Never Game

The Lincoln Rhyme Series

The Cutting Edge
The Burial Hour
The Steel Kiss
The Skin Collector
The Kill Room
The Burning Wire
The Broken Window
The Cold Moon
The Twelfth Card
The Vanished Man
The Stone Monkey
The Empty Chair
The Coffin Dancer
The Bone Collector

The Kathryn Dance Series

Solitude Creek
XO
Roadside Crosses
The Sleeping Doll

The Rune Series

Hard News
Death of a Blue Movie Star
Manhattan Is My Beat

The John Pellam Series

Hell's Kitchen
Bloody River Blues
Shallow Graves

STAND-ALONES

The October List
No Rest for the Dead (Contributor)
Carte Blanche (A James Bond Novel)
Watchlist (Contributor)
Edge
The Bodies Left Behind
Garden of Beasts
The Blue Nowhere
Speaking in Tongues
The Devil's Teardrop
A Maiden's Grave
Praying for Sleep
The Lesson of Her Death
Mistress of Justice

SHORT FICTION

Collections

Trouble in Mind
More Twisted
Twisted

Anthologies

Nothing Good Happens After Midnight (Editor and Contributor)
A Hot and Sultry Night for Crime (Editor and Contributor)
Ice Cold (Editor and Contributor)
Books to Die For (Contributor)
The Best American Mystery Stories 2009 (Editor)

Stories

A Perfect Plan
Cause of Death
Forgotten
Turning Point
Verona
The Debriefing
The Second Hostage
Ninth and Nowhere
Captivated
The Victims' Club
Surprise Ending
Double Cross
The Deliveryman
A Textbook Case

Original Audio Works

The Intruder
Stay Tuned
Date Night
The Starling Project

THE MIDNIGHT LOCK

A LINCOLN RHYME NOVEL

JEFFERY DEAVER

G. P. Putnam's Sons
NEW YORK

PUTNAM
— EST. 1838 —

G. P. Putnam's Sons
Publishers Since 1838
An imprint of Penguin Random House LLC
penguinrandomhouse.com

Library of Congress Cataloging-in-Publication Data

Names: Deaver, Jeffery, author.
Title: The midnight lock / Jeffery Deaver.
Description: New York: G.P. Putnam's Sons, [2021] |
Series: A Lincoln Rhyme novel; 16 |
Identifiers: LCCN 2021036488 (print) | LCCN 2021036489 (ebook) |
ISBN 9780525536000 (hardcover) | ISBN 9780593332627 (export) |
ISBN 9780525536024 (ebook)
Subjects: LCGFT: Novels.
Classification: LCC PS3554.E1755 M53 2021 (print) |
LCC PS3554.E1755 (ebook) | DDC 813/.54—dc23
LC record available at https://lccn.loc.gov/2021036488
LC ebook record available at https://lccn.loc.gov/2021036489

Printed in Canada
1   3   5   7   9   10   8   6   4   2

FRI

Book design by Tiffany Estreicher

For Andrew, Wendy and Victoria

There can be no higher law in journalism than
to tell the truth and to shame the devil.
WALTER LIPPMANN

PART ONE

CYLINDRICAL KEY

[MAY 26, 8 A.M.]

1

Something wasn't right.

Annabelle Talese, though, couldn't quite figure out what that might be.

One aspect of this concern, or disorientation, or mystery, could be explained by the presence of a hangover, though a minor one. She called them "hangunders"—maybe one and a half glasses of sauvignon blanc too many. She'd been out with Trish and Gab at Tito's, which had to be one of the strangest of all restaurants on the Upper West Side of Manhattan: a fusion of Serbian and Tex-Mex. Fried cheese with beans and salsa was a specialty.

Big wine pours too.

As she lay on her side, she brushed the tickling, thick blond hair away from her eyes and wondered: What's wrong with this picture?

Well, for one thing, the window was open a few inches; a May breeze, thick with the gassy-asphalt scent of Manhattan, eased in. She rarely opened it. Why had she done so last night?

The twenty-seven-year-old, who had dabbled at modeling and

was now content behind the scenes of the fashion world, rolled up-right and tugged her *Hamilton* T-shirt down, twisted it straight. Adjusted her silk boxers.

She swung her feet over the edge of the bed, feeling for her slippers.

They weren't where she'd kicked them off last night before climbing under the blankets.

All right. What's going on?

Talese had no phobias or OCD issues, except one: New York City streets. She couldn't help but picture the carpet of germs and other unmentionable critters that populated the city's asphalt—and which got tracked into her apartment, even when, as she did every day, she stowed her shoes in a carton by the door (and insisted her friends do the same).

She *never* went barefoot in the apartment.

Instead of the slippers, though, the dress she'd worn yesterday, a frilly, floral number, lay spread out beneath her dangling feet.

The front hem was drawn up, almost to the décolletage, as if the garment were flashing her.

Wait a minute . . . Talese had a memory—more hazy than distinct—of tossing the garment into the hamper before her night-time routine.

Talese qualified her narrative now. The slippers weren't where she *thought* she'd left them. The dress wasn't in the hamper where she *thought* she'd tossed it.

Maybe Draco, the bartender, always a flirt, had been a little more generous than usual.

Was the drink count, possibly, 2.5 on the scale?

Careful, girl. You need to watch that.

As always, upon waking, the phone.

She turned toward the bedside table.

It wasn't there.

No landline for her, her mobile was her only link at night. She always kept it near and charged. The umbilical, attached to the wall plug, was present, but no phone.

Jesus . . . What's going on?

Then she saw the slippers. The pink fuzzy things were across the room, each on either side of, and facing, a small wooden chair. It had been scooted closer to the bed than she normally kept it. The slippers were facing the chair in a way that was almost eerily obscene—as if they'd been worn by somebody whose legs were spread and who was sitting on a lap.

"No," Talese gasped, now spotting what was on the floor beside the chair: a plate with a half-eaten cookie on it.

Her heart thrummed fast; her breath grew shallow. Somebody'd been in the apartment last night! They'd rearranged her clothes, eaten the cookie.

Not six feet away from her!

The phone, the phone . . . where's the goddamn phone?

Talese reached for the dress on the floor.

Then froze. Don't! He—she figured the intruder would have been male—had touched it.

My God . . . She ran to her closet and pulled on jeans and an NYU sweatshirt, then stepped into the first pair of sneakers she found.

Out! Get out now! The neighbors, the police . . .

Fighting back tears from fright, she started out of the bedroom, then noticed that one of her dresser drawers was partially open. It was where she kept her underwear. She'd noted something boldly colorful inside.

She approached slowly, pulled it fully open and looked down. She gasped and finally the tears broke free.

On top of her panties was a page from a newspaper. It wasn't one she read, so he would have brought it with him. Written on it, in lipstick—the shade that she favored, Fierce Pink—were three words:

RECKONING.
—THE LOCKSMITH

Annabelle Talese turned to sprint to the front door. She got about ten feet before she stopped fast.

She'd noticed three things:

One was that the butcher block knife holder, sitting on the island in the small kitchen, had a blank slot, the upper right-hand corner, where the largest blade had rested.

The second was that the closet in the hallway that led to the front door was open. Talese always kept it closed. There was an automated switch in the frame so that when you opened the door, the bulb inside went on. The closet now, however, was dark. She would have to walk past it to get to the front door.

The third thing was that the two deadbolts on the door were turned to the locked position.

Which meant—since the man who'd broken inside had no keys— he was still here.

2

The defense attorney, approaching the empty witness stand, beside which Lincoln Rhyme sat in his motorized wheelchair, said: "Mr. Rhyme, I'll remind you that you're still under oath."

Rhyme frowned and looked over the solidly built, black-haired lawyer, whose last name was Coughlin. Rhyme affected a pensive expression. "I wasn't aware that something might have happened to damage the oath."

Did the judge offer a faint smile? Rhyme couldn't see clearly. He was on the main floor of the courtroom, and the judge was considerably above and largely behind him.

The testimonial oath in court had always struck Rhyme as an unnecessary mouthful, even with the "so help you God" snipped off.

Do you solemnly swear to tell the truth, the whole truth and nothing but the truth?

Why did swearing have to be solemn? And once one affirmed the first "truth," was there any point to the overkill? How about: "Do you swear you won't lie? If you do, we'll arrest you."

More efficient.

He now relented. "I acknowledge that I'm under oath."

The trial was being conducted in New York Supreme Court—which, despite the name, was in fact a lower-level court in the state. The room was wood paneled and scuffed, the walls hung with pictures of jurists from over the years, going back, it seemed, to the days of Reconstruction. The proceeding itself, however, was pure twenty-first century. On the prosecution and defense tables were computers and tablets—the judge had a slim high-def monitor too. There was not a single law book in the room.

Present were thirty or so spectators, most here to see the infamous defendant, though perhaps a few hoping to see Rhyme.

Coughlin, whose age Rhyme figured to be about fifty, said, "I'll get to the substance of my cross-examination." He flipped through notes. Maybe there were no books, but Rhyme noted easily a hundred pounds of foolscap between the defense and the prosecution tables.

"Thank you, sir," said the judge.

Being a criminalist, a forensic scientist aiding in criminal investigation, is only partly about the laboratory; the other aspect of the job is performing. The prosecutor needs an expert witness to present findings in an articulate way and to patiently and effectively parry the defense counsel's assault on your conclusions. On redirect, a good prosecutor can sometimes rehabilitate a witness battered by the defense, but it's best not to get into hard straits in the first place. Lincoln Rhyme was reclusive by nature, and loved his time in a laboratory above all, but he was not entirely introverted. Who doesn't enjoy a little grandstanding before the jury, and sparring with the defendant's attorney?

"You testified on direct that no fingerprints of my client were left at the crime scene where Leon Murphy was murdered, correct?"

"No, I did not."

Coughlin frowned, looking at a yellow pad that might have contained perceptive notes or might have contained doodles or a recipe for beef brisket. Rhyme happened to be hungry. It was ten a.m. and he'd missed breakfast.

Coughlin glanced at his client. Viktor Antony Buryak, fifty-two. Dark-haired like his mouthpiece but bulkier, with Slavic features and pale skin. He wore a tailored charcoal gray suit and a burgundy vest. Buryak's face was oddly unthreatening. Rhyme could picture him serving up pancakes at a church basement fundraiser and remembering every parent by name and giving the kids an extra splash of syrup.

"Do you want me to read you back your testimony?" Coughlin, who'd been hovering close to Rhyme, like a shark near chum, lifted a palm.

"No need. I remember it. I stated—under oath, I'll just reassure you—that of the fingerprints collected at the scene of Leon Murphy's murder, none could be identified as your client's."

"What exactly is the difference?"

"You said I testified that your client *left* no fingerprints at the scene. He might very well have left a million of them. The evidence collection team simply didn't recover any."

Coughlin rolled his eyes. "Move to strike."

Judge Williams told the jury, "You'll disregard Mr. Rhyme's response. But try again, Mr. Coughlin."

Looking put out, Coughlin said, "Mr. Rhyme, no fingerprints of my client were *discovered* at the crime scene where the convicted felon Leon Murphy was shot, correct?"

"I can't answer because I can't speak to whether the victim was a convicted felon or not."

Coughlin sighed.

The judge stirred.

Rhyme said, "I agree with your 'were discovered' part of that sentence."

Coughlin and Buryak shared a look. The client was taking this better than his attorney. The lawyer returned to his table and glanced down.

Rhyme regarded the jury and found more than a few looking his way. They'd be curious about his condition. Some defense attorneys, he'd heard, privately complained about his presence, given that he was a quadriplegic, testifying from a wheelchair—which, they believed, generated sympathy for the prosecution.

But what could he do? Wheelchair bound he was. Criminalist he was.

Rhyme's eyes circled to the defendant. Buryak was a unique figure in the history of organized crime in the region. He owned a number of businesses in the city, but that wasn't how he made most of his money. He offered a unique service in the underworld, one that had probably cost more lives than any other organized crime outfit in New York's exceedingly criminal history.

The *People of the State of New York v. Viktor Buryak*, however, had nothing to do with that. This was about a single incident, a single crime, a single murder.

Leon Murphy had been shot to death a week or so after a meeting with the manager of a warehouse that Buryak owned. Murphy was a psychotic wannabe gangbanger who fancied himself a descendant of the Westies, the brutal Irish gang that had once ruled Hell's Kitchen in Manhattan. Murphy had made a sales pitch offering protection to the warehouse manager.

A very bad business idea, selling that particular product to that particular consumer.

Coughlin asked, "Did you find footprints near Leon Murphy's body? Or near where the bullet casing was found?"

"Near the body, the field was grassy, no footprints could be ascertained. Near the bullet casing, the evidence collection technicians found footprints but because of a recent rain it was impossible to determine the type of shoe."

"So you can't testify that my client's footprints were found at the scene of the crime?"

"Don't you think that can be inferred from my prior comment?" Rhyme asked acerbically. He'd learned that nobody cares about badgering attorneys. That's what they're paid for.

"Mr. Rhyme, does the NYPD forensics unit routinely collect DNA at crime scenes?"

"Yes."

"And did you discover any of my client's DNA at the scene where Leon Murphy was killed?"

"No."

"Mr. Rhyme, you analyzed the bullet that killed Mr. Murphy, correct? That is, the lead slug?"

"Yes."

"And you analyzed the shell casing too?"

"That's correct."

"And, once more, what caliber was that?"

"Nine-millimeter parabellum."

"And you testified that the lands and grooves, that is the rifling of the barrel, suggest that the gun was a Glock seventeen."

"A Glock definitely, a model seventeen most likely."

"Mr. Rhyme, did you or any investigators you were working with check firearms records in any state or federal databases with regard to my client?"

"Yes."

"And does or did he own a Glock, specifically a model seventeen?"

"I have no idea."

"Explain, Mr. Rhyme."

"He might own a dozen."

"Your Honor," said Coughlin. He sounded slightly wounded that Rhyme was treating him so unfairly.

Was Viktor Buryak on the verge of smiling?

"Mr. Rhyme." The judge was growing weary.

"He asked if he owned a Glock, and I testified that I have no idea. Which I don't. I can testify that the record shows that, in New York State, he owns no *legally* registered Glocks."

ADA Sellars said, "Your Honor, the defense is straying from Captain Rhyme's contribution to the case, which is not firearms purchase records. It relates solely to his expertise in physical evidence."

Coughlin said, "Let me lay this foundation, Your Honor. It will be clear in a moment where I'm going."

Rhyme looked at his keen eyes and wondered what that destination might be.

"Proceed . . . for the moment."

"Mr. Rhyme, to recap, could you confirm that my client's DNA was not found at either the site of the body or site of the shell casing?"

"Correct."

"Or *on* the body or shell casing."

"That's true."

"And his footprints and fingerprints were not found at either place?"

"Correct."

"And no fibers or hairs that could be traced to him were found there?"

"Correct."

"And state and federal records do not indicate that he owns or owned a Glock semiautomatic pistol?"

"Correct."

"In fact the only forensic connection between the murder of Leon Murphy and my client is a few grains of sand on the ground where the victim was found."

"Six," Rhyme countered. "More than a few."

Coughlin smiled—it was directed at the jury. "*Six* grains of sand."

"Please explain again how that sand connects my client to the murder."

"The sand was unusual in composition. It was made up of calcium sulfate dihydrate, with silicon dioxide, along with the presence of another substance, $C_{12}H_{24}$, about three quarters saturated hydrocarbons and one quarter aromatic hydrocarbons."

"About that other substance, as you call it. Could you translate for us, please?"

"It's a particular grade of diesel fuel."

"But why does this connect my client to the scene?"

"Because samples were taken from the street in front of his driveway in Forest Hills, Queens, and similar sand was found there. Control samples taken from where the body was found revealed no such sand."

"Did the sand taken from my client's home match that at the scene where Leon Murphy was murdered?"

Rhyme hesitated. "The word 'match' in forensic science means identical. Fingerprints match. DNA matches. There are some chemical mixtures that are so complex that they could be said to match.

In forensics, barring those situations, we use the word 'associated.' You could also say very, very similar to."

Coughlin repeated, "'Very, very . . .' I see. So then you can't testify that the grains of sand at my client's home matched the grains of sand at the crime scene."

"I just said—"

The attorney snapped, "Can you say the grains of sand from my client's house *matched* the six grains of sand discovered at the crime scene?"

After a long moment, Rhyme said, "No, I cannot."

Coughlin brushed a hand through his sturdy hair. "Almost done, Mr. Rhyme. But before you leave, I'd like to ask you just a few more questions." A fast look to the jury, then back. "And these are about you."

3

Will it be murder or not?

Will I be watching a human being's bloody end?

The clearing is surrounded by lush greenery and, beyond, sandy fields. In the hazy distance are hills like camel humps. A jetliner's contrail slices the sky, high, high, in the air. A voluptuous storm cloud looms and there will be rain soon.

I stretch and observe closely, looking at two men, both sinewy, dark complected, black hair, Latinx features. They are wearing gray slacks and T-shirts with images and type.

I myself am dressed similarly, though my slacks are beige and my T-shirt black, with no markings.

All of us wear running shoes.

The man with the knife is in an AC/DC T-shirt. The man standing in front of him, his hands bound behind his back, is wearing a faded yellow and green shirt. I think there was a sports team logo on the breast but washing has removed it. Brazil soccer, maybe.

AC/DC is speaking loudly, in Spanish. The knife moves but not threateningly. The man is simply gesturing. Making points, emphasizing. His body language suggests he's worked up. The strident words spew from the wiry man in staccato bursts.

The man with his hands bound with long and sloppily tied rope is looking as bewildered as afraid.

The lecturer raises the knife in the air. It has a smooth edge on the bottom of the blade, a serrated one on the top.

The question remains: Will it be murder?

Maybe this is just a message. Pure, and ponderous, talk. Intimidation.

When people are about to die, they don't get desperate and try to fight or run. They're passive and perhaps cry or perhaps ask, "Why, why, why?" but little more than that. Maybe there's some negotiation: Promises of money, or sex. Promises of changed ways. Mutterings of regret.

Never begging for mercy. Which I find interesting.

AC/DC's diatribe seems to be winding down. The motion with the knife slows. The bound man is crying.

And, of course, I'm wondering what *I* should do.

Playing God means making tough decisions.

Sitting forward in anticipation, eyes on the wicked knife, which seems stained with dried blood, I ask myself: What's it going to be?

4

M r. Rhyme," Coughlin was saying, "you analyze evidence in
your town house, is that correct?"

"In a *laboratory* in my town house, yes."

"Not a bad commute," the man offered casually, smiling. Several
jurors joined him.

Rhyme dipped his head, acknowledging the tepid cleverness.

"What precautions do you take to make sure there is no contamination of the evidence gathered at the crime scene by substances
in the town house?"

"We comply with the American Forensic Institute's Committee
of Area Contamination Guidelines. One hundred percent."

"Tell us specifically how?"

"The lab is scrubbed three times a day with disinfectants. It's
separated from the rest of the town house by a floor-to-ceiling glass
divider, with positive pressurization so intake of substances from
outside cannot happen. No one goes into the lab without wearing
protective clothing—bonnets, booties, mask and a lab coat. Gloves

too. This protects them and protects the evidence from contamination."

"Booties, you said."

"Like the sort surgeons wear."

"With all respect to your condition, Mr. Rhyme, you can't put booties on your wheels, now, can you?"

"I mostly supervise the lab work of others."

"Do you ever go into the—is it called a sterile area?"

Rhyme hesitated again. He glanced at the prosecutor. Sellars's face revealed a hint of uneasiness. "Yes, sterile area. And I do go in occasionally to analyze evidence. I wear all of the other personal protective gear I just mentioned and—"

"I'd like to focus on the wheels of your chair. How do you protect them against contamination?"

"The wheels are carefully cleaned by my aide before I go inside. They're brushed and scrubbed."

Coughlin glanced at the wheelchair. It was an Invacare model with large wheels in the center and two coaster wheels in the front and two in the back. This let Rhyme turn in any direction he wished without having to drive forward or back.

"This is the chair you'd use when you go into the lab?"

"Yes, but again—"

"'Yes' is fine, sir. Now what type of tires are those?"

"I couldn't tell you."

"If they're standard, they'd be fourteen-inch Invacare 3.00-8 foam filled. Also known as flat free, or solid tires."

"I believe that's correct." Well, the man had done some homework. And when had the lawyer's private eye been spying on Rhyme?

"And Invacare is known for quality products for the disabled, aren't they?"

"Objection," said Sellars. "The witness is not an expert on a corporation's reputation. Besides, what's the point of this line of questioning?"

"I'll withdraw the question about quality products, Your Honor. I'm getting to my point now."

"Very well. With some vivace, perhaps." The judge was known to be an opera fan.

"Of course, Your Honor. Mr. Rhyme, do the tires on that wheelchair perform to your satisfaction?"

"Well, yes."

"Including good traction?"

"Yes."

"Do you think that's because of the deep tread?"

"Objection."

"Mr. Coughlin, if you want to introduce the wheels into evidence, make your motion."

"That won't be necessary, Your Honor."

Of course it wasn't. The jurors had all gotten a look at the treads, which were deep. The lawyer had made his point.

"Mr. Rhyme, how long would you say it takes your aide to clean those treads?"

"Probably twenty minutes."

"For *both* of them?"

"That's right."

"Ten minutes each."

"That's what the math would say." Getting a few smiles himself.

"I've read your treatises, Mr. Rhyme. You've written that trace evidence adheres like glue to hands, feet, hair. And can be so small that it's virtually undetectable without special equipment like powerful microscopes. Is that correct? Those are your words, are they not?"

"Yes, but—"

"Now, you made a reference to the AFI's Committee of Area Contamination Guidelines. Isn't it true that those guidelines deal exclusively with the issue of DNA contamination?"

Rhyme paused. His eyes met the prosecutor's. "This is correct."

"They say nothing about other substances?"

"No, though by following them—"

"Mr. Rhyme, please. The guidelines were not meant to address other forms of trace evidence analyzed in the lab. Is that a true statement?"

"It is," Rhyme muttered.

Coughlin's eyes lit up. "If you knew that the guidelines applied only to DNA, why would you cite them as proof of your diligence in handling the trace evidence against my client?"

"I didn't think about it."

"Could it be that you wanted to attempt to shore up your credibility because you are not in fact very confident about the evidence presented against my client?"

"Objection."

"Sustained."

But of course the jurors' memories could not be erased. They'd just heard that Rhyme was not completely playing fair.

"Mr. Rhyme, were you inside the sterile area of your lab when the analysis of this sand was going on?"

Rhyme fell silent. He looked at Thom in the back of the courtroom, his trim aide wearing today an impeccable navy-blue suit, off-white shirt and dark gray tie.

Coughlin prodded, "Mr. Rhyme?"

"Yes, I was."

"And when you went inside, did your aide scrub the treads of those tires?"

"Yes."

"How?"

"Wipes and bleach."

"Did he use a Q-tip or similar item to dig into the treads?"

"No. He used wipes."

"And that was for only ten minutes per wheel."

"Objection."

Coughlin trimmed out the "only" and asked, "And that was for ten minutes per wheel?"

"About that, yes."

"Mr. Rhyme, you must have a lot of equipment in the lab. Chromatographs, electron microscopes, drying hoods . . . Typical forensic devices."

"That's right."

"And they generate a fair amount of heat?"

"When they're in operation, yes."

"Are there fans in the lab?"

Rhyme was silent for a moment. "Yes."

"And a fan could, in theory, blow trace evidence around. So that foreign matter brought inside the lab could contaminate a soil sample?"

"Objection."

The judge: "He's an expert witness. I'll allow the hypothetical. Mr. Rhyme, please answer."

"In theory."

"Mr. Rhyme, the evidence report states that your laboratory analyzed the soil samples from the murder scene and from my client's property on April twentieth. Is that correct?"

"That sounds right."

"And on that day were you outside your town house for any reason?"

"I don't remember."

"Well, I'll refresh your memory. You gave a lecture at the Manhattan School of Criminal Justice on West Seventy-Fourth Street. This was at ten a.m."

"I'd have to check."

"Your lecture was on YouTube. It's time-stamped."

"Then," Rhyme said stiffly, "I guess the answer is yes."

"Your Honor," Coughlin said as he lifted another document and approached the bench, "I'd like to introduce into evidence Defense Exhibit One." He handed two copies to a woman bailiff, who gave one to the judge and the other to Sellars. The ADA read through the pages and then looked at Rhyme with a frown.

After skimming her copy, the judge asked, "Mr. Sellars?"

A sigh. "No objection."

Coughlin approached Rhyme and placed a copy open before him. "Mr. Rhyme, this is a report from Albrecht and Tanner Forensic Services. Are you familiar with them?"

"I am."

"Could you describe them to the court?"

"They are a private forensic laboratory. They do commercial work for construction and manufacturing companies mostly."

"Are they a respected operation?"

"Yes."

"This report was commissioned by my firm and, in full disclosure, I'll add that we paid the company's standard fee for their services. I'm reading from their report. 'Our technicians collected eighty-four ground samples from sidewalks, gardens, planting beds and public works sites.

"'These samples were stored in sterile containers and returned for analysis in our laboratory. Per instructions, our technicians were told to look for the presence of calcium sulfate dihydrate, with silicon dioxide, in combination with $C_{12}H_{24}$—saturated hydrocarbons (seventy-five percent) and aromatic hydrocarbons (twenty-five percent). Our analysts did find significant quantities of such substances.'"

Coughlin cast a dramatic glance toward the jury then to his witness. "Mr. Rhyme, what the report is describing is a particular type of sand mixed in with diesel fuel, correct?"

"Yes."

"You see the proportion of chemicals in those samples?"

Rhyme looked down.

"I do."

"And is that proportion identical to the proportion of chemicals in the six grains of sand the prosecution introduced as evidence linking my client to the murder scene?"

Rhyme looked toward Sellars, then quickly away. "It is."

Coughlin returned to the report. "Under the heading 'Location of Collection,' the report states, 'These samples of sand came from a work site on the west side of Central Park West, in the three hundred block.' Mr. Rhyme." Coughlin turned. "Is your town house, which contains your laboratory, located in the three hundred block of Central Park West?"

Clearing his throat, he responded. "Yes."

"Is it possible, Mr. Rhyme, that those six grains of sand you claim link my client's home to the site where Leon Murphy was killed came not from either of those locations, but from right outside your front door, and that they were tracked into your laboratory in the treads of your wheelchair, and that therefore no trace evidence exists suggesting my client is guilty?"

Rhyme's lips tightened.

"Your Honor?" Coughlin asked.

"Mr. Rhyme, please answer."

Rhyme cleared his throat. "What you describe is possible."

"No further questions."

5

see that, no, it's not a scare tactic.

This is going to be murder. The real thing.

Blood is about to flow.

In quantity.

AC/DC, the one with the knife, grabs the victim's hair with his left hand, pulls it back and works the knife around the neck, the way you slit the paper wrapper atop a bottle of whisky. The victim gives a squeak as if of surprise and the crimson fluid flows. Oh my, it sprays. He sinks to his side. The knife man saws and saws—the knife merely *appeared* sharp—and finally detaches the head. He tosses it contemptuously aside and continues to lecture. The body doesn't twitch or curl. It's completely still.

And now for my role in the matter.

My decision.

I hit the space bar to freeze the video. I sip some caffeine-free cola and realize it's gone warm and flat during the course of the past hour or so; I've been engrossed in videos of the sort I've just been watching. One loses track.

I sit up a bit straighter and lift one shoulder, then the other. A bone pops. I'm at my workbench in a chair that's padded but not made for long-term sitting, though I usually sit in it long-term. I've been meaning to get a new one and I will soon. I have my eye on a thousand-dollar, special-order model.

I read the comments populating the screen below the frozen video.

> Epic!!!!
>
> Los Zetas should be rounded up and shot.
>
> Was a Mexican cop who did it, the cartels OWN them.
>
> Not as good as last weeks why no closeups!!
>
> Why didnt they do his girlfriend two?

Why indeed? I think. That *was* a bit of a disappointment.
So, decision time.
I type several keys and hit Return.
The screen goes black, replaced by the words:

> This video has been removed for violating our community standards.

This will piss off a lot of our audience. I sometimes read comments complaining about the company deleting a video. They cry censorship. How can we ignore the First Amendment?

But viewers on social media are rarely constitutional scholars and they miss the significant fact that the First Amendment prohibits *governmental* censorship. My company—ViewNow—like YouTube, Instagram and all the others can delete to their hearts' delight. Completely legal. You don't like it, type in another URL and browse elsewhere.

I had debated a different route. Rather than deleting the vid, I could have put it behind an entry page. When a viewer clicked on the title, "Justice Cartel Style," a pop-up would have appeared.

Mature content. Sign in to confirm age.

But the video was, like most nowadays, high-def. The blood was vivid and plentiful, the death yelp—the last sound ever to be uttered by the victim—clear. So the execution had to go altogether.

My job as content moderator is to consider what's in the best interest of my employer. And that means striking the fine balance between the titillating, shocking and disgusting on the one hand, and the cute, funny and inspiring, on the other. Ultimately, of course, I suspect that when it comes to offense, the wunderkind execs within the Silicon Valley headquarters of ViewNow don't give two shits about producing upright content; they're terrified of scaring off advertisers if the vids are too troubling (though I was amused when a banner ad at the bottom of the Los Zetas beheading was for Family Pride Life Insurance).

One more question remains: Should I delete the poster's account because of his offense?

So far he's uploaded scenes from the video games *Grand Theft Auto* and *Red Dead Redemption*, very violent but computer generated. No real San Andreans or Old West settlers were killed in the making of those games.

However, I see his journey. From those games and violent Japanese anime, he's moved on to posting more real-life scenes of gore and death, lifted from other sites, of people killed in various genocides and mass murders—after the deed is done.

Today's cartel beheading is the first real-time murder he's posted.

Will, someday, he decide that this isn't enough and move from observer to participant?

Lust transports you.

A fact I know very well.

Cancel, or not?

I'm God. I can do what I want.

My finger hovers over the keys.

Ah, let him have his little hobby.

After I close out the beheading video another pops up in its place. A helpful algorithm shot it my way.

It's the conspiracy theorist going by the name Verum, who posts several times a week. We are on the lookout for politically inflammatory material too, in addition to the blood and sex. And the anonymous Verum certainly walks a fine line.

The figure pixelated past recognition sits at a desk. The room is white and a curtain is drawn over a large window. There are hooks on the walls, where paintings would hang when taping is not in progress.

Verum is obsessed with secrecy.

For good reason.

The deep voice is also distorted and all the eerier for it.

"Friends: I've come into possession of a classified report about a program the Hidden have created in Los Angeles, Chicago and New York. The K to Twelve Improvement Project is a secret program initiated to map every student in the system by facial recognition. The data will be used to track the whereabouts of the youngsters and their parents and will allow the government to create political, religious and economic profiles far more invasive than anything we've ever seen.

"The Hidden will stop at nothing to destroy our privacy! In the comments below this video you'll find the names and addresses of the superintendents of those schools. Don't let them get away with using our children as fodder for the War!

"Say your prayers and stay prepared!

"My name is Verum, Latin for 'true.' That is what my message is. What you do with it is up to you."

Below is a URL for a site in the dark web where one can contribute money to fight the Hidden, which Verum passionately attacks but has never quite defined. The ads are targeted: survival gear, weapons, books by other conspiracy theorists.

One could block Verum's posts for containing purported facts that are "inaccurate" or "cannot be verified."

Or—ever useful—the community standard thing.

Some of the posts have also incited followers to violence. It's us versus the Hidden.

I let it stand.

Rising, I walk across my workshop floor, worried and uneven oak one hundred and fifty years old. I get a cold cola.

The space isn't large. It has a raftered ceiling and brick walls. Wooden posts rise. The windows are covered with steel security panels. This was so that a hundred and twenty years ago no one would break into the Sebastiano Bakery Supply Company and steal equipment. The sheets serve my needs well too. I hardly want intruders, though I'm less worried about thieves than others who might come a'calling.

I keep it well lit because when it's dark it reminds me of the Consequences Room and that just makes me furious.

I happen to glance at a rough-brick wall into which I've pounded tenpenny nails and hung on them my collection of locks. One hundred and forty-two of them. Also mesh bags of keys, of which I own at least a thousand.

No other decorations grace the walls of the workshop because if you have locks and keys why would you need any other art?

Glancing at my phone for the time.

I log off and, in an instant, Los Zetas beheadings and copyright violations and Verum's anarchical rhetoric are gone.

I have plans to make.

Last night's Visit to Annabelle Talese's was a challenge. But nothing compares with tonight's.

That's going to require considerably more finesse.

6

riminal investigators call potential suspects "people of interest."
Lincoln Rhyme coined a term that was a forensic scientist's
counterpart: a "substance of interest." He bestowed this desig-
nation on a material when it was the odd thing out, appearing at a
crime scene when there was no reason for it to be there.

Hearing Rhyme's characterization, Ron Pulaski, the young patrol officer who often assisted Rhyme and Amelia Sachs, had said,
"Oh, yeah—the kids' books. What's out of place in this picture? You
know, like a shark nesting in a tree." He was the father of two.

At first inclined to belittle the simile, Rhyme had reconsidered
and said, "Exactly."

In this instance the substance was $NaClO_2$, known more com-
monly by its nickname, sodium chlorite.

The trace had been found at a homicide, the backyard of a modest mansion in a posh neighborhood of Queens. Alekos Gregorios,
a well-off owner of a chain of industrial laundromats, had been
robbed and stabbed to death. Two detectives from the 112 House on

Austin Street—Tye Kelly and Crystal Wilson—were running the case and, confronting delays at NYPD's main crime lab, had asked Rhyme if he could short-circuit the system and take a look at the evidence. Any opinions would be welcome.

He'd agreed.

Gregorios, a widower, lived alone. His neighbors reported seeing nothing suspicious around the time of death, but his grown son, who'd had dinner with him that evening, told police that his father had had a run-in with a homeless man earlier in the day. The man was tampering with the gate to the enclosed backyard and Gregorios ran him off. The man had threatened Gregorios, who had not taken the mad rant seriously.

The son had only his father's description: white with wild, unwashed brown hair and wearing a filthy raincoat.

No other details.

New York City's homeless population hovered around fifty thousand, so canvassing the streets and shelters was not an efficient way to proceed. The detectives hoped Rhyme could narrow down the search.

Enter $NaClO_2$, the substance of interest, which Rhyme had isolated.

He was presently back in his town house, on Central Park West— the very venue that had been the subject of the debate in the case against Viktor Buryak.

The stately premises dated to the era when Victoria ruled England and Boss Tweed New York, each with unchallenged power over their respective worlds, which were not wholly dissimilar, varying only in geographical reach.

Other than the paneled walls, rich oak floors and plastered ceiling, the parlor looked nothing like it would have a century and a half ago. While a portion was a contemporary sitting room with chairs and tables and bookshelves, the rest was what he'd described to attorney Coughlin: a well-equipped forensic lab, the sort that any small- or even medium-sized police department or sheriff's office might envy. Ringing the workstations were spark emission and fluorescence spectrometers, evidence-drying cabinets, a fingerprint fuming chamber, hyperspectral image analyzer, automated DNA sequencer, blood chemistry analyzer, liquid and gas chromatographs and a freezer no different from what one might find in the kitchen.

Tucked into a corner were the microscopes—binocular, compound and confocal and scanning electron—and the scores of handheld instruments that are a forensic scientist's tools of the trade.

The lab had a decidedly industrial feel to it, but to Lincoln Rhyme one word and one word only applied: "homey."

For a moment his mind wandered back to the trial and he wondered how the jury deliberations were going at that moment.

He himself had never served on a jury before. Criminalists consulting for the NYPD and FBI last about sixty seconds in voir dire.

Rhyme now studied the dry marker whiteboard on which certain details of the Gregorios killing were notated. Since Rhyme was merely an advisor, only the basics were jotted down or taped up, not all the minutiae of the case: a brief description of the suspect; the time of death (9 p.m. or so); security camera status (present in the vicinity but not aimed at the scene); the killer's mismatched shoes (not unusual among the homeless); and a stark photo of the three knife wounds in the victim's torso. The absence of other wounds suggested that the killer had hidden on the property and surprised Gregorios. In some states, like California, this would be called "lying in wait," and made the crime a capital offense. In New York the penal code made no reference to lying in wait, but the suspect's behavior would help the prosecutor prove intent.

The photos vividly revealed the eviscerated body and the Rorschach stain of blood on the broad path of white and beige pebbles.

Then there was the trace.

On his pants pocket—the hip, where presumably he'd kept his wallet—an evidence collection tech had lifted a sample, which contained $NaClO_2$, along with citric acid and cherry syrup.

Rhyme had dictated a memo to the detectives in the 112 House, a copy of which was on the board.

When mixed together, sodium chlorite and citric acid combine to create chlorine dioxide, ClO_2, a common disinfectant and cleanser. However, ClO_2 also is used as a fraudulent cure-all for a number of diseases, including AIDS and cancer. When sold as a quack cure, ClO_2 generally has added to it a flavoring agent, such as lemon, cinnamon or—as is present here—cherry syrup.

Should any persons of interest be identified and found to possess any cherry-flavored ClO_2, it would not be unreasonable to pursue additional investigation into their whereabouts at the time of the homicide and, if a warrant could be obtained, additional evidence that might link the unsub to the scene.

The response, not long after, was from Detective Tye Kelly:

Holy shit, Captain Rhyme. We owe you a bottle of whatever you drink, up to and including Johnnie Walker Blue.

Rhyme then noted the front door to the town house opening. He heard the sticky rush of traffic speeding along Central Park West.

"How did it go?" Amelia Sachs asked, entering the parlor from the hallway. Meaning not the Gregorios case, he understood, but his testimony at the Buryak trial.

"It went," Rhyme said to his wife. He gave a shrug, one of the few gestures he was capable of. "We'll just have to see."

Amelia Sachs, tall and trim, brushed her long red hair off of her face.

She bent down and kissed him on the mouth. He smelled the sweet/sour aroma of gunshot residue. She said, "You look, hm, troubled."

He grimaced. "The defense lawyer. I just don't know. Was he good, or not? Don't know."

"I won't ask how long you think the deliberations'll be."

Sachs, a seasoned NYPD detective, had herself testified in hundreds of trials. She knew the pointlessness of the inquiry.

"How'd it go for *you*?" he asked.

Sachs competed in practical shooting matches, also known as dynamic or action shooting. Contestants moved from station to station, firing at paper or steel targets, with the score based on best aim, fastest time and the power of the rounds. Shooters would fire from prone, kneeling and standing positions and often did not know ahead of time the configuration of the stations or where the targets would be. There was considerable improvisation in practical shooting.

Sachs enjoyed firearm competitions, or just plain practicing on the range, as much as she enjoyed surging around the track, or through city traffic, behind the wheel of her red muscle car, a Ford Torino.

"Not so great," she replied to his question.

"Meaning?"

"Second." A shrug that echoed his.

"Weren't there fifty people competing?"

Her shoulders rose again.

Sachs was her own toughest critic, though she did admit, "The guy got first place? He does it full-time."

Rhyme had learned from her that marksmen could make good money on the competition circuit—not from prizes but from sponsorships and teaching classes.

Thom brought in mugs of coffee and a platter of cookies.

At the moment, though, Rhyme had little thirst—not for coffee, at least.

"No," Thom said.

Rhyme frowned. "I don't recall asking a question."

"No, but your eyes did."

"Thinking I was looking at the single malt? I wasn't."

He had been.

"It's too early."

There was no medical opinion that Rhyme had ever seen about those afflicted by quadriplegia limiting their intake of alcohol, and even if such studies existed, he would have ignored them.

"It was a difficult morning. The trial. You were there."

"Too early," Thom pronounced and set the mug of coffee on the table beside where Rhyme had parked his chair. "And, by the way, I thought you handled it well. On the stand."

A sigh—too dramatically loud, Rhyme had to admit. He looked at the bottle, which the aide had left in the parlor but was too high to reach. Damn it. Of course it was well within Sachs's reach but in matters of Rhyme's health, she deferred to Thom—at least, most of the time. This morning would not be an exception, apparently.

He lifted the mug and sipped. He grudgingly admitted to himself that the brew was pretty good. He replaced the cup, not spilling a drop. With surgery and relentless therapy, he now had nearly complete control of his right arm and hand. The advancements for patients suffering from spinal cord injuries had accelerated greatly in recent years and Rhyme's several doctors had presented him various options to improve his state even more. He was not averse to doing so but knew he would resent the time that the procedure and recovery would steal away from his investigating work.

For now he was content with the functioning of the limb—and, by twist of fate, his left ring finger, which might seem an ineffectual appendage, but the digit could pilot the wheelchair expertly. Leaving his right hand to grip evidence . . . or a glass of twelve-year-old scotch.

Though not today.

He debated calling ADA Sellars. But why bother? The prosecutor would call when he heard something.

His phone hummed, and he told it to answer.

"Lon."

The voice grumbled: "Got an odd one I could use some help with, Linc. Amelia?"

"I'm here too, Lon."

In Lincoln Rhyme's town house, phones were always on speaker.

"You both free?"

Rhyme said, "First. Define 'odd.'"

"Aw, lemme do it in person. I'm pulling up now."

7

Upper East Side.

I'm walking from the subway station, not fast, not slow. Blending into the crowds, I move north.

Anyone glancing at me would see nothing out of the ordinary: abundant dark hair, longish, more unruly than curly. My body is slim, lanky. My fingers are long and my ears are bigger than I'd like. I think that's why I get few haircuts, to cover up the flaw. I also wear stocking caps a lot. In New York City, you can get away with this kind of head covering most of the year. If you're thirty or under, like me. (One difference: mine pulls down into a ski mask.)

I'm in those running shoes that are similar to the ones worn by Los Zetas. They were made in China and are an off-brand. They're comfortable enough. Mostly I wear these because I heard that police sometimes have a database of shoe tread marks and it would be easier to identify and trace a well-known style. Maybe I'm overthinking but what can it hurt?

At the moment I'm wearing blue jeans and, under a black windbreaker, a dress shirt, pink, a nice one; it was a present from a girlfriend, now former. This puts me in mind of Aleksandra. She isn't former; she's very present. Coincidentally she mentioned not long ago that pink happens to be her favorite color.

In one of my sessions with Dr. Patricia she found hope for me when, in answer to her question as to whether I was seeing anyone, I said yes and told her about Aleksandra. "She's pretty, Russian, a professional makeup artist. She's built like a dancer. She used to be one when she was little."

From Aleksandra I learned that all Russian girls are either dancers or gymnasts when they're young. "There are no exceptions to rule," she announced, her expression charmingly professorial.

I turn on 97th Street and, when no one is looking, slip through a chain-link fence and into the half-collapsed building that smells of mold, brick dust, urine.

It was formerly owned by a Bechtel, or Bechtels plural, whoever the family might be, according to the carving in the crown of the structure.

The place is pretty disgusting but suits my needs perfectly: it overlooks the service entrance to the apartment building that will be the site of my Visit tonight.

This shadowy neighborhood is the East Nineties. It's a transitional area. To me it has a thin, gloomy quality. It's illuminated by no direct sun, only reflected light. The word "diluted" comes to mind.

I have entered carefully, keeping an eye out for occupants. If there are any they're strung out on meth or heroin or crack, if anyone still does crack, but that doesn't mean they can't be witnesses. I have my knife, of course, but I hardly want to use it—who needs that fuss?

But the structure is unoccupied, as it was on my last two visits here. Not surprising. It looks like the whole place could come down at any minute.

I am, though, concerned about the trash here. The Chinese shoe tread is anonymous, yes, but I don't know how effective the rubber is in protecting against tainted hypodermic needles.

I gaze out, looking over the occasional passerby. I'm an expert at watching people and because of that I am an expert at knowing when I'm being watched. Right now, I'm not. I'm hidden behind the panes of glass, just like I'm hidden to those who post on ViewNow—invisible, but always watching.

I study her building: dun-colored stone, aluminum trim around the windows, a weatherworn green canopy leading to the street. Ten stories. Not many young people here, or retirees. This part of town—while pale and nondescript, architecturally bland—is expensive.

But Carrie Noelle can afford it. Her business is, by all accounts, successful.

Being here now is part of the way I approach my Visits. Always planning ahead.

There are two ways to pick locks: The crude approach involves either using a snap gun—which you stick into a keyway and pull the trigger until the lock opens—or bumping, bluntly pounding a key blank until you defeat the device. The second approach is rake picking—the subtle, the *artist's* approach. My approach.

Similarly there are two ways to approach breaking and entering. Some burglars improvise. They show up at the home and just see what happens.

I'm incapable of that. My Visits involve exhaustive preparation. I need to know about security in the building, front door, service door, cameras in lobbies and hallways or outside, doormen, vantage points, homeless men or women stationed nearby, who, like crank heads, might be stoned or crazy or drunk, but who can have just fine memories and describe me to a tee.

Curiously, I learned not long ago, serial killers too are divided into two categories: disorganized and organized offenders.

I see now that nothing has changed. No new cameras in or around Carrie's building. No homeless squatters in adjacent doorways. A simple Webb-Miller on the service entrance. Which hardly even counts. I call such locks hiccups.

One more thing to check.

And I have to wait but a moment. Ms. Carrie Noelle, in person, walks into view, returning from a lunch date I knew she had scheduled.

She is tall, in her mid-thirties. Her outfit today is jeans and a leather jacket. Running shoes, orange and stylish, not gaudy. Her chestnut hair's tied back in a ponytail. Not model beautiful but quite pretty. The woman walks in smooth strides. There's an athleticism about her. Catlike. She not only resembles but she moves just as elegantly as my gorgeous Aleksandra.

Every Russian girl, she is gymnast or dancer growing up . . .

Carrie is walking along the sidewalk in front of the Bechtel Building. She passes the window, not ten feet away but doesn't glance in.

And the final element of the prep: I confirm that she's alone. Carrie isn't on the arm of a man who would complicate my Visit. (I'd say man *or* woman, but I know that she's straight.)

Of course she could have a suitor stop by later tonight, but that hasn't been her style.

All by her lonesome.

She proceeds to the front of her building. She greets a neighbor, a retiree, he seems. He's walking toward the entrance too. They smile—hers is radiant—and they exchange a few words. With his key he opens the door (a silly Henderson pin tumbler).

The bags she carts are cumbersome and, gentleman that he must be, he volunteers to help her. She hands one over. As he takes it he glances in and once again smiles, lifting an impressed eyebrow.

Which says to me that the recipient of whatever is inside will be delighted with the purchase. On the other hand, noting the logo of the store on the bag, aren't children *always* overjoyed when their parents put that very special new toy into their little hands?

8

Rumpled" was the go-to word in describing Lon Sellitto, the middle-aged detective first grade who had been the criminalist's partner years ago, before Rhyme moved to Crime Scene and, later, ascended to be the head of NYPD Investigation and Resources Division, which included the CSU.

Pressing his mobile to his ear, the stocky man with thinning hair of a shade that could best be described as brown-gray made his way into the parlor, nodding greetings to Rhyme and Sachs, as he steamed toward the cookies. He tucked the phone between cheek and shoulder and broke one in half carefully, then set the larger portion back on the tray before negating the show of willpower by scarfing down the surviving half.

He was apparently on hold. He said to no one, "Oatmeal. Raisins. Damn, that man can bake." He glanced toward Sachs. "You ever bake?"

She seemed perplexed, as if she'd been asked that old saw about how many angels fit on the head of a pin, or however it went. "Once, I think. No, that was something else."

Sellitto asked, "How'd the trial go?"

Rhyme grumbled, "No earthly idea. It's in the jury's hands now." His voice conveyed the message that he didn't want to think about, much less discuss, the trial. He said, "'Odd'? You said, 'odd.'" The criminalist's heart was beginning to thud a bit faster—as always, the messenger was his temple. Lincoln Rhyme lived for "odd," along with "unusual" and "challenging." "Inexplicable" too. A case where Thug A shoots Thug B, who's then caught with the murder weapon ten minutes later, did not intrigue. His worst enemy was not a psychotic killer but boredom. Before the accident, and after, to be bored was to die a little.

Amelia Sachs was also eyeing the visitor with some anticipation, it appeared. She was assigned to Major Cases—where Sellitto was a supervising lieutenant. She could catch a job for anybody at MC who needed her but she worked most frequently for Sellitto—and she always did when Rhyme was brought on as consultant.

The detective was then speaking to the person on the other end of the line. "Yessir . . . We're on it . . . Okay . . . Well." He paced up to the immaculate glass wall that separated the non-sterile part of the parlor from the lab. He rapped on the glass absently. He nodded, as one will do when concluding a conversation, even when the person he was speaking with was off camera, miles away. "Yessir." The phone vanished into the pocket of his brown suit. The man had other colors in his wardrobe but when he thought of Sellitto, Rhyme thought of brown.

Thom appeared, with another steaming mug. "Here you go, Lon. How've you been? How's Rachel? You ever get that dog you were talking about?"

"Don't interrupt him, Thom. He's here to tell us an interesting tale, aren't you, Lon? About something *odd*."

"You make the best coffee."

"Thank you."

"Molasses in the cookies?"

"Not too much. It can overwhelm."

"Interruption, I was saying," Rhyme said in a slow, cool voice.

Sellitto said, "Rachel bakes. She made scones the other day. Which I'm not even sure what that is. Kinda dry. Good with butter. Okay, okay, Linc. A couple uniforms from the Twenty House get a call."

The precinct, a 1960s-era structure with a white stone façade, always in need of scrubbing, was within walking—or rolling—distance of the town house and Rhyme had been there on investigations more than a few times in the past years.

"Case like nothing I've ever seen before."

And Lon Sellitto had witnessed a great deal of mayhem over his years as an NYPD beat cop then detective.

"So. Here's the sit."

"The what?" Sachs asked.

"The situation. Everybody's using 'sit' in OnePP."

At another time Rhyme would have lectured his former partner about the sanctity of language, suggesting that dismembering a word spoke volumes about the intelligence and vanity of the dismemberer—nor was he particularly happy at the curious renaming of One Police Plaza. But he let it go.

"Victim was a woman named Annabelle Talese. Twenty-seven, marketing manager for a fashion company and an influencer."

"What's an influencer?" Rhyme asked.

"Do you not watch *any* television, Linc? Surf the web? Or listen to podcasts?"

"What's a podcast? . . . That I'm joking about. But influencer?"

Sachs said, "Somebody who talks about a product online. I use this mascara for my morning routine. I like this line of sweaters from ABC knitwear. They get paid by the manufacturer, or they make money from advertising. Influencers're pretty or handsome. At least, that helps. Unboxing videos're part of it too. Pam told me about them."

The young woman, whom Sachs had taken under her wing after saving her from terrorists, was presently studying criminalistics in Chicago.

Rhyme looked at her, querying.

"Somebody buys a product and then videos themselves taking it out of the box and setting it up."

"Will wonders never cease," Rhyme said and glanced at Sellitto with a can-we-move-it-along expression.

"A perp breaks into her place in the middle of the night."

"Homicide?" Rhyme asked.

"No."

"Sexual battery?" from Sachs.

"Probably not."

Rhyme and Sachs shared a glance. It was she who said, "'Probably'?"

"Here's part of the 'odd.'" Sellitto took a long drink of coffee, which apparently authorized him to chew down another cookie. "Might have touched her, but she couldn't tell. Basically what he does is he moves things around in her apartment. Personal things, clothes, hygiene stuff, sits beside the bed and eats one of these." He pointed at the pastry.

"Jesus," Thom said.

"I'll say. Kid was petrified. Thought he might still be in the apartment after she woke up."

"Why?"

"That's the other part of 'odd.' The door was locked, both the knob and two deadbolts, so she figured he had to be there. Only he wasn't."

"So," Sachs said. "He had a key."

"No, he didn't. She's sure of that. He picked the locks to get in. And used his tools to lock up after he left. What kind of burglar does that?"

9

Sachs asked, "And she's positive there's no spare key?"

"She was going to give a set to her mother but hadn't gotten around to it yet. A responding said she admitted she'd been drinking the night before. But nothing more than on a typical gals' night out. Can I say 'gal'?"

"Lon," Rhyme said impatiently.

"Anyway, her word, not mine. Then they wondered if she'd moved things herself—you know, staging it to blame an ex or the landlord. But she didn't point any fingers, so that theory's shot. And anyway, they said she was really freaked. Genuinely. She thought it might be a ghost but decided that, quote, 'wasn't real likely.'"

Sachs sat down in front of a computer and went online. After she did some keyboarding, a video began to play. It depicted an attractive woman, blond, in a low-cut sweater, sitting at her kitchen table in a bright and neatly ordered dwelling—it smacked of your average New York City apartment. She was smiling broadly at the camera. She was holding up some makeup accessory with affection.

Influencing, apparently.

Sachs froze the image and studied the woman closely. "Anna-belle," she whispered.

This was her way, Rhyme understood. Sachs wanted to know the victims in the cases she was running, wanted to know their histories, their loves, their fears, as many details of their lives as she could absorb—and wanted to know too, in the case of murder, what the last few minutes of those lives had entailed. This bonding with the victim, she believed, made her a better investigator, and the process started with knowing the name.

Though Rhyme was no less sympathetic to the victims' fates than Sachs, such details did not interest, much less motivate, him.

There were people cops and there were science cops, and the two of them were respective examples of each. This created occasional tension. But, on the whole, it could be argued that this very contrast was what made them click so well.

"So, breaking and entering," Rhyme said, eyes off the computer and on the ceiling. "Moving things around. A chance for prints, DNA, footprints. Anything else?"

"Well, stole a knife and a pair of panties."

"Hm." The suggestion of sex and violence was always troubling, even if he had not, at this point, acted on it.

"But the strangest part was he left a message. It was on a torn-out newspaper page. Left it in her underwear drawer. He used her lip-stick to write on it. 'Reckoning,' and it was signed 'the Locksmith.'"

"What was the newspaper?" Sachs asked.

"*Daily Herald*," Sellitto said. "From February of this year."

Rhyme didn't know it. He paid scant attention to news unless a story shed light on a case he was investigating or contained informa-tion that might be useful in the future. He had little patience for most media.

The lieutenant continued, "A rag. Tabloid scandal sheet. The company that publishes it owns a TV station—same thing—and some shock-jock radio shows."

"Shock jock." Rhyme had not heard the term but when he realized "disc jockey," he got it.

He said thoughtfully, "Okay, Lon. She's upset. Who wouldn't be? She caught a stalker, maybe. Or it was random. But there was no assault."

Assault is awareness of physical contact of any kind. She was asleep.

"*Probably* no battery," Rhyme continued.

Nonconsensual contact.

"But even that would be hard to prove if there's no evidence of touching. So you've got second-degree burglary."

Breaking into a *commercial* building required several conditions to make the crime a burglary, such as the perp's being armed with a deadly weapon or causing injury to someone. But no such requirements were necessary when the trespasser broke into someone's *personal* dwelling. Simple breaking and entering made the Locksmith's crime a felony.

But that hardly turned it into the crime of the century.

Sellitto caught the point. "Okay, okay, got it, Linc. He messed with her mind but considering what he could've done . . . So, you want to know what the hell'm I doing here, other than an excuse to have Thom's baked goods. It's a non-case, right? Well, there's more."

He dug out his phone and fiddled, then displayed the screen to Rhyme and Sachs. It was a picture of a social media post: the *Herald* page that Sellitto had referred to earlier, sitting in a dresser drawer, atop garments, the word "reckoning" and the nickname barely visible; the image was dark, shot without the flash, so as not to wake her, Rhyme supposed. Beneath the picture was typed Annabelle's address and the words: "Who'll be next?"

"He posted it somewhere underground but it went viral fast: Facebook and Twitter pages—newspapers, TV stations mostly. Word's out now and reporters're calling downtown. It's holy hell. The brass can't afford to flub a case that's got a press-magnet of a perp like this guy. Especially now."

Rhyme was all too aware of the scandal of recently botched investigations and trials in New York City.

Sellitto continued, "That's who I was on the horn with when I got here."

Rhyme had been wondering about the "Yessir." He said, "So it's about politics, Lon. Who has time for that? Anyway, I'm doing *my* part to take the trash out." He nodded at the whiteboard of the Viktor Buryak investigation.

"I know you are. But I'm not through pitching my case. The respondings's report ends up on Benny Morgenstern's desk."

Sachs said to Rhyme, "Gold shield, Major Cases. Been there a long time."

Sellitto said, "Yeah. He's like the wise old man of the squad. Yoda."

Rhyme frowned. "I don't know any brass named Yoda."

Sellitto stared for a moment, then, apparently deciding his former partner was serious, said, "Just hear him out."

10

Via Zoom, Rhyme—and the others in the parlor—were looking at a round man with a pale, freckled face.

Benny Morgenstern was in his fifties, not exactly the "old man" Sellitto had suggested. He wore a short-sleeved white shirt without a tie. He sat at a cluttered desk, filled with file folders and what appeared to be locks and keys, as well as metalworking tools.

A main bailiwick of the NYPD Major Cases squad was burglaries, robberies and hijackings—crimes that involved perps getting into places that were locked up for the very purpose of keeping them out.

"Captain Rhyme. You don't remember. We met a while ago. The Whitestone Brinks case."

He remembered the case—a four-million-dollar heist—though not the detective.

Rhyme's response was a nod.

"Hi, Benny," Sachs said.

"Amelia. Lon's briefed you, I guess. But here's the situation."

Ah, "situation"—not "sit." Rhyme cast a glance to Sellitto, who whispered, "Yeah, yeah, yeah," in response.

"I had one of the respondings take a shot of Ms. Talese's front door. Hold on."

He shared a screen on Zoom, and Rhyme could see a knob with a keyhole in the center and two different deadbolts, one above the knob, one below.

Morgenstern continued, "Now, this isn't going to mean a lot to you . . . not yet. Bear with me. In the knob, there's a generic pin tumbler lock. Anybody could pick that with a basic set of tools and an hour to watch YouTube videos. But the deadbolts: Hendricks Model Forty-One on top. And Stahl-Groen Sixteen on the bottom. At lock-picking conventions, they're competition models."

"Lock-picking conventions?" Rhyme asked.

"Like hacker conventions. Oh, some professional locksmiths show up, but most of the action is with the bad boys and girls. The picking underworld. Open-society activists, WikiLeaks, that sort of crew. They have contests to see who can crack complicated locks before the clock runs out. Even some of the best pickers in the world can't get through these babies in time. Some can't even pick 'em at all. And your guy, the Locksmith, couldn't stand in a New York apartment building for a half hour, working away. He'd have four, five minutes. Tops." Morgenstern's voice seemed laced with astonishment. Admiration too, perhaps.

"Now, it gets better. Or worse." The detective swiped the page and a picture of a wall appeared, with what seemed to be an electronics panel.

"He gets through the deadbolts, and then has five seconds to disable her alarm. Which he does."

Morgenstern continued, "Maybe he got her code. He could snatch her purse and it's inside, but that's unlikely. Let's assume he hacked it out of service. Her model's wireless. There're three ways to take them out. All three involve using an RF—radio frequency—transmitter. One way is brute force, standing outside and transmitting every possible combination of four-digit pins. It takes about an hour and twenty minutes to get from 0000 to 9999. But, of course, that wouldn't work in a Manhattan apartment. The second way is to hide a recorder nearby and capture the frequency of the disarm code. Then, when you go to break in, you play it back with the transmitter. But that too: hard to hide in an apartment building like hers.

"So, I think what the Locksmith did was the third way: he jammed the system. See, when you open the front door, a sensor mounted in the frame sends an activation transmission to the main box. That starts the five-second clock running; if you don't enter the right pin in that time, the alarm goes off.

"But what you can do *before* you open the door is transmit a constant frequency that jams the link between the door sensor and the box. The 'door open' message never gets through to the panel. He probably used a Hack-InRF—that's the most popular system."

"And you can just buy them?" Rhyme asked.

"Yep. Or make one, if you're electronically inclined." Morgenstern stopped the screen share and his face appeared once more in a larger window. He must've had thirty locks on his desk. Was picking a hobby for him? Rhyme wondered.

"Now, something you have to know. We're pretty sure he's done this before. Similar MO. Somebody at the Six House got a call. This was in February."

Rhyme asked, "The Village?"

"Yeah. Greenwich Street. That one, a woman came home and found somebody'd been there. Moved things around. Pulled her bedsheets down. Ate some snack food."

Rhyme asked, "And they were sure nobody had a key?"

"Correct."

"Did he take any souvenirs or leave a message?"

"No."

"Maybe a former romantic interest with a grudge," Sachs suggested.

"The responding asked but there wasn't anybody she could think of."

Sachs asked, "Did the gold shield in that case send in ECTs?"

"No, Crime Scene wasn't involved. The vic didn't want to pursue it. And if you're thinking of running it now, Amelia, the place's been scrubbed. A while ago. She moved out a week after it happened—out of town in fact, she was so freaked. And it's New York so there was a new tenant in, in about five seconds, freshly painted walls and steam-cleaned carpet."

"Were those locks as tough as the ones this morning?" Rhyme asked.

"I don't know. It was just an incident report, no follow-up, no investigation." His eyes lowered and he read from a sheet of paper. "Now, the other one, March. Midtown South, off Ninth Avenue. This MO was closer to last night's. A perp breaks into the vic's apartment while she's asleep. Rearranges her things, underwear and stuff. Get this, he made a goddamn sandwich and ate it. Well, ate half of it—to let her know what he'd done. Left the dirty plate on her bedside table."

Sachs asked, "She slept through it too?"

"She was on some kind of mood drug, she said. And I'll save you the breath. No ECTs, no investigation. And she was out of the place in *three* days. Only her sister had a set of keys, and they were accounted for. No exes as possible doers either."

"Notice a trend?" Sellitto asked. "First victim, she wasn't home. Second, she was but he didn't play with knives and underwear. Last night: he left a newspaper with a possibly threatening message and he's stepped up to flirting with sharp objects and lingerie."

Rhyme asked, "You ever hear the nickname 'the Locksmith'?"

"No, never."

"That souvenir he left, the *Daily Herald*," Sachs asked, "does it mean anything in the lock community?"

"That rag? Can't imagine what. Maybe he just needed some stationery."

"Where could we start looking for somebody had these skills?" Lon Sellitto asked Morgenstern.

"It's a guy in the trade, you're thinking. But probably not. For one thing, all the commercial locksmiths know they're the first ones we'd look to when a perp is as sophisticated as this. Also, there's a thing about tradesmen locksmiths. Pride in profession and that means not using their skills for illegal crap.

"I can get you a list of a few who've strayed, but I'd say he does something else for work and got obsessed with picking separately. Studied it on the side, and I mean *studied* it. Probably hooked up with a mentor at a convention—and one hell of a mentor, at that."

Sellitto asked, "Any trademark moves that might help?"

"No, there's no signature, as it were. He's just very, very good. The best I've seen. Basically, unless you've got guard dogs, a CIA-level alarm system *and* a door bar—you know, that rod from the door to the floor inside—you're not going to be able to keep this guy out."

Sachs said to the screen, "Thanks, Benny."

"A last word? One thing about picking: the good ones're brilliant. You have to outthink the lock maker, and outthink the lock. You've got to be a chess player. And you have to do it all with a clock ticking down. Your boy here, he's got that intelligence and he's got the skill. That's a real bad combination for somebody with a playbook like his. You want my advice, devote resources. Find him. And fast. There's some bad shit looming."

Morgenstern ended the session.

Rhyme was staring out the window. He believed Sellitto was speaking to him but he wasn't listening. What he was thinking of was another perp, a man who was as close as could be to the word "nemesis"—a characterization that Rhyme considered both profoundly unprofessional and yet completely accurate.

The Watchmaker and Rhyme had gone head-to-head several times over the years. In each instance, Rhyme had foiled his attempts at assassination or terror attacks, but the man had always escaped and gone on to commit more crimes outside of Rhyme's jurisdiction. The last time they'd met, the Watchmaker had assured him that one of them would not survive their next encounter.

Not long ago, Rhyme had learned from an intelligence source in England that someone was targeting him for a hit. The matter was still under investigation, but Rhyme now suspected the Watchmaker was involved. Was it possible that the Locksmith was working for the "nemesis"? Or was he, in fact, the Watchmaker himself.

The Locksmith's MO and obsession with mechanical devices echoed those of the Watchmaker. Had the man returned to the city to target Rhyme? But, on reflection, it seemed unlikely. His personal enemy's passion was timepieces and it seemed unlikely that he would so compulsively take up the topic of locks this late in his career.

But one thing did resonate: the Watchmaker's skills were those of a master illusionist. He kept the police and the public and the real victim of his crimes focused elsewhere.

Rhyme wondered if the same were true with the Locksmith.

What was actually going on?

Sellitto asked Rhyme and Sachs, "So. You'll run it?"

The couple regarded each other and it was she who nodded their collective assent.

Then Rhyme said to her, "Check NCIC, Interpol and our own databases."

With a parting glance at Annabelle—Rhyme had forgotten her last name—Sachs exited that page and logged on to a secure NYPD server. Her fingers, tipped in uncolored, close-cut nails, pounded hard. A moment later. "No references to 'Locksmith' as a proper name or nick or aka. Some perps were locksmiths by profession but picking skills had nothing to do with the crimes and they're either long gone or nowhere near here."

Rhyme mused, "So he's created himself from whole cloth. Interesting."

Sachs logged out of the server. "Did the page of the newspaper he left mean anything to her?"

"I don't know," Sellitto said. "They declared a crime scene and backed out, the uniforms did."

Sachs asked, "The picture he posted, could Computer Crimes trace it?"

"No, it went to an underground image board—there's no trail."

Rhyme said to Sachs, "Okay, get to her apartment. Walk the grid."

"I'll interview her too and get some uniforms for a canvass."

"Video in the building?" Rhyme asked.

Sellitto told him no.

Rhyme reflected: a canvass wouldn't do much good then since the officers would have no description. All they could ask neighbors was if they'd seen anyone "suspicious"—a line out of a shamus movie from the '40s. He didn't care much, though. He was distrustful of witnesses and their accounts anyway.

He wanted the evidence.

Sachs asked, "Where's Annabelle now?"

Sellitto said, "At her neighbors'. She won't go back to the apartment alone."

"Hardly blame her there."

Rhyme said, "I'll call Mel. Lon, can you get me Pulaski? Is he free?" Rhyme added, "I *want* him free."

"He'll be free."

"Let's get a board going."

Sachs moved aside the Buryak and the Gregorios whiteboards and positioned a blank one in the middle of the room. She picked up a dry marker. In every case in which the real identity of the perp was not known, Rhyme and the team would assign him or her a code name, usually "unsub"—unknown subject—followed by numbers representing the month and day of the crime. In this case, though, they didn't have to go to the trouble.

The perp had named himself.

She wrote *The Locksmith* at the top of the board, perfectly centered and in fine, elegant script.

11

Returning to my workshop, from the surveillance at darling Carrie Noelle's, I look up and down the scuffed and littered street. Two people with their backs to me, a couple. No worries there. I recognize them as residents, hipsters, if they still have hipsters now. The man has an elaborate beard. I'm always clean shaven. Fewer hairs for me to shed and for the police to find.

I step to the front door of the old Sebastiano Bakery Supply Company building, which is a judicious distance from my apartment.

At the door I extract my red and black keychain, a tacky souvenir, but one I have quite the affection for: it depicts the Tower of London. On it are a half-dozen keys, most of which are unusual. One of them is Swiss, and the titanium blade is rounded, and the bitting—the ridges to push up the pins in the tumbler lock—are inside the tube so it cannot be duplicated by someone taking a photograph or making an impression. This key opens the top lock.

The two below it require other keys on my chain: a dimple key and a chain key, whose shaft dangles in links, as the name suggests, making the lock it opens virtually impossible to pick. By everyone else, I mean. I cracked it in two minutes and seven seconds.

I step inside and re-secure the locks, set a steel bar from a metal bracket in the floor to one in the door, a forty-five-degree angle. One who picks locks appreciates that locks can be picked. Metal bars cannot.

On a table by the door I set the keys and my brass folding blade knife that I'm never without. I shed my jacket and hat and check the news on my phone. I'm curious what they have to say about my Visit to the pretty—no, beautiful—influencer Annabelle Talese. Oh, I'm quite the celebrity, apparently. The whole town is in a tizzy. The Locksmith this, the Locksmith that. I wondered how long it would take for the picture, once posted on one of the forums, to migrate to the popular media.

Record time, it seems.

I spend some time looking over my tools, cleaning and oiling the ones that need it. I have quite the collection: two-piece bypass lock shanks, small keyway finger lock rakes, other mini rakes, heat-shrink lock pick sleeves, glasspaper, pick handles, bump keys, bump hammers, top of keyway tension wrenches, circular tension tools, cylinder lock jigglers, skeleton keys, wafer lock rakes, picks for double-sided locks, standard rakes, dimple rakes, wave rakes, pen-style lock pick, on and on . . .

And in boxes neatly arrayed: snap guns and electric pick guns, the EPGs looking like stainless-steel electric toothbrushes with dozens of needle tips. Efficient and fast. To be used sometimes, but artless.

Also, practice locks (made of clear plastic so you can see your progress in picking).

Now I sit in the chair I will someday replace and scoot forward, greeting my opponent for tonight.

The lovely and infuriating SecurPoint Model 85. It's mounted in a slab of wood, like a doorframe, which is in turn bolted to a stand. Though I've seen it a hundred times in person, and a thousand in my mind, I look over the lock once more, perhaps the way a chess player regards his opponent before the first move.

I look at the SecurPoint as an astonishingly beautiful and coy woman whose mind is impossible to fathom and who has her own secret agenda for granting you access to her heart and her body. Or not.

Inhaling slowly, exhaling.

I pull the lock closer yet. Then pick up my tension tool and rake and slip them inside.

12

Amelia Sachs had never seen a victim looking so upset.

She and Annabelle Talese were sitting in the front seat of the detective's ruddy Ford Torino, outside the woman's apartment building.

She fidgeted—even more than Sachs herself would do when stressed, and Amelia Sachs was quite the fidgeter.

Talese would twine her pale lemon hair around her fingers, pull it back over her shoulders, release it then twist some more. Her face was fraught with worry and she examined every passerby on the sidewalk. In her eyes, suspicion vied with fear.

She had agreed to assist Sachs when she walked the grid, by gowning up herself and pointing out where the Locksmith had been and what he'd touched, though it had taken her some minutes to work up the courage.

Once the search was done, samples collected and photos taken, the woman had wanted to leave, and so the interview was conducted here, in the safe confines of a solid Detroit-built vehicle.

At one point, when Sachs adjusted her jacket, she inadvertently revealed her pistol; Talese noted the weapon and relaxed a touch.

Sachs produced a pad of paper and a pen. And a digital recorder, which she set on the dashboard. "You okay with this?" Indicating the slim Sony.

"Yes, anything."

Sachs pushed the button and a cyclops eye glowed red.

"Now you're absolutely certain no one could have keys?"

"Positive."

It wasn't an apartment, but a co-op; she owned the place and was able to put her own locks in, which she'd done about six months ago.

"Who installed them?"

She gave the name of the company.

The recorder sucked up decibels, while Sachs took notes.

Benny Morgenstern had sent the names of the victims in the Village in February and on Ninth Avenue in March. Sachs displayed her phone and asked, "Do you know them?"

"No, never heard of them."

She leaned toward the likelihood that the invasions were random. But that didn't mean he had targeted, or was going to target, one particular individual, and the others were misdirecting camo.

"That newspaper he left?"

"It's garbage. I don't read the *Herald*."

"You know anybody at the paper? Or their TV station?"

"Oh, the WMG channel? That's crap too. And, no, I don't."

"The articles?"

Sachs displayed a photo of the page.

"They don't mean anything."

"The word on the paper: 'reckoning'? It suggests somebody wanted to get even. You think of anybody in your life like that?"

"My God, no."

"Do you think the intrusion was meant to intimidate you? Have you been a whistleblower? A witness to a crime?"

"No, nothing like that."

Sachs didn't know how the Locksmith came to learn of the other women who'd been his victims earlier, but she suggested it was possible Talese had come to his attention through her influencing job. "I've seen some of your videos. They're good. They look professional."

"Thanks."

"Any fans who could be stalkers?"

"It's possible, I guess. I only use my first name but it's pretty easy to get my last—and an address. All that data-mining stuff."

"Can you go through comments and pick out the inappropriate ones?"

"Oh, I have the comments turned off. You can only look at my vids. It's the smartest thing when you're influencing. I've talked to a couple other girls in the business, friends of mine. They leave the comments on. You should see what people post; some of it's disgusting."

The woman scanned the streets, tugged at her hair. Pulled a scrunchie out of her purse, a bright red one, and started to bind her hair with it, but then stopped. She dug into the bag again and exchanged it for a rubber band, presumably so she wouldn't stand out quite so much. She sighed and lowered her head. Sachs wondered if she'd cry. She didn't.

"I'm sure you know quite a bit about computers and the internet," Sachs said.

"Not a lot. Enough to make the vids and post them is all."

"I'm thinking we could contact all the platforms you post on and talk to security there. That'd give us the IPs of everybody who's watched you. Might get us some names to work with."

Now, Talese gave an ever-so-faint smile. "Detective, the thing is, I post on five different platforms and the analytics show I have a total of, um, about two hundred and thirty thousand subscribers and fans. And you can triple that to get the number of people who just hit the site to watch me and never subscribe."

Well, that answered that.

"Anyone in the building who might be an issue?"

A shrug. "I don't know most of my neighbors. It's New York, right?"

"Have you noticed anybody following you or watching you over the past few weeks?"

"No."

"And as far as you know, he only took the knife and your underwear?"

"I think that's it. No jewelry, checkbooks, computer, TV. What a normal thief would take."

Sachs closed the notebook and shut off the recorder.

Talese stared at the façade of the building. "I'm going to stay with my mother. Long Island. Until I sell it and buy something new. Can I pack a suitcase?"

"Of course."

"Will you come with me?"

Sachs smiled. "Sure."

They climbed from the car and Talese stood with her hands on her hips, staring up at the tall building once again.

"He *did* take something else, Detective."

Sachs looked her way.

Annabelle Talese's voice dropped to a whisper. "He stole my home. I loved it so much, and he took it away from me."

13

Rhyme glanced up as Amelia Sachs entered.

He was in the hallway and he looked outside, past her, noting the remnants of construction work on the street.

These samples of sand came from a work site on the west side of Central Park West, in the three hundred block . . .

His heart accelerated some, wondering what the verdict against Viktor Buryak would be. It was so important. Lives depended on it.

Sachs had just returned from walking the grid at Annabelle Talese's apartment, which was located about five blocks from Rhyme's town house on the Upper West Side.

She was carrying a milk carton, in which she'd put the evidence bags of what she'd collected. There didn't seem to be much, he was disappointed to see.

"Amelia!" Mel Cooper, Rhyme's primary lab man, was an NYPD detective. He was slight and balding. His shoes vied with his thick-framed eyeglasses to be the less stylish accessory, though Rhyme had seen pictures of him tuxed-up in a ballroom dancing competition with his gorgeous Scandinavian girlfriend, and he cut quite the figure. He was presently gloved and was dressing in a mask, lab coat, booties and bonnet.

"I'll take that, thank you," said Cooper, lifting the crate away from her. He stepped into the sterile portion of the lab.

"Ron's canvassing," Rhyme told her.

Ron Pulaski, the earnest young patrol officer, had become an expert at crime scene work thanks to Rhyme and a solid interviewer thanks to her.

"Benny gave him a list of locksmiths in the city, and he got some himself off the internet. Quite a few, as it turns out. He's talking to them all." Pulaski was conducting a phone canvass to see if the locksmiths had any thoughts about who the perp might be, given his level of skill. Phone calls weren't as efficient as in-person interviews, but Rhyme didn't feel they had much time. Instinct told him that the Locksmith would move on another victim soon.

"Got the name of the locksmith that installed Annabelle's locks." She explained she'd texted it to Pulaski.

Rhyme said, "He's also checking out locksmith conventions— what Benny was telling us about."

But, he added, there were none in the Northeast, either presently or in the near future, though Benny had told him that the organizers often didn't advertise the events to the general public and word of the gatherings spread only on the dark web.

Lon Sellitto was canvassing too, in a variation of Pulaski's hunt. As he'd promised, Benny Morgenstern had given the lieutenant a list of locksmiths who'd been arrested for using their skills illegally or suspected of doing so. Sellitto was presently tracking them down for interviews—either as suspects themselves or to see if they had an idea about who the Locksmith might be.

So far, neither patrol officer nor detective had had any success.

In the sterile portion of the lab, Cooper was setting out the items Sachs had brought from Talese's apartment.

Lincoln Rhyme missed much about the able-bodied life. There was the contented stroll for bagels Sunday morning with your partner—at 11 a.m. after waking late. There was attending plays without half the audience staring at your elaborate contraption of a wheelchair. There was pursuing and eliminating a strafing fly.

But Rhyme missed two things most dearly. The first was meandering on foot through this magnificent playground of a city, New York, and learning what he could about its people, its geography, its economy, its foliage, its underbelly. Doing so informed his work as a criminalist and helped him match evidence to place, and place to perp.

And the second absence that tugged at his heart? Slipping on the Tyvek jumpsuit, donning gloves and picking up and examining the evidence to trick from it the truth about what had happened at the scene.

"Let's move here, okay?" Rhyme grumbled. The Locksmith was presently getting farther and farther from the Talese scene. And, possibly, getting closer and closer to another intrusion, where perhaps his goal would be different, and rather than stealing a knife he would use it.

Then too there was always the possibility that the victim might awaken and scream and fight back—a possibility that the Locksmith surely had considered; he'd be fully prepared to take a life to save himself.

Cooper first photographed the torn-out page 3 from the tabloid the *Daily Herald*, from February 17 of this year. He shot the back of the sheet too and loaded the images onto the high-def screens.

On the front, which had been signed by the Locksmith, apparently in Talese's lipstick, were five articles, with these headlines:

Secret Report Uncovered: AIDS Created
in Russian Laboratory

U.S. Senator's Intern Pregnant with Love Child

Bombshell: Actress's Divorce Invalid;
Arrest Expected

Women-Hating Group Exposed

Tech Company Has Proof of Illegal Wiretaps
by Feds to Help Campaign

The back of the page was ads. Get-rich-quick schemes, real estate ventures that smelled of scams, dating and massage services. Sex trade lite.

Sachs said, "None of the articles mean anything to Annabelle."

Rhyme skimmed them. "Not exactly hard news, is it?"

She shrugged. "Maybe he just needed something to write on. He brought it with him. She said she doesn't buy the paper."

Cooper chuckled. "Nobody who reads the *Herald* admits they read the *Herald*."

Rhyme said, "Let's call the newspaper, legal department, and see if they have any thoughts. Since he posted the picture, they might already be aware of it."

She looked up the company's number on her phone and called. The company's general counsel was on conference calls but his assistant assured Sachs he would call back. She left her and Sellitto's numbers.

Cooper was examining evidence under a blue-glowing alternative light source.

"Hm. Knows what he's doing. I'm not seeing a lot. No prints or fibers on the paper itself. And it was ripped apart from the other page folio. No cutting-instrument tool marks. The lipstick he wrote his message in is associated with what Amelia found in the apartment—the victim's."

The intercom system between sterile and non was good. It sounded as if Mel Cooper were right next to them.

Sachs wrote the findings on the whiteboard, below her notation about the absence of latents at the scene, and the fact he'd stolen a pair of her panties and a kitchen knife. A Chef's Choice model, ten inch.

Cooper continued, "Everything he touched, negative on prints and DNA. He was in gloves. The cookie was half eaten, but he broke it in half before indulging—there was no saliva. This guy is good."

More than a decade ago a brilliant French criminalist, Edmond Locard, wrote, as Rhyme paraphrased in his classes: "At every crime scene there is a transfer of trace between the criminal and the victim or the scene itself. This evidence might be invisible to the naked eye, undetectable by scent. But it's there for the crime scene officer with the diligence and patience to find it."

Locard referred to the trace as "dust" but that was as good a metaphor as any.

Most perps committing serious crimes nowadays wore face masks, shower caps and shirts with long sleeves tucked into their latex or nitrile gloves, keeping the trace evidence they'd brought with them—hairs and skin cells bearing that wonderful and damning deoxyribonucleic acid—from sloughing off at the scene. This was not that they were foundationally cleverer than in the past, or had stumbled across a website devoted to Locard, but because they could be counted on to have a cable TV subscription and an interest in police procedurals.

But the Locksmith was particularly cautious.

Rhyme thought yet again of the Watchmaker and the care he similarly took on his dark assignments.

"Shoe. Size eleven."

That would make it more likely than not that he was of average height, though he could be obese or skeletal. All investigators were, of course, aware that shoes and feet correspond only if the wearer wishes them to. Rhyme once pursued a killer who left size 12 shoe prints, while his feet came in at 8. There'd been cases where it worked the other way as well, such as when a male killer crammed his size 11 feet into a woman's size 6 flat. The smart, though undoubtedly painful ploy, confounded the investigation for several days.

"Pattern says it's a running shoe. But it's not in the database. So, no brand or model number. Four different types of dirt in the treads: one primarily sand, two basic dirt—minerals and loam—and the last is mostly clay. I'm checking on other substances now."

Up went the information on the chart.

Sachs added, "I followed his route, service door to basement, elevator, her apartment and back again."

"Video in the elevator, hallways?"

"No."

"He'd've checked that out ahead of time."

Cooper said, "Even without a camera, he was taking a chance on the elevator. Somebody else could've gotten in at any time. New York, city of night owls."

"Not if he had an FDNY fire service key," Rhyme said. "Call Benny back."

14

"Benny," Rhyme said, "you're on speaker here. We were wondering about an FDNY key."

"She was in a high-rise, and he didn't want to risk another passenger getting on, on the way up or the way down," Morgenstern said.

"Exactly. Could he've picked the fire service lock?"

"This guy could have, piece of cake. But he wouldn't need to. You can buy sets for a hundred bucks."

"Assuming there's no way to trace purchases?"

"Dozens of sellers. Take days. And anyway, since he doesn't want a trail, he probably got a set at one of those lock-picking conventions I was telling you about. And then, I don't know her building's setup, but a lot of them keep a key in a case near the elevator doors on the ground floor or basement. Of course, if you use one and you're not fire service, you're in trouble, but I don't think your perp gives a shit."

Sachs thanked Benny once more and they disconnected.

"Wonder if he *is* FDNY," Cooper said.

Sachs offered, "I don't see the Locksmith in that culture. Usually fire workers have family. They have friends. Our perp's a loner. Besides, if they want to get through a door, they don't pick locks. They use an axe."

Rhyme agreed it wasn't a likely theory.

Sachs was staring at the evidence chart. A whisper: "What do you want? Why're you doing this?"

Just like he wasn't a people cop, Rhyme wasn't a motive cop either. The why of crimes usually didn't draw his interest unless it helped uncover relevant evidence. Whether you kill for money, kill for passion or kill because you're a schizophrenic off your meds and believe you're saving the world from zombies, to Rhyme the reasons were irrelevant. Yet the "odd" nature of the case made Rhyme curious about the man's purpose.

He asked if his wife had any theories about what he was up to.

Sachs thought for a moment. "I see it going two ways. One, he's got a political or philosophical beef with the *Herald*, or maybe all media. They invade people's lives—and that's why he's breaking in. It's a message in itself. Remember, Benny was talking about lock-picking conventions? He said some pickers were like hackers. Open-society activists."

Rhyme asked, "And number two?"

"The paper's a red herring. Nothing to do with his real mission. He's an illusionist and's got something else entirely going on."

Rhyme smiled. "I was just thinking of the Watchmaker."

"So was I."

"Let's keep going with the evidence."

Slowly, despite the Locksmith's care, they made some discoveries that could be linked to the perp—by comparing them to control samples Sachs had taken from Talese's apartment. These included diesel fuel and silane, which was a cleanser, fragments of asphalt, sandstone, tiny slivers of white porcelain and rubber, small pieces of copper wire.

Rhyme mused, "Old electrical systems, early twentieth century. Porcelain's shattered by blunt force."

After another run of trace through the gas chromatograph/mass spectrometer, Cooper called, "Found triclosan, ammonium laureth sulfate, lauryl polyglucose, sodium chloride, pentasodium pentetate, magnesium and sodium bisulfite, D&C Orange dye number four."

Rhyme said, "Dish detergent."

Sachs shook her head. "Not so helpful, that."

"*Maybe* not," Rhyme said slowly. "Where was it, Mel?"

"Mixed into the soil from his shoes."

"Ah. Interesting. Dishwater on your hands, on your clothing. But how often do you *walk through* it? At home, rarely. Working in a restaurant kitchen, yes, but I have a feeling he's not a busboy or dishwasher." He closed his eyes and leaned his head back. "Where, where . . ." Rhyme's lids opened quickly. He asked Sachs and Cooper, "Do you know about the gates in Central Park?"

Neither of them did.

He explained that when the park was being developed in the mid-1800s, twenty sandstone gates were built, though they were more entrances than gates, since they had no physical barrier such as bars. Each was named in honor of a group, an activity, a calling—among them Artisans, Women, Warriors, Mariners, Inventors. There was even a Stranger Gate.

"Every year in May, the city scrubs the gates with diluted dish detergent. It cleans sandstone but doesn't damage the rock—it's very soft. Then they hose down the surfaces, leaving pools of detergent on sidewalks."

Ever since he began with the NYPD many years ago, Rhyme had made it a professional mission to learn as many of the intricacies of the city as he possibly could. As he wrote in his book, "You need to know the geography and workings of the city the way a doctor knows the bones and organs of the human body."

"We're onto something here," he whispered. "More. Keep going. I want more."

Cooper, bending over the lab's compound microscope, said, "Have something here. I'll put it on the screen."

After some keyboard taps, a number of grainy objects appeared on the monitor. The image was of what Cooper was looking at through the eyepiece: bits of some red substance, the shape of grains of sand. According to the scale at the bottom of the monitor, they would be the size of dust particles.

"From his shoe again?"

"That's right."

"GC it," Rhyme ordered. "I want the composition."

After analyzing a sample, Cooper said, "Silica, alumina, lime, iron oxide and magnesia. In descending amounts."

Rhyme announced, "Brick. Silica's sand, alumina's clay. The red comes from the iron and lower baking temperatures of nineteenth-century furnaces. So it's old."

"Well," Cooper said slowly, with emphasis in his voice, "one other substance." He looked toward Rhyme. "Dried blood. Ninety-nine percent sure it was on his shoe. Amelia got samples in two places."

"Species?"

"Human."

"TSD?"

The time since deposition—how long has passed since blood was spilled—could be determined by Raman spectroscopy. The technique, relatively new in the armory of forensic scientists, works by hitting a sample with a laser beam and measuring the intensity of the scattered light. Rhyme particularly liked the technique as it was nondestructive and the sample could later be tested for DNA.

Cooper ran a sample and read the results, in the form of a chart. "It's five, six days old, more or less."

Rhyme's eyes swiveled to Sachs's. Her face was troubled. She said, "Maybe he cut himself accidentally . . . Or maybe he's already started using a knife."

Cooper then ran the DNA and sent the results to the CODIS database. They soon received the message that there were no matches.

Closing his eyes again, Rhyme let his head loll back against the padded rest. He thought past the blood. He would assume that the Locksmith was in fact dangerous, if not deadly. His sole concern now was finding him. What did the evidence have to say about that?

Soap.

Brick.

Tiny shards of porcelain.

Copper wire.

Rhyme's phone buzzed, and he answered.

The caller was Assistant District Attorney Sellars, the prosecutor in the *People of the State of New York v. Viktor Buryak.*

"Lincoln. The jury came back with a verdict."

"And?"

"They found him not guilty. All counts."

15

Not good enough.

It's taken me fifty-nine seconds to pick the SecurPoint 85.

Way too long.

Carrie Noelle's apartment door is held fast by two locks, as are most residences in New York. The simple one in the knob and the SecurPoint.

They are both pin tumblers, one of the oldest designs in history. The man who earned the patent for the design in the U.S. was the famous Linus Yale Sr. The lock he created and his son's refinement of it are basically the same as are in use today, even after a hundred and fifty years.

In these locks there's a rotating plug into which the key is inserted (through the "keyway," not "keyhole"). The plug and the surrounding casing each have corresponding holes drilled into them and inside the holes are spring-loaded pins, which keep the plug from turning and opening the deadbolt or latch. The serrated ridges on the key push the pins up to the shear line, which frees the plug to turn.

To pick a pin tumbler, the process is simple: You insert a tension wrench into the keyway and twist the plug, which puts pressure against the pins and keeps them from springing back into the secure position. Then you use a thin rake—which looks like a dentist's pick—to push the pins upward until they're above the shear line.

Ah, but the SecurPoint . . .

It's similar to the famed Medeco. The ends of the pins within the lock are cleverly chiseled and, even more challenging, they rotate, so the tip of the rake must not only catch the sharp end of each pin but must twist it to free the plug and allow it to open. (When a Medeco executive patented the design, in the 1960s, he offered fifty thousand dollars to anyone who could pick it—a popular promotional gambit of lock makers. At the time, only one person in the world was able to do so—an NYPD detective, as a matter of fact.)

Cracking the SecurPoint in fifty-nine seconds?

That's probably a world record. But it's still too long.

Tonight, for my Visit, I need it to be thirty or under.

Not that an alarm would go off. It's just that I've assessed that for Carrie's size of apartment building, the number of residents, the time of early morning, I can afford to be crouched in front of her door for no more than a half minute. Beyond that time, the risk is unacceptable.

SecurPoints can be bumped—that is, opened by brute force, achieved by jamming a blank key into the passage over and over and occasionally hitting the key with a hammer or mallet. But I despise bumping. Again, the artistic element. The elegance.

It's also noisy.

I know very well—from the incident in 2019—the disaster that noise can lead to during a Visit. A simple thing like a latch clicking can result in tragedy.

No, I'll rake open the SecurPoint, and I'll do it quickly and silently, so that Carrie Noelle won't hear a thing and will continue to slumber in innocence. And vulnerability.

I inhale and exhale slowly, concentrate all my being on the Secur-Point 85.

Locks have been picked by actually looking into the keyway. The greatest picker of all time, a lock salesman named Alfred C. Hobbs, cracked the supposedly unpickable Detector lock at the Great Exhibition of 1851 in Britain. Some of his tools had tiny mirrors on them (which was considered cheating, and the event became known as the Great Controversy).

I don't have such tools. But I do "peer" inside the lock in a way. I close my eyes and visualize the pins and tumblers with the same clarity as if seeing them under a brightly lit microscope.

I become one with the device.

Lock picking has been called a dark side of zen.

A tap on the stopwatch.

In goes the tension tool, in goes the rake.

Five seconds, ten, twenty, twenty-five . . . thirty, forty.

Click.

The lock opens.

Forty-one seconds. At a recent lock-picking convention, the record for cracking a SecurPoint 85 was one minute and four seconds.

I've done it in nearly half that time.

But still not good enough.

I step back, make a cup of herbal tea. As I do I picture Carrie Noelle, who is a tea lover too. She's wildly appealing in spandex—hip huggers and tank tops are her outfits of choice. She tends toward bright colors.

I wonder what kind of kitchen knives she has. She'll have some. Everybody does. They're a perfect Christmas present.

Once again I study my prey, the SecurPoint.

Seductive, sexy, coy.

Whom I want to be inside, *need* to be inside.

From my hundreds of tools, I select a different rake.

Inhaling and exhaling. I reset then hit the stopwatch again.

Tension bar inserted.

Rake inserted.

The tools are moving slowly, back, forth. Up, down.

My eyes are closed, feeling the pins as if with the tips of my fingers.

Click.

Eyes open. Twenty-eight seconds.

I'm filled with indescribable warmth.

Well, Carrie, it appears that you're going to have some company tonight.

"Friends: The Hidden have a new way to strike. The news made it all the way out here to the West Coast: in New York a vicious organized crime boss was found not guilty of murder, which there's no doubt he committed. And how did this happen? The state's expert witness intentionally got him off because he manipulated the evidence!

"And why? Because this criminal has ties to senior politicians and, more frightening, employees of our national security agencies.

"Yet another weapon the Hidden wield to subvert justice!

"I've found a classified report that states that this is the dozenth time in the last few months the police have bungled investigations or prosecutors have dropped the ball.

"But of course they haven't 'bungled' anything. They're infiltrated by the Hidden, which decides what is and is not justice.

"New York is hardly alone. In Minnesota, the Health and Human Services Division of domestic abuse shelters had been infiltrated by the Hidden and used as a cover for sex trafficking. In Orlando the Hidden have

formed alliances with gangs, paying them to riot and to burn the businesses of legitimate, hardworking Americans. And no one is ever prosecuted.

"Say your prayers and stay prepared!

"My name is Verum, Latin for 'true.' That is what my message is. What you do with it is up to you."

16

Rhyme's phone hummed. He noted the area code and exchange. What was this about?

He shared a glance with Sachs, who turned the volume of the TV down. They'd been watching the breaking story of the Buryak verdict. The mobster in the glorious suit and colorful vest was shown walking out of court. He wasn't smiling. His brow was furrowed, as if the trial had been an irritating distraction and he was once again concentrating on projects that lay ahead.

Rhyme ordered the phone to answer. "Yes?"

"Mr. Rhyme?" a woman's matter-of-fact voice asked.

"That's right."

"Commissioner Willis would like to set up a Zoom call. Are you free?"

Another glance between the two of them.

"When?" he asked.

"Now."

"Send me the link." He gave his email address.

"Thank you."

They disconnected.

"What's up?" Cooper asked.

"No idea."

"What do you know about Willis?" he asked them both.

Cooper shook his head. Sachs said, "Sally Willis, first deputy commissioner."

The NYPD has two sides. One, headed by the chief of department, handles criminal investigations. It includes the detective and patrol bureaus. The other is civilian; it takes care of all non-criminal administrative matters. The first deputy commissioner heads this operation.

Sachs continued, "She's tough. She came out of Internal Affairs. At IAB, she was by the book. She'd write you up for pocketing a bribe or wearing white socks. Made no difference."

The footwear reference, Rhyme knew, meant citing an officer for a minor uniform violation.

"Known as the Iron Maiden."

Lovely.

A moment later the pulsing tone echoed through the parlor. Rhyme said, "Command. Email."

A window popped up on a large screen.

"Command. Open." Then, after the Zoom invitation appeared, Rhyme said, "Command. Cursor to hyperlink. Command. Enter."

He joined with computer audio and clicked on the video camera icon and a red light on the webcam glowed. A moment later he was looking at a nondescript conference room, presumably somewhere in One Police Plaza. The wide-angle shot revealed several people around the end of a conference table. A blond woman in her mid to late fifties was in the center.

He knew the other two. To her right was a solidly built Black man of about forty-five. Francis Duvalier was a senior assistant district attorney. Rhyme had testified in some of his trials; he was good and a preferred prosecutor for high-profile cases. The other was Alonzo Rodriguez, whose official title was commanding officer at large in the Detective Bureau. He was round and balding and his face was squat, distinguished by an odd attempt at a handlebar mustache. All three were in dark jackets and white shirts. The men wore ties in different shades of blue. Willis wore a pearl choker.

"Captain Rhyme, I'm First Deputy Commissioner Willis." Her voice was gravelly. Rhyme noted she used the mouthful of a title. Others might have said "Dep Com" or just their first name.

Noted too that she'd used his title as well. Perhaps a sign of deference, perhaps not.

"Commissioner. And Francis, Al."

"Lincoln," they said simultaneously.

The trio was stony faced.

Rhyme said, "I'm here with Detectives Sachs and Cooper."

"Good."

A curious comment. He waited.

"Captain Rhyme, first, I think I can speak for the entire department when I say we truly appreciate your contributions to investigations and prosecutions over the years."

He tipped his head again.

"I assume you've heard about the Viktor Buryak verdict."

"I have."

She looked at Duvalier, who said, "Lincoln, there was a jury poll taken after the verdict." He was hesitating, which Rhyme had never known him to do. "Eight members of the jury said the reason they couldn't convict was because of your testimony. They said that the evidence was questionable."

Rhyme was silent.

The man continued, "You and I, we both know that juries can be tough to figure. But that many of them, focusing on the same issue?"

Willis continued, "Somehow, the poll went public. I guess some jurors talked to the press. It became an issue. There've been stories: a man nearly convicted of murder on the basis of erroneous evidence. You know we've had problems in the past."

She was referring to incidents in the NYPD lab where evidence technicians were sloppy or lazy, or who in a few cases were bribed to intentionally alter evidence.

"Captain, we needed to do something. To shore up the department's credibility. This comes from the top. I've met with some people here, including the commissioner. It's been approved by the chief of department too. We've come to a decision. A press release is going out as we speak. Effective immediately, the NYPD will no longer be using civilian consultants in criminal investigations."

Rhyme said coolly, "If I'm not mistaken, you wanted me on the Locksmith case. Weren't you feeling that he'd thrown the home invasion in your face and you wanted him collared as fast as possible? *Was* I mistaken about that?"

The trio looked toward one another uneasily. Willis continued, "Circumstances changed."

Amelia Sachs was blunter. "Bullshit."

"Detective Sachs, this decision was not made lightly. And it's not just you, Captain Rhyme. No outside contractors at all—not for investigative work."

Sachs persisted: "So you'll shoot yourself in the foot because of the . . . what? Optics? One mistake out of thousands, and you hit us with this?"

"Detective, maybe in the future we might be able to put some quality control measures into place and revisit the decision. A year or two."

"Commissioner, name one investigator who hasn't fumbled a lead or missed the boat with a sample of trace or DNA . . ."

This was true. Yet the situation here was more complicated, because of that series of missteps in investigations and prosecutions Lon Sellitto had referred to earlier. These had been embarrassing for the NYPD and, worse, they had proved deadly. Several drug dealers who'd gotten off went on to kill rivals and bystanders. One sex trafficker had raped a teenager after his acquittal and fled to a Latin-American country with no extradition to the U.S.

This move, banning consultants, was clever. It would lay the blame for the Buryak screwup at the feet of someone not directly with the NYPD. And by banning consultants, the city—that is, the mayor—would be seen as taking strong action to clean house.

Willis's harsh voice continued, "I should bring up another policy we've instituted: that any employee of the NYPD who employs or works with a civilian will be subject to discipline, including suspension and firing."

Mel Cooper said, "And what do the PBA attorneys say about that?"

"They're in agreement."

Well, this had certainly been thought out.

Rhyme found himself looking at Al Rodriguez, who grimaced, gave a faint shrug and thumbed at his thin mustache.

Willis said, "Also effective immediately, Detectives Sachs and Cooper, you're to have no communication with Captain Rhyme."

"Commissioner," said Sachs, "Lincoln and I are married." Her voice registered disgust.

"You know what I'm saying, Detective. No *professional* communication. I'll be having the same conversation with Lieutenant Sellitto and Patrolman Pulaski. The officers on the Locksmith case will continue to run it. But all forensics will be done by department personnel at the lab in Queens."

Sachs sighed and sat in a rattan chair.

Willis said, "I'm sorry about this."

Rhyme now understood from her voice that "this" referred to something yet to be.

It was for someone else, Rodriguez, to tell him.

In a rather imperious voice he said, "The commissioner and chief of department have been in touch with the district attorney. His policy is that any officer who intentionally uses civilian consultants in an investigation may be indicted for obstruction of justice. The consultant too." Rodriguez added, "I've been put in charge of enforcing that policy."

An assignment that he would not be pleased about.

Still, he said what was inevitable.

"Detectives Sachs and Cooper, pack up all the evidence there and have it transported to Queens. Thank you for your time, Captain," Willis said. "I am sorry it worked out this way."

The Zoom screen vanished.

17

V iktor Buryak was in his lovely Tudor home in a leafy section of
Forest Hills, Queens, the most idyllic suburb of New York
City, in his opinion, apologies to Staten Island.

Buryak was sipping strong English breakfast tea, his second favorite drink. The brew was wonderful. It warmed him, heart and belly. His wife ordered this brand online for him. After he'd had a serious bout of the flu some years ago, coffee became repulsive and he began drinking tea. A man curious by nature, Buryak had looked into the origin of the beverage. His research, hardly academically rigorous, revealed that English breakfast tea was misnamed in several ways. It came from India, Sri Lanka and Kenya, not England. It was imported to the British Isles by the Portuguese, who drank it in the afternoon. A Scotsman popularized its consumption at breakfast. Victoria was responsible for bringing the seductively fragrant leaves south, and it was the Americans who had given it the name "English," which made sense because why would the Brits refer to it that way? To them it was just "tea."

His two cats chased each other briefly, amusing Buryak. They were grayish Maine Coons and massive. Brick, the female, was dominant and feisty. The male, Labyrinth, was younger and was happily bullied. Lab had replaced Mortar when he passed, several years ago.

He turned to his computer—a high-def model the size of a small TV—and began the meeting.

"Gentlemen."

There were five windows open on the monitor. Buryak's face was in one—the upper right—and from three other squares, faces peered out as well. He received in reply nods or greetings as perfunctory as his had been.

As each person spoke, a red outline appeared around the window. The program was similar to Zoom, but had been created by Buryak's IT people and was virtually unhackable. As far as tracing went, if you rode the coattails of the proxies, you ended up somewhere in Europe but there the trail would end.

In the upper left was Harry Welbourne, a sinewy and sour fifty-five-year-old. He radiated impatience, here and in person. He would be in his office in Newark. In the lower left was Kevin Duggin, whose face, very dark, was as round as Welbourne's was narrow. There was no telling where youthful, muscular Duggin might be. His businesses were scattered throughout East New York and Brownsville. But judging from the background—a Miró-like modern painting—he was probably in either his town house in Harlem or his house on the South Shore of Long Island. In the final occupied window were the Twins—Buryak always thought of them in upper case. Stoddard and Steven Boscombe. Both of the thirty-seven-year-olds wore their blond hair shoulder-length and middle-parted.

The center window was black.

"I heard about the verdict, Viktor. Congratulations, man." This was from Stoddard. Fortunately—for those wishing to tell them apart, if not for the man himself—Steven's cheek was disfigured by a two-inch-long scar.

Duggin was nodding. "I feel for you, man. Been there. Nothing worse than sweating out those verdicts. Who was the ADA?"

"Prick named Sellars."

Stoddard: "Murphy had to go. No loss to the world there. Wonder who did it."

"Don't have a clue. It's being looked into."

Welbourne rarely spoke and he didn't now.

Buryak said, "Let us get down to business, okay?" He'd been in the U.S. for thirty years. His Ukrainian accent had all but vanished and his English was flawless. Occasionally, though, he tended to speak more formally than colloquially.

"Got my checkbook," Duggin said.

Stoddard offered, "You're playing with the big boys now." His brother snickered.

Welbourne might have grunted. Buryak couldn't tell.

"First lot . . ." He typed and a picture of a yellow articulated dump truck appeared. "This is a Volvo, ten years old. Payload capacity 28 short tons. Gross weight 104,499 pounds. Max engine gross power 315, gross torque 1,505. Max speed of 33 miles per hour. As you can see it's in fair condition. The reserve bid is fifty thousand dollars, and I'll accept increases of five."

"Fifty," the Twins said simultaneously. Their high voices, coupled with their cold blue eyes, made the stereo effect just plain eerie.

Duggin: "Five five."

"Sixty," scarfaced Steve said.

In his rich baritone voice Duggin said, "Sixty-five."

Buryak was watching Welbourne, who was looking at another part of the screen. His eyes narrowed. He wrote something on a piece of paper and handed it to someone off camera.

The Twins regarded each other and chimed in with, "Seventy."

Buryak said, "Come, please. It is a once-in-a-lifetime chance. This truck can turn your businesses clean around. Did you hear? Three fifteen horsepower? Three fifteen!"

He enjoyed playing auctioneer.

Duggin said, "Come on, you motherfuckers. You're killing me. Seventy-five."

No one looked at the camera; Duggin and the twins were gazing at their upper left-hand corners, trying to see if they could get a clue as to what Welbourne was up to. The New Jerseyan was reading another portion of the screen, maybe some personal information, a spreadsheet or a website. He jotted another note and handed it off.

The brothers muted their call and began conferring.

"It's at seventy-five, Harry."

"I'm aware."

"You heard that torque."

"I heard."

"Viktor, my friend," Duggin said, "ain't it time to bang the gavel?"

"Not yet, Kevin."

Duggin slouched back in what appeared to be quite a luxurious black leather chair and sipped from a mug. "I think it oughta be fucking gavel time," he muttered.

The Twins unmuted. "Eighty."

Duggin: "Eight five."

"Crap," Steven spat out. "You don't even know what the fuck to do with a truck like that."

"Now, gentlemen, pretend we're at Christie's. A little civility."

The brothers looked at each other once again. They shook their heads simultaneously.

Buryak was disappointed. He'd thought this lot would do better.

"Going once . . ."

Welbourne took a slip of paper from a hand that ended in red polished nails. He read it.

"Going twice."

Welbourne looked into the camera. "One hundred ten thousand."

Yes!

Duggin grimaced, and the twins exchanged perplexed glances. All three remained grudgingly silent.

"Sold!" Buryak slapped his desktop in lieu of a gavel.

"I'll wire the money now," Welbourne said in his quiet, unemotional voice.

"It will take about a week to ten days for prep."

"All right."

"Now, let's move on to lot two." A picture of a twenty-foot cabin cruiser on a trailer appeared. It was old, the paint job uneven, missing some windows.

"This is what is called a fixer-upper, but well worth the investment. Let me give you the details."

18

Shortsighted, foolish . . .

Lincoln Rhyme was staring at the triptych of evidence boards.

In the corner was the Alekos Gregorios killing. Behind it, the Viktor Buryak–Leon Murphy case.

Which was, of course, not a case any longer at all.

Front and center was the Locksmith. It contained scores of notations, which Sachs would photograph and transcribe onto a similar board in the crime scene main facility in Queens—now that the case had been stolen away.

Rhyme knew he probably wasn't the best criminalist in the world. Out there somewhere—France, Botswana, Singapore, Brazil, the U.A.E., or, likely, in the borough of Queens, at the main NYPD lab—there was a man or woman with forensic skills that outshone his. But one thing was undeniable. Rhyme knew the city of New York as well as he knew this town house. And it was that knowledge base, combined with his natural talents for chemistry, physics and deduction, that made him unique.

Was some of this assessment ego?

Yes, of course. But ego and skill do not, by any means, exist in opposition. A good argument could be made that they have a correlated, and possibly causal, relationship.

"Here."

He looked up. Thom handed him a glass. Inside was amber-colored liquor. He smelled peat . . . but not too much. One of his favorite Glenmorangies, and a double pour. His aide, who'd been fired as often as he'd quit yet was still here, could read moods.

He sipped. It helped some, but Lincoln Rhyme's fiercest genre of anger was reserved for stupidity, even more so than corruption and deceit.

And with this sociopath roaming the streets of the city for reasons unknown, it was reckless in the extreme to sideline him.

He and Thom were alone in the town house. Cooper had packed up the evidence and had taken it to Queens. Amelia Sachs was at Major Cases. She'd gone down there to hand deliver a particular missive to Lon Sellitto.

His phone hummed and not the sound but his glance at the caller ID made his heart stir.

"Lon. Tell me."

The pause delivered the answer.

"Sorry, Linc. They're not budging. I got all the way to the commissioner."

Rhyme had figured this would be the answer. In fact, he nearly smiled at the image of the rotund, rumpled detective lieutenant insisting his way into the commissioner's office and pleading the case for Lincoln Rhyme's reinstatement. Sellitto would have wanted to mutter, "Are you out of your fucking mind?" But, of course, he would have brought all the negotiating skills of a seasoned homicide detective to the game.

"I found something else. You heard about this blogger? Verum?"

"No."

"Crank conspiracy guy. Posts online, these videos about politics, society, all kinds of bullshit. Lies, but people eat them up. He's got thousands of followers online."

"'Verum'? Latin for 'true.' Except what he says isn't."

"You got it. Looks like he's in California, maybe L.A., but he's been posting about New York. There's this conspiracy he calls the Hidden. Some movement trying to destroy American institutions. He said that's why Buryak got off. The trial was thrown."

"I'm part of a secret state, hm? I missed the thank-you cards from Buryak for doing my part to set him free."

"And then he's saying that the police aren't doing enough to stop the Locksmith because they're part of it too. City Hall."

Ah, he got it now. Rhyme barked a sour laugh. "It's not the brass, is it, Lon? The ban-the-consultants didn't come from the brass; it was the mayor. He wanted me out because of the election. I'm a fall guy."

Rhyme knew next to nothing about politics—it didn't affect his universe of forensic science—but he did know a special election for governor was coming up soon, and Mayor Harrison—a Bronx-born lifelong shirtsleeve politician—was going head-to-head with billionaire businessman Edward Roland, who lived in a posh portion of Westchester County.

"Looks like it." Sellitto scoffed.

So, Rhyme found himself a pawn in a political contest, a role he didn't think he'd ever played before.

"Listen, Lon, you seen Amelia yet?"

"She dropped it off." His voice was low.

"You take credit. Don't tell anybody it came from me."

"Fuck, Linc. I take credit all the time for shit you come up with."

"Night, Lon."

The call was disconnected.

He was staring at the Locksmith whiteboard when his computer dinged with the sound of an incoming email. It was a Zoom invitation from a man he hadn't spoken to in some time. NYPD Commanding Officer Brett Evans—the same rank as somber Rodriguez, of the handlebar affectation.

Rhyme took another sip of scotch and, manually this time, clicked on the link.

Soon he was looking at a man in his mid-fifties. Evans was the epitome of police brass. He had a lined, lean face, broad shoulders and hair going gray. His eyes were forever calm. This was a chest-up-only angle but Rhyme remembered him as having slim legs. "Dapper" was the word that came to mind.

"Lincoln, sorry to bother you at night."

"No worries, Brett." Rhyme rarely littered conversations with pleasantries like "doing well?" or "what's happening?," and he didn't now. He waited.

"I heard what happened, Lincoln. Jesus." His face was troubled.

Rhyme couldn't help but chuckle. "Aren't you afraid of getting busted, Brett, talking to me? Obstruction of justice, conspiracy . . . *treason?*"

"You always did have a sense of humor. Anyway, Lincoln, as soon as I heard I called Sally Willis. I put in a word for you. Nobody's changing their mind."

Evans had worked his way up from patrol to gold shield and beyond. Commanding officers, or "commanders," perched in the loftiest aeries of NYPD hierarchy.

But their power did not trump City Hall's.

"No, it's set in stone. Nothing to do. You can't appeal a business decision."

Evans mused, "The O'Neil case? Hell's Kitchen?"

"Remember it, sure."

Rhyme—yes, as a *consultant*—had handled forensics at a scene detective third grade Evans had run near the West Side piers. In walking the grid at a warehouse, long abandoned by the ruthless Eddie O'Neil, Sachs had discovered an unusual feather. After several days of analysis and research—and eyes-closed pondering, Rhyme was able to trace it to a neighborhood pet store, where O'Neil, they learned, bought his illegally imported birds. The owner of the store—after some horse-trading (Rhyme liked the animal motif)—agreed to be a confidential informant against the mobster. O'Neil got collared minutes before a shootout with rivals that could have led to the deaths of dozens of innocent pedestrians and drivers on Ninth Avenue.

That had been the case that made Evans's career.

"I owe you for that one. Always have. So, listen, Lincoln. I've got some buddies in New Jersey State Police. *They* use consultants, no problem." He chuckled. "And, I mean, plenty of homicide in New Jersey, right? *The Sopranos*."

Rhyme had no idea what opera singers had to do with murder in New Jersey, but there was no disputing his premise.

"They'd love you on board."

"Appreciate it, Brett," Rhyme said, not adding that he wouldn't take a job with that outfit, as fine as it was, because his expertise was New York City and he was not inclined to begin his education anew into infrastructure, geography and culture.

And then there was the commute . . .

"I also know some people at commercial forensic operations in the city," Evans added. "That work can be just as challenging, right?"

No, it didn't come close. He said, "I'm sure it is. But for now I just need to think about things for a bit."

"Sure. I understand. You should know, there're more than a few of us here think this is bullshit."

But there were some important ones who did not.

"Thanks for the call, Brett."

Rhyme was tired, bone tired. He summoned Thom, who escorted him upstairs in the tiny elevator and got him ready for bed.

Soon he was lying on the elaborate, mechanically operated mattress and starting to doze off. Just before sleep arrived, though, he thought: Yes, indeed he was a pawn in the chess game of state politics—a piece that had been removed from the board, without sufficient tactical forethought.

And, unable to avoid belaboring the metaphor a bit longer, he wondered: Just how would his sacrifice affect the endgame?

19

When is a truck not a truck?

Viktor Buryak was alone, cats excepted. He was jotting notes on the results of the auction and he was pleased. The wire transfers from the three bidders were already in. With Buryak, customers always paid up front.

Everyone had bought something. Welbourne, the truck. The twins, the boat. And Kevin Duggin picked up a backhoe.

Buryak was, he felt, part of a new generation of mobsters. That didn't mean he was Gen ZZ or whatever was current, of course. Buryak was in his fifties, conservative, a traditionalist. He wore a suit every day, usually with a stylish vest. He polished his shoes. He never indulged in illegal substances—and why would he when he had tea and his *first* favorite beverage, fine brandy?

And neither did new generation mean developing and selling state-of-the-art designer drugs to those who were under thirty but who had a six-figure disposable income.

No, the innovative part was what his company, VB Auctions, actually sold.

The bidders in tonight's auction had no need for any such equipment and wouldn't even take delivery. Buryak was cautious to the edge of paranoia and so he'd come up with the idea of a phony auction.

What the men had really been bidding for was the commodity that was Viktor Buryak's specialty, and perhaps the most dangerous product in the city. Worse than drugs, plastic explosives, poisons, machine guns.

Information.

The "dump truck" that stone-faced Welbourne bought was really a file that Buryak and his employees would assemble. It would contain exacting details of shipments of fentanyl and OxyContin from a warehouse in Pennsylvania to Virginia to New York and on to its ultimate destination in Connecticut (the circuitous route, which involved using separate trucks decorated with fake signage, was for security).

The file would also include the names of the drivers, their personal information (family members too) and the names of police in each jurisdiction the trucks would roll through, including, in New York City, a few precincts with cops who could be counted on to turn a blind eye, or even help Welbourne's hijackers.

The "boat" the Twins had bought was a dossier on a man named Suarez who'd come to New York from Miami, with a small crew, and was planning on starting a drug operation that catered to the Latinx population. It was small-time and not much of a threat to any of the bidders, but the dossier could be used to guarantee that the man would have to kick over a good portion of the take to the winner. It contained sexting messages between the married Suarez and a mistress. Selfies too of both of them, several naked in bed, the bath, the floor, the kitchen island (really? Buryak had thought). The girlfriend was, literally, that: a girl, sixteen, which made the pictures child pornography and their self-documented activities statutory rape.

Suarez would pay big.

Duggin had gone away happy too. The "backhoe" was a year's worth of monthly reports on when and where the NYPD vice and drug teams would conduct raids. Duggin's specialty was sex trafficking, and his crew ran more than a dozen massage parlors in the city. Buryak had been amused when, after he won the auction, Duggin had brayed a laugh. "Bought myself a back-*hoe.* Damn."

As a cover, yes, VB did move industrial machinery and made a fair profit doing so. But the golden kernel of the operation was what took up ninety percent of the time, resources and space: the research department, which operated much like a corporate espionage/private eye/data-mining firm. His people conducted interviews and performed surveillance and collected data. But they dug much, much deeper to unearth sensitive information that no one else could provide.

Admittedly, some of the practices were questionable—using Bulgarian and Czech Republic hackers (they were the masters). And then there was always the ever-popular business model of extortion, blackmail and broken limbs or threatened children.

Knowledge is power, and armed with Buryak's facts and figures, the crime bosses in the New York area were thriving. Arrests were down by thirty percent and an outfit paying for Buryak's services could count on hobbling an upstart competitor before they got a toehold in the territory. And the products and services that Buryak didn't deal in, but that his clients did, proliferated all the more abundantly on the streets of New York, Bridgewater, Newark, Trenton and every other supermarket catering to consumers with that insatiable need for drugs, guns, sex, stolen credit cards and merchandise.

His success, he knew, put a figurative price on his head. The police and FBI wanted desperately to stop him. Look at that bullshit Leon Murphy case. Utterly trumped up. But no one was more security minded than he was, a lesson learned early, on the streets in Kiev when his father—a loud and proud organized criminal—was arrested in front of the family home by police who decided that lifting his hands and crying *"Ne zachepy moho syna!"* warranted bullets in his head.

At least they heeded his plea and did not in fact hurt his son. They told the boy to stick to the straight and narrow—well, an equivalent Ukrainian cliché.

But, of course, he did not. The fourteen-year-old knew only his father's calling, but from that blood-spattered moment on, he followed what he called "prophylactic practices" to stay safe, alive and out of prison.

He convinced his mother to move to the U.S., where at least due process would give you a fighting chance and lawyers could be miracle workers. He identified a pretty and moderately sexy woman who was Ukrainian American and he became a citizen of the country. On the surface he was a legitimate businessman, running a successful company. He was active in church. He donated to good causes and served on charitable boards.

None of which fooled a single soul. There was no doubt among the authorities he was data-miner-in-chief to the gangs—the "Godfather of Information," some paper dubbed him—but proving it was another matter. This, he knew, was why the prosecutor clutched at straws and tried to bring him down with that bogus murder charge.

He himself never stepped over into the dark side of his operation. He had minions for that. They were well paid for their loyalty. But more important they were mostly married or had children. There was the unspoken whip: that if they broke the watertight seal and Buryak got damp, very bad things would happen. (Only once had he transgressed, murdering a contractor who'd come across a stash of unaccounted millions in his country house and tried to extort him. He'd successfully turned the man's death into an accident, but the effort that took, and the anxiety it caused, told him he would never take matters into his own hands again.)

This was why he'd been mortified and infuriated to have been arrested—and tried, no less—for the death of a punk like Leon Murphy. Killing someone for trying to sell protection at one of Buryak's warehouses? No point. He would've sent a lieutenant to sit down with Murphy in a bar and explain about the dangers of identity theft. "Such a problem, such a hassle . . . People lose everything. They even end up on the street, Leon."

Why waste ammunition?

His phone—an encrypted satellite—hummed.

It was his head of research department. "Willem."

"Sir. Are you free?"

"Yes."

"Well, I need to talk to you about the Chemist. Our reception team picked up some information you need to know about. The tap in the courthouse prosecution room."

"All right."

"They didn't get as much as they'd hoped. He doesn't talk much. At least the audio quality's good. He said that if you were acquitted, he would find *some* evidence to quote 'nail you' for something."

"The Chemist said that?"

"That's right."

"I see. Anything specific?"

"No."

JEFFERY DEAVER

"That was it. He left the room. After that, we powered down the bugs. They sweep occasionally and we couldn't afford for them to be found."

"Thank you, Willem."

"You need anything more, sir, let me know."

They disconnected.

He rose and walked into the huge Mediterranean-style kitchen, the cats following like dolphins beside a cruise ship. His wife was not home to make him tea, so he boiled water and made a fresh pot himself. He took it and a porcelain cup back to his office.

So. The Chemist would continue to be a problem. This wasn't a surprise to Viktor Buryak. He'd seen in the man's eyes humiliation and the pain of defeat when the clever lawyer, Coughlin, cut him to pieces on the stand. And the man couldn't get him for Murphy's death again; double jeopardy guaranteed that. So he would come after him some other way.

Would he go so far as to *plant* evidence against him, set him up for another crime, even another homicide he didn't commit?

This didn't seem far-fetched.

He now took a sip of the delightfully hot tea and sent an encrypted message to Aaron Douglass. If anyone could make a problem like Lincoln Rhyme, aka the Chemist, go away, he was the man to do it.

PART TWO

MASTER KEY

[MAY 27, 4 A.M.]

20

I ntent.

That's the main thing—the "key," you might say—that defines the crime of possessing lock-picking tools. In New York, the law is clear:

> *Possession of burglar's tools. A person is guilty of possession of burglar's tools when he possesses any tool, instrument or other article adapted, designed or commonly used for committing or facilitating offenses involving forcible entry into premises, or offenses involving larceny by a physical taking, or offenses involving theft of services . . . under circumstances evincing an intent to use . . . the same in the commission of an offense of such character.*

Nearly all states have laws like New York's. You can buy whatever you need to pick locks, provided you do not plan to use them in furtherance of a crime. It's the prosecutor's job to prove that and it's a task that can be difficult.

If for some reason an officer of the law were to have stopped me as I was walking down the street toward Carrie Noelle's apartment and poked through my backpack, noting the tools, I would simply hand him the business card that reads *Day & Night Locksmith Services*, which is a complete fake, by the way. He might be suspicious and call the number. An answering service would pick up, taking the sting out of the suspicion. And he'd be thinking: Hard to prove intent, so the DA won't be interested.

He'd let me go. He might be curious about—and troubled by— my locking-blade brass knife but, then again, I follow the law and keep it concealed, a must in New York. And its length of 3⅞ inches is permissible in the city (it's also a length that's not a problem for me, as I know full well what kind of damage that much razor-sharp metal can do).

You don't need a Los Zetas serrated hunting knife to get blood to spray.

On the other hand, if, at the moment, a cop were to find me as I am now, in stocking cap and clear latex gloves, with those selfsame tools, and a page from the *Daily Herald*, he would deduce intent to forcibly enter into premises to commit a felony.

Which is why I'm crouching once again in the abandoned, unstable Bechtel Building, across from Carrie Noelle's apartment and not making a move until the street is deserted, until there is no one to note my presence.

I scan the surroundings. Present are some cars, some late-night revelers, a homeless man pushing a cart.

I grow impatient until finally, an opportunity. I'm across the street and, in a matter of seconds, through the service door. Some locks don't even deserve the name.

Soon I've climbed to Carrie's floor and am waiting in the fire stairwell, listening carefully.

I hear some clicks, some thuds. I'll wait for silence.

I unzip my backpack and open my tool case. I feel the brass knife in my pocket.

I'm breathing slowly. Concentrating, all too aware of the greatest challenge I—and all trespassing lockpickers—face: time.

Historians can't say for certain when and where the first lock was made, but they can say when the earliest lock was discovered. It was in the palace of Dur-Sharrukin, now called Khorsabad in Iraq—the site destroyed by ISIL a few years back. The lock dates to about 4000 B.C. It secured a massive door, which probably weighed hundreds of pounds.

The key was equally imposing and had to be carried on a guard's shoulder. It wasn't particularly sophisticated. In fact, it was so easy to duplicate by thieves and intruders that the royals took to installing multiple keyways in the door—only one of which worked. The purpose of this was to keep the intruder on the premises trying keyway after keyway for so long that the guards would find and then gut him after the briefest of trials, or no trial at all.

This is the reason most burglars are caught: because they can't breach their target before being spotted or heard. If you hear a *clink-tink* in your hallway and you rise from your TV-viewing spot to peek out and see nothing—because the picker is already inside your neighbor's apartment—you put it down to a cat, a rat, a settling building.

If you see someone in a ski mask and gloves, irritated because he can't defeat the lock, well, the results are obvious.

Speed . . .

Hence my agonizing practice with the SecurPoint 85.

Time is one enemy of the lockpicker; noise is another.

I have no idea what the wooden locks of ancient eras sounded like (wood was phased out in Roman days), but metal on metal undeniably makes noise, when inserting, when turning, when unseating.

Clink-tink . . .

So I need to make the process as silent as possible.

If I don't, it could be the disaster of 2019 all over again.

And I cannot let that happen.

In the stairwell of Carrie Noelle's building, I listen closely.

Silence.

Now. Go.

Fast, I'm into the hallway and at her door.

First, the knob lock. Three seconds, it's open.

And the SecurPoint 85?

Well, let's not get ahead of ourselves.

People are lazy and often don't bother to lock the deadbolt. Or they're forgetful.

I twist the knob and push.

Ah, but Carrie Noelle has been diligent, turning the latch before it was jammy time. The SecurPoint 85 is snug.

Go . . .

In goes the tension wrench, and I turn it, putting torsion on the plug with my left hand.

My right inserts the sharpened rake. Feeling the pins as I move the rake up and down, back and forth. *Seeing* them in my mind's eye—I've dismantled a hundred locks, touched the pins, smelled the metal, felt all the parts heavy in my hand.

I lose myself in the process of becoming the key.

A dark side of zen . . .

I'm not religious but I consider lock-picking mystical, akin to the transfiguration of Jesus from man to spirit. Buddha from ignorance to enlightenment. Gandalf the Grey to Gandalf the White.

Click, click.

There are ten pins in this lock—two in each hole. Manipulating them.

I have not been breathing since I started.

Little finger, left hand, keeps taut the tension wrench, while the rake probes.

Fifteen seconds . . .

Push, push . . . But gently. Don't anger those pins that have yet to be tricked up into their tunnels. You can't bully them. They have to be seduced.

Click, click . . .

Then the wrench swivels, and the one-inch-throw deadbolt leaves the strike panel.

I've done it!

The SecurPoint is a disgrace to its name.

In twenty seconds, no less.

I stand, shoot graphite on the hinges. Then I'm closing the door with outer-space silence.

Carrie is not an alarm kind of girl, so there is no need to flood the house with RF waves, or to spend the first five seconds of the Visit cutting wires.

A few steps inside. I listen.

I hear the hum of the refrigerator. The bubbling from the aquarium.

It's dark but not black. One thing I've learned is that unless you mount thick shades on all the windows, New York—Manhattan particularly—is filled with illumination. Light from a million sources bleeds inside through dozens of tiny fissures. This is true every minute of every day.

When my eyes acclimate I walk, cautiously, farther into the apartment itself.

I'm moving through a long hallway. I pass a door, closed presently. It leads to a small bedroom. Beside the door sit a half-dozen children's toys, among them an eerie-faced doll, a wooden locomotive, a puzzle, also wood, in which play involves rearranging letters to spell words.

I continue past the bedroom down the corridor. The kitchen is to the left, living room to the right. Comfortable couches and chairs, fake leather. A pommeled coffee table, covered with magazines and makeup and socks and more toys. The aquarium is impressive. I know nothing about fish but the colors are quite appealing.

In the back is the larger bedroom.

I take my brass knife from my pocket and open it, giving the faintest of clicks (I have graphited it too). Gripping the handle hard, the blade side up.

If I had been heard and was about to be attacked, now is the moment when it would happen.

I step inside.

But here she dozes. Pretty Carrie Noelle. She's sprawled on the bed in a tangle of purple floral sheets and a bedspread that seems too thick for the temperature in the apartment, which is not that cool. But this is what she's chosen for swaddling. People wage a war against insomnia and will use whatever weapon or tactic gives them advantage.

I fold the knife and replace it in my pocket.

Then look over Carrie once more.

Most women I've observed in the Visits sleep on their sides, a pillow or bunch of blankets between their legs. This is not a sexual thing, I'm convinced. Also, no one wears pajamas, much less nightgowns, unless it's a sexy garment and there's a man on the sinister side of the bed (as happened once—a surprise discovery that resulted in my fast retreat). No, the de rigueur outfit for bed among the female persuasion is sweatpants or boxer shorts and a T-shirt. And you'd be surprised at how many single women, of all ages, are accompanied to slumber with a stuffed animal or two.

I return to the living room. I look at her bookshelf. Carrie enjoys murder mysteries and bios and cookbooks, and—as in every apartment I've visited—she has a thousand-dollar collection of self-help and exercise books. Most, hardly cracked.

In the kitchen I find a bottle of red wine, an Australian shiraz. It's a good one—and it features a screw top. (Those from Down Under, I recall from the formal and fancy meals of my childhood, my father lecturing, are not afraid to sell fine wines in easy-to-open bottles. And why should they be? It only makes sense.)

I dig for a crystal glass and fill it halfway. I sip. It's quite decent. Then I correct myself. It's quite *good*. "Decent" does not mean quality. It means only the opposite of indecent—that is, not obscene. Anyone who practices the science of locksmithing knows that precision is everything. A thousandth of a thousandth of a millimeter of error in the bitting of a key will render it useless—except for steadying a wobbly table leg.

I walk to the front bedroom, quietly open the door. I look in and see all the children's toys. And the crib in the corner.

Children can make the Visits problematic. Waking up at all hours and screaming for attention.

I'll get back to this room but for the moment I return to the bathroom outside Carrie's bedroom.

There's a lipstick on the counter that describes itself as Passion Rouge. I'll use this to sign my calling card, the page from the *Daily Herald*.

I wonder what the police think of it. If they're diligent, and they probably are, they'll be considering the articles on the signature page, the ads on the reverse side, who the editors are, who the publisher is . . .

Are they thinking about more than that? Are they thinking page 3, the February 17 edition?

3
2/17

I suspect—no, I *know*—they aren't.

Where should I leave the paper? I wonder.

I decide, unimaginatively: underwear drawer again. I'm sure that results in tears. Then the newspaper slips from my mind and, gazing around the cozy bathroom, I fantasize about another outcome for Carrie Noelle.

I'm recalling the famous murder scene in the movie *Psycho*. The victim is in the shower when the killer slips into the bathroom, holding high the knife with which he plans to slash her to death. The tension is unbearable . . .

I imagine a variation. I *don't* leave the signed newspaper at all and slip into the darkness, as planned.

No, I'm standing *in* the bathtub, hiding behind the drawn shower curtain. There I wait—for Carrie to walk sleepily inside to start her morning routine . . . and make that pretty face all the prettier.

21

She awoke at dawn.

Some noise from the street broke her slumber.

Squinting at the bedside clock. Nearly 5 a.m. Damn.

Groggy from the pill last night, Carrie Noelle sighed. If I fall asleep now, I can still get one hour and twenty minutes.

Staring at the ceiling.

If I fall asleep *now*, I can still get one hour and eighteen minutes.

Noelle gripped the long pillow she embraced when she slept and rolled to her left side.

She gasped and reared back.

The eyes of a Madame Alexander doll—on its side as well—were staring at her.

While no one can dispute the artistry of these works, they are just plain fucking scary when they're twelve inches from your face, and you don't remember propping it on your neighboring pillow when you hit the hay at midnight.

Couldn't help but think: Two glasses of wine and the Ambien before bed (I know, I know, not good).

She must've been picking up some of the toys and carted it in here without thinking.

Noelle pressed her lips together. Morning mouth—like she'd eaten sand, which she'd actually done, once, on a dare by a cute fellow middle-schooler.

She reached for the bottle of Fiji water on the nightstand.

Not there.

She looked around. Wait. It was on the *left* bedside table—the farthest from the side she slept on. Why did she leave it there?

It was full, so she hadn't taken a sip in the middle of the night and then set it on the table after a fit of tossing and turning.

Noelle rolled upright and climbed from her bed. From the floor she retrieved the pair of jeans shed last night and a sweatshirt that was sitting on a small Queen Anne chair that was her de facto clothing caddy.

She gasped once more.

Beneath the sweatshirt, sitting spread out on the seat of the chair, was a bra. It was pink and decorated with tiny embroidered red roses.

The garment was one she had not worn for years—it was too small now. There'd be no reason for her to dig it out from where it spent its days, along with other skinny apparel: in a tied bag in the bottom of her closet.

Doll, water, bra . . .

What the hell were you doing, girl?

No more duets of alcohol and pharma. Period.

Maybe she'd been sleepwalking. It did happen. She'd read an article in the *Times* about the phenomenon. True, mostly adolescents and children were afflicted. But the condition did occur in adults sometimes.

Sleepwalking . . .

Or chardonnay-walking.

She turned to where her phone was—or was supposed to be: on the floor, plugged in and charging, beneath the bedside table.

No. Not there.

She'd probably kicked the iPhone under the table or bed after the jeans came off.

Well, look.

I can't.

Deep breath. The childhood fears, the clichés about the boogeyman under the bed.

Get. The. Damn. Phone.

On her knees fast, truly expecting a sinewy hand to zip from the dust-bunny world and close around her wrist.

No one—no *thing*—attacked.

But there was no phone either.

She walked to the doorway that led into the living room. Noelle froze.

A gasp. The phone was stuck in the sand on the bottom of her aquarium, standing upright. The fish circled it like the apes examining the monolith in *2001: A Space Odyssey.*

Heart pounding, sweat pricking her scalp, beneath her arm, she leaned forward. On the coffee table, before the beige couch that faced the aquarium, was a glass that appeared to contain the dregs of red wine.

Carrie Noelle did not drink red wine. A headache issue.

And even if she did, she wouldn't have used *this* glass, her mother's Waterford, which had been tucked away in the sideboard, under several layers of tablecloths and napkins, as inaccessible as the 32B bra.

Then she understood.

He'd been here!

The story in the news!

Some man had just broken into an apartment on the Upper West Side. Some psycho who called himself the Locksmith. He could get through even the most sophisticated security systems—even, apparently, the expensive top-of-the-line model deadbolt that Noelle had had installed.

She stepped into her Nikes and started down the hall.

But she stopped, fast, at the sound.

What . . . What is that?

She cocked her head and made out the faint notes tinkling from the second bedroom.

It was Brahms's "Lullaby," and the tune was coming from the mobile above the baby crib.

Lullaby and good night,
You're your mother's delight,
Shining angels beside
My darling abide.

Son of a bitch, she thought. Now more angry than scared. She ran into the kitchen for a weapon and stared at the countertop.

The butcher block knife holder was there.

All of the knives were gone.

Glancing at the second bedroom, she noted that the door was open—it had been closed when she went to bed. *That* she remembered clearly.

Jesus, he was in there now, with the knives!

It was then that she remembered the toolbox, which rested in the bottom of the bathroom closet. No knives inside but there was a hammer. It was the only weapon she could think of so it would have to do. She turned and stepped into the bathroom fast, closing and locking the door.

Thinking, fat lot of good that'll do. If he got through a four-hundred-and-fifty-dollar deadbolt, how long would the knob lock stop him?

As she flung the closet door open and dropped to her knees to dig for the tool kit, she paused and looked up.

The shower curtain, which she'd left open last night, was drawn closed.

Soft and warm is your bed,
Close your eyes, rest your head . . .

22

Amelia Sachs finished walking the grid at the crime scene, Apartment 4C, 501 East 97th Street.

She'd done the Bechtel Building, the Locksmith's entry and exit routes into and out of Carrie Noelle's building and had just completed her apartment itself.

Wearing white Tyvek overalls and other standard crime-scene gear, she carried a dozen paper and plastic bags out into the hallway, and handed off to an evidence collection tech—a young, talented Latina, whom Sachs had wanted to recruit to work regularly with her and Rhyme—a plan put on hold now that her husband had been summarily fired.

She tried to quash the anger she felt at the brass's foolishness. No, that was too mild. Their *idiocy.*

This she was not able to do.

Politics . . .

"Terrible," Sonja Montez said, somber faced, as she looked at a large plastic bag containing a baby's rotating mobile of angels. She had a four- and a six-year-old at home.

"Do the CoCs and get them into the bus."

"Sure, Detective." She put the bags, from which chain-of-custody cards dangled, into a large plastic tub and walked to the elevator.

Sachs spent another fifteen minutes in the apartment, then she too left and descended to the main floor. Outside, she noted the large crowd, staring at the police activities.

Reporters too. As always, the press hovered, and . . . *pressed.*

"Is this the Locksmith?" one called.

"Detective Sachs!"

"Was there a *Daily Herald* page here too?"

She said nothing and began stripping off the overalls.

Ron Pulaski approached. The young officer ran a hand through his short blond hair and absently worried the scar on his forehead. He'd suffered a head injury on the job years ago, and it had been a long slog back to full health.

"Sucks about Lincoln."

"Yeah. Any luck with locksmithing shops?"

"No. Just that they were all impressed at the perp's skill."

Sachs scoffed. "Not helpful."

"No."

She glanced up toward the window that would be Noelle's. "He was drinking her wine. Just like he ate Annabelle Talese's cookies. Sitting on the couch with his feet up on her coffee table."

"Drinking?" Pulaski was frowning. "He's careful about friction ridges. But careless about DNA?"

"Maybe. Maybe not. We'll have to see."

"Brother. What's the guy about?" He thought for a moment. "I think he's flaunting. Home invasion, sitting there, throwing the intrusion into the victims' faces."

"Throwing it in our faces too." Sachs had run serial perp cases before. Narcissism was a key component to their personalities. They believed they were special; they could play God.

Her eyes slipped to the reporters.

She happened to glance behind the throng and notice a gray Cadillac, one of the newer ones. It was stopped in a traffic lane, which wasn't odd, since there were other curious drivers slowing or pausing as they or their passengers eyed the police action. Given the dark windows, she wasn't one hundred percent certain but it appeared that the driver—in shades and a black hat—was videoing or photographing her. While others in the crowd were filming the ambulance, the crime scene van, the police cars and the white-gowned techs, his phone was aimed directly her way. She knew that it was not uncommon for the perp to return to the scene during an investigation. Sometimes this was to glean what the cops were discovering. Other times, it was to bask in their handiwork.

Narcissism . . .

When he seemed suddenly aware she was observing him, he set the phone down, put the car in gear and sped on. Sachs stepped into the street but caught only the tag's state—New York—not the number, before it disappeared around the corner.

"Something?" Pulaski asked.

"The gray Caddie. More interested in us than I would've liked."

"You think our perp drives a *Cadillac*?"

"Why not? Locksmithing's just a hobby, according to Benny Morgenstern. Who knows what he does for a living? You find anything here?"

Pulaski said, "We've talked to a couple dozen neighbors, businesspeople, deliverymen. Nobody's seen anything."

He and a half-dozen officers from local precincts had checked escape routes the Locksmith might have taken. It appeared that he'd broken a window in the back of the building and dropped into an alley to escape. The fact that he hadn't used either the front entrance or the service door meant he'd left just minutes earlier—the police presence would have surprised him.

"Security cameras?"

"None that're working."

Half the cams one sees in stores and on the street are fake or not hooked up. Recording security video is a time-consuming and complicated job. And cameras and boxes can be expensive.

"What we talked about before," she whispered. "You okay helping?"

"Absolutely, Amelia."

"Fourth floor. East stairwell." Sachs nodded at Noelle's. "Then the Bechtel Building. Front lobby."

"Got it." The young officer walked off.

Her eyes scanned once more for the gray Cadillac. No sign of it. Sachs stepped to her Torino, from which she retrieved her dark blue sport coat, pulling it on over the black sweater. She also wore black jeans and boots. Then she walked to a nearby blue-and-white and sat down in the backseat.

"How are you doing?" Sachs asked Carrie Noelle.

"Okay, I suppose." The woman returned Sachs's phone and thanked her for its use. Her own, which Sachs had retrieved from the aquarium, would be going into evidence on the off chance that the Locksmith had touched it without gloves.

Noelle said, "I have to ask. How'd you get here so fast? My neighbors heard me calling for help and they said you were downstairs in seconds. How on earth did that happen?"

23

Lincoln Rhyme.

That was the answer to Carrie Noelle's question.

"We had leads that the Locksmith might have some connection to your block."

Sachs let it go at that and didn't share that, as his last act as a criminalist, before he was furloughed, Rhyme considered the evidence collected thus far: the dish detergent, shards of old-time porcelain insulator, the brick dust. Then he'd composed the memo that Sachs—his "special envoy"—had taken downtown to hand deliver to Lon Sellitto, as email couldn't be trusted. The instructions were to have the lieutenant send patrol officers in Midtown North, the 19, 20, 23, 24 and 28 Houses to search for a demo site involving an old, red-brick building. Those police precincts bordered Central Park, which Rhyme had targeted as a focal point because of the dish detergent used in cleaning the park's gates.

Early this morning, 4:30 a.m., Sellitto got a report of a possible location. A patrolman responded, telling the lieutenant that his beat included the red-brick Bechtel Building on East 97th, half demolished and awaiting a new developer, since the existing one was in bankruptcy. They knew of the structure because it was the site of drug activity and they would occasionally roust the pushers. The resourceful officer had sent pictures of that and surrounding buildings.

Sellitto had in turn forwarded them to Sachs, keeping Rhyme out of the chain, though in the predawn hours she had, of course, shared everything with her husband.

"He doesn't live in the place," Rhyme had said as he lay in bed. "And if there's no active demo going on, he doesn't work there."

"Which means he might be using it for surveillance." Sachs had pointed to one of the pictures—of the apartment at 501 East 97th. "The service door's right across from one of the windows."

"Get down there now."

Twenty minutes later she'd pulled up in front of the Bechtel Building, meeting Ron Pulaski and two blue-and-whites. They'd done no more than huddle to come up with a plan of action, when a call came in from Dispatch, reporting a break-in, in the very building she was gazing at.

She, Pulaski and the uniforms had responded, covering the exits and hurrying upstairs where a hysterical Carrie Noelle sat in a neighbors' apartment. Escorted by Pulaski downstairs, she'd waited in the back of the squad car while Sachs and the ECTs walked the grid.

The woman described a break-in that was identical to Annabelle Talese's. She had no idea when the suspect had left.

Sachs asked Noelle the same questions that she'd asked Talese—about stalkers, exes, anyone who might wish her harm.

Sachs suspected the answers would be the same as well: Noelle could think of no one who had a motive to harm or threaten her or invade her home. Which gave credence to the theory that the intrusions were most likely random, though his purpose was still a mystery.

"It was so terrible," Noelle whispered. "My job, I sell collectible toys. He put a doll in bed next to me. And he turned on that mobile, you know, over a baby's crib? The Brahms 'Lullaby.' I'll never be able to hear that music again." Noelle dug for a tissue in her purse and dabbed her eyes. She opened a bottle of some medication and took two pills, swallowing them dry.

Thirty feet away, Evidence Collection Technician Sonja Montez had removed the Tyvek coveralls. Stripping off the cocoon had revealed a striking woman of dark complexion, bright pink lipstick and blue eyeshadow. She wore a striped black and red blouse and burgundy side-zippered slacks. She caught Sachs's eye and gave a thumbs-up. Meaning the evidence was in the CSU bus, all the chain-of-custody cards filled out.

Sachs noted a car pulling up. It was roughly the same shade as the Cadillac and, at first, she tensed, but then noted it was a different make. A woman was behind the wheel. She spoke to a uniformed officer and he guided her to the curb. She parked and climbed out. Noelle's sister, it seemed.

Noelle asked, "Is it okay if I go now? I don't want to be anywhere near here."

Sachs recalled Annabelle Talese's words.

He stole my home. I loved it so much, and he took it away from me . . .

"Of course. I'll call if I have any more questions. And if you think of anything else, let me know." They had exchanged cards.

It was then that she heard a male voice. "Detective Sachs."

She turned to see Commander Alonzo Rodriguez walking toward her. His dark eyes, close-set in a round and balding head, took in the evidence in the back of the CS bus. With him was a slim man—also balding—in a fine suit. Sachs knew him. Abraham Potter. He had some job in the mayor's office, probably an aide. He looked imperious but she suspected he didn't possess particular power, and was probably a skilled tattletale.

Camera crews were filming their way. Rodriguez seemed more than aware of that.

With a faux smile beneath his odd, stringy mustache, he said, "I know there was a little friction in yesterday's meeting. I just wanted to say one thing."

"Okay."

"When word comes down from on top, there's not a lot that can be done about it."

"Is there anything I can help you with, Commander?"

He cleared his throat. "Detective, there's an officer at the crime scene lab in Queens. He's expecting that evidence"—a nod at the cartons—"to be logged in, in thirty minutes, with all the chain-of-custody cards duly executed."

"Noted."

"You know the consequences if that doesn't happen."

She didn't answer.

"You've given all the evidence you've collected to the collection technicians." A nod at the bus.

"Yes," she said coolly.

Then in Rodriguez's moonish face, split in half by the handlebar, a smile, of sorts, appeared. He walked toward her car. "But before you go, indulge me." And he gestured her to follow with a crooked finger.

24

At 5:04 a.m., with Carrie Noelle snoozing contentedly one room away, I turned on the hanging mobile in the room where she stored the children's toys she sold online.

I heard the bleat of a police siren and looked out the window to see several police squad cars and unmarked ones driven by plain-clothes cops descending in front of the Bechtel and Carrie's apartment buildings.

I thought, again, of 2019. The disaster.

And my palms, in the expensive clear surgical gloves, began to sweat. My heart to pound.

Then more officers were descending on the block where the Bechtel Building stood. They were looking round.

Looking for *me*?

Impossible.

Or perhaps not.

The more I considered it, the more I believed this wasn't a coincidence.

Those in the lock industry don't believe in omens. Locksmithing is science, it's mechanics, it's physics. Pins retreat because we make them retreat. The third time—or the thirtieth—is the charm only because that's the time we've achieved just the right combination of tension and raking.

Then, with the bleat of a siren, I heard Carrie stir in her bedroom.

Out!

I took all of the knives from the butcher block, slipped one in my bag, along with the panties I'd taken earlier, and hid the others in the freezer. This would slow her down because she'd think I'm armed—if I took just one, she might not notice.

Then a look out of Carrie's front door. The hall was empty, so I left. This time without relocking the SecurPoint 85. No time for dramatic flourishes.

I couldn't leave by the front door to the street, so I did via the back window. Breaking a window to escape is like bumping a lock. But I comfort myself with the thought that it was painted shut; there was no lock to pick. As I climbed out I reflected that I probably shed evidence, but, fortunately, there was a hose on the ground, beside some trash bags. I pointed the nozzle at where I landed and turned the stream on full. Hairs and DNA that I might have left would soon be down the storm drain.

Now, an hour later, I'm on crowded 97th Street, along with curious spectators and the press.

I learn that I was right; this is no coincidence. A tall redhead detective—there's a gold badge on her hip—is talking to a young blond officer in a uniform. He calls her Amelia and he's Ron and she mentions Carrie Noelle by name.

In fact, there she is, mouse-timid in the back of a squad car.

How the hell . . . ?

I know for a fact that Carrie didn't call them; when they arrived she was still Sleeping Beauty and her phone had been drowned in the aquarium.

Nobody could have seen me break into the apartment or they would have called the police much earlier.

Somehow, they figured out that I was targeting her.

I consider this.

Figuring out my assault on Carrie specifically was impossible; only I knew I had a Visit to her planned. But what *isn't* impossible is that they decided I was going after someone in this neighborhood. No. On this *block*.

This has to be it. Amelia points to someone in one of those space-man crime-scene suits and then to the Bechtel Building. And he, or she, begins to encircle the front with police tape.

Of course!

I glance at my feet.

My betraying shoes.

I picked up some dirt or mud or something telltale on one of the earlier visits here and tracked it to Annabelle Talese's. The police traced it to the Bechtel Building. This seems incredible to me, but then to a layperson picking a SecurPoint—or, for that matter, any stout deadbolt—would be akin to magic.

I call up Google. All it takes is "crime scene" and "Amelia" and "NYPD," and I'm inundated with references to Amelia Sachs, decorated detective, daughter of a decorated patrol officer, married to the decorated former detective, now consultant, Lincoln Rhyme.

Their specialty is forensics.

I'm furious with myself. What if this Rhyme and his wife had made the deduction earlier and sent officers here then, when I was crouched in the dank front lobby of the Bechtel Building, waiting for the chance to start my Visit?

It wouldn't have taken long to get to the "intent" question. Once the officers discovered the tools—my stocking cap that pulls down into a full-face mask, page 3 of the *Daily Herald* and, of course, the knife, technically legal though it may be—I'd be on my way to jail.

Which would be, for me, pure hell.

My hands are actually tremoring.

And that is a condition that no lockpicker can tolerate.

So, in the future, shoes with plain leather soles.

Amelia spends some time talking to Carrie Noelle in the back of the car. I can imagine the exchange, as they each try to figure out the why-me question.

I calm and focus on the situation. After Carrie—still pretty but pale and with hair askew—drives off with her ride, I edge closer to Amelia. I want to learn more about my pursuers. It's a risk being here, though no one seems to pay me any mind. Sunglasses—and the morning is in fact sunny—a turned-up collar on my sumptuous leather jacket. On my head I've swapped the stocking cap for a more common Mets baseball hat. I have never been to a game, not that team, not any. My father, I happen to reflect, was too busy to take me to any amusement, especially a common one. That, however, was the least of his sins, and the fact is I would have hated his company anyway.

I notice some tension between Amelia and a man who has the smug quality of someone in power. I guess he's a police captain or some other brass. The rotund man sports a self-conscious handlebar mustache. Maybe he fancies himself Agatha Christie's Belgian detective Poirot. He's dark-complexioned. Latino, I gauge. Or possibly Mediterranean.

There's another suited man, skinny and bald, and he stands by, observing with unemotional eyes.

The exchange between them is not a full-on argument but he's lording something over her, louder than he needs to be, with the result that the nearby press continue to film.

Poirot reminds me of my father.

My impression is that police department politics are more involved than the art of crime solving.

The dispute seems to be about the evidence she has collected.

He walks to an old-time car, a Ford Torino. It's hers. I've just seen her take a jacket from it and tug the garment over her appealing figure. Poirot is saying, "But before you go, indulge me." He gestures condescendingly for her to follow.

The skinny man joins them, and a flash of sunlight fires from his smooth skull.

Poirot peers into the interior of the vehicle like a traffic cop hoping to spot some weed or an open beer. He then points to the trunk.

Hands on hips, she regards him closely.

More video cameras are gobbling up the scene. How ironic: I see a crew from WMG—the Whittaker Media Group channel—a part of the empire that publishes the *Daily Herald*.

There's a standoff for a moment between Amelia and Poirot. It seems his condescending poke toward her trunk proves nearly to be too much for Amelia. She is a few inches taller than him, and she leans close, glaring. He doesn't give an inch.

After a moment she pulls keys from the pocket of her black jeans. Most cars back then—the '60s—came with two different keys: one for the ignition, one for the doors and trunk. The reason for that has been much debated, and I don't have an answer to the mystery.

Amelia opens the trunk. Poirot glances in and doesn't see what he'd hoped to see.

She slams the lid and walks toward the front of the car, removing her phone and making a call. Poirot remains nearby, watching her with his arms crossed, like a principal before a high school student possibly guilty of an infraction.

Ignoring the man, Amelia finishes her call, then drops into the low car. The big engine fires up crisply and she skids into traffic.

Poirot looks after her and then walks away, his face both smug and disappointed as if he *wanted* to catch her in a no-no. Baldie is at his side, now on his mobile.

The Belgian detective ignores questions from the press, several of whom ask again—nearly demanding—if this was the work of the Locksmith and if, this time, he murdered anyone.

In truth, my thoughts are still on Amelia. I understand she's married but that doesn't stop me from picturing her alone in bed, as she sleeps in a T-shirt and boxers, on her side, a long pillow or curled duvet between her slim legs. In the video playing in my head, I'm in the room, just a few feet away, staring down, enjoying what I'm seeing, her mouth slightly open, her knees drawn up and—particularly vivid—her red hair splayed out upon the pillow, arcing and glossy, like a hawk's unfurled wings.

25

What's she doing here? Lincoln Rhyme wondered.

Amelia Sachs was walking into Rhyme's town house. Apparently, given the timing, she would have come directly here from the scene on East 97th. Rhyme was surprised. He thought she'd go straight to Queens to supervise the processing of the evidence at the main lab, per fiat from Willis and Rodriguez—and ultimately, the mayor. She should be in their lab; the team needed to move fast. The Locksmith was smart, and careful, but he'd stumbled once, leading them to his next victim. Maybe he'd slipped up again, this time directing them to his home or office, or revealing his identity.

It was odd to watch her enter without the evidence cartons. Perhaps she'd come here to pick up some things she needed before going on to Queens. Even though Rhyme's lab was a small fraction of the size of the main NYPD operation, his was better financed per square foot and had newer and in some cases more sophisticated instrumentation. If she took any—fine, she could help herself—but damn it, the city was going to pay for transport and recalibration. And he'd want a receipt.

Sachs said, "Carrie's fine."

"Who?"

"The vic. Carrie Noelle."

He knew she was all right. He'd heard.

Not relevant.

"But this one was more troubling."

"How so?"

"He moved all her knives—hid them. And shorted out her phone in the aquarium."

Rhyme considered his wife's words. "He didn't want her to have a way to communicate and didn't want her to have weapons. Because this time he was considering attacking her."

"That's what I think."

"Why *didn't* he?" Rhyme asked.

"Maybe he heard we were there. One of the blue-and-whites hit the siren, to move a car along. He heard it, saw us and got out fast."

"The siren, really?" Rhyme grimaced. "At least, if that's the case, Sachs, I suppose we saved her."

She nodded.

"Did he leave a newspaper?"

"He did. In her underwear drawer again. Same page. Same message—in lipstick."

"The hell's that about? I'm voting it's a misdirection."

And then recalled that his vote would not be counting for anything in the investigation.

The doorbell sounded and Rhyme and Sachs glanced at the security monitor. Thom had heard too and he appeared in the hallway, looking neat and trim, as he always did. Dark slacks and a blue dress shirt, a blue and purple floral tie. "Answer it?" he asked, noting that they continued to look at the monitor and had not unlocked the door themselves.

The caller was a large, tanned man, with a shaved, or naturally bald, head. After a moment he held up a gold NYPD shield.

Sachs and Rhyme shared a glance. She said, "Don't know him."

On his chair arm controller, Rhyme hit the intercom.

"Help you?"

"Captain Rhyme?"

"That's right, Detective."

"You have a minute?"

A pause. "Sure." A nod to Thom, who walked to the door and unlatched it.

A moment later the man, with broad shoulders and a handsome, thoughtful face was in the parlor, looking past Rhyme and Sachs, who stepped away and typed on her phone. He said, "Well, that's impressive."

He meant the lab.

Rhyme knew. Nothing to comment on.

The large man turned and nodded to Sachs and Rhyme. She slipped her phone away and focused on the visitor.

"Detective." A glance to Sachs. Then back to Rhyme: "This won't take long, Captain. I'm Richard Beaufort, the One One Two. I'm following up on the Buryak case."

We, the jury, find the defendant not guilty . . .

"Are you?" Rhyme reminded himself to keep a lid on the impatience and anger.

"Yessir. I'm contacting everyone involved in the trial and putting together a file of all the documentation they have about it. Pain in the ass, I know. For me too. Do you have anything here? Evidentiary reports, anything like that? Copies are fine. You can keep the originals."

"Postmortem, hm?" Rhyme wheeled closer to Beaufort, who towered. The height disparity was one thing about his condition that had been so very hard to get used to: he was always lower than those around him. Rhyme's personality had been forceful—if not domineering—and being looked down at was a blow. Oddly, though, over the years he'd come to realize that he actually had *more* power in the chair; those talking to, or arguing with, him lowered their heads, which was, in a way, an act of submission.

"I honestly don't know what they have in mind, sir. I was just told to collect any documentation."

"I think we gave the prosecutor everything." He looked to Sachs, who nodded. Then Rhyme said, "But there are some evidence charts we did, flow diagrams, you know. It's secondary material. Would they want that?"

"I think they would. Is that a scanning electron microscope?" He walked to the glass partition. "And a chromatograph. In a Central Park West town house. I'll be damned."

Rhyme continued, "They're photos—digital—of the charts. Like those." Rhyme pointed and Beaufort looked toward the whiteboards on easels. One was of the Locksmith case, the others about the Buryak and the Gregorios case—the murder by the homeless man. There were crime scene photos of the bloody body. They were explicit and bright and stark. Beaufort gave no reaction.

He asked, "A thumb drive, or something?"

"Sure." He wheeled to the computer, instructed it to call up the Buryak file. He scrolled through to find the JPGs of the charts and, after Sachs had loaded a blank thumb drive into the USB slot, copied the files and pasted them. She handed the drive to Beaufort.

"Thanks, Captain, Detective . . ." He pocketed the small rectangle. "Appreciate it." He started to leave, then paused. "I'm sorry about what happened."

The Hindenburg? World War Two? The Great Recession? Rhyme reined himself in and said, "Thanks."

"They didn't ask me but I would've told them it's a bad idea. We need you, a lot of the line people say so. Brass too."

"You take care, Detective," Rhyme said.

"You too."

Thom showed him out.

As soon as the door closed, Rhyme turned to Sachs. "So?"

"Take a look. I'll send it to you." She typed on her phone and a moment later a ding rang out in the lab. Rhyme called up his email.

He was looking at what she'd just downloaded from the NYPD personnel database and sent to him.

Richard Beaufort was indeed a detective, third-class, with the NYPD. And, yes, he had been assigned to the 112 House, the precinct in which Buryak's mansion was located. However, he'd never had anything to do with the Buryak case. In fact, for the past four months, he had had nothing to do with criminal investigation. He'd been transferred to a different job.

He was on Mayor Tony Harrison's security detail.

Rhyme muttered, "Son of a bitch was here to see if I was working the Locksmith case."

"Rodriguez was at the Noelle scene, playing it up for the cameras. Potter was there too, the mayor's aide."

"To report that we're toeing the line." Rhyme scoffed. "The press's really playing it up big. They like notorious bad guys. Looks better when they get caught. The Zodiac Killer, the Boston Strangler. And here we've got a nefarious serial perp. The Locksmith gets collared on the mayor's watch—and without my help—his poll numbers go up. I don't know why any human being would run for political office."

Rhyme again reflected: I'm fucking housebound, no work to do, no desire to look for alternatives.

He thought of what Commander Brett Evans had said last night.

New Jersey . . .

Commercial lab work . . .

Jesus Christ.

He said, "You've got to get to Queens. That blood trace Mel found? If he used the knife once he's going to use it again. That's a given."

She didn't answer but glanced down as her phone dinged with a text. "Just a second." She walked into the hallway and then out onto the front porch. On the monitor, he saw her looking up and down the street. She returned and, head down, sent yet another text.

"Sachs. I'm serious. You need to get started."

Now, she held up a wait-a-second index finger and walked to the front door once more. He heard it open. He heard voices.

And into the lab walked Ron Pulaski and Mel Cooper. They were each carting crates containing evidence bags.

"The hell's this?"

Sachs told the men who had just entered, "I watched Beaufort drive off. He's clear. And I don't think they're going to waste manpower surveilling us." She turned to Rhyme. "They may not like you at the moment, but they don't *dislike* you enough to spend money spying on and busting you."

Cooper walked to a locker and donned a face mask and gloves, booties, lab coat. He carried his crate into the sterile part of the lab and then took Pulaski's and did the same.

"I'll repeat my question," Rhyme muttered.

Sachs: "I double-dipped the evidence. Took two samples of each. From the Bechtel Building and Noelle's."

"You did *what*?"

"I hid the second set in both scenes," Sachs continued. "Ron went back and got them after I left."

Rhyme looked from one to the other.

She said, "We talked about it. Lon too. We know the risk. Are they going to fire us? Maybe. Arrest for obstruction? Not likely."

Cooper said, "Let's face it, Lincoln, we didn't have a choice. The Queens lab is good. But not as good as we are."

Pulaski said, "Maybe some of your ego's rubbing off on us, Lincoln."

Sachs then said, "We never did ask *you*, of course. Your ass is on the line too. What do you say?"

The three were looking his way.

Rhyme, not a man of many words but rarely speechless, said nothing for a moment. Finally: "Thank you."

26

Rhyme was listening to Sachs's description of the Carrie Noelle home invasion.

"He did the same thing as at Annabelle's. Moved personal effects, stole underwear and a knife. No dessert, but he drank some of her wine."

"Left the glass?"

"He did."

Rhyme grunted affirmatively, thinking: Possibly DNA.

Sachs pulled on booties, gloves, a cap and a white lab jacket and stepped into the sterile portion of the parlor, where Mel Cooper was logging the evidence in and signing his name on the chain-of-custody cards.

The items that the Locksmith touched were a doll, some clothes, a wine bottle and glass, a wooden block and the knives it had contained, a tube of lipstick, a children's mobile in a second bedroom that served as a storeroom for the toys she blogged about and sold online.

"He started it playing."

Cooper said, "Must have freaked her out. Imagine."

She said, "Had to let that go to Queens, the mobile. Couldn't cut it in half, her phone too, but we've got almost everything else."

"Footprints?"

"Everything but the bathroom was carpeted, and there he stood on the rug."

"Friction ridges?" Rhyme called. This was just a formality, and Sachs and Cooper confirmed he'd worn gloves and left no fingerprints.

"I want that DNA," he said. "Check the wineglass."

Sachs handed Cooper the heavy goblet. "Couldn't afford for that to go to the lab. I wanted it here."

Rhyme agreed. "Hold it up," he called.

The tech lifted it to the camera and Rhyme wheeled to a large monitor. He noted a smear around the lip.

"Swab it and give me the analysis."

Cooper did as instructed. Soon he had an answer. "Sodium carbonate peroxyhydrate."

"Goddamn it."

Pulaski, the scribe manning the whiteboard, looked his way.

Rhyme continued, "It's oxygen bleach."

"Hell," Sachs muttered.

"What's the matter?" the young patrol officer asked.

"Well, it's obvious, isn't it?" Rhyme grumbled. "He can't leave touch DNA because he's wearing gloves, and he's got some head covering so we can't get a hair. The only chance to snag his DNA was from imbibing the vic's wine. And he cleaned the rim off with one of the few substances in the universe that destroy deoxyribonucleic acid."

"Doesn't alcohol?" Pulaski asked.

"No, Rookie. Alcohol is used to extract and store DNA. Regular bleach won't do it either. You need to start reading my book."

"I have. You don't mention oxygen bleach."

"Oh." Rhyme hesitated. "It's in the eighth edition."

"I didn't know there was an eighth. I have the seventh."

Rhyme muttered, "The eighth's not out yet. I'll make sure you get a copy."

Pulaski said, "If he's that worried about DNA, it might mean he's in CODIS."

The database repository of DNA, accessible to law enforcement agencies. Unlike the fingerprint database, which logs the prints of millions of both criminals and innocent citizens (like those applying for government jobs or a concealed carry permit), nearly all those in CODIS have broken the law.

"Possibly, but most smart perps—like the Locksmith—are going to want to leave as little of themselves behind as possible as a matter of course."

"Why didn't he just take the glass with him?" Cooper wondered.

Sachs offered, "I'd guess he wanted to make sure she saw it. The intrusion was more invasive that way. He wants to cause the most damage he can. There's a sadistic side to him."

Pulaski said, "So the glass is useless as evidence."

"Who said that, Rookie? Mel, the bleach. Give me the percentage breakdown of the sodium carbonate and peroxyhydrate."

The tech told him the concentrations of the two ingredients.

Rhyme sighed. "*Now*, it's useless. In those proportions, it's off-the-shelf commercial oxy bleach. If they'd been unique amounts we could have deduced he made it himself and, therefore, had a degree or training in science. But this?" He gestured impatiently. "It tells us . . . he's got cash and the address of a home improvement or drug store."

Sachs's phone hummed, and she answered.

"Lon. You're on speaker."

"Hey. I'd say hi to Lincoln, but I know he's not there. On vacation somewhere, I'll bet."

Rhyme called out, "Hello, Lon. I understand you're a co-conspirator too."

Sellitto chuckled. "I didn't hear that. Listen, I talked to Whittaker Media's legal department. The chief general counsel, a guy named Douglas Hubert. They don't have any names yet but he's putting together a list of possible suspects who might have a gripe with the paper or the TV network. Going to be a long one. A lot of folks don't care for the rag."

"Disgruntled employees?"

"Hubert's looking at them too. And he said that the head of the whole shebang, Averell Whittaker, is retiring and selling the company. I'm wondering if maybe a buyer hired the Locksmith then leaked the story to drive down the value of the company. Might be worth looking into."

"We'll do that, Lon."

"Any leads?" Sellitto asked.

"Not yet."

"All right. Keep me posted."

After he'd disconnected, Rhyme said, "Let's keep at it."

Sachs and Cooper began examining each item for foreign substances the Locksmith might have left on the carpet or the objects he touched.

"More dried blood. From the carpet outside her bedroom. It matches the sample from the Talese scene."

"Suggests that there was a fair amount of it he stepped in. Maybe he wiped at it but didn't bother to seriously clean his shoes. Okay, what else?"

Pulaski added the discoveries to the board, which Rhyme now studied.

—*Blue Victoria's Secret panties and knife—Zwilling J.A. Henckels brand—were stolen.*

—Daily Herald *newspaper, page 3 of the February 17th edition, same as at A. Talese scene. Message, the same: "Reckoning—the Locksmith," in victim's lipstick.*

—*Brick dust.*

—*Blood, DNA match with that found in the Talese intrusion.*

—*Limestone.*

—*Sandstone.*

—*Asphalt particles.*

—*Motor oil.*

—*Sesame seeds.*

—*Oxygen bleach.*

"Secondary scenes?" Rhyme asked.

Sachs and Cooper examined next the evidence collected from the Bechtel Building.

—*Size 11 shoe print in pattern the same as at A. Talese's.*

—*Sandstone.*

—*Limestone.*

—*Motor oil.*

—*Detergent.*

—*Microscopic particles of brass.*

—*Crushed common fly.*

Sachs said, "Nothing at all at the entrance—the service door, the floor leading to the stairwell, the stairwell itself. And the exit?" She scoffed. "It was a back window he broke. He jumped into the alley-way and turned on a hose. Flooded the whole area."

Water destroys trace as efficiently as fire.

Rhyme sighed. "What does all this tell us? That he walks around the streets of New York."

He was angry. His wife and his friends were risking their jobs to bring him evidence, and the evidence was not paying off.

"We need more."

"Have a thought," Sachs said. "I had the impression somebody was watching me."

She explained about a gray Cadillac whose driver seemed a little more than casually interested in her and the scene.

"Can't say for sure—the car may have been a coincidence. But I'm going with the assumption he never left. He wanted to know who was investigating him, and how."

"Bechtel Building," Rhyme said.

Sachs nodded. "We know he used it as a vantage point before. Maybe he used it again, to keep an eye on the investigation. It'd be perfect. The windows're smeared—you can see out, but looking inside, it's just blackness. I'm going back. Who knows? Could be, this time he got careless."

"Friends: Back to New York, Have you heard about this crazy man, the Locksmith? He breaks into people's apartments for rape and murder. Or are they just SAYING he's crazy? I've heard reports he's working for the Hidden, a soldier to rain terror down upon the citizens of the city to further the movement's agenda of destruction.

"And does he have an ally in City Hall? If New York has the best police department in the world—as they claim—why haven't they been able to stop him?

"I submit it's because they've been infiltrated by the Hidden too. They don't want to find him.

"I say this to those of you living in the Big Apple: Next time you hear a click or a footstep or a breath in the middle of the night, you might not be alone. The Locksmith—and the Hidden—may have come for you.

"And is the policeman you call on your side? Or theirs?

"Say your prayers and stay prepared!

"My name is Verum, Latin for 'true.' That is what my message is. What you do with it is up to you."

27

Now, Labyrinth chased Brick.

Drawing a smile from Buryak.

In Kiev, teenage Viktor had a dog, a terrier mix, and leaving Let behind was the hardest part of the trip to the New World, though he walked three miles through city streets to bestow the dog on his cousin, Sasha, who loved it and who, he knew, would give it a good home.

Then animals past and present slipped from Buryak's mind as the landline phone hummed with the tone from the intercom at the front gate.

"Yes?"

"Aaron."

A moment later Buryak watched a man stride up the walk from the driveway in front of the garage. He was wearing a dark suit and a white shirt, a pink tie. His facial features suggested he was of mixed race, though his pallor was light—close to that of Buryak's own. He wore headgear you rarely saw: a beret, black. He was tall, over six feet, and broad chested and beefy. He wasn't overweight as such; he was simply big.

Buryak had cultivated multiple sources who would gather the information he auctioned off under the guise of tractors or smelting irons. Aaron Douglass manned a narrow but decidedly helpful conduit; it was also undoubtedly the cleverest in the organization.

"You think of that yourself?" Buryak had asked the man, speaking of his inspired idea for gathering data. "You are fucking brilliant in the head."

Douglass was also called on from time to time to handle special assignments. As an enforcer. He came up with solutions that minimized risks to Buryak. Problems were solved and nothing ever got traced back to him.

The man was a firewall. No prosecutor or investigator would ever turn Aaron Douglass, because Buryak had information on *him* too.

Buryak's mansion featured two entrances. On the inside of the gate, the driveways split, the right leading to the formal front door, the left to Buryak's office. His wife, Maria, was out, but she knew the rules. He'd instructed her to circle the block if there was a car parked in front of the office—as Douglass's gray Cadillac presently was.

The meeting wouldn't take long.

Douglass now walked to this office door and knocked.

Buryak rose and let him in, and, as he did with every human being who entered, he wanded him for recording devices and transmitters. Douglass scored negative; like all employees and contractors, he knew the rules and had left his phones and weapons in the car.

"Aaron."

Douglass pulled his beret off and stuffed it into his jacket pocket. Maybe the unusual headgear made him feel like a soldier.

"Mr. Buryak. Congratulations on the case." He eyed the cats, now preening, with the eye of someone who had never owned an animal in his life. The bulky man sat on the couch, where Buryak indicated.

Even the laudatory comment set off a match-rasp of rage within him.

"Came close, too close. Word on the street about him? Murphy?"

"Maybe revenge for a hijacking a year ago, maybe because he was fucking Serge Lombrowski's wife."

"My lawyer, Coughlin, didn't want to go there. He said it is not our job to prove who did it." He snickered. "How desperate was Lombrowski's wife? For Christ's sake, look at Leon's face." A sip of tea. "So, the Chemist situation?"

"I'll lay out what I've found. His wife, the detective, she's working this crazy case, the Locksmith."

"He's married?"

"That's right."

"Is he not . . . ?" Buryak hesitated. Not trying to be politically correct. He just couldn't recall the man's condition.

"Quadriplegic," Douglass said. "Tetraplegic, they say in Europe. But that doesn't mean he can't be married."

"No. Of course not."

Married. An interesting fact, a *helpful* fact. Maybe.

"And this Locksmith case?"

"That's what he calls himself, or the media calls him that. He breaks into women's apartments and rearranges shit in their house and then leaves. He can get through any lock in the city in like thirty seconds."

"Pervert."

"I guess, but no rape, no assault. He doesn't kill anybody."

"So. Robbery?"

"No. He fucks with their minds."

Going to all that effort and risk . . . and not making money? Insane.

"Why?"

"No idea." Douglass shrugged. "I spent the morning following her—Amelia. Oh, here's her picture, by the way. I took it at the scene."

"Attractive."

Douglass shrugged. He had never mentioned women, or men, in his life. Maybe sex didn't interest him. He was one of the few men over whom Buryak did not have the leverage of a vulnerable family.

But Douglass had another secret that kept him in line.

"Her name's Amelia, like I said. Detective. Works crime scenes, mostly. So I followed her to see if she was running something to do with us, with you."

"Did she make you?"

"No, she might've seen the Caddie, so I swapped out for my SUV."

"Then the big question I must ask: Is Rhyme—and her, too, I guess—looking into me?"

"I think so. Here's what I found. Amelia went back to his town house, where he works. He's got a lab—"

"Yes, yes, I know it well," Buryak said darkly. "The three hundred block of Central Park West."

Douglass cocked his head. Then, when Buryak said nothing more, continued, "Only there was something odd. There was a cruiser parked up the block."

"A Land Cruiser? What is that, Toyota?"

"No, I mean, a police cruiser. Two guys inside, was all I could see. After a while, this guy leaves Rhyme's apartment and Amelia comes out and waves the guys in. They grab some crates from the trunk."

"Crates?"

"It was NYPD evidence inside. I could see the bags. Chain-of-custody cards."

"Why do you think it's about me?"

Douglass looked at him, as if Buryak had missed something. "You did hear, didn't you? . . . Oh, no, sure. You don't watch the news."

Buryak was impassioned about the commodity he sold: factual information, hard, verifiable data. Not speculation, not rumor, not guesses.

Media . . .

Douglass continued, "Rhyme got fired. He's not working for the department anymore."

"Because—"

"He screwed up at your trial, and that fucked with the mayor's ratings. So whatever they're up to, it can't be an official NYPD case. You were right, I think—about what your research picked up in the prosecutor's office. He's gunning for you."

"He is an arrogant prick. And now he's lost his job. All the more reason to bring me down."

Brick approached. Buryak bent to pull her onto his lap, but she walked away. He remembered that villain from the James Bond movies, holding the cat. The cat just sat there and took the creepy stroking. It wasn't a Maine Coon; they had minds of their own. You could pet them if they wanted to be petted. Otherwise, forget it.

Buryak sipped tea. When Douglass had first started working for him, he'd been offered a beverage. He declined. On the second visit, he did the same. Buryak had stopped offering.

Buryak said, "That trial made me quite tense. I wish I could just get a little peace. Maria has a masseuse she goes to, Palm Beach, when she is upset. Ah, what I wouldn't give for a little peace . . ."

The man had mastered the language of speaking as if a prosecutor was listening to every word.

Aaron Douglass had, in turn, mastered *understanding* the language of Buryak. It was like a code, perfectly clear when you had the key.

Now, Buryak was sending an unequivocal message to Douglass, who easily translated: Find muscle, somebody good and discreet, and make sure that person "corrects" the situation with this Rhyme and his wife, all the while keeping Buryak insulated.

"There's a masseur I use sometimes," Douglass said. "He's very good. And I know he's available. I'll call him now."

"A massage, yes, yes." Buryak stretched and rose. He glanced at the cats. "Better feed my livestock now. Do you have pets, Aaron?"

A very brief hesitation.

Was he thinking of the wisdom of giving away some personal information?

"No."

"Ah, they can add a great deal to your life."

"I'll remember that."

28

As Sachs piloted the Torino to a curb on East 97th Street she was aware of flash of white: a Lexus SUV turned quickly west on a cross street and drove out of sight.

She believed she'd seen it earlier, close to Rhyme's town house. Had this vehicle been following her? She'd had her eye out for the gray Cadillac, which she hadn't seen, but she now wondered if she was being double-teamed.

By whom? And why?

Nothing to do about it. Except stay aware.

She parked up the street from the Bechtel Building and tossed the NYPD official business placard on the dash, then stepped out. Sticking to shadows and looking around frequently for gray sedans or white SUVs—and any other pedestrian surveillance—she made her way to the building. A few doors down, she paused and studied it carefully, with an eye out for threats.

Human threats, she meant. The building itself—oh, it was a

given that the place was a death trap. The stone façade, three stories tall, was pitted and soot stained, and the crowning cornice piece into which was carved *Bechtel* was cracked horizontally. It seemed that not much beyond a gust of wind could topple the broken portion and send it crashing to earth. The glass was missing from most windows. A portion of the north wall had collapsed into a vacant lot, and sizable chunks of ceiling and walls had come down inside.

She saw no movement.

Sachs radioed Dispatch and reported, "Detective Five Eight Eight Five. I'm ten-twenty at Four Nine Nine East Nine Seven. K."

"Roger, Five Eight Eight Five."

Then she clicked her Motorola to mute; inopportune crackles had betrayed any number of officers.

The front double door, scrawled over with graffiti, was nailed shut, but one could gain entry from the lot—the route the Locksmith would have taken to get inside and surveil Carrie Noelle's building.

She ducked under a large, rusty sign.

DANGER. NO TRESPASSING. DO NOT ENTER.

She made her way through the chain-link fence gate, in a contortionist's maneuver that sent a pang through her arthritic bones. Some medical procedures had helped but certain maneuvers reminded painfully of the temperament of her joints.

Sachs was prepared to collect evidence if the Locksmith had returned, but she was not in Tyvek overalls. Hardly wise to wear a white outfit when there was a possibility her prey was still inside the dark rooms. Her concession to forensic propriety was the black latex gloves she wore, hair tucked up under a baseball cap and rubber bands around her boot soles—to differentiate her feet from the perp's. If a long strand of red hair contaminated the evidence, it could be easily excluded. The same with a fiber from her jacket.

Once inside, she paused at a collapsed wall and a pile of rubble.

Listening.

A drip of water, a faint creak that she put down to settling structure.

No breathing, no footsteps.

She pulled her short Maglite from her jacket pocket and clicked it on, holding the black tube in her left hand, so her right was free to draw. The beam swept over the first-floor lobby. Nothing appeared to have come down since she'd been here a few hours ago. Making minimal noise, she returned to the window where the Locksmith had stood to view Carrie's building.

A tile sign on an intact wall told her that the Bechtels had made home appliances a century ago. Now the structure was used for something quite different: Needles and crack pipes littered the floor, and some cardboard cartons had been broken down into homeless mattresses. Wads of filthy cloth were piled up against some of these. Empty malt liquor and booze bottles too. Vodka seemed to give the most kick for the buck.

But as she swung the light back and forth on the floor and around the large room, she spotted something that told her, yes, somebody had been here since her first search: a small candy wrapper, Jolly Rancher, in green apple flavor.

Had it been the Locksmith? Junkies might have a sweet tooth like anyone else but they would probably not crash a building with police tape around it.

The wrapper went into a bag. She collected trace from around where it had lain with an adhesive roller. She tore the sheet off and slipped it into a second bag.

She moved on, searching slowly, looking for prints of a size 11 running shoe. If he'd been observing the police activity, the front window would not do him much good, but the windows on the building's west side would offer a good view of where she and the ECTs had staged.

She would check there, but first a thought occurred to her. Was it possible that the building *did* have some inhabitants——perhaps someone who'd gotten a look at the Locksmith?

Sachs started into the darker reaches of the building, leaving daylight behind and relying on her flashlight. She paused every so often to listen for the sound of footsteps, the sound of a breath, the sound of an unhappy board under shoes.

The sound of a pistol being cocked, or a knife flicking open.

29

Deep in the Bechtel Building, the man watched the flashlight beam swinging slowly back and forth.

He saw the woman pause and cock her head, listening. Moving on once more. She was cautious, as one would be in a place like this. Walking, pausing, walking on.

Lyle Spencer was a large man, six feet four inches tall and he weighed two hundred and forty pounds. He was sustained by the physical; he had been—throughout all phases of his life. Muscle, you could count on. Muscle worked.

His face was long and striking and stern, with dark eyes set off by pale skin. On his head was a dusting of close-cropped hair of gray-blond hue. His muscles were bulky, earned with old-fashioned weights on bars. He had a contempt for exercise machines but couldn't say why. His hands were wide, fingers long. He had once broken a man's wrist using only two of those fingers and a thumb.

Because he was here illegally and because of the clammy atmosphere inside the Bechtel Building he thought of an incident years ago, involving another woman, one he'd shot to death with a carefully placed round in the back of her head. The second slug was accurately placed too, but he was sure the first had killed her.

Spencer's eyes were now accustomed to the dark and he moved in a general direction around behind the woman. He studied the floor before each step.

Something in the southwest corner of the manufacturing space had caught her attention. Spencer wondered what it might have been. In any event this was good. If whatever she'd seen would hold her attention for a little bit longer, he could get behind her. He looked at the floor and noted a pipe, about eighteen inches long. He lifted it silently.

He now moved through the dim showroom where years ago solidly built ovens and refrigerators and dishwashers had sat, probably all white, though maybe pale green or pink, which he believed were popular colors for domestic devices in mid-century.

BECHTEL INCORPORATED
Appliances for the Homemakers of the Nation
Est. 1925

Dark passages, the smell of wet stone, the smell of mold.

He recalled the scent of the blood from the woman he shot. Her husband's too. He'd killed them both that day.

Now, he eased forward silent and studied her flashlight beam, and from the width of the bright disk on the wall he knew approximately where she was standing, examining whatever it was she was examining. If she stayed in that corner, yeah, it would be good. Though he was a large man, Lyle Spencer could move quickly. Much of his height was in leg, not torso. His strides were long.

He considered options.

There really was only one.

Get behind her.

The beam of her light was sweeping slowly over the floor. She'd be facing away from the door he was near.

Now, he told himself. And stepped forward.

30

Lyle Spencer's world lit up with white fire.

"Drop the rod. Now. I am armed and I will fire." Her voice was razor raw.

He turned, glaring into the brilliant light in her hand.

Ah, clever. He glanced to the side. The woman had tied up the flashlight with a grocery bag—there were dozens on the floor—and left it dangling from an old piece of skeletonized machinery to trick him. Her new flashlight wasn't one at all. It was the app on her phone.

He shook his head in dismay and looked calmly at the muzzle of her pistol, aimed directly at him.

The rod, pointed toward the ground now, swung back and forth in his hand, the way a baseball player casually carries the bat to home plate.

"I'm a police officer. Drop the rod now. You move one step, I will fire."

He had no doubt that she would.

Back and forth, back and forth.

She held the weapon perfectly steady. The bigger Glocks, he knew, were not light weapons.

Back and forth.

"Do it now." Not shouted, as another cop might have done. The voice was calm, icy. Her final warning.

A moment longer. He dropped the rod, which hit the concrete and bounced, ringing twice, with the sound of a dull bell.

I'm walking along a street on the Upper East Side, my eyes on the vehicle I'm about to break into, a block away.

Seeing the model and make of the car, I can't help but think about Englishman Joseph Bramah, who created a cylindrical key lock in the late 1700s that was so sophisticated it's still in use today. (He offered a sizable challenge reward to anyone who could pick it. The reward stood for sixty-seven years, until the great Exhibition of 1851, where it was picked by none other than my idol, Alfred Hobbs.)

Bramah found a huge market for his lock but he wasn't able to make them fast enough to turn a profit. So, the brilliant inventor (beer draft pumps, modern toilets, banknote presses) invented something else that turned his business around: the assembly line.

Which supposedly inspired Henry Ford, and the industrialist began using the technique to manufacture cars.

And it happens to be a descendant of Ford's Model T that I'm about to break into just now.

If you need to crack a vehicle lock, you can often use a jiggler, also called a tryout key. They look sort of like standard pin tumbler keys but are flat. My set includes fifteen on a ring. They're in my jacket pocket right now and I'm fingering them as I approach the car.

And, oh, yes, Officer, I'm carrying lock-picking tools with illegal intent . . . just for the record.

It's quicker to use a rake and tension tool in a car lock—faster yet to yank the cylinder out with a dent puller—but neither would work here. With a jiggler, you insert it and, just like the name, work it back and forth with one hand, like you're using the proper key. If somebody was watching you, they might wonder what you're up to, but if you pretend to be making a phone call and absently playing with the key, you can get away with it.

Out comes my cell phone in one hand and the jiggler keys in the other. I look around. The street isn't deserted but it's not crowded either, and even more important, I know the owner of the car is busy elsewhere.

The door opens with the second jiggler. There's no bar on the steering wheel, which I find odd. A car like this one would be easily stolen. That's the thing about locks and security devices. Anybody can get burglarized; you'll never be able to keep yourself completely secure. You just need to make your car or apartment a little bit harder to burgle than your neighbors'.

I suspect there's a cutoff switch to the ignition hidden somewhere under the dash. Maybe two. Might even be radio controlled.

No matter. I'm not here to steal the car; I'm presently driving a very nice luxury set of wheels myself.

All I care about is one thing. And it takes me just a few minutes to locate what I seek. I find it not in the glove box but rubber banded to the back of the driver's sun visor. I memorize what I've found, and in ten seconds the door is closed, relocked and I'm walking down the street, reciting the address.

Oh, this is very good news.

Since Lincoln Rhyme, I've read, lives on the Upper West Side, and the address I just memorized is in Brooklyn, this means that even though she's his wife, Crime Scene Girl Amelia must spend some nights by herself.

The fantasy I conjured earlier has a basis in reality.

She has a bedroom all her own.

31

As they stood in the decrepit, half-collapsed manufacturing room of the Bechtel Building, Sachs handed the man back his driver's license and employee ID card.

Lyle P. Spencer, forty-two, was the security director for Whittaker Media Group, the publisher of the *Daily Herald*. Not being able to see her clearly, just someone in street clothes, he'd thought she might have been a dealer or an addict.

"Or the Locksmith." His voice was a resonant baritone.

"Locksmith?" she asked.

He asked, "You have proof it's a man?"

Interesting thought. Assumptions.

"Size eleven man's shoe. But in answer to your question. No, we don't."

"I was just trying to get out of the place, the door behind you. And call the police from the street. Tell them there was an intruder here."

"The pipe?" A glance at the floor.

"In case it came to that."

She asked why not a firearm.

"Don't own one."

"You're security. But no carry ticket?" It's almost impossible to get a conceal carry permit in the city, but there's an exception for those who need a weapon in their line of work.

"I run the New York security operation. I don't get into the field much."

Spencer added that if he happened to do so—like now—he wore personal protection gear, which was plenty for him.

Sachs reflected that his size alone would be a deterrent. His arms, chest and legs were massive.

"You realize you're violating a crime scene."

The man shrugged. "Technically, being within a defined crime scene isn't an offense. Guilty of civil trespass, yes, but the complaining witness is the owner of the place and he's busy with bankruptcy, it looks like. The only crime *you'd* be interested in is tampering with evidence, which is to alter, destroy, conceal or remove it with the purpose of hiding the truth or making it unavailable for a proceeding or investigation."

The recitation told her a great deal about Lyle P. Spencer.

"We'll move on," she said. "Why're you here?"

Spencer explained that when his boss heard that somebody'd left *Herald*s at both of the intrusions, he wanted him to investigate. "His—for the time being I'll go with male—his MO, from what I've heard, paints him an organized offender. That means he would have surveilled the building before the intrusions. I couldn't find any sites he might've done that from for the first incident, on the West Side. Annabelle Talese's."

"He was probably in a deli across the street, but it'd been scrubbed by the time I figured that out."

He nodded, then looked around. "But this was a perfect spot to stage for the intrusion last night."

"We found brick dust at the prior scene. That's what got us here."

"Sure. Picked it up in his shoe and left it at the first scene, and you narrowed it down to the Bechtel Building. Smart." He seemed impressed. "And he came back."

"The candy wrapper. You noticed that?" Sachs asked.

"No crime scene officer'd miss it first time around. If it was his, he probably was here to watch the operation, check out who was after him."

"Why I'm here now. Where were you L.E.?"

"Albany. Patrol after the navy, then got my gold shield. But, with a family, I decided private security made sense. I basically doubled my income and haven't been shot at." He glanced at the Glock on her hip.

"Military police?"

"No. I was special ops, a SEAL."

"You searched the entire place?"

"Ground floor. No way to get upstairs, not safely, but that would be true for him too. I didn't see any other footprints or evidence, other than the wrapper."

"Does Mr. Whittaker have any thoughts on who the Locksmith might be?"

"We've talked about it and, no, he doesn't."

Sachs said, "We've been in touch with your legal department. They're pulling together a list of threats and complaints."

"I know. Doug Hubert's people're doing it. They'll be thorough."

Sachs said, "Can you get me in to see Averell Whittaker himself?"

"I can. Yes."

They completed a walk-around and she saw no suggestion the

Locksmith had been anywhere else but in the front. Spencer had been careful to stick to the gravel, avoiding the flat portions of the floor, thick with telltale reddish brick dust.

She'd been watching his eyes and noted his alert body language when a rat nosed out of a pile of rocks, regarded the two visitors and retreated slowly, with apparent irritation.

They returned to the front of the building and she stepped outside—away from the cringey sense that the whole place was about to come down and bury them alive.

She said, "Oh, here's something else I have to ask."

Spencer preempted. "What time was the break-in? Early, wasn't it?"

"Around four a.m."

"I have an apartment in Whittaker Tower." He withdrew a notebook and pen and jotted a name and phone number. He tore off the sheet and handed it to her. "That's the head of building security. He'll show you RFID entry records and video. I got home at one a.m. and left for work at six."

She pocketed the sheet.

As if he couldn't resist, he said to her, "Now what was your question?"

32

W ell. *This* is a set of wheels."

Lyle Spencer was sitting shotgun in her red Ford Torino Cobra. They were on their way to Rhyme's to drop off the evidence that Sachs had collected at the Bechtel Building, and then they would go on to lofty Whittaker Tower to meet with the head of the media empire.

"What's under the hood?" Lyle asked.

"A four-oh-five."

"Beautiful."

"You know cars."

"Follow Formula One." His tone was: But then again, who doesn't? "Used to do some showroom stock when I was upstate. I'm guessing you know what that is."

Amelia Sachs only smiled.

Stock cars come in a number of different categories and are raced in many types of circuits. Originally "stock" meant just that—the car came from the dealer's stock of inventory and wasn't modified in any way. Then the various racing organizations—NASCAR being the biggest—allowed modifications. "Showroom stock" or "production stock" required that the car be nearly identical to what a consumer could buy, with only a few safety modifications, like a roll cage.

She felt his eyes on her as she slammed through the four-speed shifter, then hard dropped into second, turned and casually steered into the skid. The wheels responded handily.

Spencer was nodding. "You can see. I'm not exactly built like a jockey. My biggest problem was fitting into the cage. Wanted to have the steering column shortened but couldn't get a ruling on that one." He patted the dash. "I drove one of these in a couple races."

"A Torino?"

"That's right. A Talladega."

Sachs exhaled a fast laugh. "No."

"Uhm."

There was no more famous stock car in the early days of racing than the redesigned 1969 Torino Cobra, which was renamed the Talladega, after the famed racetrack. The car dominated NASCAR in '69 and '70.

"You race anymore?"

"Nup. Don't even own a car now. Sold my SUV when I moved into the city. Four parking tickets in one day. I go to Avis or Hertz if I need wheels."

His tone was wistful. He would miss driving. She could understand. The power of the pistons, the whine, the speed, the sense of a vehicle always on the edge, always a half second away from flying out of control. The consuming feel of that car that you were a part of and was part of you . . . It was wholly addictive.

She said, "Maybe, it works out, you can take it for a spin."

His eyes shone. "I may think about that."

She swerved around a texting yellow cab driver who veered into her lane, saw in the corner of her eye that Spencer's left leg extended just a bit, while his right arm moved back, subconsciously mimicking her fierce clutching and the downshift.

In ten minutes they were at Rhyme's town house.

Spencer said, "You're going to want to check that alibi."

Sachs slipped the shifter into first gear, killed the engine and set the brake. She tapped her phone. "I already did." She'd texted Lon Sellitto about the man and asked him to call security at Whittaker Tower.

"That was fast."

"We don't have much time. I needed to know whether to trust you or bust you. I'll be five minutes." She stepped out then turned back to the huge man. She bent down into the open window. "I'm going to have to ask a favor."

"Anything I find out about a threat, even if it leads somewhere in the company, I'll let you know ASAP."

"Okay, I meant to say, I'm going to ask you *two* favors. One is what you just said. The other is not mentioning to anybody that the evidence I just collected ended up here."

"Which is where?" He was looking at Rhyme's stately town house.

"My husband and I live here," she said. "Lincoln Rhyme. He's a criminalist. Former NYPD."

"Wait. Lincoln Rhyme's your *husband*?"

She nodded.

"Damn." He appeared both impressed and mystified. Then he gave a smile. "What evidence? I don't know anything about any evidence." He shrugged and she wondered if the massive shoulders had ever torn a garment seam with a gesture like that. "I tend to get amnesia. I was going to see a doctor for it but I kept forgetting to make the appointment." Delivered deadpan.

She dug black nitrile gloves from her pocket and pulled them on. "Aren't you curious why I asked?"

"You're running a renegade operation you don't want the brass to know about. Maybe you're worried about corruption, maybe politics, maybe you shook a stick at the wrong person. Been there, done that." Lyle Spencer—the man who, she'd calculated, had had four hours' sleep last night—yawned and, to the extent he could, stretched back, crossed his arms across that massive chest and closed his eyes.

33

"Here are the tax consequences," said the man who looked like he would know everything there was to know about tax consequences.

He had the pale complexion of somebody who spent his days in offices in front of computers and calculators. Gray suit, white shirt, trim hair. In his forties. His glasses, Averell Whittaker decided, should not be called glasses at all but spectacles.

The two men were in Whittaker's home office, high atop the tower that bore his family name. The structure was on opulent Park Avenue.

The accountant had his hand on the thick document as if it were a bomb with a spring trigger and were he to let go the results would be disastrous.

Which they would be indeed.

Whittaker said, "Thank you, John. I'll review it."

This he wouldn't do. He knew exactly what was going to happen, and he knew exactly what the consequences, tax and otherwise, would be. It was John's job—along with his team of a dozen other people—to look out for Whittaker and his companies. And to stop him from doing something stupid.

But stupid in one man's eye is noble in another's.

Whittaker said, "Langston, Holmes says the papers'll be ready next week."

A pause. "All right."

The two words were spoken as if Whittaker had just told him he was about to rappel down a thousand-foot cliff.

At night, in a rainstorm.

After the accountant was gone, Whittaker picked up his cane, which was ebony and topped with a brass sculpture of a woman's head. He'd selected this one, rather than the lighter and rubber-tipped version recommended by the doctor, because the woman bore a passing resemblance to Mary.

He rose and limped his way to the window. He caught a glimpse of himself in the antique mirror decorating one wall. His face was gray, the unhealthy visage mocked by the perfect, thick, white hair, the imperial nose, the wizard brows and, beneath them, piercing black stones of eyes.

Then he stared out the window at a vista that included perhaps three hundred thousand people.

And where are you?

He returned to his computer and, not sitting, logged in to his email.

His heart sank yet again. Not that he truly expected a reply.

But he'd hoped. Oh, had he hoped.

Where? . . .

Kitt:

Please, hear me out, son. I've made mistakes. I've treated you badly. I didn't listen to you. And I will be honest. I can't plead ignorance. I understood at the time what I was doing and that my actions were transgressions. They were sins. I can't plead ignorance. But I'm wiping the slate clean. I'm dissolving everything. Not much time to make amends but that's what I fervently desire . . .

The missive went on and on.

It also went unanswered.

He recalled the last conversation they'd had: in the bar at Donelli's, a posh place, filled with posh people—most of them media kings and queens and princes and celebs.

Whittaker was there often and to him it was simply a watering hole.

Given his son's feeling about his father's profession, it was also the absolutely wrong place to meet with Kitt. And, making matters worse, the boy had shown up in jeans and flannel. Even the help was dressed better.

I should have picked a different place, he'd thought.

The conversation had struggled and stalled, like the muddy Range Rover during that photo safari the family had taken years ago.

Idealist Kitt, activist Kitt, ever perplexed why his father refused to abandon the Whittaker Media Group brand of "journalism," the quotation marks supplied by his son's thin fingers.

Whittaker had, for an instant, nearly said that the company is what put him through a good school and bestowed upon him an ample trust fund.

Thank God he'd held his peace. Though apparently whatever had transpired during that uneasy meal was enough to create a deep, perhaps irreparable, rift.

They hadn't spoken in eight months.

Finally Whittaker had worked up courage. And, just the other day, sent the email.

Kitt, please hear me out . . .

And, shamefully, he had included the line, I'm sorry to say the doctor isn't hopeful.

Playing *that* card was a sign of his desperation.

Son, you're largely the reason I'm dissolving the company. I realize I wasn't the father I should have been. The husband or brother too. I was cruel to employees, I was cruel to the subjects we wrote about. I was cruel to my family, to you especially. Your absence finally let me see. Please, let's sit down . . .

Where are you?

His mobile vibrated. Since he'd gotten sick—well, since the sickness decided to stop being coy and chose to blossom—he'd developed a sensitivity to loud and jarring sounds.

He glanced at the caller ID.

"Jo."

His niece's low, even voice said, "That policewoman's here. The one Spencer called about."

"All right. I'm coming out."

A sigh. The police . . . About that man terrorizing people, leaving *Daily Herald*s . . .

The crows were coming home to roost. In droves.

No, the *vultures* . . .

Gripping the cane, he moved slowly across the rich Persian carpet, predominantly blue, a shade that reminded him of Mary's eyes.

34

A wide door of rich mahogany opened slowly and a man stepped out of what seemed to be a home office.

He was using a brass-headed black cane for support. He was not old. Amelia Sachs guessed he was late sixties, maybe early seventies. He'd been a handsome man at one point but was now sunken and fragile. The skin was loose and gray. Cancer not cardio, she guessed. He was attentive to personal details, though. His hair was perfectly coiffed and he was smoothly shaven. She smelled floral cologne. His dark suit and white shirt were not baggy. Photos on the mantel and walls told her he'd lost much weight lately, which meant that the garments were recently tailored or purchased, despite his numbered days. We fight disease on many fronts.

Averell Whittaker nodded an affectionate greeting to the couple Sachs had just met: Joanna Whittaker, the man's niece, and her fiancé, Martin Kemp. A nod to Lyle Spencer too.

One other person as well: Alicia Roberts was the armed guard assigned for Whittaker's personal protection. The solidly built blond woman, with hair in a tight bun, wore a dark suit. She seemed to be ex-military.

Sachs identified herself and shook Whittaker's dry, firm hand. He sat, adjusted his paisley pocket square and then gestured everyone to sit. Sachs eased into the cream-colored leather chair. She and Rhyme had pursued a perpetrator to Italy not long ago and she'd had a chance to sit on some very upscale furniture. This chair would have stood up quite nicely to any of those.

When Lyle Spencer sat, the chair creaked.

The apartment was in the residential portion of Whittaker Tower. The building was commercial to the top ten floors—the Whittaker Media Group newspaper, TV and radio operations—and above that private residences. The massive living room was decorated with subdued elegance. She saw a Picasso on one wall. The artist who did that pointillism thing—Sachs could never remember—was responsible for another. From the north-facing floor-to-ceiling windows you could see the Bronx and—given the lofty height of sixty-four stories—maybe an outer ring of Westchester.

Her entire town house in Brooklyn could have been tucked tidily into this room.

Whittaker began, "This person calling himself the Locksmith, leaving the newspapers, he hasn't hurt anyone?"

"Not in the two cases over the past couple of days. He breaks in, rearranges things and lets her know that he's been there."

"Lord," Joanna said.

"We did find a small amount of blood, but no other direct evidence of violence."

Sachs took a notepad from her inner pocket and clicked a pen to ready. She held up her Sony and, when there were nods all around, pressed Record. "The two victims say they don't have any connection to anyone at your paper or TV channel. They don't know why he's leaving the newspapers." She gave the names and asked, "Do they mean anything to you?"

The family members regarded one another. "No," Whittaker said, and Joanna shook her head. Martin Kemp did as well.

Sachs asked about the progress of the legal department in pulling together the list of threatening letters and complaints the media company had received.

Whittaker replied, "Doug said it should be ready in an hour or so." He sighed. "It will be a big file. We've tread on many toes for many years. And then the equal opportunity issues. Whittaker Media has not had the most diverse and felicitous workplace environment."

Joanna said, "Maybe it doesn't have anything to do with us. Like that man who shot Reagan. Hinckley? He was inspired by *The Catcher in the Rye*. But there was nothing in the book that called for violence." The woman had long brunette hair, tied back severely into a ponytail. The strands were thin and the tail swayed when she looked over the visitors, which she did in a staccato way. Her gray eyes, beneath close-knit brows, were keen and her mien stern. Her dark navy suit was cut like a man's. The face was square and she had a prominent nose. Sachs liked that she wore her features proudly and hadn't given in to pressure from anyone, society included, to change her contours.

Sachs said, "Possibly." She explained her thinking that the Locksmith might be using the *Herald* as a token—to protest media's intrusion into people's lives.

"Ah," Whittaker said sadly, "he's breaking in—just the way *we* do."

Sachs shrugged. "Just a thought I had. Also, he could be planting the papers as a complete misdirection."

"How's that?" Martin Kemp asked. He had a voice that could earn him a slot as an FM radio host.

"He could be up to something else entirely, not involving you, and he's focusing attention on the newspaper."

"What would the something else be?" Whittaker asked.

"We don't have any theories yet. We also know that you're selling the company. Is it possible that a potential buyer hired the Locksmith to put you in a bad light, reduce the value?"

He gave a laugh, which to Sachs seemed almost sorrowful. "Buyers . . . Well, it might be helpful, Detective, if you knew a bit about Whittaker Media. I have to confess that the brand of journalism we offer isn't quite up to the *New York Times* standard."

"Averell," Joanna said kindly and touched his knee.

"No, she should know." The man shrugged, which resulted in a minor wince. He continued, "Charlotte Miller. There's *one* example. Of many."

The name was familiar, Sachs said, but she couldn't place it.

"It was about a year ago. Aide to a U.S. congressman from Alabama. Marvin Doyle."

That too echoed. She said nothing and let Whittaker continue. "One of those terrible things. He assaulted her. Drugs in her drink, something like that. The police investigated but there wasn't enough evidence to go forward with a prosecution. Charlotte didn't give up, though. She wanted to tell her story and expose him. I bought it and paid her for exclusivity. Put a top writer on it. We promised it was going to be serialized. But it never ran."

"Why not?"

"Because I killed it. Do you know buy and bury?"

"No."

"It's when a newspaper or TV station buys the rights to a story with no intention of running it. Basically they lock up the story and the subject forever. You can't sell it anywhere. That's what we did with Charlotte."

"To protect Doyle?"

Whittaker was somberly regarding the brass figurehead of a woman on his cane. "Exactly. He was our friend in Congress. He supported legislation to make it easier for media companies to capture and sell viewer data and harder for us to get sued."

The memory came back to her. "Wasn't there a death or something? Related to it?"

"A few months after the story would have run Doyle tried to rape another woman, an intern. She fought back. He killed her. Negligent homicide. If the story had run maybe that wouldn't've happened."

Silence in the room, so high in the stratosphere that you could hear not a single horn, not a single growl of a truck engine.

"Averell," Kemp said softly.

But the man would not be deterred. "And then there's the quality of our reporting. I put 'quality' in invisible quotation marks. A *Daily Herald* reporter went down to Virginia on a story. It was about a teacher running a satanic cult in her high school history classroom. There were reports of sex and animal sacrifice. A man in North Carolina read the article, drove there and shot up the school. Killed the teacher and a girl in the class, wounded three."

She shook her head.

"You know how the rumor started? She was teaching her students about the Salem witch trials. That was all. A simple history lesson, but the reporter—with his editor's blessing—couldn't resist the satanic hook. Turned out that the teacher was gay and a couple of students in her class came from families that didn't approve. *They* started the rumors and just plain lied. The reporter quoted the teacher's denial, but that, obviously, had no effect on the shooter. I said the editor approved the story, but I gave him full rein."

Grim-faced, he said, "It was incidents like those that finally made the decision for me. A month ago I decided it was time to put the empire to sleep. Forgive the long answer to your question, Detective, but I'm not selling to anyone. There are no buyers—except for our production equipment, trucks, computers. I'm liquidating and sinking every penny into a foundation for ethical journalism."

Sachs jotted notes. Then she looked up. "So unless we come up with another motive, we'll have to go on the assumption that he's motivated by revenge for something the paper's done. The word 'reckoning' *does* suggest that."

Lyle Spencer said, "I was thinking: If they were different pages with each invasion, it might be the newspaper or company in general he's angry with. But since he's leaving the same page, It's probably something about one of the articles there."

Sachs had been about to make the same observation. She pulled up the picture of page 3 on her phone again and locked it open.

SECRET REPORT UNCOVERED: AIDS CREATED
IN RUSSIAN LABORATORY

U.S. SENATOR'S INTERN PREGNANT WITH LOVE CHILD

BOMBSHELL: ACTRESS'S DIVORCE INVALID;
ARREST EXPECTED

WOMEN-HATING GROUP EXPOSED

TECH COMPANY HAS PROOF OF ILLEGAL WIRETAPS
BY FEDS TO HELP CAMPAIGN

Whittaker said, "Ever since Doug told me, I've been thinking about the stories. Well, can't be the Russians. They'd probably happily take credit for weaponizing AIDS. The second headline is true, but it's not the *senator's* love child. We make that clear in the story somewhere. The third one? The actress didn't fill out a form right in her divorce affidavit, and she was investigated but never charged. And that's hardly the sort of transgression that leads to psychotic stalkers. The last? Every media outlet from *Car and Driver* to the *Wall Street Journal*'s got proof of illegal wiretaps by the feds. That's used chewing gum."

"So, the fourth story."

"I think it's possible. It's about the Apollos, a group of Neander-thals who're anti-feminist. They feel women should stay in the home, et cetera. It's acceptable to beat your wife if she quote 'misbe-haves.' Which is anything that displeases the husband. A wife has to have sex on demand."

"Why do you think this story motivated them?"

Whittaker grimaced. "Again, journalistic standards. Our re-porter was . . . less than diligent. He made up some quotes. Painted them *even* worse than they really are. There was a huge backlash and attacks on members of the group—I mean physical attacks. The Apollos named in the story were bullied and beaten up. One of the leaders was shot and paralyzed."

"So the Locksmith could be an Apollo."

"Or hired by them," Spencer pointed out.

Whittaker shrugged, wincing once more. Was it the cancer? Maybe arthritis. Amelia Sachs knew the malady only too well.

Sachs said, "I want the names of everybody the reporter inter-viewed for the story. The reporter's name and number too."

"I'll get that for you," Whittaker said.

The group sounded despicable, but a crime was a crime.

Whittaker asked, "And with what he posted on social media, ask-ing who'll be next, he's going to keep going?"

"We have to assume that."

Joanna closed her eyes briefly. "And think what would happen if a victim woke up when he was there."

Sachs said, "We should assume that he"—a glance toward Spencer, thinking of his earlier gender comment—"or she is targeting not only the company but you personally. You should be aware of any threats. Anyone following, observing you." Pointing toward the mantel, Sachs said, "That picture is of you and your wife?"

Whittaker replied, "Yes. Mary passed a few years ago."

"Who's the young man in it?"

"My son, Kitt." A deep breath. "We're estranged. He's been out of touch for eight months or so."

Sachs could now see a different kind of pain in the man's eyes. "Do either of you talk to him?" she asked Joanna and Kemp.

His niece and her fiancé shook their heads.

Sachs got his mobile number and then asked, "You have a work number for him?"

There was a pause. Joanna said, "We don't actually know what he does. He's a lost soul. When we were in touch, it seemed like he jumped from job to job: he was going to do something for the environment, then he was going to fly commercial drones—"

Kemp said, "Then it was gas and oil leases, remember? And something about videography and computers."

Whittaker said, "I'm sure nothing came of them. I have no idea what he's doing now. Probably living off his trust fund."

"Social media?"

Joanna said, "He doesn't have any accounts. Doesn't trust them—or *didn't*."

She asked the woman and her fiancé if they worked for Whittaker Media too. Joanna did, but not on the media side. She ran the company's charitable foundation. Kemp worked in real estate on Wall Street.

Sachs supposed they weren't in as much danger as Whittaker or the journalists on the paper, but still advised them to be watchful as well.

Spencer's phone sounded and he read a text. He replied. "Doug Hubert's got the threat list compiled. We can pick it up now. I can take you over there."

Sachs handed out cards to each of them. "Please, call me if you can think of anything else." Pocketing the recorder and pad and pen, she walked to the door with Spencer, and both nodded goodbye to Alicia Roberts, the quiet woman guard.

They were in the alcove when she heard, "One minute, Detective." Whittaker was up and walking after them slowly, listing into his cane. He glanced at Spencer, who got the message and said, "I'll be in the hall."

He said, "Detective, this is . . . I know we don't know each other from Adam, but I want to say one thing. I don't have a lot of time left. And my only son's become a stranger to me. I haven't been the best father . . . No, I've been a terrible father. I want him in my life again, to try to make up for what I've done. If you find him, could you tell him that? It's not your business, I understand, but . . ."

"I will."

His face softened in gratitude. He turned away, but not before Sachs caught a glint of what might be tears in his eyes.

"Excuse me."

Sachs was on Park Avenue, heading toward the north side of Whittaker Tower, which was the business entrance to WMG. Lyle Spencer was at her side.

They had just made their way through a small crowd of protesters outside Whittaker Tower. The majority of signs took aim at fake news, some about diversity hiring.

She glanced back at the voice.

The man, wearing blue jeans and a black windbreaker, had a lean face framed with curly dark hair. Sideburns. The word "ferret" came to mind.

"Excuse me, Officer Sachs."

She stopped and turned to face him.

The ferret approached, eyeing Spencer's bulk. Speaking quickly, he said to Sachs, "I see your eyes, you're thinking. But, no. We haven't met. Among cops, you're a celeb. Can I say 'cop'? Nothing offensive about that, right?" He talked a mile a minute. "Sheldon Gibbons. I'm with *InsideLook Magazine*." He displayed a press badge. She noted the last name, which added another mammal to the equation. Wasn't that a monkey or orangutan?

"Is this your partner?"

Neither Sachs nor Spencer answered.

"Can I help you?"

Gibbons said, "And sorry, it's 'Detective' Sachs. I called you 'Officer.'"

She was going to give him a few seconds' worth of polite but that was it. She cocked her head.

He brandished a digital recorder, much like hers.

"Were you seeing Averell Whittaker about the Locksmith?"

She said, "I'm asking permission to see that."

Gibbons frowned. "I'm sorry?"

"Can I see your recorder?"

"I guess." He handed it over.

She hit Stop. And gave it back to him.

He offered a conspiratorial—and maybe admiring—grin.

Sachs asked, "What do you want?"

"Whittaker Media is one of my beats. I was asking if you were talking to Averell about the Locksmith."

"Why do you think I was seeing him? It's a big building."

"You came out of the south hallway. There's only one elevator there and it goes directly to his suite."

She said nothing.

"Come on. This is a great story. A guy breaks into apartments and leaves one of Whittaker's papers? Like a journalistic Batman villain? What angle are you following? Do you think the Locksmith's a former employee?"

"I have no comment. On that. On anything."

"Is Whittaker himself in any danger? How about his niece, Joanna? Was she there? She visits a lot." A coy smile. "Maybe the Locksmith's extorting her charity. It's well endowed."

"On anything," she repeated.

Gibbons offered a card. "I tell it like it is, Detective. I don't trash cops in my stories. I report the facts, unlike some news institutions." He nodded toward the skyscraper. "Threats against Whittaker and Joanna, that's a valid story. I want to report it. Help me out. Who knows, maybe publicity'll drum up some witnesses for you."

"Goodbye, Mr. Gibbons." She slipped the business card away, thinking that if she threw it out now, a scene might ensue.

"Take care, Detective Sachs. Keep me in mind."

She and Spencer continued to the entrance. She looked back and noted that Gibbons did not circle back to the crowd to fish for stories. He'd apparently given up on his reporting duties for the time being and had vanished from sight.

35

So the Locksmith *had* returned to the Bechtel Building.

Mel Cooper was analyzing what Sachs had found on her second visit to the place, where she had happened to meet the Whittaker Media security chief, Lyle Spencer.

"What do we have, Mel?"

"Wrapper from a Jolly Rancher piece of candy."

"Why do we think it's his?"

"Bit of dish detergent on it, same profile as earlier. And some graphite—the grade that locksmiths use."

"Prints, DNA?"

"None."

"So he carefully unwrapped the candy before popping it into his mouth. Couldn't he tear it open with his teeth, and be helpful? So this delicacy? Is it rare? Limited sources? Will it lead us someplace?"

Cooper bent over the computer and typed. "The number-one hard candy in America. One million two hundred thousand dollars' worth of revenue every year."

Rhyme sighed.

"Halloween? A million pounds're sold."

"Thank you, Mel," Rhyme said acerbically. "I could have deduced the wrapper's uselessness evidentially from the revenue stat, without the weight information."

Cooper, unfazed, continued, "Around it, on the floor, Amelia found traces of boron, copper and iron. It was probably his since the control samples from the building don't show any of these."

"Put them on the board," Rhyme called to Thom, their current scribe, and up went the notes.

The significance?

That he couldn't say. Not yet. These were among the most common materials in the manufacturing industry.

So little evidence . . .

Rhyme couldn't sweep from his mind Sachs's earlier speculations.

The paper's a red herring. Nothing to do with what he's really up to. He's an illusionist and's got something else entirely going on.

He tried to put himself into the mind of the man who was the Locksmith's doppelganger—the Watchmaker.

How do the cogs fit together?

Newspapers, knives, tricky locks, lingerie, two innocent, unrelated victims (and possibly more), days-old human blood . . .

What are you trying to construct?

But he had no answers. Rhyme's eyes went to the photo of the splashy newspaper page and his mind to a place where it had gone, reluctantly, earlier: the question of what was motivating the Locksmith to commit these complex and risky crimes against the paper—and, ultimately, against the Whittakers?

"What's the story behind the family?" Rhyme asked.

Cooper said he didn't know much. He was not a consumer of

Whittaker Media Group products. He read the *Times* and the *Wall Street Journal*, and he and his girlfriend watched little TV news; mostly they listened to NPR and podcasts.

That was basically Thom's journalistic diet too, the aide reported. "You want me to look into them?"

"No. I'll do it." Rhyme went online and engaged in some high-school-level research. In a half hour he had a rough picture of the Whittakers and their empire.

Averell and Lawrence had inherited a modest chain of newspapers in the New York suburbs from their father, a few radio stations too. The operation was only marginally profitable. The brothers, Ivy League grads (both academically and athletically distinguished) were ambitious. They'd never wanted anything to do with the mundane and profit-neutral chain and pursued careers other than journalism. Averell in manufacturing, Lawrence in investing.

But when their father passed away and left them the papers, they decided to exploit the opportunity given them.

The business model of reporting about Westchester County planning and zoning meetings and covering light opera and modern dance left both brothers cold.

It was time for a makeover. Averell was quoted as saying, "The *New York Times* promises to deliver all the news that's fit to print. And *Rolling Stone* delivers all the news that fits. We're going to deliver all the news that people *want*."

Overnight most of the employees were fired and the local papers sold. All the resources went into founding the *Daily Herald*, a national paper in both print and online editions. Its stories were classic tabloid fare, with one exception: it took no political stance whatsoever editorially. They wanted advertisers and readers from the entire spectrum, and so the reporters focused on, or sank into, the world of celebrity and scandal.

Almost from the first day—the banner headline being about an actor who had evicted his own mother from his home so his girlfriend could move in—the *Herald* hit big, and the cash flowed.

Several years ago, Whittaker Media acquired a limping TV station and created the WMG channel, its content as tawdry—and appealing—as its print counterpart.

The Googled articles Rhyme skimmed—and there were many of them—were punctuated with photos of Averell and Mary, and their son, Kitt. There were nearly as many of Lawrence and Betty and their Joanna. Athletically built, with fierce eyes, Averell looked every inch the captain of industry or ruthless prosecutor, while alcoholic Lawrence was retiring and unkempt and dowdy. Their wives were always photographed as if they were on their way to a fundraiser. Kitt seemed sullen and he dressed down. Joanna was her mother's daughter, smiling for the camera and, sometimes, wearing a gown that matched Betty's.

It was a lush life. The homes were palatial and in one series of pictures Betty and Joanna hosted a garden party in a greenhouse that was bigger than Rhyme's town home. The company rose to the ranks of the Fortune 500, and the foursome appeared at galas, the White House Correspondents' Dinner, the Academy Awards and untold black-tie events in Manhattan.

Then harder times.

Betty died, a heart attack, and her husband proved not to be the savvy Wall Street investor he fancied himself. He racked up severe debts and only by selling his brother his shares in the company did he avoid bankruptcy. Averell kept Lawrence on as a highly paid employee—while Joanna, a junior reporter for the paper, was given a huge raise and put in charge of the company's charitable arm. Averell even signed over a vacation house and one of his yachts to that side of the family.

Then several years ago, Mary died from cancer, and after that Kitt largely vanished from the pictures of Averell, Joanna and her fiancé, Martin Kemp.

Recently the company itself began to unravel. Rhyme read about the consequences of false or careless reporting, resulting in assaults, suicides, even murder.

Complaints about Averell and his management approach began to surface too. He did not want women in any senior positions—he felt they created a distraction in the workplace—and the company's minority hiring was a sham. One article in a competing newspaper called it the *"White*-aker Media Group."

Finally, Averell underwent an epiphany and decided to liquidate the empire and put the proceeds into a foundation, which would promote ethics and minority education in journalism and create a watchdog group to oversee the threats to reporters around the world.

"Averell Whittaker Does a 180," read one headline.

Rhyme logged off.

"Anything helpful?" Thom asked.

"Not really," Rhyme muttered, his eyes on the Locksmith evidence board. He wondered again if the Locksmith's whole plan was misdirection.

Looking to the side, he scanned the board that had been devoted to the Viktor Buryak matter.

And what, Viktor, are you and yours up to right now?

A question that could not be answered, of course, so Lincoln Rhyme let it vanish from his thoughts and turned back to the mute evidence board devoted to the Locksmith.

36

"Y ou know," Aaron Douglass was saying, "you think about Austin. They claim to have the best food trucks in the world. Or at least more of them. Not true."

He and Arnie Cavall were on a corner of Madison Avenue in the eighties, the poshest of the posh. Shorter than towering Douglass, Arnie looked up, confused by the lecture, but attentive. He was the "masseur" that Douglass had told Buryak about, which meant he wasn't one at all.

Douglass continued, "New York wins. You've got lángos—that's Hungarian fried bread with a bunch of stuff on it. Out of this world. Then, of course, tacos, Korean bowls, gyros, empanadas, pupusas— El Salvador, the best are with cornmeal—lobster rolls, though they're pricey and you have to watch for too much mayonnaise."

Arnie might have been short but he was strapped with muscles. He wore a denim vest over a white shirt. Tight-fitting jeans, cowboy boots. Just the thing for stomping, Douglass guessed. He wore three rings on his right hand. Big ones. Were they for punching?

Douglass was wearing what he usually wore—nods to the villain in the movie *The Matrix*, dark suit and white shirt and tie (now pale blue, unlike the film). You couldn't see the tie, though; a napkin was tucked into his collar. Douglass was presently eating a maple-flavored tempeh burger with kale, tomato and garlic aioli on spelt bread. As he was enjoying it, occasionally bits of sandwich escaped.

Arnie was studying the elaborate sandwich.

"You should get something." A nod at the truck. Their other specialty was artichoke lentil cake with barbecue sauce. Douglass wasn't vegan, but people who were made some very good dishes.

Arnie shook his head.

Douglass adjusted his black beret. He didn't know why more people didn't wear them. Comfortable. Stylish. Easily stashed.

"You need an app or have to go online and find out where particular trucks will be. It's kind of a game."

"That right?"

This was one of the ten trucks that Viktor Buryak ran, making some money from the food, but that wasn't the point, of course. Everybody in the organization knew that Buryak was always looking for smart ways to collect information he could broker, and Douglass had scored big-time by coming up with the idea.

You think of that yourself? You are fucking brilliant in the head . . .

Yeah, Douglass was—at least with this. Food trucks were perfect for espionage and intelligence gathering. No one ever paid attention to the presence of a food truck. Drivers could suck up all sorts of information and take pictures to their heart's content.

Douglass enjoyed doing this particular job for Buryak—handling security and collecting intelligence at the trucks—because he loved to eat. He made the rounds of the trucks in the city, collecting information that was too sensitive to be sent via phone, and taking care of any risks to the drivers. And he was always comped dishes. He must have had five meals a day.

"There she is."

Amelia Sachs, and the oversize guy with her—also in a *Matrix* dark suit—were walking out of Whittaker Tower. He was carrying a large folder. They were stopped by a skinny guy with a grin that Douglass thought was phony. They had a brief conversation and Detective Amelia and the companion continued down the sidewalk.

"Got a good look at her?"

"Yeah. Who's the big guy?"

"Don't know."

Douglass finished the food and wiped his face. Doing the dishes, for him, was wrapping everything up and dropping it in the nearest waste container. He fished a bottle of water from his pocket and sipped. He supposed eating this way wasn't healthy, always on the run. But this was the least unhealthy thing about his life.

Detective Amelia started the car and spun it one eighty, went right past the food truck without glancing at it. Everybody did this. Unless of course they were hungry.

"And I get five K for it?" Arnie asked.

"Five K."

The man appeared uncertain. "What you told me, it sounds risky."

"Life's risky. Maybe I'll get salmonella from that sandwich. I'm not negotiating."

A sigh. Arnie said, "Okay."

"And I need a complete loss of memory when this's over with."

"I sometimes forget my mother's birthday."

"I'm not joking." Five Gs buys you the right to crack the whip occasionally.

"I got it, I got it. Everything'll go away after. When and where?"

"I don't know yet. It'll have to be deserted and we can't have witnesses."

"She didn't look like a cop."

"No, she doesn't. Here's a down payment." He handed the man an envelope. "A thousand. And another thousand for a beat-up van. And score some other plates for it. Don't put 'em on now. You do that just before the job."

"I've done this before. How big?"

Douglass supposed it didn't matter, and he said this. Then: "You clear the deck for the next two days. You don't take any other jobs."

"What if—"

"You don't take any other jobs."

"I don't take any other jobs." Arnie nodded quickly.

"I gotta talk to my associate here."

Arnie looked around.

"The driver," Douglass snapped. "The food truck."

"Oh. Yeah, okay. You know, I had an idea. I'll get a white van. That's the most common color. What do you think?"

"It's a fine idea. Now leave."

After Arnie left, Douglass told the food truck driver that he'd done a good job with the sandwich and asked for a Cuban coffee.

Douglass sipped the coffee and thanked the driver, who also handed over an envelope—the results of some espionage work. Money changed hands. Smells wafted from the truck. As much as he loved food, he was a terrible cook and was, at the moment, between wives (he was good at getting married but not so great at *staying* that way).

"What's the bestseller today?"

"Creole-grilled tofu, I'd say."

"Make me one and wrap it up. I'll have it for dinner."

37

Back in the womb of my workshop.

A change of clothes, some peanut butter cheese crackers, some decaf coffee.

I'm looking over the knives I've acquired—Annabelle's and Carrie's. They're of a functional design, nothing fancy. Carrie's is the sharpest. I have their panties too. One pair blue, one pair pink. But I'm less interested in them than the blades.

The knives and the garments are sitting on a table beside my workbench. There are also two copies of the *Daily Herald*; they both still have page 3 intact.

That is one very troubled newspaper.

I feel the weight of my own knife, the beautiful construction of brass, in my pocket.

I content mod for a bit. I peruse a video of a woman who's lip-synching a top 40 song. She's good. The autobot has sent it to me not for any violent or sexual issue, but because she's violating the copyright law. She doesn't have a blanket ASCAP or BMI license, which would give her the rights to "sing" the tune. However, I will leave it up for a few days. I have spotted a mole on her neck that I believe is cancerous. I don't want to go to too much trouble, so I simply log on like any other person and leave a comment that she ought to have it checked out.

My mother died of that disease.

I watch some more vids and play God for a bit.

Delete . . .

Sign in . . .

Let stand . . .

We content moderators spend hours upon hours looking for vids that violate either the law or that famous "community standard," which is quite the odd phrase, since there must be a billion distinct communities in cyberspace, ranging from ethereally noble to disgustingly depraved. The company sends us guidelines, but basically community standards are what I decide they are.

I say I play God, and I do. Often posters, desperate for likes and shares, fling up buckets of content that I have to loose my lightning bolt of judgment upon.

I've seen hundreds of executions, suicide attempts, rapes, child beatings and molestations, people shooting up and OD'ing, survivalists giving step-by-step instructions about bomb making, animals hurt, racial invective, calls to revolution, facts cited by politicians and pundits and bumpkins that even I—smart but hardly an expert—know are blatantly false.

Hours upon hours.

There is no end in sight.

My company, ViewNow, is smaller than YouTube and not owned by one of the mega-tech outfits, but it's not insignificant. Over two hundred hours of videos are uploaded every minute, and each day millions of people watch four billion videos. If you watched every video that was available on ViewNow today, it would take thousands of years of nonstop viewing to see everything.

It's really breathtaking.

All social media platforms employ content moderators.

We're the grunts in the front lines of battle, like the grad students somebody told me about, with sledgehammers at the first nuclear reactor at the University of Chicago with orders to go into the radioactive pile and break it apart before a reaction melted the Second City.

Their plight may be apocryphal. Ours isn't.

Some platforms stash their content mods in boiler rooms, which might be located anywhere in the world. Many of these sites are in Manila and India. Those mods used to work in call centers throughout South Asia but grew tired of irate customers and insults about accents and they flocked to the moderating profession, hoping it would be a springboard to a good job in tech.

This never happens for the vast majority. Content modding is not a springboard to anything . . . except—for most—depression. After all, we don't spend ten hours a day watching vids on how to make a sponge cake or snowboarding. We root out the bad stuff. I mean, the *really* bad stuff—videos that can never be unseen and that sit, festering, in our heads forever.

I know of four mods who've committed suicide, another two dozen who've tried. Marriages have ended and livers grown distended from cirrhosis. ViewNow has a counseling department. Nobody uses it because there's no time, not when a billion hours of video remain to be viewed.

Otherwise gentle people have turned violent after a few months at CM work.

As for me?

Of course, I have no problem whatsoever with the job.

I'm a born content moderator and always have been. Real life or a high-def monitor. Not a bit of difference to me.

I've never liked the verb "peeping," much less using the word in the silly-sounding combination with "Tom." According to the myth, or factual history (no one knows), Tom was a tailor who was the only person in Coventry to catch a glimpse of the naked Godiva riding through the city (to get her husband to lower rents on his tenants, a strange form of protest and one that sounds pretty far-fetched, to say the least). The scenario was somewhat skewed since *she* was the one outside and Tom was peeping, if you can call it that, from the privacy of his tailor shop.

Tom was struck blind by God or fate or whoever, though there was no particular statute he'd broken, it seemed. As for today, the offense of peeping falls somewhere within the laws of trespass and invasion of privacy and if there's a participle it's usually "peeking," not "peeping." The laws have now been expanded to include spying by drone and hacking into webcams, as well as revenge porn and posting without permission.

I knew as a boy that what I did was wrong and creepy and embarrassing and, if I was on someone else's property, a crime (you can stare and leer at someone, drooling and grinning madly to your heart's content, if you do it from the sidewalk). But nothing would stop me. I had to get closer. I snuck up to houses in the pleasant suburban village where we lived and peered through windows. Hundreds of times. The problem with the offense is that if you're close enough to see, you're also close enough to be seen. The more my outrageous dangling from trees or hovering on trash cans became, the riskier were the ventures, and the police might be summoned.

Overburdened, as always, officers recognized I was weird but not a physical threat and tended to treat me as a nuisance. They left the matter of discipline and reeducation up to my father.

The self-described captain of industry was not a moral man so he was not concerned about the wrong of what his son did; it was the embarrassment and the bruising of his reputation that stung. Had his boy been a shoplifter, a pot dealer, a teen drunk, he might have been fine with those younger-days misbehaviors. But the creep factor, coupled with the fact that there was no significant police involvement and punishment meted out pushed him over the edge. He took the law into his own hands and jailed me himself. If he found out that I'd transgressed, it was solitary confinement in our house.

Not just house arrest, free to roam from room to room. Oh, no, I was locked into bedrooms, then pantries, then bathrooms, then closets—one in particular so reeking of naphtha and cedar, I'd get high. He'd leave a bucket for the personal functions.

It was on the second or third detention that I learned I could pick the locks and escape. They were mostly Home Depot hardware that could be opened with a knife blade or a straightened coat hanger. My bedroom had a rim lock—the sort with the traditional keyhole-shaped opening, the design dating back hundreds of years. This was more challenging but, well, I managed.

The first time took me an hour. The next five minutes.

I didn't necessarily want to go anywhere but I needed to know I could.

Then the tipping point.

I had been caught at the house of a prominent lawyer. His sobbing daughter believed she had seen me gazing at her naked from outside the bathroom window. Her father sped to our house and, once inside, confronted me and my father. Denials streamed and I was tearfully upset—that I got *caught*, of course.

The lawyer paid little attention to me, as if I, being a mere thirteen-year-old, were a virus unable to make choices about where to float and whom to infect.

The man's fury was focused on my father.

"Your son's a pervert," the lawyer muttered, which was patently untrue. My obsession isn't and never was about sex; I want to get inside people in a different way. In fact, it was the daughter Heather who pranced into the bathroom and disrobed, while I was observing a fight between the parents in an adjoining bedroom. I blamed her. But that was not an argument to raise in the moment.

The man then said he represented powerful unions. His clients had "associates," a benign word sculpted ominously. Did my father get the drift? If I weren't punished, his business would be "disrupted." The tone of his voice suggested violence was a possibility.

My father turned to me, sitting beneath the two powerful men, though he spoke to the lawyer. "Don't worry, there'll be consequences."

And, yes, there were.

38

Rhyme looked up at the man accompanying Sachs into the parlor. He was huge and imposing, a born fighter or wrestler. He was gazing at Rhyme with . . . what was it? He seemed intimidated. Odd, as he outweighed Rhyme by a hundred pounds easily, and was purely physical.

Then his eyes swayed to the equipment on the sterile side of the room. The look shifted to awe.

Sachs introduced Rhyme to Lyle Spencer.

So this was the security man she had told him about.

He set down a thick file folder. "The Whittaker Media complaints and threats, from the public and from employees."

"That many?" It had to contain five hundred documents.

Spencer said, "And these are just the ones in the past year."

Sachs said, "We'll scan them and get started." Rhyme's turning frame could handle bound books but there was no device in the lab that could display and sequence single sheets of paper. She took a call on her mobile.

"Mel Cooper," came the voice from inside the sterile portion of the lab.

"Lyle Spencer."

Lincoln Rhyme rarely thought to introduce people.

Spencer studied the lab. "Quite the setup. But you've heard that before."

"It suits. When I need something sophisticated, we farm it out."

Spencer said, "My first job, we didn't have anything like this in the entire county. Everything had to go to the state lab. Took forever to get results."

"Amelia said you were L.E."

"Detective. Albany."

Just like Rhyme, he'd left law enforcement for a different, though allied, job. In his case, though, the move would have been voluntary. More money and less risk.

Disconnecting the call, Sachs joined them.

"That was the super of Kitt's building."

She'd explained that Averell's son, the slim, gaunt-faced young man Rhyme recalled from the online pictures, had not been seen for several days. The superintendent knew this because his mailbox was full and the postman complained to him.

"Think it's related?" Rhyme asked.

Sachs said, "The papers in the two apartments set the stage, then the Locksmith, or the Apollos, or somebody else kidnap or kill Whittaker's son? Makes sense."

She asked Spencer, "And he has hardly any connection to the family?"

"Not that I ever heard of."

Rhyme said, "Where does he work?"

Sachs explained that the family didn't know what he did. All she had was the one mobile number and email and he wasn't responding.

"DMV," Rhyme said.

Sachs went online to the state's secure website and entered her username and passcode.

"He owns an Audi A6. I'll send the tag to LPR."

The NYPD's license plate recognition system was made up of cameras mounted to squad cars. As officers drove through the streets of the city, the cameras constantly scanned for license plates and recorded images of the tags, along with the time and the location of each one. The result was exabytes of data. The system was a big help in finding cars whose drivers had fled accidents or were registered to suspects or those with outstanding warrants. The whole concept was controversial in that it sucked up and recorded hundreds of thousands of innocent citizens' plates too. Civil liberties groups complained, raising privacy concerns.

Rhyme understood this worry. But, in the end, he sided with the LPR system. It had helped them close a half-dozen cases.

"He's red-flagged now. If any cruisers have a hit I'll get a call."

Spencer said, "I have a meeting with Mr. Whittaker." A nod toward Rhyme. "Confession. I could have messengered over the file or given it to Amelia. But, to be honest, I just wanted to meet you. We had some of your books in our library in Albany. I studied them."

"Ah," Rhyme said.

He started for the door then stopped. "Amelia told me about the Locksmith operation. It's sensitive. If anyone asks, you're not involved in the case."

"Thanks."

With another nod, to Sachs, the large man walked into the hallway and out the door.

"I checked him out," she said.

"Assumed you would. What's his story?"

"Not sure," Sachs said. "Something happened. Not the military,

I think—he was a SEAL. Something more recent. PD in Albany, I'd guess." She told him that he'd been trying to leave the Bechtel Building, armed with a brain-beating pipe, when she'd lit him up. "It was odd. I targeted him center mass. Identified myself. Had him blinded by the flashlight on my phone. But he didn't drop his weapon. He just stood there."

"Deer in the headlights."

"Nope. I thought he was thinking of coming at me. Never seen anybody looking so relaxed with muzzle gaze."

"Any idea why?"

"Scar on his head. You see it?"

"No."

"I'd guess he was in a bad firefight. PTSD."

Rhyme, a lab man, a crime scene man, had occasionally experienced violence in the line of work. But ironically the only serious injury he'd experienced had come from an outright accident, not a gunshot. A beam had fallen onto his neck in a construction site he was searching. He could not imagine the panic, the noise, the chaos, the horror of a firefight. Sachs—no stranger to combat—had told him that the average length was three to seven seconds, though it seemed like long minutes.

She said, "I don't think he wants to be a security guard."

"A well-paid one, I'll bet."

"He mentioned a family, so I'm sure he needs the money. But he's like us. Blue is in his blood. He misses it."

Then Lyle Spencer and his inner angels or demons vanished like morning mist as Rhyme's eyes scanned the file.

"No other P.E. to analyze." A sour glance toward the sterile portion of the lab. "Let's read the complaints and threats. How many are there? Two million? Three? Thom! Thom! I need you to scan some documents. Let's go!"

39

on't worry, there'll be consequences.

My father might have gotten me into treatment. Lord knew, he had the money.

But instead he hired a locksmith and had three of the most expensive locks in the craftsman's stock installed on each of the two basement doors—one into the house and the other into the garden.

They were, however, installed backward.

Anyone outside simply could use the latch to open the door; the person *inside*, though—which would be me—would need keys, the only copies of which my father kept with him. The locksmith was perplexed and, before he started the job, asked a few questions.

He stopped his inquiries when handed ten one-hundred-dollar bills, on top of his fee.

Our mansion was large but the cellar was not—about twenty by thirty feet with a finished bathroom and wood floors and paneling, though there was no ceiling. Just black painted beams and pipes overhead.

A bed. A three-legged dresser, propped against the wall. A television, with basic cable. No computer. Father was afraid I'd email someone for help and I would have. Food would be set at the top of the stairs three times a day. There was a bag for laundry.

My father was serious about my being a prisoner and told me to pack up clothes, books, games, whatever I wanted. I was going to be taken out of school for "health" reasons but I would read my lessons and take tests at the end of the semester.

I did as ordered and collected two boxfuls of items and clothing from my room and descended into the prison.

"You ruin your life, that's your choice. But when you threaten my life's work, that's the end of it."

He added that he was sorry it had come to this. But actions have consequences. The first sentence was a lie. The second, obviously, he passionately believed in.

The air was either too chill or too warm and always damp. The solitude was a worm. The quiet was a scream. The boredom was like pepper in my throat. The mindless television killed my spirit and, I was convinced, my brain cells. I'd start books. I'd lose interest.

I would scream at times, cry, sit in a dark corner huddled for hours. Think about killing myself. What would be the most efficient way to die?

What saved my sanity—and my life—were locks.

The DeWalt 345, the Morgan-Hill, the Stoddard. The elegant impregnable devices became the center of my subterranean world. I found a safety pin in one of my boxes and tried to pick each one. I had no idea what I was doing and thus had no success. I remembered the satisfaction of opening the bedroom door with a modified coat hanger key but, with these devices, I was unable to duplicate that warm, marvelous sensation of the latch clicking home and freeing me.

I would stare at them for hours—the ones on the back door were just past the foot of my bed. After some hours, they appeared to begin to move, to swell in size, to shrink into dark holes, to sway or to shine with sparkling, swirling light.

I began to talk to them, and I believed they replied to me. They had three different personalities.

After five months, my father released me, I'm sure at the behest of my mother, who was largely cowed by him but had argued strongly against my imprisonment. I could hear them upstairs—the tone and the give-and-take, if not the actual words. He issued a stern warning that I'd go back inside if I ever peeped again.

I nodded, agreeing submissively, but felt no contrition whatsoever.

My solitary had let me see who I truly was. The deprivation—and the ensuing ordeal—convinced me that only peeping could bring me comfort.

Those terrible months had also taught me I had to be smarter. And to make sure I would never be imprisoned again.

At a secondhand bookstore I bought the *Ultimate Guide to Lock-picking, 10th Edition*, the most comprehensive tome on the subject ever written. At a home improvement store I bought a set of lock-picking tools, surprised they were available over the counter.

What better locks to hone my skill on than the three models that had kept me imprisoned? I still remember that day when I raked open the Morgan-Hill pin tumbler, which was described in the book as a nearly unpickable lock. I was in heaven. After a few weeks I was able to open all three locks on the doors in minutes.

Nothing could keep me in.

I began making Visits once more, now far smarter and more careful. I only went out late at night, when Father and Mother were asleep. I would dress in black and choose only the houses that I could approach under cover.

What I saw made little difference. Sometimes it was mundane, girls sipping soda. A grandmother knitting. Boys at a computer game. Sometimes men and women together, coupling, sweaty and lost to the world. The occasional fight.

Sometimes I did more than spy. One night I left a condom in the backseat of the car owned by the wife of the lawyer who had been responsible for the imprisonment. Let the couple make sense of that but whatever happened I think it didn't end well for either of them.

Consequences . . .

Other people who had crossed me would get a Visit too. I'd leave knives outside their doors. A doll in their window. Once I painted a swastika on the right rear fender of a Mercedes owned by a man who'd yelled at me about something. The man would probably get all the way to work before he'd begin to wonder about the staring.

Those Visits were about justice. The others? They just made me feel good.

Then, finally, I was away to college, a good one, given my father's money, and into the real world.

I made half-hearted attempts to get well. All I wanted was meds, to get the peeping under control. I'd tell the doctors a variation of a story, substituting an addiction to video games for peeping but describing in detail my imprisonment, which raised a shrink eyebrow or two.

Dr. Patricia dressed in beige, unoffensive outfits and had an utterly unsexy but engaging way about her. She might have been thirty-five; she might have been sixty.

"You were thinking about a job change?" she once asked me.

I told her the truth—that unlike my father I was not career minded. "I flit." I actually said that, and added, "Like a butterfly."

"You're young. You have time. Just ask yourself: What might you like to do, what's enjoyable that you can earn a living at?"

I told her I'd think about that.

And being the strategic therapist that she was, she inquired: "And how is Aleksandra? Things are going well with her?"

"Yes. Very good."

Dr. Patricia diagnosed me as suffering from anxiety and depression, laced with some ADHD—all very fixable. She gave me Wellbutrin, which has fewer sexual side effects than other antidepressants. I guess she didn't want to hamper my relationship with my Russian beauty.

Then toward our last session, she said, leaning forward for emphasis, "But there's one thing you have to do. You'll never be free until you confront the issue of what your father did to you in the basement. You need to talk to him about it. Tell him how the cellar affected you. It could be that he'll beg for forgiveness. You'll reconcile."

I told her I would think about her suggestion. I tucked the idea away and dusted it off from time to time.

Now, I glance at my phone for the time. It's afternoon. My Visits only work, of course, after midnight. But sometimes you get an urge to peep, to peer, to possibly do more.

Sometimes you need to hurt.

For the simple joy of it.

I take a shower and then dress. I pick up my knife. It's not only a helpful weapon, and tool, but it has great sentimental value.

It was given to me by Dev Swensen, my lock-picking mentor. He machined it himself. Brass is an unusual metal for a weapon. Unlike its stronger cousin, bronze, brass is rarely used in weapons. Not that it can't be honed to razor sharpness; it's just that it won't hold an edge very long. It needs to be sharpened after each use.

Into my pocket it goes.

Completely concealed, Officer. And short enough to be legal.

I don the Mets cap, sunglasses and a raincoat. I collect my gaudy, precious souvenir keychain and step outside, making sure, as I always do, the locks are nice and snug.

40

Was that guy following her?

No . . .

But maybe.

She'd noticed him about halfway on the walk to the school—four blocks total. She'd turned back absently at the sound of a horn and noted that he had looked away slightly, as if he'd been gazing at her.

A block farther along she peeked again. What made it suspicious this time was that he was the same distance behind her. Had he slowed down intentionally to keep pace?

Taylor Soames was savvy in all the ways that a Manhattan woman had to be, especially a single woman. The brunette was attractive enough, she felt, and dressed in outfits that displayed her figure, which she worked hard to maintain and was proud of. But they were never overtly suggestive or revealing. She attracted eyes, which was okay—it was the nature of men and women—but she was sharp enough to know when a look crossed the line.

With this fellow, she just couldn't tell. The sunglasses . . .

She arrived at the school where she was going to pick up her daughter. Roonie had stayed late after class for chess club. Rather than going inside, though, Soames waited. She wanted to see if she was truly being followed.

The man ducked into the Korean deli on the corner, pulling a phone from his pocket.

To make a call?

Or pretend to?

She assessed: A raincoat on a day of no rain, shades with little sun. A baseball cap pulled low. Younger, rather than older. More creepy than slavering. But she was standing outside a school, so "creep" took on an intensified meaning.

She just couldn't tell.

How embarrassing if the police confronted an innocent man.

Maybe, she thought, it's my ego that's the problem.

Though usually her radar was correct.

Damn it, was he now looking out at her through the milky plastic window of the deli?

She chatted with a few of the other moms, also picking up their middle-school children.

Checked her phone for emails and texts.

A man's voice behind her. "Oh, you're Roonie's mom, right? Hi."

The parent had stepped out of the front door of the large red-brick school. He wore the sticky visitor's ID badge plastered to a very nice suit.

"Ben." They nodded. "I'm Meghan Nelson's dad. We met a month ago. PTO. Before the great schism."

She laughed, with a shake of her head. The power play among the parents in a middle school had all the high drama of a royal court coup.

"Is Meghan in Roonie's class? I don't remember, sorry."

"No, she's sixth grade."

Soames's eyes returned to the vegetable stand. The stalker was either gone or had walked deeper into the deli.

Ben said, "We went to the gymnastics meet. The one at Hunter. Meghan thinks Roonie totally rocks." He laughed at his dip into teen speak.

Soames smiled. "Really, how sweet. Is that her sport too?"

"She wishes but she's big-boned. And too tall."

His daughter, he explained, wasn't into sports, but she was a wiz at singing and dancing. "Meghan's the theatrical one in the family." He gave a laugh. "Second only to my ex."

Then Ben looked past Soames—toward the deli.

"All okay?" she asked.

"Nothing. Just . . . this guy was staring at me."

"Was he wearing sunglasses?"

"Yeah, like he was some kind of player. He stepped back inside."

"And a raincoat and baseball cap?"

"That's him, yeah," Ben said.

"I think he was looking at *me*." She explained about the suspected following.

"Well . . . you want me to go talk to him?"

"God no."

Ben offered a smile.

"I knew a stalker once, *my* ex." Soames was feeling relaxed talking to him. "It was just that he wasn't inspired to stalk *me*, only his secretary."

He touched his bare ring finger. "Five years for me."

"Three."

Ben was a good-looking man; his thick dark hair was swept back, with premature gray streaks. Which, Soames had always felt, added to the sexy quota. And the suit was truly gorgeous. He had money.

"You want to call the police?"

"No. It's probably nothing."

Silence arose between them. Ben was looking up the street. She could feel his mind working. And she wasn't surprised when he said, "Look, I don't know your situation, but . . ." Funny how even the handsome ones grew positively bashful when about to ask the question. "You like Broadway?"

"Who doesn't?"

"Meghan's got a part in *Annie*." He nodded to the school. "The end of school play. Interested in going?"

She laughed at the Broadway reference. "I'd love to."

When he looked up the street, she scanned his body fast. Athletic.

And she loved graying hair.

She thought back to the last time she'd been with a man. Fortunate I have a good memory, she reflected.

Then she looked again at the deli.

Imagination, or not?

There were so many crazy people in the world, and particularly in such a densely packed city like this. She'd read in the *Times* about the number of people who were true sociopaths. Quite a few. The story said that most were harmless but some could snap for virtually no reason whatsoever.

"Nine one one?" he asked.

A faint laugh. "You're reading my mind. But no. I don't even see him anymore."

"You said you lived near here?"

"Four blocks." She nodded south.

"I'll walk you."

"Oh, no, you don't have to. You've got to pick up Meghan."

"She's staying at the ex's tonight. I just came by to drop off a backpack. Maybe if this guy sees me he might think I'm a boyfriend and leave you alone."

One terrible thought flashed through her head. What if the sunglasses man was dangerous, and, in a psychotic rage, jealous of Ben, attacked him?

"I'm insisting. If you don't agree, then *I'll* have to start following you."

She smiled.

They chatted for another few minutes until Roonie stepped out of the school. The slim girl, hair pulled back in a ponytail, had a large backpack over her shoulder.

"This is Mr. Nelson. His daughter's in the sixth grade."

"Meghan. You know her?"

"I think, yeah."

Soames was not, of course, going to mention the stalker to her daughter so she said only that their apartment was on Mr. Nelson's way home and he was going to walk with them.

He glanced in Soames's direction with a wink at the white lie.

"Cool," the girl said, and they started on their way.

"Hey, let me carry that." Ben nodded at the backpack.

"Really?" Roonie asked.

"You bet," he said, and lifted the heavy pack off her shoulder and slung it onto his own.

The threesome started south.

"So, Roonie, what routine do you like best in gymnastics?"

41

O h, I don't know," the girl tells me. "Balance beam, I think. Un-evens, too."

I nod at Roonie's response.

I could tell her what Aleksandra said, about Russian girls: dancers or gymnasts.

Better not to.

Come to think of it, both Taylor and Roonie have a slightly Slavic cast of face.

Of the two, the girl is the prettier. Mom isn't jealous of you. Not yet. I have a feeling it may happen.

As I walk along beside them—enjoying playing the role of Ben Nelson—I glance over pretty Taylor and skinny Roonie, thinking they have no idea what's hit them.

It was just like picking a lock. I followed her from her apartment, trying to get Taylor to notice me. I actually had to step in front of a taxi to get him to honk. At last she turned and noted me and seemed to grow suspicious.

She looked once more a few minutes later and I knew the hook was in.

"And tell Mr. Nelson about the camp you have coming up."

"Oh," she says, smiling. "It's the best. We're going to Wilmington. It's a famous place. There'll be a hundred of us from all over the East Coast. Jenna Carson trained there."

"No way," I say, exhaling with the breath of the impressed.

After she arrived at the school, I ducked into the deli. Off with the coat, sunglasses and hat—all cheap and disposable. I stuffed them into a plastic bag I bought for a dollar from the clerk. Underneath was a Brooks Brothers suit.

When she wasn't looking, I slipped around the corner to the back of Hawthorne Middle School and dumped the bag in the trash. I picked the Steel-Tec lock on the school's service door in three seconds. Pasting a parent's ID label on my chest, I climbed the stairs to the main floor and stepped outside.

Oh, you're Roonie's mom, right? Hi.

I stoked her paranoia about that sunglasses-wearing creep who might have been following her. If you think you're being stalked and someone independently confirms it, well, then you *are* being stalked. Set in stone.

Almost too easy.

"Like, what's your daughter's sport?" Roonie asks.

I tell her, "She takes after my side of the family. Zip athletic skill. But she likes to act. I've done a little of that myself."

"Cool." Now it's balance-beam Roonie's turn to be impressed.

Taylor looks at me admiringly.

"We saw your gymnastics meet. You were really good. You nailed your routine!"

She grins shyly and I believe she's blushing.

Taylor now chats, as they walk along the gritty, damp sidewalk and I'm in heaven. I've picked the lock of these two females' lives.

I see that Taylor has fallen silent. She seems troubled and I wonder if she's suspicious, even if she doesn't know that the man beside her is not who he seems to be and has a very sharp knife in his pocket.

It occurs to me that maybe what's bothering her is that by frustrating the stalker, he decided to assault someone else.

Is her gut pinging with guilt at the moment that she might have set in motion a chain of events that will end in an assault, a rape, a murder?

Well, I think, that faint trickle of remorse is nothing compared to the pain you're going to feel, Taylor.

And, Roonie, you too.

The girl now pulls her phone from her back right pocket and shows me a video of some famous gymnast. Jenna Whoever.

"She's amazing."

"That's the routine I'm working up now."

"Maybe Mr. Nelson and Meghan can come to your next meet?"

"Yeah, like, sure."

We cross the street. Taylor points ahead and says, "That's our building, right there."

And I think: I know.

"Friends: Follow-up to my news from my home, the West Coast. Remember the post about the government contracts for infrastructure projects around the country, using steel produced by a well-known company, based in California? They were using pig iron from eastern Europe in forging beams for bridges and highways, recall?

"Well, now I've learned that in a construction site in Northern

California, two workers are in serious condition after beams, made with the substandard steel, shattered. And what was the project? A highway bridge over a two-hundred-foot chasm.

"Next time you drive over a bridge, ask yourself: Was it built with defective steel?

"This is corruption at its worst.

"Why isn't the General Services Administration in Washington doing anything about it? Because, of course, they're controlled by the Hidden!

"Say your prayers and stay prepared!

"My name is Verum, Latin for 'true.' That is what my message is. What you do with it is up to you."

42

There but for the grace . . .

One of the two lead shields on the Alekos Gregorios homicide, Detective Tye Kelly, stood in the double doorway of the old gym, now a homeless shelter, brightly lit and clean but smelling to the back of his nose like disinfectant. Men were the only occupants here. The Department of Homeless Services—a very different DHS than the one that first comes to mind—wanted no trouble. Homeless people were just like homed people with regard to impulse control, or lack thereof. The problem here was that there were no doors you could hide behind and lock.

His partner, the other detective on the case, walked up behind him and looked over the huge room.

"Cleaner than I thought," Crystal Wilson said, hands on her trim hips. Today, coincidentally, they both wore dark gray suits. Her top was a black sweater, his a powder blue shirt. Each had jet black hair. His was thinning. Hers was done in neat cornrows. Kelly was at first surprised she'd never seen a shelter, but she'd come up in the 112, where there were none.

This one, the Deloitte House, was in a different precinct, west, where there were several official and unofficial shelters.

Wilson said, "It's bed B-eighty-six."

He wondered if she'd be thinking the same thing as he, a play on Bingo.

But under the circumstances—the location and their mission at the moment—neither of them acknowledged the thought.

Kelly was aware of the eyes following them and certain hand movements, as things were slipped away. Weapons, drugs and alcohol were forbidden in the shelters of New York City, but that had nothing to do with the *reality* of weapons, drugs and alcohol— especially in a shelter that was woefully understaffed and featured virtually no security. Still Kelly knew from experience that there was little to be gained from rousts and as long as no one flaunted their contraband, or threatened anyone, then let them be.

Leave them *something*, Kelly thought.

After all, there but for the grace . . .

Michael Xavier, his age somewhere from thirty to forty-five, sat on the edge of his bed, chewing his lips—from the antipsychotic drugs—and muttering to himself. He was not alone in this. Xavier was a bulky man. He was in a T-shirt that revealed arms that were both fat and muscular. He had an unruly beard. On his feet were shabby leather shoes. These matched, unlike the footwear of Alekos Gregorios's killer. But leads had to start somewhere.

Tye Kelly was big and imposing and his brows met in a line. They were arched high above his unsmiling eyes, all of which made him look like an irritated boxer. Wilson was petite and affected a gentle expression, both amused and curious, giving her the appearance of a first-grade teacher, not first-grade gold shield. He let her talk.

"Mr. Xavier, I'm Detective Wilson and this is Detective Kelly." Badges were displayed. Across the hall came a shout, "Get the fuck out!" But it was apparently directed to something invisible floating near the ceiling.

The man grunted, looked them over and said, "Is what it is."

"I wonder if you could tell us where you were last Tuesday night? Do you recall? Around nine p.m.?"

He chewed some more and stared at them. He muttered something.

"What was that, sir?"

Xavier fell silent and played with a fingernail.

"Where did he say he saw it?" Kelly asked Wilson.

His partner answered, "Under the bed."

Kelly got down on one knee and swept the beam of his small tactical flashlight under the cot. Damn. Cleaner than the floor at home.

Detectives from the 112 House had called a dozen shelters—located within five miles around the home of murder victim Gregorios—and asked if any staff had seen bottles of any brand of cherry-flavored chlorine dioxide, the fake medicine, in the possession of any white male residents who matched the description of the homeless man that Gregorios's son had told them about.

The director of Deloitte had seen the email and called the 112 and reported seeing a bottle of cherry-flavored Miracle Sav.

After Lincoln Rhyme had told him that there'd been trace of the stuff found on Gregorios's clothes—and none recovered in the man's house—Kelly had looked the substance up and, while it could be used as a legitimate cleanser, some people were stupid enough to drink it like medicine, causing kidney failure, vomiting, shedding of internal mucous membranes. It had even been given as enemas to children to cure autism and had seriously injured scores and killed several. (Kelly wished he'd been called in to run one of *those* cases.)

"Mr. Xavier, do we have permission to go through your locker?" she asked.

This was dicey. If the bottle were inside and could be linked to the murder scene, a defense counsel would leap on the search as unconstitutional because, in his current mental state, Xavier was not able to give consent.

On the other hand, the vicious nature of the killing meant that if he were the perp, he needed to be collared—and now.

"Is what it is, is what it is, is what it is . . ."

She sat on the unoccupied bed across from his. "Mr. Xavier?"

Kelly then froze. He said, "Never mind. Glove up and open it."

"But . . ." she protested. She'd be thinking probable cause. And, because she was in law school at night, Fourth Amendment.

"We got it. Plain sight."

He'd shined the light up into the springs of the cot and saw something tucked under the mattress. He pulled on blue latex gloves and reached in, removing the bloodstained wallet.

It was Alekos Gregorios's.

Wilson opened the locker. Underneath two mismatched shoes was a bottle. She lifted out the Adidas-Nike pair of joggers, and the partners looked down at a bloodstained knife, about eight inches long, and a bottle of Miracle Sav.

In bold red print was the legend that reported that, among eliminating other maladies, the potion had been "proven to cure all forms of mental illness and dementia."

43

L on Sellitto was on the speaker.

"The Apollos're the lead suspects."

He explained that after the hit-piece *Daily Herald* article about the "women haters" had come out and senior members had gone into hiding, the officers whom Sellitto had assigned to find the potential suspects were having trouble tracking them down. "They're posting plenty of threats, though. One guy in particular, nicknamed 'Chosen,' is calling for Whittaker's beheading."

A trace of his IP address, though, ended at a proxy in Europe.

He added, "And the psych department chimed in. They think it's somebody connected to the group because of the profile. The Locksmith steals underwear. That suggests he's sexualizing women. And the knife he takes: he wants to hurt them, subconsciously."

"Doesn't seem all that subconscious," Rhyme observed.

Sellitto added that the reporter who'd written the story and the editor who'd assigned and approved it had left Whittaker and were not returning calls. They were no longer in New York.

As for the WMG legal department file that Doug Hubert had prepared, not a single one of the 495 complaints and letters of threat pointed the spotlight toward a perp like the Locksmith.

Most of the employee complaints were about equal employment, diversity and discrimination. A few OSHA issues. The threatening letters from those who had been the target of articles raised the issue of defamation, and the majority were sent by attorneys. The Locksmith's assault on the company—if that's what the home invasions were—wouldn't arise out of any conflict he'd put his real name to via a lawyer's letter. The others' grievances came out of journalistic sins the paper had committed, but were minor, and the remedy was retraction.

"Waste of time," Rhyme had muttered. He had returned to his waiting state: skeptical of all crime-solving techniques that did not involve evidence. The witch-doctory of psychological profiling, for instance.

Sellitto continued, "On the forensic side, I'm not getting shit from Queens."

The NYPD lab had its set of the evidence from the Carrie Noelle scene, though nothing from the man's second visit to the Bechtel Building. The techs there were top notch but the Locksmith was one of thousands of cases they were running. Rhyme could dedicate himself fully to the investigation—even if illegally.

"So," Sellitto grumbled. "Do not get your ass busted. You're our only source for the nitty-gritty."

"By which I assume you mean incisive forensic analysis."

"I'm serious, Linc. There're people who want heads to roll."

"As quickly as clichés."

Sachs said, "We're being careful."

Sellitto scoffed, "You know what's inevitable?"

"Death and taxes is always a good answer, though, of course, that's a cliché too."

"If *we* collar the Locksmith, the question's going to come up how we did it. And since Queens isn't giving me squat, the whole world'll be looking right at you, Linc."

"Allow me one more hackneyed turn of phrase: we'll cross that bridge when."

"Well, let me just say, forewarned is forearmed."

"Touché, Lon."

They disconnected.

Sellitto was right. But what choice did they really have? This man had to be stopped before he put to use one of those knives he was so fond of.

Sachs took a call and jotted some notes. She edited an entry note on the whiteboard, replacing the number 22 with 26.

R. Pulaski, canvass of locksmiths/locksmith schools in tri-state area.

26 canvassed, no connection to anyone fitting profile of Locksmith.

Rhyme asked, "Mel? That graphite on the Jolly Rancher wrapper? You ever run it?"

The tech had not, other than to confirm it was professional grade, and he did so now.

Rhyme then was looking at some pictures of trace on the flat-screen monitor. The tiny slivers of deep yellow metal had taken his attention.

"What?" Sachs noted his gaze.

"That brass. We know it's been machined. Metals don't *shed*."

She snapped her fingers. "Key-making machine."

"He might work at a home improvement or hardware store. That's one lead but we don't have the manpower to survey them all. We'll keep it in mind if we find something to narrow down the geographic field. But another lead is that he might privately own one himself. Are they rare, Sachs? Are they expensive? Let's hope so. I want to know how many key-machine manufacturers there are and what their records of private sales are like."

She called Lon Sellitto back with this request, and, after a conversation, she disconnected. Rhyme knew that the detective would assign canvassers right away.

He turned back to the chart.

The Locksmith was intelligent, given to planning, careful, and he was aware of, and he studied, his pursuers.

Rhyme thought again of the Watchmaker. The Locksmith was truly his heir . . . But then he corrected the notion, which suggested that their present perp had somehow replaced the earlier. But that wasn't the case at all. Oh, yes, the Watchmaker might have met his fate in one of his enterprises gone wrong. Rhyme, however, couldn't believe that. He had a feeling that the man was very much alive . . . and very much involved in other plots.

He wondered again if one of which might have to do with the intelligence from the UK, relayed to Rhyme by the FBI. The gist was that unknown Person X had hired unknown Person Y to kill Person Z.

Person Z's identity was quite well known, according to the report. Lincoln Rhyme himself.

Sachs, reading a text, said, "Bad news about the key-cutting machine."

"You can buy them for a thousand dollars and they're sold at dozens of retail locations so he could pay with nice tidy untraceable cash," Rhyme guessed.

"More or less."

"Hell."

Sachs scrolled through her phone and apparently found a number. She placed a call. And hit the Speaker button. Rhyme heard it ringing.

"Hello?"

"Lyle?"

"Amelia," Spencer said.

"I'm here with Lincoln and Mel Cooper."

"Any breaks in the case?"

"Nothing much. None of the complaints Legal found panned out. The lead detective's focusing on the Apollos, but nothing solid. I'm calling to see if anybody's heard anything from Whittaker's son."

"I'm with Mr. Whittaker and his niece right now."

They heard him pose the question. And the answers from both Whittaker and Joanna and her fiancé, Martin Kemp, were negative.

"I'd like to take a look at his apartment. Does anybody there have a key?"

No one in the family did.

"The building have a super?" Sachs asked.

Joanna said, "Yes. Lives there."

Sachs told them, "I can get a warrant for a welfare check. Spencer, you free tomorrow morning?"

"What time's good?"

"Make it nine."

"See you then."

They disconnected.

She shook her head. "Hope nothing's happened to him. They had a fight and his father wanted to reconcile, then he goes missing."

"What did they fight about?" Rhyme asked absently.

"Seems he didn't like his father's muckraking and running a

media empire that was light on women on executive row and heavy on them in short skirts in front of the camera. Well, you saw the complaints." She nodded at the file folder the WMG legal department had provided.

But Whittaker Media's policies and practices didn't interest Rhyme much. He was gazing at the chart, gazing at the crime scene photos on the monitor, gazing at the evidence bags in the sterile portion of the lab, lined up in a way that for some reason suggested to Lincoln Rhyme cattle at a slaughterhouse.

Something had to be there.

Something . . .

His eyes then turned toward the photographs, once more, in particular the ones she had taken at the Bechtel Building crime scene.

"Mel," Rhyme called sharply. "I've got a job for you."

"What?"

"An autopsy."

Cooper paused and cleared his throat. "Well, Lincoln, I don't do postmortems." The tech was uneasy.

"You need to rise to the occasion," Rhyme said solemnly. "Just this once."

44

'm in my workshop.

And staring at my Tower of London keychain, a prized possession.

The Tower has always been special for me because of the Ceremony of the Keys:

In the Tower, every night at 9:53, the chief yeoman warder—a Beefeater—locks the outer and tower gates, then marches to the Bloody Tower. A sentry challenges him and he tells the sentry he's got the Queen's keys and is allowed to pass. The ceremony ends at exactly 10 p.m. In hundreds of years it's never been canceled.

I am lying on the firm futon, thinking of Taylor Soames.

And her pain.

Oh, not physical.

No, a subtler kind.

And much more enduring. You gut someone with a brass knife and the agony is fleeting.

What I did was much more satisfying.

After I dropped them off at her building Taylor would have trekked upstairs with her Roonie, euphoric at the wonderful turn of events.

So damn hard to meet decent men in this city, but she'd pulled it off!

Ben Nelson ticked all the right boxes. Divorced five years, so the domestic drama was largely a thing of the past. He had a daughter close in age to that of her own child. A gentleman. No beer gut. A pelt of natural hair—to which I'd added a little gray makeup, because I know she likes that in a man. Resources (the Brooks Brothers suit—and any woman who says she doesn't want a man with money? Liar!). Humor. And, on first blush, not a perv. I didn't examine boob or leg. Well, once—the former—but she was looking away and didn't catch me. We're all human.

And chivalrous. Walking them back home, protecting them from that stalker! And even carrying slim Roonie's backpack.

Ben was just the man for the job.

But soon that anticipatory joy would begin to evaporate.

I wouldn't call—and my burner is already battery-less and destined for landfill, so when she works up the courage to phone me, nothing. She'll try to recall the name of my employer. Good luck with that. Even I can't remember the name I made up.

Then she'll check with the Hawthorne school.

No record of any parent named Ben Nelson. Or daughter Meghan.

She'd begin—by tomorrow night, or so—to be feeling the searing effects of the betrayal: the sorrow that the relationship she'd hoped might come to be was now a bonfire.

And poor Taylor would be feeling utter terror too.

Because she would have been thinking if they'd met when Roonie was out of town, she might have asked him in for a drink. And one thing would lead to another . . .

There's sexual assault by force. There's also assault by misrepresentation.

And, my God, Ben had even met her daughter—the petite girl with the odd name and a daunting and elegant routine on the balance beam.

He'd even touched her shoulder, when he lifted off the book bag!

No . . .

That thought will bring tears.

The victory was as delicious as the thought of Annabelle Talese seeing the cookie plate beside her bed and Carrie Noelle waking up to the stare of a holy-shit Madame Alexander doll.

Delicious . . .

At the moment, though, all is good. Taylor's and Roonie's lives are proceeding on a course of hope.

And what are my ladies up to at the moment?

I know very well. Taylor has tucked petite Roonie into a bed covered with a lavender and white bedspread, just a touch threadbare. The bed rests against the blue wall on which are three racks that were meant to hold dog leads but are now festooned with colorful ribbons at the end of which dangle gymnastics medals.

The girl is wearing fluffy pajamas, in pink. They came with a detachable hood with a glistening satin unicorn horn and horse-like ears, as apparently unicorns and equines share DNA. Roonie's tablet is charging on the bedside table, which is painted pale green.

Her room is not as cluttered tonight as it has been. The girl *can* be a bit of a slob.

She's not ready for sleepy time yet, though, and she's doing some kind of weird pantomime—like dancing with your hands and arms only, to rock songs.

Taylor herself is having a glass of wine—a sauvignon blanc—and a late-night treat of hers: mint Oreos. She is in sweats.

How do I know this?

Because mother and daughter are telling me. Via their phones.

Roonie is posting thirty-second clips on a platform like TikTok, one right after the other.

And Taylor is doing a livestream on my very own ViewNow. She is talking about books—she's in a club and volunteers at a library—and fielding the comments that come streaming in, ignoring others.

Which, it's no surprise, is how I am able to execute my Visits, whether in someone's bedroom anonymously, or in person on the street like tonight.

Videos are one of the most efficient keys ever invented.

Keys to opening up lives.

With Taylor and Roonie, I learned in the brief span of a few days all the facts I'd ever want about the mother and daughter. I caught some of the girl's posts about gymnastics and then Taylor made a few appearances. I did some light internet diving and found names and interests and career details. Segueing to other social media told me all about her. Public divorce records too. Pictures of her on social media with five different men in the past year explained she was likely single.

Some bordered on risqué, which told me even more.

Roonie was an avid poster on sites like YouTube and ViewNow. Gymnastics routines, stretching exercises, recipes, makeup tutorials, outfits of the day. I learned so much about mascara and lasagna and how far your money will go at Claire's, Justice and Forever 21 that I could be her father.

I found out too about the play, in which my fictional Meghan would appear (though sadly not in the lead).

And—from videos posted by the school and the PTO—I learned

what the school visitors' passes look like, not high definition, but sufficient to duplicate into a reasonable facsimile. I discovered the controversy within the parent-teacher organization.

Sitting back and watching the videos for hour after hour after hour, I can see the types of locks and deadbolts and alarms people have. I can see who has dogs and door bars, I can see who keeps a shotgun nearby (rare in New York City but occasionally). I know where the knives are, and the toolboxes. I can see who has carpet—for silent stalking—and I can hear who lives on busy streets to cover up my noise (remembering the 2019 disaster, as always). I know the layout of every apartment before I approach. I know who has young children, who might need a bit of nursing or potty and might destroy my perfectly good evening.

I can even see who delivers the pizza (handbills stuck to the fridge with silly little magnets), who their doctors are, who has diabetes (insulin needle reminders), and who has a little too much love of the bottle.

I knew Carrie Noelle had the lunch date because she wrote it in red marker on a wall calendar.

People share so very much . . .

In college, I remember, I became fascinated with Darwin's theory of natural selection.

People think it's about ape-like creatures becoming humans. Ah, but the broader view about survival of the species is what so gripped me.

The theory is quite simple. It has four components:

One, individual creatures within a population differ.

Two, those differences are passed on from parents to their offspring.

Three, some of those individuals are more successful in surviving than others.

Four, those successful ones have survived because of traits that they have inherited and that they will in turn pass on to their subsequent generations. The unsuccessful die off.

In the wilderness, deer that are the color of the surrounding woods will tend to survive, while albino deer, which stand out to predators, will not.

This is exactly my worldview. People who don't post anything online are invisible to threats like me. Those who do? Well, think of poor Annabelle Talese, the influencer, online day and night. And Carrie Noelle running her mini-QVC toy-shopping show out of her home and Taylor Soames and Roonie, who post in hopes of meeting mates or friends or because of ego or boredom or loneliness or . . . who knows why?

The difference is that by posting, they *choose* to be the albino deer.

So that if the wolf, the coyote, the human hunter, were to take them as trophies, well, their deaths would really be of their own making.

This is simple logic to me.

45

The cause of death was asphyxia," Mel Cooper reported to Rhyme.

Cooper, in the sterile portion of the parlor, was staring down at what was left of the corpse. Which was not of the human variety, but rather a *Musca domestica*, the common housefly discovered by Sachs in one of the Locksmith's footsteps in the Bechtel Building.

The tech explained that it had perished because its muscles had frozen up in a state of tetany, which is essentially a nonstop contraction. It could neither fly nor breathe. The immediate cause for this was the blocking of acetylcholinesterase, an enzyme that allows the muscles to relax. The reason for the blockage of the multisyllabic enzyme was a particular organophosphate, a fancy name for insecticide.

Cooper continued, "The substances in the toxin are parathion, malathion, diazinon, terbufos."

Amelia Sachs laughed. "Sounds like the names of the bad guys in a superhero movie."

Rhyme had never seen a superhero movie but on the basis of that observation alone he thought he might give one a try, though he guessed his respect for logic and science and rational thought might dampen the careless treatment of the natural world that the filmmakers would rely on.

The insect's demise had given them a lead, possibly, if not an earthshattering breakthrough. A search revealed that only one product contained the "bad guys" in the same proportions as those found in the dead fly. It was Fume-Assure, and it was used by large-scale fumigation companies, of which a half-dozen operated in Manhattan. One helpful executive, intrigued at being part of a police investigation, explained that that particular insecticide was used almost exclusively for fumigating old, unoccupied buildings, which would be renovated and put up for sale.

"You can't tent in Manhattan but you seal the windows and doors. Pump this stuff in. Let it sit for a week then vent."

"Apartment buildings? Offices?"

"Anything. High-rise, low-rise."

In Rhyme's mind, the chain went: The fly was found within the Locksmith's footprint at the Bechtel Building. No one would have fumigated a building that was about to be torn down, so it was most likely that he had picked it up someplace else. Could that location be helpful? No way of knowing. But Rhyme decided to make the assumption that it was. Why not? The case wasn't overflowing with leads. So, they would look for an old building that was unoccupied and up for sale. He wouldn't live there, unless he was a squatter, which didn't seem likely, but would have another connection with it. Maybe staking out the next victim.

Or perhaps, it now occurred to Rhyme, it was a building somehow related to his profession.

He commanded his phone: "Text Pulaski." The screen dutifully appeared and the blink of the cursor encouraged him to continue:

> In addition to looking for existing locksmiths with
> connections to LS, look for those that have closed or gone
> out of business, especially those in old, unoccupied
> buildings, possibly ones for sale.

A moment later, the young officer responded.

> Will do.

They closed up shop for the night and a half hour later Rhyme was in bed, Sachs beside him, already asleep. As he closed his eyes and let his head ease against his wife's, smelling a floral shampoo, he reflected that deductions arising from the fly's demise were somewhat unlikely, but that didn't mean they weren't worth considering. After all, "long shot" was a phrase that could be applied to nearly all aspects of policing, especially that odd and esoteric art form known as forensic science.

"Friends: Poor New York. The Locksmith is still at large and I have discovered why. I got access to a classified report from the highest sources. The Locksmith is working with the authorities. He breaks into your apartments and houses and plants listening devices, and their signals go directly to the CIA and FBI and other top-secret agencies deep in the bowels of nondescript office buildings in Washington. If he's crazy, he's crazy like a fox. But don't think you're safe. He murdered two people when they discovered him planting the bugs.

"Demand that the authorities answer for this. And buy surveillance detectors!

"Say your prayers and stay prepared!

"My name is Verum, Latin for 'true.' That is what my message is. What you do with it is up to you."

PART THREE

PIN TUMBLER KEY

[MAY 28, 6 A.M.]

46

I n my workshop, I awake early, chilled.

In two senses: From the draft in the old bakery supply building.

And from a thought.

Specifically the image of red-haired Detective Amelia as she went about her meticulous business at the crime scene outside Carrie Noelle's apartment.

She seemed sharp, giving no-nonsense orders and carefully assessing the bags of evidence, which I am pretty sure, but not positive, contain nothing that can lead them to me.

But I'm not taking any chances. After all, she and her husband, this Lincoln Rhyme, placed me at Carrie's as if by magic.

It wasn't magic, however. It was cold science that they practiced. While there is a mysticism about locks and keys, which derives from what or who the lock is guarding, the workings of the devices run by the laws of nature.

I need to take precautions.

I roll from the bed. The simple futon is hard, good for a back often aching from spending hours hunched over a workbench or computer—in a chair that I *will* replace with the ergonomic one. I really will. Someday.

I hit the bathroom, my bare feet stinging on the chill black-and-white hexagonal tiles. Then I dress and make some decaf coffee and eat half a bagel with cream cheese, considering the problem I face.

If this problem were a lock to which I had no key I would first consider: Do I need to open it? Can I do without what's in the apartment or steamer trunk or car that the lock is guarding? If yes, then I move on.

But if what's being protected is significant and, especially, life-threatening, then I decide that I need to take on the task of picking.

In this case, the lock—well, the problem—is the danger of the police finding my identity.

Yes, there is a place containing damning evidence, and redheaded Amelia and the wheelchair-bound Lincoln Rhyme could in fact find it.

How could I have been so careless?

What's the solution going to be?

The three types of lock picking: the snap gun, a snake rake or a bump key.

In this instance, I don't have time for the subtle approach.

What I'm about to do would correspond to using a bump key.

Brute force.

That's my only option, no matter the risk—to me or to whoever might die in the process.

A half hour later, I am in an area of downtown Manhattan where a number of buildings are being razed for yet more commercial/residential developments.

My destination, ahead of me, is the ancient Sandleman Building, on the top floor of which is Dev Swensen's long-closed shop. After my father opened my eyes to the esoteric world of lock picking, I eventually learned of Swensen, a lanky, wild-haired Scandinavian. He was renowned for his picking skills but he existed far outside the mainstream of the community. The blond former pro snowboarder was eccentric and politically active—extremely libertarian. He believed in open access to everything. There should be no secrets, governmental or otherwise. And so over the years he learned how to pick virtually any lock in existence. He was never caught but it was suspected that he picked the locks of hundreds of military installations, banks, corporate headquarters, media outlets and politicians' and executives' homes. He never entered a single facility. He simply turned what was closed into what was open, and then he left.

I studied for several years with Swensen, coming regularly to his shop in the Sandleman Building. We became friends.

Swensen did more than locksmithing, however. He was also a renowned computer hacker. Using an alias, he had spent years breaking into government databases and private accounts and published whatever he found.

No secrets . . .

Then three years ago he learned he was about to be arrested for some hacks. He took his go-bag and fled to Norway, leaving behind everything (the brass knife was a farewell present to me). The authorities seized his shop but they had no interest in the locksmithing tools and equipment, only the computers and storage devices. After they left, they simply sealed the place up, leaving all items non-digital untouched, apparently waiting for his family or business associates to remove everything. But there was no family and Swensen's shop was forgotten.

Not by me, though.

I kept returning, hiking up to the twelfth floor of the deserted building. Originally I was going to take Swensen's books on lock picking—a wonderful library—and help myself to tools and hard-ware. I grew interested, though, in what was against the back wall: a collection of safes and safe doors. Dial locks were something I had little experience in, so I returned frequently to the shop to practice safecracking, using Swensen's notebooks to learn the art.

But I was careless. I brought food and drink. As I practiced on the safes, I never wore gloves. I left receipts and possibly even mail!

Now, on this overcast, damp morning, in a workman's yellow jacket, hard hat, clear gloves and smooth-soled shoes—no telltale treads—I walk to the chain-link gate barring entry to the back of the building, carrying the two-gallon can of gasoline. The padlock is one of those with a combination, so it takes time—twenty or so seconds—to open it. Another look around. No people. No cameras.

Then into the loading dock of the building, where I shut off the electricity at the main panel and the water supply, to disable the alarm and the sprinklers—if there are any. Then I pour the fragrant gasoline onto a pile of wood scrap at the foot of the stairway. I use a candle lighter to ignite the liquid and instantly a rage of flames sweeps through the scrap pile and starts upward. Forty minutes from now every micron of trace I've left will be gone forever.

47

Kitt Whittaker lived in a high-rise about five blocks from his father's complex on the Upper East Side.

Sachs's Torino pulled up at the same time as Sellitto's NYPD unmarked. Lyle Spencer, the autoless former racer, was on foot.

The officers got out and Sachs looked up at the building, a slab of shiny glass and metal.

Sellitto brushed at his gray overcoat as if trying to smooth the wrinkles. His expression was sour. "I got a call from downtown. You heard about this asshole? He goes by Verum."

Spencer said, "He posts some kind of conspiracy crap."

"Never heard of him," Sachs said.

Sellitto continued, "He says we're working with the Locksmith. Some deep movement. Called the Hidden."

"Us, the police? Seriously?"

"Oh, yeah. He's planting bugs in the apartments and he's killed a couple of people who've found him."

"Listening devices?" Sachs sounded incredulous.

"All bullshit," Spencer said.

"Yeah, sure. But tell that to the seven thousand five hundred and fifty people who've called OnePP and their local precincts to complain. The mayor, commissioner . . . they're livid. That number by the way came directly from Dep Com Sally Willis."

"Livid enough to put Lincoln back on duty?"

"That's part of it too. He's working for the Hidden. I told him earlier."

"What?"

"He got Buryak off because he's working for the governor and the CIA or some shit like that. Nobody believes it but it's drawing attention to Linc. So, yeah, in answer to your question, he's still out."

Sachs said, "Next thing, we'll see the Locksmith was at Ford's Theatre the night Lincoln was shot."

Sellitto grumbled. "Big problem is witnesses're going to freeze up if they think we're working with the Locksmith."

Spencer muttered, "Jesus."

They met the super of Kitt's building outside and Sellitto displayed the warrant, which had been issued on the grounds both of a welfare check and that Kitt might be a material witness. The slim man, who spoke in an eastern European accent, glanced at the papers, without reading. He led them to the fifteenth floor and down a subdued copper and oak corridor to 1523.

She nodded to Spencer who placed a call to Kitt's landline.

They could hear it ring inside. After four tones, it went silent.

"Voice mail."

"We're going in," Sachs said.

The super stepped forward, but she shook her head and took the key from him and motioned him back. Standing to the side, she unlocked the door and pushed it open an inch. She handed the key back to the uneasy super and he retreated.

Sachs glanced at Sellitto, who nodded. Her hand was near her Glock. Sellitto was on the left side of the door. Spencer, a civilian, stood ten feet back, arms crossed. She wondered how many dynamic entries he'd done as a cop in Albany. His eyes, evaluating them and scanning the hallway ahead of and behind them, told her: quite a few.

Just before she pushed the door open she drew her weapon. Maybe nerves, maybe a sixth sense. Sellitto, glancing her way, paused a beat and then drew his as well.

Sachs shoved open the door. "Police! Serving a warrant! Show yourself!" They were pushing inside, weapons up, swinging the pistols back and forth, always dipping or raising the muzzles when they crossed before one another. This was as automatic as blinking.

The living space featured a large, rectangular living room/dining room, kitchen to the right. Out the window was a panoramic view of Brooklyn and looking south she could see where her own town house was, in general location, not the ancient structure itself.

His father's living room was only marginally larger.

"Kitchen clear," Sellitto called.

Though obvious, Sachs said, "Living room clear."

The choreography of settled procedure.

Then on to the bedrooms, both of which were unoccupied. One, the bed unmade and cluttered, would be Kitt's, while the other was prepared for guests but had not been used for some time.

"Bathroom clear," Sellitto called.

"Second bathroom, clear."

There remained one more door, on the far side of the living area. Maybe another bedroom. They regarded each other and walked to it, stood once again on either side—a somewhat futile precaution because bullets penetrate Sheetrock like this about as fast as a needle pokes through silk. She glanced and he nodded.

Door open, weapons up.

An office. Empty as well. It was small; no "clears!" were required.

"I'll check in here." She holstered her gun and pulled on latex gloves.

Donning gloves himself, Sellitto said that he'd go through the kitchen.

The office contained a desk and several file cabinets. She went through drawers and found office supplies, real estate listings, a catalog of drones, various computer hardware parts. Also reams of business documents, many of them government contracts, requests for proposals. Evidence of the pipe dreams of making it as a tycoon in an industry so very different from tainted journalism, she guessed.

She remembered Kitt's cousin and father saying he had never really found a career that suited.

He'd given up on all of these, she guessed, and was now on to some other hope.

She opened all the cabinet drawers. Filled with tax and accounting and investment records.

She started to close one and noted the tops of the files were slightly higher than the lip of the cabinet; they brushed against it. When she lifted out several folders, and shone her pocket flashlight down into the drawer, she saw why.

A false bottom.

Maybe where he hid drugs.

She lifted out all the files and with her knife pried up the white plastic sheet.

"Lon. Take a look at this."

48

The lock was bigger than he'd expected.

Ron Pulaski, still breathing hard after the climb to this, the top floor of the building, was now trying to jimmy the hunk of a padlock with a twenty-four-inch crowbar.

It didn't budge.

He stepped back. And surveyed the wall. This was the only office on this side of the hallway and there was only one door. Across the hall were two other offices, but they were completely empty and showed no signs of recent habitation. The prints leading from the stairs to this shop door, though, indicated that somebody had been here recently—maybe the past week.

But how to get in?

He set to work once more.

He had to.

Lincoln Rhyme believed it was important—because of a dead fly. Pulaski wasn't exactly sure how that had worked, but the man had decided that certain pesticides in the fly's corpse suggested this building might have a connection to the Locksmith.

And it seemed pretty likely that this was the case because the door he was trying to break into had this sign painted on its wooden façade:

DEV SWENSEN'S LOCK SERVICES

INSTALLATION

REPAIR

LOCK-OUT SERVICES—RESIDENTIAL, COMMERCIAL AND VEHICLE

CLASSES AND INSTRUCTION

Pulaski tried once more, and this time one of the hinge screws seemed to move a fraction of an inch. A few minutes later one flange on the middle hinge was slightly loose. One more. The bar slipped out and whacked him in the thumb. Pain exploded.

He inhaled deeply against the sting.

He paused.

The young officer smelled a fire nearby. He turned his eyes to the stairwell, from which wisps of smoke were now curling.

Amelia Sachs pulled the hood of the crime scene overalls back, tossed her hair. For her, this unique, piquant smell of the plastic garment would forever be associated with the curious combination of challenge and tragedy. She dialed Rhyme's number and when he answered said, "Averell Whittaker's son Kitt—he's the Locksmith."

"Tell me."

She explained what they had found hidden in the filing cabinet, all the drawers of which had false bottom panels. There were books on lock picking, sets of lock-picking tools. Panties matching the description of those stolen from Carrie Noelle's and Annabelle

Talese's apartments. Also two copies of the February 17 edition of the *Daily Herald*, missing page 3.

In the closet was a pair of brandless running shoes whose tread seemed to match the pattern at the earlier scenes.

"And it looks like there's red brick dust in the treads, Rhyme. Flecks of dried blood too."

"He learned his lesson and went to plain soles, so he doesn't pick up as much trace."

"In a basket in the kitchen, Lon found a packet of green-apple Jolly Ranchers. Looks like there's graphite on it."

Rhyme said, "You mentioned the underwear he stole. What about the knives?"

"They're not here."

She was holding a small carton containing plastic and paper bags of what she'd collected. Chain-of-custody cards dangled from some items, like *From . . . To* tags on Christmas presents. She added, "But there's not much else, no computer, no phone. He's got to have more tools too. A workshop someplace else."

"Any leads to where?"

"No."

"Get the evidence in. Send out his ID on the wire. But I wouldn't announce it publicly. That'll spook him."

"Agreed," she said.

Sachs had declared the apartment a crime scene, and that would now be information accessible to everyone at OnePP. Willis would hear and send Beaufort and Rodriguez to make sure that any evidence from the scene would be logged in to the Queens lab. She'd have to move fast.

A crowd was gathering, a couple of dozen people. Reporters too. Always the press, calling questions. She ignored them.

Lon Sellitto joined her. "Still nothing on Kitt's Audi in the vehicle recognition system."

Sachs removed the booties and they went into an evidence bag for later examination. Occasionally key evidence was picked up from places the crime scene investigators had trod. Then the gloves came off and she blew on her hands to dry the sweat.

Sachs walked to the front of the CSU bus and spoke to the tech who was behind the wheel. She was a tall woman with mahogany-colored skin and an elaborate tattoo of an iguana on her forearm, now concealed under her jacket.

"Izzy, need you to do something for me."

"And that tone tells me there's something shady going on." She was amused.

"Shady might be an overstatement. Can we go with hazy?"

"I can live with hazy. What d'you have in mind, Amelia?"

"There are going to be people at OnePP who want that evidence to get to the lab quick as a lick."

"What my grams used to say."

Sachs was frowning. "I may've heard there're some traffic jams—accidents, maybe. Everything's slowed up. That tunnel—it's always dicey. And the Fifty-Ninth Street Bridge? Forget it."

Izzy said, "So what you're saying is it might be better for me to take a different way?"

"Only a thought."

The tech said, frowning, "Maybe the Triborough. I could go north in Manhattan, cross the bridge, then south to Queens. Maybe take Central Park West."

"That's an idea. And you know Mel Cooper's visiting Lincoln Rhyme at the moment. You could say hi."

"Mel is a dear. And that man can *dance!*"

"You might even show Mel what you've got." She nodded at the cartons. "You know, he's working the case. Give him a preview."

Cooper's name, not Rhyme's, would go on the chain-of-custody card. One could assume that the technician had examined the evidence in the Queens lab, not Rhyme's parlor.

Sachs grew serious. "You know there are people who've threatened to reprimand anybody who helps Lincoln on a case."

"Rodriguez." She scowled. "Always thought he was a stand-up man. But now he comes on with 'nobody's supposed to work with Lincoln.' Lord, you know, Lincoln Rhyme is the *whole* reason I went into crime scene work." The woman's broad face blossomed with a coy smile. "I'll be on my way now. Ah, all that traffic. The Queensboro, the tunnel."

"That tunnel can be a bitch."

"Sure can be, Amelia." The woman turned and whistled—it was really quite piercing. The other CSU tech, an older Anglo, turned and jogged to the bus and jumped into shotgun. Sachs slammed the rear doors shut and thumped the side with her palm.

The vehicle's tires actually spun and squealed and off-gassed pale smoke. With blue lights flashing, it skidded onto the street, under Izzy's expert touch.

Ignoring reporters' calls about what had happened, she walked to Lyle Spencer, who was standing beside the Torino.

Sachs said, "You shocked at the news? About Kitt?"

Spencer exhaled air through puffed-out cheeks. "Putting it mildly. You heard, a lot of friction in the family, the estrangement. But never in a million years . . ."

"If you were going to have a workshop/safe house, how would you handle it?"

Spencer said, "Something small, off the books. I'd pay cash. No application process or credit check. With Kitt's resources, trust fund, he could pay whatever the landlord wanted."

"I didn't see anything inside that gave me any clues. Let's hope Lincoln'll find something in the evidence to narrow it down."

A cheerful voice called: "Detective. We have to stop meeting like this."

She turned to see the man she'd labeled a ferret.

The reporter. Sheldon Gibbons. A name as memorable as his face.

How the hell had he found her?

He was armed with his digital recorder once more. While other reporters would jab their cameras and recorders forward like fencers and pepper their subjects with shouted questions, Gibbons was calm, almost eerily calm, though he still spoke quickly. "Kitt Whittaker lives in that building. First, you were talking to his father and Joanna—did you mention she was there, at the tower the other day? I don't remember?"

There was no response.

"Well, now you're here, but in crime-scene regalia. Is he all right? Has he been assaulted?"

"You do remember, I don't make comments for the press?"

"Has he been injured—maybe by the father of the Hunter Mill student who was killed? That fake satanic cult story. You know about it?" It would be utterly exhausting to listen to this man for any length of time.

"No comment. There'll be a press conference later, I'm sure."

"I'm sure of that too. But I happen to be here *now*. Why wasn't there a guard on Kitt, in light of the Locksmith's threats? Are you guarding Joanna too? And Averell himself?"

"Go away," Spencer grumbled ominously as he stared at Gibbons.

The reporter held up a hand and said in a smooth voice, "First

Amendment. I have a right to be here. Who're you? I saw you with Detective Sachs earlier. Are you NYPD? Do you work for Whittaker Media?"

Spencer said nothing.

"Have you heard what Verum, the vlogger, is saying—that the NYPD has been infiltrated and is purposely not investigating the Locksmith case vigorously? I know *you're* involved in that case, Detective."

Gibbons looked around with narrowed eyes. "Hm. No ambulance or medical examiner. I guess Kitt isn't hurt. Or dead. Has he gone missing, by any chance?"

The reporter suddenly ceased to exist to Sachs. She noted that Lon Sellitto had taken a call and was staring at the ground, his usually expressionless face a mask of concern.

He disconnected and sighed.

"Lon?"

The rumpled detective turned to her. "Amelia . . . I have to tell you. It's Ron."

49

Sachs skidded her Grand Torino off Hudson Street and aimed toward the Sandleman Building, rising about ten or twelve stories into the gray sky. It was narrow and grimy. A large banner read *For Sale. Commercial.*

Sachs could see no flames but smoke flowed from floors about a third of the way up. Two helicopters hovered nearby.

Spencer gripped the dashboard as the muscle car skidded to a stop two blocks away on a deserted street. She wanted to leave the way clear for more emergency vehicles if they were needed.

Sachs and Spencer trotted forward, moving over and around the snaky hoses. Patrol was keeping back spectators and most of the uniforms knew Sachs and, as Spencer was with her and he looked like a gold shield in his undertaker suit, let them both through to the command post.

A panoply of emergency vehicles, fire trucks mostly, sat like discarded toys. Dozens of firefighters were running hoses. The command post was an FDNY van that read *Battalion Chief* on the side.

Spencer said, "He knows we're onto him and he destroyed his workshop?"

Sachs said, "Probably not. Lincoln found a lead to an old locksmith company. Must have some connection to him, though, since I'll bet he's behind the fire and wants to erase the evidence he was there."

She looked at a broken-out window on the top floor. Pulaski's head was visible, and white smoke flowed past him. Not terrible yet. From here, she could see flames in the windows of the seventh and eighth floors. They were thick, tumbling orange and black masses.

She knew the battalion chief, Earl Prescott. Nodded to her side. "Lyle Spencer, he's with me."

A nod to Spencer.

"The situation?"

"It's bad. I've been in touch with your officer. He's on the top floor, but he can't get on the roof—it's sealed—and he can't go down. All the stairs are burning and it's too hot. I can't get my people up there either. We're pumping fast but the place is a hundred years old. A tinderbox. The building has sprinklers, but looks like the perp shut the water off and the control's buried under tons of burning debris. No doubt about the arson. We found the remains of a gas can in the loading dock.

"Wish the news was better." He gestured to the helicopters. "No LZ on the roof. And they can't lower a rescue team because of the fire. Too much heat turbulence. One crew said they'd try. I vetoed it. I had to. Bird comes down hard here, you can imagine."

Sachs noted that there were two hook and ladders. The chief followed her gaze and said, "Their reach is only a hundred feet into the air and change. And look." He pointed to a one-story building, an abandoned storefront, that was under Pulaski's window. This meant the ladder truck couldn't get directly beneath him. Because of that angle, the basket would only get fifty feet in the air, and even then it would not be directly under the window.

"We're pumping all we can into the higher floors. Maybe it'll knock down the fire. But even with his head out the window, the smoke's going to get him soon."

She made a call on her phone.

A coughing voice answered. "Amelia, I was almost into the office. The locksmithing office." More coughs. "I couldn't get in. Was it arson?"

"Had to be. Found a gas can."

Pulaski: "Means there's some evidence inside."

"Don't worry about it. We just want you down. Are there any other windows you can get to? They can't get the basket close."

"This is . . . the only one." The voice was a rasp.

"Okay. Save your breath. We're working on it."

Prescott said, "There's a mountain rescue team with the state police. They're in a chopper on the way. Should be here in a half hour, probably less."

Spencer was studying the building. "He doesn't have that kind of time." He turned to the chief. "You have a line gun?"

The chief looked him over, then glanced to Sachs, who nodded.

"We do, sure."

The yellow plastic device looked like a child's toy gun with an eight-inch orange projectile, like a light bulb, on the end. To the tail of this was tied a thin yellow line that fed from a spool. You put a .22 cartridge in the gun and when it was fired, the projectile carried the line to the person needing rescue. The twine was too thin for that purpose, but rescue workers then tied their end to a more solid rope, which could be pulled up by the person in distress.

"He can haul up a Sterling self-rescue," Spencer said.

Sachs was aware of the device. It was an emergency rappelling unit. It was used as a last resort for firefighters trapped in high floors when—just like now—the stairs were blocked. You donned a harness and hooked one end of the device's rope to a pipe or beam. Then climbed out the window and using a hand brake lowered yourself to the ground.

He asked Sachs, "Has he ever used one?"

"I have no idea." She pulled out her phone again and placed the call. "Ron? Have you ever used a . . ." She looked at Spencer, who said, "Sterling self-rescue."

She repeated it.

"No."

Spencer said, "Okay. Hang tight. We'll work something out."

She told him this and disconnected.

The fire was worse now. The smoke thicker. Her heart was pounding hard. She'd known Pulaski for years. She'd mentored him. She thought of breaking the news of his death to his wife and children, to his twin brother, also a cop.

No, she'd think of—

Spencer said to the chief, "Fire the line gun and have him haul up a climbing line."

"Climbing line?"

"At least three-quarter inch. You have that?"

"We do, but he can't shimmy down it."

"He's not going to. I'll climb up, rig him with the Sterling."

"How do you mean?"

Spencer was impatient. He repeated what he'd said then added, "We've got to *move*."

"Nobody can climb a rope a hundred feet in the air."

"I can."

"Well, sir, you're civilian, aren't you?"

Sachs said, "He's deputized."

Though there was no procedure for conferring that status in the NYPD handbook, the fire department chief either didn't know this or decided if there was any time to circumvent procedure it was now.

She continued, "Get him what he needs."

"Give me oxygen, a mask and two Sterlings. And gloves with wrist straps, and boots. Size thirteen if you have them."

The radio clattered. "Chief, water's not doing shit. It's flowing down the stairs on both sides; the fire's in the core. We can't reach it."

"Roger." Then to Spencer, "Okay, we'll get what you need." He ordered two of his men to do so.

Spencer said, "Can you call him?"

Sachs did and handed over the phone, on speaker.

"Yes?" Coughing, hard breathing.

"Officer, this is Lyle Spencer. We're going to fire a tie line to you, then you're going to drag a climbing rope up. What can you secure it to?"

"There's a . . ." Fierce coughing. "A radiator under the window."

"Good. I'll get back to you." He handed the phone to Sachs.

A flash of white on the street as a large van turned the corner. It was Lincoln Rhyme's Sprinter—his disabled-accessible vehicle. It parked and a side door opened and an elevator lowered Rhyme and his chair to the sidewalk. He rolled away from the van, which curled its accessory up. Thom drove off to find a parking space out of the way of the official vehicles.

Rhyme approached. The chief nodded.

He said to Sachs, "When I heard, I had to come. How is he?"

Sachs briefed him, and together the somber couple watched Spencer get ready for the climb.

The security man said, "Call Ron. Speaker."

She did.

"It's Lyle, Officer. Stand back from the window. Grab the yellow projectile that's coming up. Then pull up the climbing line."

Spencer pulled his suit jacket and tie off and dumped them on the ground, kicked his shoes off and pulled on the boots, then gloves. As he was fitted with an oxygen tank, he nodded to a firewoman who held the line gun in a ladder basket about forty feet in the air. The first shot missed by a yard or so. She compensated and the second zipped through the empty window.

Immediately the thin yellow line began snaking through the window, taking with it the much thicker climbing rope.

Spencer borrowed a knife and cut a length of rope from another coil. About ten feet. He tied this around his chest, letting the tail dangle. He called toward Sachs's phone, still open. "How you doing, Officer?"

"Hanging in there."

The coughing was fiercer.

"What I need you to do is tie the thicker rope to the radiator."

She heard Pulaski say, "Look, mister, you're not going to try to—"

"Quit talking, son. Save that air. See you in a minute. Oh, and by the way, when you tie the rope to the radiator, keep in mind: really fucking tight."

50

Lyle Spencer ran up the ladder to the roof of the one-story building.

There, holding the climbing line, he looked up.

The rope rose straight to the twelve-inch ledge outside Pulaski's window. He shook it, like a battle rope, and the sine curve headed upward, dissipating about forty feet up.

Get to it, sailor.

Spencer leapt into the air, two feet or so, and gripped the rope. He did a pull-up, then lifted his legs and gripped the rope between the top of his left foot and bottom of his right—the classic S-hook climbing technique.

He then straightened his legs and rose a yard or so up the rope.

Lift . . . grip . . . straighten.

Only one hundred feet to go.

Well, one hundred and change.

Breathe. Exhale.

Now, only ninety.

And change.

Lift . . . grip . . . straighten.

Already his arms were feeling sore but no muscle was screaming.

"Evacuate, evacuate, evacuate," the chief called over a loud-speaker.

At this the trucks blared their intersection horns three times, which was the universal signal to get the hell out. Always done, in addition to the transmission, in case of a radio malfunction or a particularly loud conflagration.

Well, guess that meant his opinion was that the building was about to come down.

Nothing to do about it now, except climb.

Lift . . . grip . . . straighten.

Eighty feet wasn't so far. Less than a third of the length of a football field.

Seventy feet.

Sixty feet.

Have to say, Trudes, it *is* pretty damn far.

Fifty.

Jesus, Lord, the hurt.

Lift . . . grip . . . straighten.

"I don't know, Dad." The girl's voice is uneasy.

"Come on, hons, you can do it," Spencer says to her.

They're fifty feet off the ground, he and twelve-year-old Trudie, blond and slim and ponytailed. They are rising at about the same pace upward.

"I don't know," she gasps.

"One step, one grip at a time," he encourages.

"I got it," the girl says and lunges for another rock above her head.

And she falls, gasping and calling out.

The spotters, who have her well under control, slow her descent and she does a rather stately abseil to the floor, which is covered in green padding.

"You good?" he calls, looking down.

"I'm good."

Up ten more feet and Spencer rings the sixty-foot bell and descends. The soft surface always struck him as pointless since if you hit anything except marshmallow at more than thirty miles an hour, you can say goodbye to a lot of portions of your body.

"Want to head home?" he asks his daughter.

"No, kinda want to try it again."

That's my girl, he thinks, but doesn't dare say. Instead, he nods to the wall. "Beauty before brains."

Lift . . . grip . . . straighten.

Spencer looked up at the twelfth-floor ledge.

How far?

Thirty-five feet.

Lift . . . grip . . . straighten.

Twenty-five.

His record in the SEALs was one hundred and fifty feet. But, okay, that was a few years ago.

Gasping. How much more could his arm muscles—and his back—take?

Fifteen.

He looked up.

Now, ten feet.

Lift . . . grip . . . straighten.

Now six, five, three.

Finally he was at the ledge.

"Hey," he shouted.

Jesus, was the officer passed out? That would be a high-magnitude complication.

"*Hey!*"

Ron Pulaski's face appeared in the window. Eyes streaming, he was coughing. His face was a mask of resignation, fear and bewilderment.

Gasping, breathing hard. "Listen. I'm going to throw this rope to you. I need you to catch it. So dust off those outfield skills. All right?"

"Sure."

Spencer took the tail of the rope tied around his chest. His feet were twisted around the climbing rope into a good S-shaped pinch and his left hand gripped it hard.

"I'm going to need you to pull me over the sill. Pull like a son of a bitch. Get on your back under the window, bend your legs and then straighten them. I'll help with the main rope."

"Maybe I should tie it around me."

Spencer nearly laughed. "You don't want to do that, son. Here it comes."

"I'm ready."

Spencer stared at his hand, inches in front of him and thought, Come on, Mr. Right, do your stuff! Which was a softball field joke between Trudie and himself.

Releasing his grip with his right, he took the chest rope and tossed as hard as he could into the window.

"Got it!"

"How's that, Trudes?"

"Knew you could do it, Dad."

"Pull!"

"Watch out for the broken glass on the window frame," Ron called.

Least of my worries.

The kid might have been skinny but he was strong. Soon Spencer could grip the windowsill with his gloved hands.

"Again."

Summiting was the tensest moment of a climb.

Spencer tugged himself upward as Ron pulled fiercely.

Then he was tumbling on top of the officer.

"We've only got minutes. We need to move."

He turned on the oxygen and slapped the mask on Pulaski's face. The officer inhaled deeply and his color returned. After thirty seconds, Pulaski handed it back and Spencer too inhaled the sweet nothing.

He mounted the gray and red Sterling FCX around Pulaski's waist, then showed him how the lever worked to release tension on the rope and lower himself slowly.

"You cool with it?" The smoke was getting worse even in the time Spencer had been here. Sparks and heat flowed from the stairwell.

He nodded.

Spencer put on the mask and inhaled deeply, blinked away the tears from the smoke. He saw a crowbar on the floor and he used it to crush the rest of the broken glass on the bottom of the frame. He then clamped the hook of the FCX to the radiator and helped Pulaski into the window, and, gripping the man's belt tightly, eased him around so that the front of his body was facing the building. "I've got you. Okay . . ." He saw that the device was properly rigged. And let go of the belt. "You're free. Easy with the lever. Down you go."

"Hey, look, Lyle . . . I don't know what to say. I—"

"Later. Now get the hell out of here."

51

park the glistening black Audi A6 at the curb and climb out, cautious. Looking around.

Police.

Fire.

Responding to what I'm responsible for.

The conflagration within the Sandleman Building.

It's not burning as fast as I'd hoped but it's fast enough. Flames are crawling up the core and I'm sure no one will get to Dev Swensen's shop in time to save anything incriminating against me.

But I'm not here because of the building.

I have another mission.

To take some photographs.

I need a set of keys. Many people are sooooo careless, and leave them in glove compartments, in cup holders, tucked above sun visors.

Or, in this instance, in the ignition itself.

Shame on you, driver. What's the good of locks if you leave the keys within the fox's grasp.

Of course, he's not a complete fool. He's kept the engine running for the air-conditioning and taken a second set with him to lock the door.

I look up and down the street.

I'm invisible. Who wouldn't be when there's a burning high-rise and a thousand flashing lights? Crouching, I open the door with the jiggler. I pluck the keys out and I take dozens of pictures from all angles. People think you make a wax impression of a key—they've seen that on TV. In fact, that works only for the most rudimentary skeleton keys. For pin and tumbler, you need high megapixel pictures.

To augment my efforts, I take a sixty-second video.

I have enough.

I slide them back into the ignition, start the engine, lock the door with the button inside and ease it shut.

In sixty seconds I've fired up the Audi and am headed away from the excitement. As much as I'd love to watch the building come down, I have some pressing errands.

Ron Pulaski was safely down, being given oxygen and water.

But there was no sign of Lyle Spencer, still on the twelfth floor. The fire was rising and the smoke was growing black and thicker.

"What's he doing?" Rhyme muttered.

Sachs said, "Jesus. The flames'll be at his floor any time now."

Two minutes passed.

Three.

Five.

"Call him."

As she lifted her phone, it hummed with an incoming call. "It's him." She put it on speaker. "Lyle. Are you all right?"

"I broke through the door Ron was trying to get into." He paused, presumably for oxygen. "The lock shop—it's burning. Only had time to scoop up some dust and dirt from in front of a workstation. Got it in a bag. I'll pitch it down."

"Get out, Lyle," Rhyme said. "The flames're one floor below you."

Spencer disconnected without responding that he'd heard.

Rhyme saw him appear in the window and toss a weighted paper bag out. It sailed to the street and landed near one of the firemen who picked it up and, seeing Sachs wave, brought it to them.

She put it in an evidence bag. She noted the fireman's name, Rhyme saw, but tucked the bag away; they'd do chain-of-custody later.

Sachs said, "Why isn't he coming down? Is he still looking for something?"

Is he still *alive*?

They stared at the window.

Come on, Lyle.

Inside the building, the ninth or tenth floor collapsed with a mammoth roar, firing smoke and embers from windows. The building groaned.

It was then that Spencer appeared in the window. He seemed to be breathing into the mask deeply, filling his lungs. Then, curiously, he lifted his head and was gazing out over the city, like a tourist on the Empire State Building's observation platform. His body language was serene.

Spencer looked down at the assembly of fire trucks.

Rhyme said, "Send him a text. We need him down now. And repeat 'Need.'"

Sachs looked at her husband and then sent the message.

They could see him fish his phone from his pocket and look at it for a long moment. Then he slid it back.

Again studying the cityscape.

And down at the roof of the one-story building a hundred feet below.

Another floor collapsed. The building seemed to rock.

At last Spencer bent down and hooked the escape rig to something inside the hallway. He doffed the mask and tank—to lose the weight for the journey downward, Rhyme supposed—and then turned and scooted himself over the sill then ledge.

While Ron Pulaski had descended in a jerking fashion, Lyle Spencer returned to earth with balletic elegance, as casually as another man might cross the street, assured by a radiant green light that his passage was safe.

52

Well, it's Lincoln Rhyme."

Turning the chair, he found himself looking at two men approaching. They appeared troubled, but Rhyme's impression was that they were affecting that expression artificially.

Maybe they thought he was here in an official capacity.

The speaker was big, tanned Richard Beaufort. Rhyme now realized he looked like some star he'd seen on a TV show—about police, as a matter of fact. Also present was Abe Potter, the mayor's aide, a slim, balding man with dark tufts of straight hair above each ear. He resembled no one memorable.

Sachs glared toward them, but Rhyme said, "It's okay," and drove to meet them.

"Detective Beaufort . . . Congratulations."

"On . . . ?" The officer frowned.

"Your assignment to the mayor's office security. I assume it's new. You said you were working follow-up on the Buryak case just the other day, out of the One One Two House." Rhyme remembered Sachs told him Beaufort had been transferred some time ago.

"Well, I have several assignments." He rubbed his fingers together, a sign of stress probably. Once again Rhyme thought of Sachs's edginess, though in her case it didn't arise because she lied.

"I remember, from my days on the force, it was always a challenge. All that juggling."

Potter wasn't a physical force but his voice was firm. "Mr. Rhyme, it was made clear to you that you can't work on any case for the NYPD."

Nice touch, the "Mr.," reminding that Rhyme was a civilian. At least Willis had captained him.

He cast a querying look toward the two men.

"There's been an arrest in the Gregorios murder."

The killing in Queens.

"A homeless man?"

"That's right. And this was displayed on the brag board at the press conference." Potter looked at Beaufort, who brandished his phone.

The photo depicted a table and a whiteboard, on which were a mug shot of the homeless suspect, looking dazed, and pictures of a bloody wallet, a filleting knife, also crimson, and of a bottle of cherry-flavored Miracle Sav. Beneath the bottle of the gut-destroying "medicine" was a printout of Rhyme's email to Detectives Kelly and Wilson.

When mixed together, sodium chlorite and citric acid combine to create chlorine dioxide, ClO_2, a common disinfectant and cleanser. However, note that the ClO_2 also is used as a fraudulent cure-all for a number of diseases, including AIDS and cancer. When used as a quack cure, ClO_2 generally has added to it a flavoring agent, such as lemon, cinnamon, or—as is present here—cherry syrup . . .

Rhyme had never approved of brass's showing off at press conferences: the stacks of drugs, the bags of money, the pictures of SWAT apprehending the suspect, the evidence. It was arrogant and unseemly. It also gave away techniques. Bad guys owned TVs too.

Beaufort muttered, "Dep Com Willis and the mayor feel this is a violation of the prohibition you are well aware of. It was highly embarrassing. And it was an insult to the chain of command. Not taking them seriously."

Rhyme looked up at Potter and asked, "Did the mayor make a statement condemning my involvement in the Gregorios case?"

"Well, he did, yes."

"What's his opponent's name, again, in the race for governor?"

Potter regarded Beaufort but finally answered, "Edward Roland."

That's right, the billionaire.

"Who, in turn, issued a statement attacking the mayor."

"I don't know what your point is here, Mr. Rhyme."

He asked, "Do either of you play chess?"

They exchanged glances once more. Frowning, Beaufort asked, "I'm sorry?"

"Never mind." Rhyme noted Sachs was looking at him. He gave her a brief it's-okay nod. "So the mayor's press comment about me was based on my email on the brag board."

"That's right," Potter said, a bit imperiously, Rhyme thought. "You didn't think it'd make the news, did you?"

"And he sent you here to . . . arrest me?"

"At this point, a public statement of contrition."

"Mea culpa and I promise I won't do it again."

"We need to make an example of flouting the rules."

Rhyme looked over Beaufort's photo once more. He was studying the brag board carefully.

When it appeared that the two men realized his interest was bordering on analytical, Beaufort tucked the mobile away.

Rhyme was thinking there were a few things he wanted to mention to Detectives Tye Kelly and Crystal Wilson, the shields from the 112, about the collar. But the pair in front of him were the last people on earth to bring the topic up with.

"Lincoln," Beaufort said, "you don't seem to appreciate the trouble you're in."

"Time stamp," was the criminalist's response.

"What?" Potter asked.

"You saw the date of the email, but not the time. Detective Kelly has the original. If you'd thought to look at it, you'd see that that email was sent several hours before the fiat—which by the way means a *legal* and definitive declaration. And I'm not sure that's what the mayor and the commissioner issued. But that'd be a matter for a different day."

"Time stamp." Potter's face tightened and he would undoubtedly be thinking of the conversation he would be having with the mayor, who would likely blame his aide and Beaufort for not checking something as simple as the timing of Rhyme's memo.

Beaufort tried, "Well, what are you doing here now?"

"I'm here—"

A voice boomed. "He's here to see me."

The three men turned to Commanding Officer Brett Evans. The tall, distinguished man, with a military bearing, nodded a greeting to Rhyme, then turned and looked coolly at the other men. "I was going to meet Lincoln and his wife downtown for lunch. Then this call came in." He looked at the flaming building. "Their colleague was in danger. They both came down here to see about him. I did too."

Evans continued, "I'm hooking Lincoln up with my friends at

New Jersey State Police. The OFS. They're interested in hiring him." Evans added some heft to the word as he said, "Consulting."

Potter looked at Beaufort.

Without a word, the two men returned to their car, Potter dropping into the driver's seat. They didn't depart, though. They'd be watching to make sure Rhyme didn't prowl the scene.

Rhyme nodded his appreciation to Evans, who grinned. "How'd I do?"

"Oscar quality."

"How's Ron Pulaski?"

"He'll be fine. Whittaker's security man saved him."

"Really? No one was hurt?"

"No."

The two men watched several more floors collapse in explosions of dancing embers and shrouds of orange flame. Evans asked, "The Locksmith was behind this?"

"I'm sure."

"I do have some names, Lincoln. New Jersey State Police."

"Thanks, Brett. I will think about it."

"Will you really?" Evans kept a stone face for a moment. Then laughed.

"But I appreciate it."

The man then grew serious. "Just be careful."

Rhyme glanced toward Beaufort and Potter. "I will."

"Well, *them*, yes. But that's not what I mean. I heard that Buryak isn't happy he was brought to trial and one of the people he's the least happy with is you. Some blogger was saying that there was a conspiracy to get him arrested and convicted. And you might be involved."

Now Rhyme was the one who smiled. "Lon told me about that. Crazy. But I'm sure I'm well into Buryak's rearview mirror by now."

53

Forty minutes ago Aaron Douglass had watched Lincoln Rhyme, accompanied by a trim, athletic man in a nice shirt and slacks and tie leave the town house. They got into a Sprinter, which featured a wheelchair-accessible ramp, and pulled away from the curb.

Once again driving his gray Cadillac, Douglass had put the sleek car into gear and followed. The vehicles made their way south—eventually arriving here, the site of a building fire.

He had no idea what was going on but he did note with pleasure that someone else was present too—the person he was actually most interested in seeing and had hoped to catch: Amelia Sachs.

Parking on a side street, he'd called his "masseur," broad-chested Arnie Cavall. "Need you. Now. With the van." And gave the address.

Douglass had joined a small crowd, where he asked what was going on.

A man said, "Heard it was that serial killer, the Locksmith. He tried to kill somebody in the building."

Ah, the man who could break into any place, the man Amelia

Sachs was pursuing when she and Rhyme were not trying to nail Viktor Buryak. He asked, "Did they catch him?"

A toothy middle-aged woman in a large hat muttered, "They'll never catch him. He works for the police."

"You're crazy." This was from somebody else in the crowd.

"I heard that online," the woman countered angrily. "It's a trusted source!"

Douglass left them to have it out—or not—and stepped to a vantage point where he could see both Rhyme and Sachs. They were near an FDNY command post. There was a cluster of firefighters and police—some uniforms and some detectives. He then circled the scene, spotting her distinctive car parked not far away, on a side street. Douglass watched Rhyme have a conversation with two men in suits, who left when a third man showed up. Finally Rhyme returned to Amelia and the mountain climber—the man who'd accompanied her from Whittaker Tower when he and Arnie were at the maple-flavored tempeh burger food truck.

The big man had just rescued someone from the building.

A spectacular feat.

The man was massaging his shoulder and taking occasional whiffs of oxygen.

Douglass noted with interest that Rhyme's wheelchair had climbed right over thick fire department hoses. It was quite a piece of machinery.

He texted Arnie.

Where are you?

The reply:

Three minutes.

He walked slowly around the neighborhood and side streets, studying the layout. He thought, Yeah, it could work.

Soon Arnie pulled up to the intersection Douglass had sent him. He was in a battered Econoline van. He parked and nodded.

Douglass looked over the beat-up vehicle, perfect for transporting meth or disposing bodies or delivering flowers. Whatever it was ordinarily used for, the important thing is that it was nondescript and looked like a thousand others on the streets of the city—just the sort of vehicle to use when you ran down a policewoman.

And, as Arnie had recommended, it was nondescript white.

"Good," Douglass said, nodding at the wheels.

"I figured this'd be best." The small, wiry man looked over at the rescue workers, all the cars and trucks, the millions of lights.

He continued, "That's them. The ones we saw when we was at the food truck. She's hot."

Echoing Viktor Buryak's more elegant observation about the policewoman.

"The fuck's that got to do with anything?"

"Yeah, but," Arnie said, going nowhere after that.

Douglass pointed. "There's her car. We'll wait until they head back to it and the Sprinter. That's Rhyme's. I need them together."

"Can he drive?"

"No. The guy with him. He's his aide or something."

"Does it have a ramp?"

"Let's focus, here, Arnie."

"Sure. When they're headed back to the car and the van."

Douglass was now pointing to the middle of the block. "That's a good spot. When she's right about there."

"By the containers and trash."

"That's right." He thought for a moment. "How fast should you go to hurt somebody bad but not kill them?"

Arnie considered this.

"I'd say forty."

"Too fast. Thirty."

Amelia Sachs looked once more at the ropes dangling from the rappel window, now filled with flames. First one cord then the other fell to the roof of the building before, their ends burning.

"Don't know I could have done that, Rhyme."

Her essential fear was claustrophobia and she had no particular concern about heights, other than the usual. But still.

The criminalist said nothing but his eyes too strayed to the window.

"What'd they say?" she asked.

"Beaufort and Potter? Wanted a public apology because I wrote a memo for the Gregorios case."

"Seriously?" Her lips tightened in disgust.

"It's gone away. But they're persistent. Oh, and Brett Evans wants me to move to Trenton or Newark. Or some such. It's a curious time, Sachs . . ." His voice lowered. "So, Kitt's the one?" he asked.

She nodded. "All the bad blood within the family, I told you—hating his father's brand of journalism. Always an activist, they said. Did Izzy drop off the evidence at your place?"

"Mel divided it in half, and she went on to Queens. He's working on it now."

"I'll get back there," she said and turned, heading for her car.

Rhyme accompanied her, wheeling at her pace. Her Torino was parked at the end of the block.

As there was no traffic, they remained in the middle of the street; Manhattan sidewalks were difficult for Rhyme's chair. They were narrow, cluttered with refuse bins and frequently cracked and uneven.

"You seem doubtful that Kitt's doing it to make a political statement."

"That's part of it in a way. But you ask me, it's something else, deeper, between father and son. Remember what he wrote? 'Reckoning'?"

After a moment, she gave a laugh. He looked her way.

"His cousin or her fiancé said Kitt's problem was he dabbled, jumped from job to job. Looks like he finally found the one thing he's good at. Lock picking and home invasion. He's not bad at arson either."

They were going west, against traffic, so there was no need to worry about approaching vehicles behind them. Still, Amelia Sachs had been a street cop, patrolling places like the Deuce—West 42nd Street—before it became the Disneyland that it was today. And so situational awareness ranked high among her innate survival skills. She glanced about frequently, eyes constantly moving. Instinct.

Now, they came to an intersection and she looked down a side street.

And froze.

"What is it?"

"Block away, a gray Cadillac."

She reminded Rhyme about the possible surveillance at the Carrie Noelle scene.

"It wasn't here an hour ago. And this isn't a new-Cadillac kind of street."

"No."

They heard a sound behind them, a vehicle. A battered white van started their way.

Rhyme asked, "At Carrie's? You make the driver?"

"Never got a good look. Male. Hat, maybe. That's it." She unbuttoned her jacket, so her Glock was exposed. She scanned both sides of the street, over and between the cars that lined the curb. "Something feels wrong here. Rhyme, move to the curb."

He did.

Sachs stepped into the middle of the cobblestoned street, crouching slightly, like a soldier looking for a sniper nest or a hidey-hole from which an attacker might emerge.

54

Lincoln Rhyme, his chair banked against the curb, between two cars, watched Amelia Sachs, moving slowly toward the entrance to a narrow alley.

But apparently she saw no sign of any threat from there or any of the windows facing the street.

Then Rhyme focused on the approaching white Econoline.

Was *that* the threat?

"Sachs! The van!"

She turned as it grew closer. Her hand started to draw her Glock.

Just then the vehicle eased to a stop. The doors opened and two men got out. One was large, tall, in his forties. He wore a black beret. The Caddie driver? Rhyme wondered. She'd mentioned a hat.

The other was smaller—age impossible to tell.

"Detective Sachs, Captain Rhyme," the taller one said. He stepped forward. Sachs kept her hand gripping her weapon.

They approached, both keeping their hands visible. In his right he was displaying something. What was it? A wallet?

No, a badge holder, with an ID on one side and an NYPD gold shield on the other. "I'm Aaron Douglass, Organized Crime squad."

He stopped but Sachs gestured them forward. Rhyme joined them too.

They looked closely at the ID, which seemed legit. Then they simultaneously took in the smaller man.

Douglass continued, "And this is Arnie Cavall. He's a CI, works for me some."

"Hey," Arnie said in a cheerful voice. "How ya doing?" He was speaking to Sachs, ignoring Rhyme.

Douglass said, with some awe in his voice, "Captain Rhyme, a real honor to meet you, sir. And Detective Sachs."

She said, "You've been tailing me. From that scene on Ninety-Seventh Street."

"That's right, I have."

Rhyme muttered, "What the hell's this all about?"

"We need to shoot a movie."

Sachs called Lon Sellitto, who apparently called somebody else. Maybe another call was involved.

A moment later she got a text with Douglass's picture and the confirmation that the detective, assigned to NYPD Organized Crime, had been embedded for six months within Viktor Buryak's organization. The mobster knew he was NYPD but believed he'd caught himself a crooked cop, having no idea he was undercover.

"Slowly I've been getting Buryak to trust me. I run part of his information-gathering operation. A small one. But everything I give him, I tone it down or change the details, so nobody innocent gets hurt. He has me do some enforcement work, like this. But that I fuck with too so there're no injuries."

"You said, 'enforcement work, like this,'" Rhyme said. "Explain."

It seemed that Buryak was convinced that Rhyme, with Sachs's help, was out to get him because he'd been embarrassed in court. The mobster couldn't be tried again for the death of Leon Murphy, but believed Rhyme was on a mission to nail him for some other case or even frame him. Apparently Buryak hadn't heard, or didn't buy, the conspiracy blogger Verus's theory that both he and Rhyme were working for the Hidden to sow chaos in the streets.

Rhyme scoffed. "I don't have any time for crap like that. And even if I did, I'd need a whole team to get something on him. He's the slipperiest fish I've ever seen."

Douglass exhaled a sigh. "I know that. *Everybody* knows that. But Buryak suffers from a serious case of paranoia. He doesn't think in specifics. All he knows is that one of the best forensic cops in the world has decided to bring him down and I'm supposed to discourage that. Make sure you're too scared or upset to pursue him anymore." He glanced at Sachs. "By running you over. Not killing you. He doesn't want that to happen. Just hurt you bad and scare the hell out of you both."

Rhyme believed he saw his wife smile slightly at this.

Amelia Sachs did not scare particularly easily.

She asked, "What do you mean by 'movie'?"

Buryak, the undercover cop explained, wanted a video of the "accident."

"He doesn't trust you?"

Douglass snickered. "I think it's more he wouldn't mind seeing you get wiped out—for his own personal enjoyment. He's pretty pissed off that you've got this *V for Vendetta* action going on."

Rhyme said, "We've got work at home." They had the evidence from Kitt Whittaker's apartment and the trace that Lyle Spencer had just risked his life to collect.

She said, "All right, let's get it over with. What d'you have in mind?"

Douglass's plan was that he was going to make a phone video as if he were surreptitiously spying on her. He would then shift the camera to the van speeding down the street. She'd stand in a doorway nearby and the van would slam into the containers where Sachs had been standing. She would then lie down on the sidewalk, as if she were unconscious and hurt.

"Won't he be expecting a story on the news?" Sachs asked.

"If somebody took a shot at you, maybe. But just a traffic accident, no fatalities? Not really newsworthy. Anyway, you have a better plan?"

Sachs looked up and down the street, then said, "Okay, cameraman. Where do you want me?"

"Friends: Thomas Jefferson wrote, 'What country before ever existed a century and half without a rebellion? And what country can preserve its liberties if their rulers are not warned from time to time that their people preserve the spirit of resistance? Let them take arms. The remedy is to set them right as to facts, pardon and pacify them. What signify a few lives lost in a century or two.'

"The Hidden will not win!

"Say your prayers and stay prepared!

"My name is Verum, Latin for 'true.' That is what my message is. What you do with it is up to you."

55

One take.

That's all they had time for.

As Sachs, Rhyme and now a curious Thom waited across the street, Douglass called his stunt driver, Arnie, who had apparently fallen madly in love with the leading lady in the space of a mere ten minutes.

While the cop manned the phone's camera, Arnie got the van up to about thirty-five or so and careened into the construction waste bins, scattering wood, cardboard, metal scraps and coffee cups and fast-food wrappers everywhere. He parked. Sachs and Douglass walked to the mess and she lay down on the sidewalk. Douglass got some footage of her, apparently unconscious.

A woman's voice from a window, "Are you all right? You need some help?"

Sachs rose and called up, "No we're all good, thanks. We're shooting an independent film."

The elderly woman said, "You have a permit?"

Douglass said, "It's on file."

"I don't see any crew."

"That's why it's an *independent*," he replied.

"The mayor has a film office. I know. I read about it."

"That's who we have the permit from."

She continued watching for a moment. "You're going to clean that up, aren't you?"

"Sure, we will." Douglass then said to Arnie, "Take care of that." The slight man grimaced but got to work.

The woman turned back into her apartment and shut the window.

Douglass looked at the video. "Good job. Maybe you could be a stuntwoman."

Sachs grunted. Rhyme could tell she felt faintly ridiculous, but he couldn't fault the undercover cop's plan. An alternative might have Buryak actually ordering a hit on Sachs or himself.

Rhyme said, "The Murphy case was the best chance we had to get him, and we saw how that turned out. Do you have anything at all on him?"

"Zip. He's the most careful OC boss I've ever investigated. Nothing's committed to paper or computer or phone. He doesn't even give direct orders when he's alone with his crew. He hints, he suggests. He has layers of people insulating him. He assumes everybody's bugged, even me, and I've gotten about as close as anybody can. Metal detectors outside his office. Scramblers, encryption."

Rhyme said, "Well, his business is selling information and data. If he knows how to mine it, he knows how to keep it from being mined."

Sachs waved to the trash. "But here—Buryak ordered assault with a deadly weapon. Conspiracy. Even if *you* didn't intend it to happen, Buryak did. And you know conspiracy. It's a wide net."

It was Rhyme who spoke. "Ah, Sachs, but I'll bet Buryak didn't actually *tell* Detective Douglass to attack you, did he?"

"Exactly. Didn't say a single word that can be traced. The worse he said was he wanted a 'masseur.'"

"Euphemism," Sachs said, shaking her head.

Rhyme thought for a moment then said to Douglass, "You're after Buryak . . . You following the Red Hook drops?"

"No, what's that?"

"Buryak's name came up. Remember, Sachs?"

She nodded. "When we were working the Murphy case, a CI mentioned him. Buryak. Something about shipments of product at the Red Hook piers next few weeks. It wasn't part of the homicide so we just sent it to Narcotics."

Rhyme said, "Couple hundred kilos."

Sachs corrected, "Bigger, I remember."

Douglass shook his head. "Well, Buryak never touches product himself. You'll never catch him buying or selling anything other than information. But maybe we'll catch somebody in the net who'll dime him out." He gave a wry smile. "I've spent six months of my life trying to roll up Buryak and I've got nothing. Then this tip comes out of left field and maybe *that's* how he's going to get collared. Hell of a line of work we're in, don't you think? Hell of a line."

56

Four people were in on the conversation.

Lincoln Rhyme was supposedly off the case, yes, but since those on the call were only Sachs, Averell Whittaker and his niece, he'd decided to take the chance of an appearance, though he let Sachs handle the lead.

She explained about their discovery that Kitt was the Locksmith.

The gasp was from Averell Whittaker. "No."

Joanna Whittaker said, "That's not possible."

Sachs explained about the evidence she'd found in his apartment— the shoes, the victims' underwear, picking tools, the *Daily Heralds*.

"It can't be . . ." His voice faded.

Then Joanna was whispering, "Jesus. I just realized something."

Her uncle was saying, "What is it, Jo?"

"The newspapers. Page three, February seventeenth. Aunt Mary died March second, two thousand seventeen."

Rhyme said, "It's a *code*. Damn it. Missed it completely. Page three represents the third month, March. The February issue?

February's the second month, so we get the number two. And the date, the seventeenth, is the year. Three/two/seventeen."

Sachs said, "We were focusing on the content. It had nothing to do with the Apollos or Russian hacks or anything else on the page."

"Oh my God . . ." Averell Whittaker cleared his throat. "I didn't mention this, but the reason Kitt walked out of my life, our lives. It's my fault—"

"Uncle—"

"No, it is! I was busy buying that damn TV station and wasn't at Mary's bedside when she passed."

Silence between uncle and niece. Finally Joanna said, "She wasn't alone. Kitt was there. And—how could you know? The doctors themselves couldn't say for sure how long she had."

"I . . . I feel that it's my fault. The way I treated him. The neglect . . ." Did the man choke a sob? Rhyme could only imagine the shock of a father learning his son was a felon and potentially a murderer.

"Averell . . ." Joanna coddled. "Don't think that way. Nobody forced him to go off the grid, to do the things he's done."

Rhyme glanced Sachs's way, and the look meant that they needed to move things along.

She said, "We're pretty sure he's living out of a workshop in the city. Do you have an idea where he might have some place like that?"

Silence again. Joanna spoke. "No, like we said, we've been wholly out of touch . . . seems like forever. Uncle Averell?"

The man was struggling to speak. "No, nothing."

"Is your fiancé there?" Sachs asked Joanna.

"No, he's at work, but I'll call him. I'll do it now." There was a pause as she made another call on a different phone and broke the news to Kemp. A moment of silence. "I know, I know . . . but they're sure. They found evidence and . . . you know how he's been . . ." Her voice faded as if she didn't want to be too hard on her cousin in front of his father. She asked about a workshop or someplace else he might be staying. Another pause. "Did he say where? Anything more? . . . All right, honey. I'll see you later." She came back on the line with Sachs and Rhyme. "Martin works in real estate. Late last year Kitt asked him about subletting an artist's loft or workshop. What neighborhoods would be the most out of the way? He said he didn't want distractions."

"Why did he want it?" Rhyme whispered, and Sachs repeated the question.

A moment later, Joanna said, "Kitt didn't say."

"What did Martin tell him?" Sachs asked.

"He recommended Long Island City, Spanish Harlem, the South Bronx. But he never heard back from Kitt about what he decided on."

Sachs said, "Please keep this to yourself for the time being. We don't want to tip our hand. We want to find him and bring him into custody safely."

"Thank you for that," Joanna said.

"Ah, Kitt," Whittaker whispered.

They ended the call.

"So," Rhyme said, offering an exasperated sigh, "our perp, he's hiding out somewhere in an area that's about sixty square miles. What could the problem possibly be?"

The gas chromatograph/mass spectrometer is a remarkable merger of two devices essential to forensic scientists.

Lincoln Rhyme had always insisted on having one in the lab, though the units are quite pricey. They're used to find out what an unknown sample of evidence might be. Chromatography, which was invented in Russia in the early 1900s, has been described as a horse race. An unknown sample is vaporized into a gas, which then begins a journey through a column filled with a liquid or a gel. Different substances within the sample move at different speeds through the column. The result is a graph of the materials. Each one is then analyzed in the companion device, the mass spectrometer, which identifies them.

In the sterile portion of the lab Mel Cooper and Amelia Sachs were using the GC/MS to unlock the secrets of the evidence she'd collected from Kitt Whittaker's apartment and the site of the Sandleman Building fire that had nearly been Ron Pulaski's funeral pyre.

As they waited for the results, Cooper confirmed that the running shoe in Kitt's closet was the one he'd worn in the first two apartment invasions and the Bechtel Building, replaced now by smooth-soled shoes, which held less trace—as Rhyme had speculated he'd done.

Outside, Lyle Spencer and Rhyme watched. The criminalist hoped some unique geographic trace would adhere to something Sachs had bagged and tagged and this would lead them to the man's workshop. Even if they could narrow down only a five- or six-block area, the canvassers, armed with pictures of Kitt Whittaker, could then go to work.

Spencer had pulled a shoulder muscle in the climb—that remarkable ascent—and had stripped to a T-shirt as he applied an ice pack Thom had fixed up for him. He was perhaps the most muscular man Rhyme had ever seen. On one biceps was a tattoo of an anchor; on the other were the initials *T.S.* in Old English type.

Spencer coughed yet again. The smoke was still embedded in his lungs.

"From *The Towering Inferno*," Cooper called.

Another popular cultural reference, Rhyme deduced. He was

referring to the evidence that Spencer had lifted from the floor, just before his descent to the ground.

"We've got ammonia, urea nitrogen, phosphate, soluble potash."

"Ah," Rhyme said, "fertilizer. I didn't know what to make of the boron, copper and iron from the Bechtel Building. Now, combined with these, it's fertilizer." He asked Spencer, "Your arm okay to write the notations on the board?"

"Sure." He did so, then stepped back and reviewed the entries. "Bricks in a wall."

Rhyme's very expression. It meant small bits of evidentiary discoveries, while not dispositive in themselves, could be combined into a formidable case for the prosecution. The more bricks the better, even if one duplicated another. Redundancy was good. Rhyme knew all too well that defense attorneys always managed to cast doubts on some of the evidence.

What you describe is possible.

No further questions . . .

Rhyme said, "Any hits on the accelerant he used?"

Cooper ran some of the ash Sachs had collected near the point of ignition. Shortly the results were displayed on one of the high-def monitors.

Rhyme studied the results. "Hell. I know the brand. He could've bought it from any one of a hundred stations in the city. Useless."

There was nothing else from the *Inferno* building. Cooper and Sachs were now looking at trace she had found in Kitt's apartment.

Reading from the computer analyzer, Cooper said, "Have water. In addition to H_2O, there's sodium, chloride, magnesium, sulfate and calcium."

Sachs took the sample and peered at it through the other staple of any forensic lab: the compound microscope. Compared to the chromatograph, this instrument was simplicity itself. you looked through lenses and something small became big.

She pushed a button and the image she was seeing went up on the screen for Rhyme and Spencer to view as well.

Rhyme called, "I recognize this. Algae bloom. So, seawater."

Cooper said, "And one more thing: additional water, in which are suspended aluminum oxide, hydrotreated light petroleum distillates, glycol, white mineral oil and methyl-four-isothiazoline."

Spencer looked toward Rhyme, expecting a repeat display of his knowledge.

"Don't know it, but we've got a special database we use."

Spencer seemed impressed. "Interesting."

Rhyme turned to Cooper, and called, "Google."

Spencer and Sachs both laughed.

No more than ten seconds later they had the answer: it was most likely an expensive polish used to protect wood from the elements. It was particularly popular with collectors of wood-sided cars and boats.

Spencer wrote this up on the chart.

The two in the sterile portion of the room prepared more samples.

Rhyme was looking at the photographs Sachs had taken at Kitt Whittaker's apartment. "That stain. In the front entryway. Do you see it? You get samples from the rug there, Sachs?"

She flipped through the clear glassine envelopes. "Here, yes." She held one up.

"Burn it."

She prepped a sample for the GC/MS.

Rhyme shot a serious gaze to Lyle Spencer. "I need a drink. And—more important—a hand to reach it."

A few minutes later the men were in the far corner of the parlor.

Rhyme had his single malt, Spencer a Bulleit. Rhyme was a peat person. Bourbon didn't appeal.

Sitting at a ninety-degree angle to Rhyme, the security man settled into the rattan chair that he had decided years ago to have Thom discard. Yet here it still was.

"You run many homicides?" Rhyme asked.

The man coughed briefly. "Albany? Lord, yes. Mostly street crime. Amazed some of those bozos weren't picked up years before. But there was some sophisticated stuff too. An assassination attempt of the governor. A bill he was going to sign, don't even remember what it was for, but not so popular among certain circles." Spencer's hand went to his scalp, just above the right ear. "Got clipped on that takedown. The slug singed my hair. I remember the smell as much as the fright. Vile."

Rhyme recalled Sachs's mentioning the scar.

PTSD . . .

He fell silent, eyes taking in the notes and photos on the whiteboard devoted to the Alekos Gregorios murder, for which Michael Xavier, the homeless man, was now in jail.

Then Rhyme turned his wheelchair slightly, and moved it closer to the security man's, so that they could not be heard by Cooper or Sachs.

Spencer lifted a questioning eyebrow.

Rhyme said, "Tell me why."

57

N o elaboration was necessary.

Lyle Spencer, it was clear, knew what the criminalist was referring to.

Rhyme was talking about what he'd seen at the burning building. Spencer, standing in the top-floor window, looking out over the city. He hadn't been thinking about how to best rappel down. He'd been thinking about leaping into the void.

Suicide.

A sip of the caramel-colored bourbon. Spencer said, "I've been *somewhat* honest with you and Amelia. Not completely honest. Yeah, Navy SEAL. Decorated. A detective in Albany. Decorated. Funny when you use that word. What does 'decorated' mean? You were an NYPD captain, right?"

Rhyme nodded.

"So at dress events you got to wear a lot of cabbage on your chest."

"*Some* cabbage."

"That's what it is. That's *all* it is." After a lengthy pause. "Let me tell you about Freddy Geiger. How's that for a name?"

"Memorable."

Spencer was now focused on the rim of his glass. "We have a big problem in Albany with meth, fent, oxy. Also sniffing gasoline and paint thinner. Geiger stepped into the market. He wanted to class up the city." A dark laugh. "His product was heroin.

"We had a credible tip about a deal going down, quarter million worth of H. Maybe that's small change here, in the city, but that was a lot for the Five One Eight. I was the lead gold shield. It was a hard takedown. All went to hell.

"Make a long story short, our intel didn't tell us Geiger's brother and his wife were in town from Buffalo. They took off and my partner and I went after them, chased 'em to this abandoned mill—the Bechtel Building reminded me of it. We went in after them." He shook his head. "Should've sealed it and waited, but we didn't. We walked into an ambush. My partner took a load of buckshot in the chest. He had a plate but he went down and the wife tried for a kill shot, missed, and I took her out. Two shots in the back of her head. Her husband turned the scattergun my way and I took him out too." A grimace. "No choice."

"Tough."

A slow nod.

"Then came the bad part." He offered a sour laugh.

He had Rhyme's full attention.

"Waiting for the rest of the team to get there, I looked outside. I saw a kid hiding in the bushes. I was afraid he'd rabbit so I circled around, solo, and came up behind him."

"Your SEAL training. It helped."

"I'm good at that, yeah. Got behind him, took him down and zipped him. Then I saw he was doing something funny. Looking at me, then into the bushes. It was a backpack he'd dumped. Cash. Three hundred K, give or take."

Spencer took another sip, then the whisky seemed to turn on him. His face tightened and he put the glass on the floor beside the chair. "Do you get as bored with confessions as I do?"

"They can be excruciating. This one isn't—if that's what it is."

"No surprise endings here, Lincoln. I cut his restraints and he took off. I hid the backpack on another part of the property and got back to my team. I picked it up the next day. The crown molding's nice here." The security man was looking up.

Rhyme glanced too. It was an elaborate zigzag pattern. If anyone had asked him to describe it without looking, he could not have.

"My daughter, Trudie, was diagnosed with an orphan disease. You heard of that?"

Ah, the tat: *T.S.*

"No."

"It means an illness that affects less than two hundred thousand people in the country. Very rare." He gave a soft laugh. "Trudie was proud that it was exotic. She said, 'Don't give me no stinkin' ordinary disease like everybody else gets.' Well, because there's a small market for orphan pharmaceuticals, the companies can't spread development costs around. So a year's treatment for some of the diseases is off the charts. Some are seven hundred K a year.

"Trudie's wasn't that high but it was a hell of a lot more than insurance and what I could scrape together from friends and family—and refinancing. Then came Geiger's money. From heaven. It covered the treatment—and helped with her lifestyle. She was active, athletic. We'd bike together and rock climb. The disease caused muscle atrophy. But we could afford good PT."

"You laundered the money?"

"Eight banks, invested in a couple of quote 'businesses.'" Spencer rocked his neck from side to side. He winced, this man who had just climbed a hundred feet straight up into the air.

"I mentioned no surprise endings."

"The skel you let go got busted for something else and dimed you out."

He nodded. "I didn't do the one thing that anybody serious would have done: claimed he went for a weapon and took him out. Couldn't do that, of course.

"If there was any good news, it was that my daughter died a month before I got busted. She never knew what I'd done."

"I'm sorry."

"I cut a deal. I pled guilty and the state waived restitution. They could have taken our house, car, pension, everything. See, I didn't technically steal from Geiger: I stole from us. Confiscated money goes into the police budget, or somebody's budget in Albany. I was never too clear on that. Anyway, the prosecutors thought it'd look bad with our daughter dying to penalize my wife too.

"I got thirteen months. Medium security upstate. My wife divorced me, married a nice guy and they've got a kid, his."

"Amelia said you talked about a family."

"Technically. They're just not mine. I needed the security job to give them something every month. They don't have a lot of money." He looked Rhyme in the eyes. "So if it seemed like an ex-cop—a disgraced but *decorated* ex-cop—died saving another cop from a burning building the insurance company wouldn't say suicide and deny the claim. That's what you spotted when I was up in the window."

"I could tell."

"Amelia didn't. She lit me up in the Bechtel Building and this thought came over me. Fuck it. That'd be it. I had the pipe. I could've gone for her. And that would be it." A shake of his head. "I remember her eyes. She was wondering why I was hesitating. She didn't get it."

"No. That's not something that would occur to her."

Amelia Sachs might dig a nail into her skin, she might drive on the edge, she might be first through the door in a dynamic entry, but Rhyme knew she had never asked the to-be-or-not-to-be question.

Spencer continued, "It wouldn't've been right under those circumstances. Not for her. And the insurance company would probably've balked. Suicide by cop. They know about that."

Rhyme nodded.

Spencer asked, "But you . . . you got it."

"I knew, yes."

"Because of what happened?" A nod at the wheelchair.

"That's right. I've been there."

"Why'd you change your mind?"

Rhyme sipped the scotch. "Funny thing happened. A while ago there was a serial kidnapper here in the city. The Bone Collector."

"I know about him."

"He was targeting me because of a mistake I made at a crime scene. I cleared it too soon. A perp was still there. When he tried to escape he killed the wife and the child of the man who'd become the Bone Collector. He decided to come after me. Revenge. But then he discovered I was planning on killing myself."

"Put a crimp in his plans, didn't it?"

Rhyme chuckled. "How do you get revenge by killing someone who *wants* to die? You're doing them a favor. So, he planned a series of crimes."

"The kidnappings?"

A nod. "And ones that I was particularly suited to run. And so I ran them."

"And, because of that, you changed your mind about killing yourself."

"That's right."

"And *then* he tried to kill you."

"Exactly. That plan didn't work either."

Spencer eased back in the chair. Rattan is noisy to start with and under his weight the piece of furniture groaned. "I lost the three things that mattered to me. My daughter. My wife. My cop job. That's why I'm always a footstep away from rappelling without a rope."

It was odd to hear the voice of a man so big, so imposing, crack.

"Sometimes it's tough," Rhyme said softly. "I can't say I never think about it anymore. But I always end up with: What the hell—why not enjoy a meal or conversation with Amelia for a little longer? Why not bicker with Thom for a little longer? Why not watch the peregrines and their nestlings on the ledge outside my window a little longer? Why not put some despicable perps in prison? Life's all about odds, and as long as the needle's past the fifty percent mark, being here is better than not."

The big man nodded, retrieved his glass then held it up like a toast.

Rhyme had no idea if his words, every one of them as true as the periodic table of the elements, registered. But he could do nothing more, or less, than tell Lyle Spencer what had saved him—and what continued to do so.

Spencer had a brief coughing fit. He rose and walked to a table near the sterile portion of the room where he'd left his water bottle. He drank from it, as he absently looked over the evidence chart.

"Rhyme," came Sachs's voice from the sterile part of the parlor. It might have been his imagination, but it seemed that there was an urgency to it. "I've got the results of that carpet sample in Kitt's apartment. You're going to want to see this."

58

I do love my workshop.

Yes, there are echoes of the imprisonment in the Consequences Room, but most of the time the anger is more than compensated for by all of my friends here: the 142 locks, the keys, my tools, my devices, my machinery.

It's especially nice when I'm engaged in a project, as now. I'm making pin tumbler keys that will open a knob lock and deadbolt.

Working with a sharp file and steel brush.

Pin tumbler keys are the most common of them all, those little triangular pieces of metal that jangle from all our keychains, the ones virtually no different from those that opened the lock created by Linus Yale and son.

I have a blank in my vise and I'm bitting by hand with a file, leaving tiny brass shavings on the workbench.

I'm engaged in the art of duplicating a key when you don't have the original . . . or the all-powerful code. Every key has a code that will allow it to open the lock that has the corresponding one. There are two layers of coding. The blind code is gibberish, KX401, for instance. You can announce that code to the world but no one can cut a key from it. The blind code has to be translated, via esoteric charts or software, into the bitting code, like 22345, which together with depth and spacing numbers allows you to cut the appropriate key, even if you've never seen the original.

But there's another way to copy a key, and that's what I'm doing now. You can work from a photograph and if you've had experience, of course, like me, it's possible to create a working duplicate. (A big scandal recently: On TV, an election official unwisely displayed the key to his county's voting machines, to assure voters of the security of the devices. Within hours lockpickers re-created the key—not to alter any votes, but to simply fulfill what God put them on this earth to do: open what was closed.)

I compare my work every ten or twenty seconds with the photos I took of the keys in the ignition at the Sandleman blaze. It takes some time but finally, I know that these are perfect duplications.

Good.

It's a very special door they will be opening tonight.

I have a little time so I decide to do some content moderating. I'm not in the mood for a beheading, but it's always fun to check in on politics. I wonder what kind of crazy post Verum put up lately. I find it amusing in the extreme that I stand accused of being part of that secret cabal known as the Hidden.

Joanna Whittaker walked into her uncle's apartment, whose view she had always admired.

New York City at your feet.

She smiled to Alicia Roberts, the security guard. "Where's Averell?"

"In his office."

"Alone?"

"Yes, making some calls."

"I won't bother him just yet."

Joanna walked to the couch and sat in the embracing, luxurious leather. She wore a sober suit of black wool, an Alexander McQueen. She happened to glance at a picture of herself and her father, Lawrence, on the wall nearby. Together they were holding up a copy of the *Herald*, open to a page on which was a story she'd written exposing a philandering politician. She was smiling and pointing at her byline. In her younger days—which were, of course, not so long ago—she was quite the terror as an investigative reporter. Those were the days when her father was an equal partner in the company and you found more women in the halls of Whittaker Media.

She smiled at the memory of the assignment. Leveling her eyes at the squirmy politician, she'd asked, "You're not answering my question, Senator. Did you tell your wife you were going to the Adirondacks with her attorney's daughter?"

"It was nothing."

"That's not responsive. My question was: Did your wife know you were going to the Adirondacks with her attorney's daughter?"

"I'm not going to answer that question."

"I'm giving you the opportunity to counter her claim that you lied about the trip."

"I . . . the girl, she was eighteen. It was just . . ."

"Did you tell your wife that you were going to the Adirondacks with her attorney's daughter?"

"No, I fucking didn't, okay?"

"When you two got to the Rosemont Inn—"

"This interview is over with."

"I'm running the story. This is your last chance to comment."

And on and on.

That job had been so much fun. Making the foolish squirm.

Seeing her byline too. That was a rush.

She looked over at the coffee table, which was stacked with documents about the Foundation for Ethical Journalism.

Nothing like it presently existed, at least not in the scale her uncle envisioned—and quite the scale it would be, since he was using ninety percent of the proceeds of his multibillion-dollar media empire to fund the nonprofit.

And what would her father, Lawrence, have thought about his brother's grand plan?

Not much, she knew. He'd found nothing wrong in journalism as titillation and leer, which both brothers seemed to be fine with for so many years. The indisputable fact was that far more people cared about sex scandals and conspiracies than cared about the G20 or an antitrust investigation into Facebook.

Unless of course there were sex scandals and conspiracies at the G20 and within the halls of the SEC.

Joanna smiled at that thought, since, perhaps, there were. And they were just waiting to be reported on.

Her phone sang with a text. It was from her fiancé, Martin Kemp.

Just here, coming up now.

She replied:

Okay.

Joanna rose and walked to the front alcove.

Alicia looked up from the padded bench she was seated on, where she'd been reading emails or texts. "Ms. Whittaker, can I help you with anything?"

"No, nothing."

From inside her jacket Joanna pulled the lengthy, razor-edge butcher knife and holding the handle in a plastic bag, she drew the blade quickly around the woman's neck, once, twice and then again, severing veins and arteries.

Spitting blood, choking, eyes wide, the woman reached for her gun, but Joanna had dropped the knife and was holding the guard's arm still with one hand. With the other, protected by the bag, she pulled the weapon from its holster and slid it far away from her reach, across the floor.

"Why?" Alicia whispered.

Joanna didn't answer. Her thoughts had moved on.

PART FOUR

BUMP KEY

[MAY 23, FIVE DAYS EARLIER, 3 A.M.]

59

am through the Andersen door lock and the EverStrong deadbolt in twenty-seven seconds. The door opens and closes with a click.

Five, four, three, two, one . . .

The wireless alarm, a sophisticated one, is under the spell of my RF box. The panel continues to emit its calming green light, oblivious to the intrusion.

I look around me. The apartment is magnificent. The blinds are now closed but I know the view is breathtaking; I've seen it in the day thanks to a video blog the owner has posted.

The door click troubles me some, so I pad fast to the bedroom.

The woman is all trundled and bundled, mouth open.

Her face is not beautiful, not like, say, Annabelle Talese's.

But that has never been important to me. A woman asleep is a woman asleep.

And being inside their abodes is what I really care about.

Being inside . . .

I return to the living room and survey the sumptuous place.

Original art is on the walls, sensuous marble sculptures sit on black lacquer tables that are polished to dark mirrors. There are leather couches and chairs. A bank of extraterrestrial orchids sits against the window, their colors pink, white, blue.

I silently walk to the windows and, just as silently, draw the curtains.

Tonight is different.

Tonight is not like the Visits in February or March, where I intruded and moved things around and destroyed the tenants' spiritual connection with their abodes.

Tonight I'm arriving where I belong.

I lift the brass knife from my pocket and open it with a click, just like the opening of a deadbolt.

Until now I've been fine opening doors.

Tonight I'll use this brass key to open what I'm meant to open, explore what I was born to explore.

The lock of flesh.

I step to the kitchen pass-through to unplug the landline. It would be quite the coincidence for her to get a call at this hour. But the organized offender, the tension-bar-and-rake-picker within me, is taking no chances.

I freeze. I believe I've heard a noise behind me.

Then: a loud pop and an agonizing burst of pain and my vision is filled with yellow light, perhaps what a Los Zetas victim sees in the moment before there *is* no light.

The Taser barb has buried itself just above my kidneys. I drop to the floor as the searing pain rises through my chest and finally finds a home in my jaw and my world goes black.

From the floor where I'm sitting, my hands bound behind me—tied tight—I understand that she was faking sleep the whole while.

She'd heard me enter, I suppose. Goddamn click. Then she'd grabbed a Taser from the bedside table and slipped from the bed as soon as I stepped to the landline.

In the minutes I was out she'd changed clothing. I can see pink pajamas on the floor in the bedroom. She is now in black slacks and white blouse. She emptied the contents of my wallet and pockets on the kitchen counter and is photographing them and then, it seems, uploading or texting the images somewhere. On the island next to her is the Taser. Something else: A pistol. A semiautomatic kind.

She seems to be in no hurry to call 911.

And she's wearing blue latex gloves.

Both of which mean that I'm fucked.

Slipping the pistol into her back pocket and picking up the Taser, she returns to where I'm sitting on the floor. The pain from the electric jolt remains.

The woman is large and formidable. Her gaze is focused and cold.

She looks me over clinically. "First. Anyone else?"

"Here? Tonight?" It's never occurred to me to make a Visit with a partner. It's an odd thought. "No."

"Downstairs, anywhere?"

I repeat the word.

"Who're you with?"

"With?"

She snaps: "Work for, your employer?"

"Nobody."

The woman aims the Taser at my groin.

"Wait!"

"Who?"

"No one! Really. I swear." The pain was astonishing. I don't want it to happen again.

She considers. And after a moment she seems to decide to believe me.

"The agenda? Burglary? Rape?"

I remain mum.

Her look conveys impatience and I suppose there's no point in being coy.

"It's what I do. I break into homes."

"Obviously. I asked why."

There's a question for you. "Because I need to."

Picking up my brass knife, she studies it. Her unattractive, though magnetic, face is intrigued. She puts the knife down.

"Why here? Why me? Give me answers or you're dead."

"Because of who you are: Verum, the conspiracy poster."

She blinks in utter shock. "You know that?"

I nod.

"And you came here to kill me."

I debate and, after a moment, tell her the truth. "That's right."

Curiously, she smiles. She taps my wallet. "Your name, it's unusual."

"I just go by Greg."

"Nice to meet you, Greg," she said with a chill, wry smile. "My name's Joanna Whittaker."

60

This young man was, it seemed, a content moderator for a video upload platform, one that Joanna used regularly for the Verum posts, ViewNow.

It was a poor man's YouTube.

"So you're the one who deletes them, right?"

He winced and gave her a perplexed look. "Your posts're lies, conspiracy theories, nonsense. The Hidden want to start a new civil war? They're infiltrating the schools, they're subverting religion, the voting process. You slander politicians and celebrities and CEOs. 'Say your prayers and stay prepared'? You don't think some bad things could come from posting that? They breach our community standards."

"But deleting them wasn't enough for you. They offended you and you wanted to kill me."

Now he laughed. "Those are my *company's* standards. Personally? I couldn't care less what you say."

"Then why?"

His thin shoulders rise and fall. "The challenge."

"Explain."

"You have an EverStrong deadbolt, SPC alarm. I've never cracked them before. And then there's the precaution you took to keep from being recognized. It was like waving a red flag at me. You took down all the pictures from the walls when you posted. The videos are ninety-nine percent pixelated. You use voice distortion. I tracked through one proxy but got stalled in Bulgaria."

"Then how?"

"You claim you're in California—to lead people off, I'm sure."

A nod.

"But in one of your early posts you left the curtain open. I got a screen shot of the view outside the window—the harbor. I could see the New Jersey waterfront. I checked out angles of sight. You had to be in Battery Park. I could also see the brass topper of a flagpole about even with your window. I wandered around the neighborhood and found it—on top of a government building two hundred feet in the air. That meant you were about on the twentieth floor. Only one building near here is that tall and has that view—this one."

"But—"

"In one of your posts I saw a blue Coach backpack on the floor."

Joanna glanced to where that very backpack, a present from her fiancé, now sat. She wasn't happy at her lapse.

"I just waited in the lobby a couple of nights until I saw you with the backpack. Then I followed you up here. I was dressed like a repairman. You looked at me once and didn't pay any attention."

She thought back and had a vague recollection of someone—perhaps.

"I saw your locks and the sign: 'Protected by SPS Security.' That's a bad idea, by the way."

"That explains why you wanted to break in. Why did you want to kill me?"

He considered this for a lengthy moment. "I needed to," he repeated.

"Where are the police on all of your . . . activities?"

"I've only done it a half-dozen times. I imagine some people've called nine one one, when they realize I've broken in. But I'm always very, very careful." He held up his hands, encased in gloves, and Joanna noted the stocking cap.

"Does *anyone* know you're here? Anyone on earth?" She asked this sternly, the tone that sent shivers down the spines of the interviewees when she was a reporter and now of her underlings at the Whittaker charity.

"No."

"There's a security camera downstairs."

"Not the service entrance. Stupid in a building like this."

She told Greg, "I could kill you and nobody would blink. Or I could call the police."

"You could. Most people would."

"But I think there's another way to handle this, Greg. Something that'll work for both of us. You'll stay alive and out of prison." She looked at him levelly. "But listen to me. I own you. If you don't do what I tell you, exactly, if you say anything about what I'm going to tell you, there will be . . . consequences."

For some reason, he blanched at the word.

"I've uploaded everything about you to a secure server and sent instructions to a third party." She nodded to the wallet. "I'm a very wealthy woman and as Verum you know how many followers I have. They're fiercely loyal and more than a little rabid. If anything were to happen to me, they will find you and kill you . . ." Her voice faded as she had another thought. "No, not kill." She smiled coldly. "You live to pick locks? Well, betray me and you won't be doing any more of that, with both your hands mangled, and a few fingers removed."

His eyes widened in horror. He nodded.

"But get this thing for me right and you'll be free to go on with your life." She tilted her head and brushed the dark hair from her face. "However sick it is." She considered. "I don't need to sweeten the pot. But I will. You'll get a half million dollars in cash. Because you'll need to move out of the area afterward. *Far* out of the area."

"And what is it that you want me to do?"

What indeed? she wondered.

Joanna walked to the bar. She poured a single malt—Lagavulin, very smoky—and taking the weapons in her other hand walked out onto the patio. She swiveled the rocker so she could see both the harbor and her prisoner.

Is it possible? Could this really work?

Joanna had been wrestling with the problem: the old bastard, Averell Whittaker, had been struck by conscience and was going to shut down the entire empire, which her father had worked himself to death building.

Joanna detested her uncle. His treatment of his family ranged from condescending to indifferent to cruel. When it was clear that Mary Whittaker, his wife, had only a day or two to live, he devoted every minute to negotiating the deal for the purchase of the TV station that would become the WMG channel.

Professionally Averell was no better: he seized a controlling interest of Whittaker Media from his brother, Joanna's father, by leveraging Lawrence's debts.

As for Joanna herself, when Averell took over, and began skewing the empire to male domination within the company, he booted her out of her reporter job on the *Herald* and put her in charge of what a "girl was best suited for": the company's charitable wing.

Which did have its advantages, since she made a good salary, had perks and because of the job she met Martin Kemp, who was good-looking and wealthy and marginally talented in bed. Oh, and who did everything she told him to. Also the charity wasn't tightly overseen, which gave her a chance to siphon funds to what she truly loved—playing the role of Verum.

Joanna Whittaker had had what she believed to be an insight about journalism as a business. If the rag *Daily Herald* outsold the *New York Times* and *The New Yorker*, if the WMG channel garnered far more viewers than PBS, then what would happen if you abandoned truth altogether? If you served up a diet of conspiracies, secret movements, dark operatives, hate and fear and schadenfreude—who doesn't just *love* others' misfortunes?

She decided to try it and, in a moment of inspiration—laced with a dash of contempt for the viewership—dubbed herself Verum.

True . . .

And was hugely successful from day one.

Martin, who funded much of the operation, had asked her if she believed any of her posts.

"Did you really ask that?" she'd replied, put out. "Obviously it's bullshit."

But she believed in the money that poured in from contributions and subscriptions and advertising.

She believed in the power she wielded over her thousands of followers, ranks that continued to grow.

She enjoyed too the creative side of the blog: coming up with her fake news.

From time to time she thought of what she could do with the Verum business model and the resources of Whittaker Media.

The possibilities were endless.

But not if the old son of a bitch, with his change of heart, was dismantling the empire and giving it all away.

For a month she'd debated. If Averell died before the dissolution papers were signed next week, his fifty-one percent of the stock in the company would go to Joanna and Kitt, split evenly. But if something happened to both Kitt *and* Averell, all the stock would be hers. She could take the company wherever she wanted.

Hurt them?

Of course she couldn't do it. Impossible.

And yet . . .

Hadn't dear Uncle Averell stolen the company from her father? Hadn't he destroyed her career as a journalist?

Hadn't he himself killed that young intern because he bought and buried the Charlotte Miller story, and because of other fake stories, paralyzed one of the leaders of the Apollos and killed a teacher and student in the Virginia satanic cult disaster?

Those were reasons, of course, *justifications* for the death of her uncle.

The bigger question she had to confront was: Could she take a life?

That question sat, rocking slowly within her, like the moored yacht she was looking at now, rising and falling in the gentle current of the Hudson River.

And suddenly she realized she could. The idea of killing was not horrifying or exhilarating; it sparked no emotion whatsoever.

She was utterly numb to the idea.

What had made her that way? she wondered briefly. But the anesthesia within her apparently extended to the motivation to ask that question.

And so she discarded it.

She now wasn't asking "if" but "how?"

Joanna now sipped more smoky liquor and studied Greg, as she told herself: You've been given a gift. What are you going to do with it exactly?

It was almost a sign. A *lockpicker.* Joanna remembered sitting with her father, drunk and tearfully muttering, "My own brother . . . he's locked me out of my own company. Locked me out and thrown away the key."

The idea now slowly emerged. She thought of it as a headline:

Estranged, Reclusive Son Kills Father and Self

It could play . . .

Kitt, the story would go, was never the same after his mother's death. In his search for some career, he'd learned lock picking and, recently, snapped. He'd break into apartments and leave a page from the *Daily Herald*. Then a moment of inspiration: it would be page 3 from the 2/17 edition; 3/2/17.

The day Mary Whittaker had died.

Joanna smiled.

He would leave several of these calling cards, and then, a grand finale, kill his father and himself.

Would it work?

What of Martin? That was a non-query. He'd do whatever he was told, even be a party to murder.

What of timing?

Kitt was flighty. He'd disappear for days, weeks sometimes. They'd need to make sure he stayed put. She and Martin Kemp could kidnap him and stash him on their boat until the climactic final act of the tragedy.

Joanna's palms began to sweat and her heart beat in excitement.

For ten minutes, she thought of refinements, removing some elements, adding others. It was as much fun as creating a Verum post about some presidential conspiracy.

61

I watch Joanna walk back into the room.

It's a very masculine stride.

She sits on the couch and looks down at me.

"Here's what's going to happen, Greg."

And she spins quite the tale.

I'm supposed to play the role of enraged son, furious at my father. (Well, that's hardly a stretch, though she's speaking of someone *else's* dad, of course.) I'm going to break into two more apartments and leave a particular newspaper page.

I ask, "You have anybody in mind for the break-in?"

"No."

"And do I . . ." My eyes stray to the knife, and I feel a pleasing warmth in my gut.

She frowns and her voice is threatening. "No. Absolutely not. You can't hurt a soul. The point is to send a message: that the newspaper you're going to leave is full of lies and fucks with people."

I nod.

Joanna looks at my latex gloves and hat and when she speaks she sounds like a stern schoolmarm once more, condescending. "How do you pick your victims?"

"From what they do online. Women, who live alone. I study their posts: locks, the doors, windows, alarms, that there're no dogs, no weapons. It's good if they drink—makes them sleep sounder. Even better if I can see a package of sleep aids or prescriptions."

"So they're random." She seems pleased at my forethought. Then the stern façade returns: "You have to be very, very careful. Nothing you do can lead back to me."

I nod. I'm beginning to see where this is headed. "So I stalk two."

I think immediately of an influencer, Annabelle, whom I've had my eye on for some time. Who else? There's a woman who sells toys from her Upper East Side apartment. Several others come to mind.

I ask Joanna, "And what do I do then?"

"That will be it. You'll have finished your obligation. I'll handle the rest."

So she'll kill the third victim herself, as if I did. I wonder who she's planning to murder? A husband, a lover, a business rival, someone who insulted her prominent nose?

I think of Lady Macbeth.

And the other question: Who is she setting up to take the fall for that murder?

"I want you to generate press. I need a splash." Joanna continues: "Come up with a name for yourself. Write it at the scene—no, I know, write it on the newspaper pages you're going to leave."

I think for a moment "What about 'Key Man'?"

"No," she mutters. "That's a business term."

Was it? I'd never heard of that.

"You'll be the 'Locksmith.' It'll mean something to my father."

I don't know what that's in reference to but I like the name.

"And add the word 'reckoning.'"

No reason for this is offered either, but since it's her circus, I say, "Okay. Oh, how about if I write it in the victims' lipstick?"

Thinking, as I just was, of influencers.

"Perfect. Now, evidence."

"I said I'm careful."

"I don't mean that," the schoolmarm snapped. She explains she wants me to steal some underwear and knives from the two victims.

Of course, to plant at the third crime scene, the one with the body or bodies.

"And I want everyone in the city to know about you right away. Post a picture of the newspaper in the apartment. Include her address. Reporters on the police beat'll see it and take up the story from there. Can you post anonymously?"

"I'll use one of the image board chans. It'll go viral from there."

"Good. And I'm going to get you some car keys too. An Audi. You can use that to drive around. Just remember to wear gloves when you do. Or wipe it down."

She disappears into the bedroom. This time when she returns she's holding a thick envelope. "Two hundred thousand. A down payment."

The cash isn't as heavy as I would have guessed. Where to go? Silicon Valley, possibly. Huge need for content moderators there. Or maybe Manila. I could live like a king, and I suspect the police there are less than diligent about break-ins and eviscerated bodies.

Joanna helps me up. She cuts the string binding my wrists, and I sit on the very nice couch. Then she steps away and grips the pistol.

I hardly blame her for being careful. I was going to knife her to death, after all.

"Any questions?"

"Can I have that?"

I'm looking at a small red and black plastic object sitting in a metal basket filled with iPhone chargers, earbuds, pens, pencils, aspirin packets.

"The keychain?"

"Yes."

It depicts the Tower of London and seems to be a cheap souvenir. I love the Tower.

She lifts it from the basket and sets it next to my wallet.

"Oh, and one other thing. Don't delete any more of Verum's posts from ViewNow."

"I won't."

"You can leave."

I gather up my brass knife and other possessions. Then down the long hall and out, closing the door to apartment 2019 behind me.

PART FIVE

SKELETON KEY

[MAY 28, PRESENT DAY, 11 A.M.]

62

A clatter outside the door. Voices, but hushed.

In the den that served as his home office, Averell Whittaker glanced at the closed door. Perhaps Joanna had dropped by. She did that some. It wasn't the maid's day. Maybe his niece and the security guard, Alicia Roberts, were making tea or coffee.

His eyes returned to the sales contract he was reviewing. Eighty pages, plus addenda. And this was just one of a dozen contracts for disposition of the equipment, the vehicles, the computers . . . endless.

How hard it was to do the right thing. You couldn't just push a button and turn the Whittaker Media empire into a do-gooding nonprofit foundation.

But he'd get it all done in his time left. He was so energized about the project. It would scrutinize print and broadcast stories in the U.S. and abroad and flag the ones it found inaccurate, after a rigorous review by fact-checkers. It would expose threats to reporters (which had multiplied exponentially in recent years). It would have a legal defense fund for reporters jailed or threatened. It would report ties between politicians and corporate interests and media companies. It would examine the FCC and other governmental entities to make sure that the regulations and laws did not limit First Amendment rights. And it would champion minority education in journalism.

But, as often, his mind soon wandered to his son.

It seemed inconceivable that he was the psychopath the police said he was.

Yet there was no doubt about his son's resentment for him. An idealist all his life, Kitt never liked the brand of journalism that Whittaker Media hawked.

Of course, that alone wasn't enough. It was also his father's neglect.

But how could I do otherwise? Fifteen-hour days keeping the business going, weathering the storms all media is subject to. A world Kitt didn't want and was unsuited for. He was collateral damage.

And, of course, there was that terrible incident with Mary's passing.

Dying without her husband by her side.

3/2/17.

He thought: But it was so important for the family. I had to buy the TV station, and it had to be done that day, or the option would have lapsed and . . .

He gave a hollow laugh. Even now I'm making excuses.

And, yes, I did it for the family . . . but mostly I did it for myself.

He looked out over the vast city, today muted by a milky complexion, the vast, bristling horizon foreshortened.

And now his son was a criminal . . . and, the police said, a threat to him and others.

At least in making his statement to—and about—his father, he'd done nothing more than *upset* several people. Whittaker prayed the police would find him before he actually hurt someone.

Or himself.

Oh, Kitt. I'm sorry . . .

He heard another scrape from outside.

Who was there?

He stood and, assisted by his cane, hobbled across the carpet. How he hated the accessory, a sign of dependency, a sign of weakness.

Pushing through the doorway, saying, "Hello, who's—"

Averell Whittaker froze at the sight of the tableau before him.

"Kitt!"

His son sat in a wheelchair. The young man's head lolled and he stared straight ahead. He seemed drunk or drugged. Behind him, gripping the handles, was Martin Kemp. The baby-faced man was swallowing and looking typically uncertain. And on the floor just inside the living room lay the Alicia Roberts her throat cut. Ample blood was drenching the blue and gold rug Mary had bought in Jordan so many years ago.

"No . . ."

Then he heard a sound from behind him and as he turned, his niece stepped forward and shoved him down the low stairs that led to the living room. He stumbled and fell hard onto the marble, crying out in pain.

63

My shoulder," he moaned. "It's broken . . ."

Whittaker climbed unsteadily to his feet and, grimacing, struggled to a chair. His head drooped and he was breathing heavily. "The pain . . ."

Joanna paid no attention to her uncle. She looked toward Kemp. "Is she dead?" She was impatient.

"Well, I mean . . ." He gestured at the still body, the soak of blood.

She scoffed. "Check and see? All right?"

"They'll . . . won't I leave fingerprints on her?"

Joanna closed her eyes briefly in irritation. "Why would you *not* check to see if someone who'd been stabbed was alive or dead? Wouldn't everybody do that? If your prints *weren't* there, that would be suspicious."

"Oh. Yeah."

He bent down over the woman, pressed his fingers on her neck. "There's no pulse."

"Check her eyes."

He hesitated.

"It's not a horror movie, Marty. She's not going to possess you with her gaze."

He grimaced at the verbal slap and nervously rubbed his hands together then lifted the woman's lids.

"I don't know . . . It . . . Yeah, I guess she's gone."

Whittaker whispered, "Jo, please . . . What are you doing?"

The woman turned disappointed eyes upon him. "It's reckoning time, Averell."

"What?" He winced.

"For one, stealing the company from my father . . ."

Whittaker snapped, "Your father was a drunk! He pledged shares for loans to cover his bad investments. Illegally. It took two years to get that nullified. I gave him a generous allowance."

"He was humiliated."

Whittaker muttered, "He made his bed. Some would've cut him off completely."

"And dissolving the company? Everything Father worked for?"

"We wrote stories that cost lives. I can't be a part of that anymore."

He looked away, as Joanna continued, "Your foundation's a joke. Nobody cares about the press, about news, about facts."

"That's not true."

"It is, yes."

"I wasn't going to dissolve your charity."

Her face flared with rage. "Where you can count on your little niece to keep her head down and not get into any trouble."

He looked at his son. "What's wrong with him? What've you done?"

"He's drugged."

"We'll work something out. Please . . ."

Her stern face, with the fleshy nose and thick eyebrows, gazed at him with what might perhaps be a modicum of sadness.

Then he thought of the security guard and knew there'd be no negotiation.

He saw the scene unfolding. They would kill him, using the same knife, then Kitt—probably injecting him with more drugs, an overdose. It would look like a suicide. The empire would go to Joanna.

"You'll keep the company running," he whispered.

"Yes, though, in a different direction. Verum?"

"The conspiracy theorist, the crank. Do you know him?"

With what Whittaker believed was a modicum of pride, she said, "I *am* him."

"Jo . . . no! You don't believe that crap."

She scoffed. "And you don't believe that stories about secret love children and the vice president's grandfather helping Lee Harvey Oswald kill John Kennedy belong on a front page. But there they are. And that made you a very wealthy man."

"It's different," he raged.

"You're right, Averell. I'm the next generation."

"Fah . . . Father . . ." Kitt was more aware now. He glanced at his wrists strapped to the wheelchair arms. He shook his head, took a breath. "Father?" His head drooped.

Joanna walked to her fiancé and was speaking to him. She appeared impatient.

Whittaker couldn't hear what they were saying exactly. *She* apparently had killed the security guard, and it was now Kemp's task to murder Whittaker and Kitt. But he was balking. Her face was filled with contempt.

He'd check pulses and eyes, he'd corroborate stories, but he wasn't going to wield the blade.

"Martin," Whittaker called.

But when the man looked his way, a pathetic expression on his face, and appeared about to speak, Joanna snapped her fingers and he fell silent.

She looked at him with disgust and, using a bloody plastic bag, picked up the knife that she'd used to kill Alicia. Striding across the sumptuous carpet to where he sat, she studied him, as if deciding to slash the left side of his neck or the right.

Whittaker slumped in the fake Chippendale chair, which he and Mary had bought in New England and refinished together after taking a class in doing trompe l'oeil and faux painting furniture. It had been a happy weeklong project.

Whittaker called in a weak voice, "Kitt?" Louder, "Kitt?"

His son opened his eyes.

Joanna stood over him and Whittaker, who looked up, expecting to see a hint of regret in that face, which bore a passing resemblance to that of his brother.

But there was none. Only regal impatience.

"Just let me say one thing," Whittaker whispered, wincing as he shifted a few inches.

She paused and cocked her head toward him.

"I'm sorry, son."

Kitt blinked slowly.

Averell Whittaker grabbed his cane in both hands—he'd been feigning injury to his shoulder—and swung the top, the brass head, with all his strength into his niece's face.

64

Joanna was on her knees, howling in rage and pain.

She was still gripping the knife and slashing toward Whittaker's legs as he rose. The blade did not connect and he launched his foot into her belly, doubling her over.

He turned to face Kemp, who was ashen white. The man had picked up another kitchen knife. He was advancing slowly. But his terror vastly outweighed his aggression.

Please, God, for the next ten minutes give me whatever strength You can. Let me save my son and then You can take me . . .

Brandishing the cane, Averell Whittaker strode across the room to meet Kemp head-on.

Joanna was struggling to stand. She spat blood.

Martin asked, "Honey, are you okay?"

"What a stupid fucking question. Kill him."

Stopping six feet from Kemp, Whittaker said, "Martin, you can save yourself. It's not too late. Call nine one one."

The man debated a moment. Whittaker thought he might actually do so. But no. He'd never disobey Mama.

Holding the knife forward, he lunged, his face an odd mix of determination, anger and utter fear.

Whittaker stepped aside and swung the cane, forcing him back a few feet. Then looked past him and with wide eyes called, "Alicia, you're alive!"

Kemp gasped and, before he caught himself, he turned to where the body lay.

Joanna shouted, "No, you idiot!"

It was only a half-second distraction but it was all that Whittaker needed. He swung the cane like a baseball bat and connected with the hand that held the knife. Kemp screamed—an actual high-pitched wail—and the blade fell to the floor, as Martin dropped to his knees, cradling his shattered fingers. Whittaker tossed away the cane and picked up the knife.

He turned to face his niece, who was scanning the entryway. She was looking at the floor.

Whittaker spotted the gun before she did, a small black pistol.

Joanna staggered toward the weapon. There was no chance that Whittaker could beat her to it. He did the only thing he could, slipped the knife into his pocket and stepped to Kitt, then pushed the wheelchair into the closest room, a library. He slammed the door and locked it.

He heard a crash as one of the two, Martin probably, kicked the wood hard.

Would she shoot her way in? That would hardly play, according to the fiction she'd created, but she was desperate.

The kicking stopped. He heard Joanna say, "Good idea."

Whittaker looked around and spotted the landline phone. He lifted it and heard: "At the tone the time will be . . ."

Martin Kemp had apparently done something right.

Whittaker hung up, jammed a chair under the knob. He moved his son out of the line of fire in case Joanna did decide to shoot.

The kicking began again. One of the panels cracked.

Averell Whittaker withdrew the knife from his pocket.

65

My computer beeps.

I've been summoned by a ViewNow algorithm, so I put on my content moderator hat. I scoot the laptop closer and maximize the screen.

It's a VNLive post. Tammybird335 is streaming in real time. She's a pretty woman around twenty, I'd guess. Her long brown hair is flyaway and some strands are pasted to her face from tears. She wears a bulky sweatshirt with a high school crest on it—from a better place and time in her life.

Either she or somebody in the comments have used the word "suicide," which the algorithm spotted.

Tammy's at her desk. Behind her is an unmade bed. Pictures of some tropical locations are on the wall. A ragged stuffed dog sits on the floor. Weeping, she says, "My mother's out with her boyfriend all the time, like she doesn't give a shit about me. And he tries to hug me all the time . . . And at school, the kids're so mean . . . I'm shy. I can't help it. It's too fucking much! Nobody cares. I mean, nobody! I think I should just do it. I don't know . . ."

The comments are rolling in.

> OMG, get help now!
>
> Do it live!
>
> Does your mom's boyfriend fuck you? Post pix.
>
> Call the police!
>
> Take ur top off.

In the chans—the underground message boards, where you can find just about everything—there are a number of lengthy forums devoted to suicide; they don't exist to get people help. They're how-to guides. Hundreds of thousands of pro-self-harm fans. The chans are text and still photos, a few GIFs, so they tend not to end up on ViewNow, but occasionally there's a video post that makes its way here.

In the comments I see someone has courteously sent Tammy a hyperlink to one of the forums.

She continues, "There's no point to anything. My boyfriend said he hates me. He called me fat."

Tammybird begins to sob.

> IM me we'll talk, get you help!!!!
>
> Your beautiful, you dont want to die!!
>
> UR hot! ♥ ♥
>
> You have pills?

Pills r so fucking lame. Hanging. Its the only way. IM me I'll walk you thru it.

At ViewNow we can access the IP address of everyone who posts. I can send Tammybird's to the cops and they can get a warrant so that the poster's internet providers will hand over her physical address—as long as she's not using a proxy, which she isn't. A welfare check ensues. This can happen fast, especially in a case of looming suicide. The authorities could be at her door within the hour.

But now I have a dilemma. If I push the button to save her, my name appears on the reports the police will read. And I absolutely don't want this to happen.

On the other hand, if Tammy takes the advice of some of the helpful commentators and does the deed and it's discovered that I reviewed the post, questions will arise as to why I didn't get her help.

The police again.

So?

Out of self-interest, I decide I'll send it to our law-enforcement liaison department.

But I'm in no hurry. I tap the keys to unearth her ISP slowly, thinking, if I'm lucky they won't get to her in time.

And, if I'm *particularly* lucky, she might even kill herself on the livestream.

66

The tactical team approached the door.

Quiet. Utterly quiet.

Sachs, in the lead, knew they were pros. Any metal that could clink had been wrapped in strips of cloth or electrical tape. All phones and radios were on mute.

The entire six-person team, four men, two women, plus Sachs, were even breathing silently. That's easy—even if it appears comical—you just open your mouth wide.

The op had all come together quickly.

"Rhyme, I've got the results of that carpet sample in Kitt's apartment. You're going to want to see this."

He'd looked over her discovery and he, Sachs and Spencer began discussing the totality of the evidence from the scenes.

Rhyme had said, "That's our answer. Call Lon and get an ESU tac team together. Hurry. We're out of time."

And now here they were.

They paused and listened at the door. She nodded to an S&S

officer, Search and Surveillance. The man tried to find a gap between the door and the threshold, but there wasn't enough space through which to fish a fiber optic camera stalk. He shook his head.

Nodding, Sachs stepped close and examined the door. She thought of the subtle touch of the Locksmith. The fine tools, the delicate manipulation of the intricate mechanism inside. Sachs put an electronic stethoscope against the door and listened.

Good enough for her.

She stepped back and whispered, "Breaching team. Ready?"

You never shoot the lock out of a door, as actors do on TV and in the movies.

Amelia Sachs knew that doing so was useless at best, disastrous at worst, given that bullets ricochet or fragment on deadbolts and lock surfaces, which are, after all, made to withstand the impact of blows, including gunshots. That shrapnel will put your eye clean out.

But hinges . . . that's another matter. When taking out a door, a breaching team will use special rounds, usually fired from a twelve-gauge shotgun. The slugs are made from sintered material—metal powder suspended in wax. This will blow the hinges out, tout de suite. No one has a better sense of humor than cops and within the New York City Emergency Service Unit, they were known as "Avon's Calling" rounds, a reference to a door-to-door makeup sales business that Sachs had heard about from her mother.

She whispered to the lead breacher, "Go."

He placed the muzzle against the bottom hinge and pulled the trigger. Sachs had turned away but felt the muzzle blast on the parts of her back that were above and below the bulletproof plate she wore. The sound was astonishingly loud in the closed area of the hallway. A second shot on the top hinge and then the coup de grace was the battering ram in the middle. The door collapsed inward and landed with what was probably a loud crash—who could tell after the stunning report of the scattergun?

Sachs, in the lead, and the other ESU officers streamed inside, dispersing to avoid the bottleneck of the door, known as the "death funnel." They cried, "Police on a warrant! Police! Show yourself!"

There was no one in the massive open living area of Averell Whittaker's lofty apartment, other than the body of the security guard, Alicia Roberts, whose death was not unanticipated, since she hadn't picked up the calls from her boss, Lyle Spencer, to warn her that she might be in danger.

One ESU officer went to the body. "She's gone."

Sachs then noted a parlor door kicked open. She and two other officers approached.

"Police! Show yourselves! Come out, hands above your head."

A voice behind her. "Security guard's weapon is missing."

Sachs called, "I want that gun on the floor now. Throw it so I can see it."

"I'll kill Averell!" It was Joanna's voice. "Let us go."

Sachs said to the S&S officer beside her, "Video in."

He unhitched the small camera once more and turned it on, then extended the flexible lens cable. He and Sachs approached the doorway, she covering him. He fed the lens in and, on the screen, Sachs saw Joanna Whittaker, her face stained with blood, standing behind her uncle, holding a pistol toward the door. Her fiancé, Martin Kemp, gripped a knife uncertainly as he stood over a young man—Kitt Whittaker, she recognized—who was strapped in a wheelchair.

"Drop the weapon!"

"Back off! You arrest me and there'll be trouble! You'll regret it!"

What on earth did that mean?

Sachs turned to the woman ESU officer who'd checked on the

body of the security guard. "Flash-bang. I want this over with. We're not negotiating."

"Okay, Detective." She drew from her belt a stun grenade, which looked very much like a canister of pepper spray. The body of the device was cardboard and contained a powerful explosive charge. To use one, you held down the lever on the side—the "spoon"—and pulled the pin. Then you tossed it into the desired location. In three and a half seconds it exploded, with a huge flash and a report that was around 140 decibels. Being next to one when it detonated was an extremely unpleasant experience.

Joanna said, "I'm not kidding. I have friends you don't know about. Back out now!"

Sachs nodded to another officer. "You too. Flash-bang."

The man hesitated. "A space like that, you'll only need one."

Joanna was ranting, "It'll be the biggest mistake of your life."

Sachs smiled. "Let's go with two. Pull the pins."

67

Joanna Whittaker joined Kemp on her belly.

Two officers approached and cuffed them both, rolling them over and muscling them into a sitting position.

Her face wasn't scared, or angry, or frustrated. It was completely emotionless, though would occasionally reveal pain. Apparently Averell Whittaker had delivered quite the blow. Her cheek looked to be broken.

Martin Kemp was whimpering, leaving no doubt who wore the pants in this criminal household, Sachs reflected, even if the observation was a throwback, and possibly politically incorrect.

Kitt Whittaker had been drugged. Sachs helped him onto a couch, while other officers cleared the apartment. She and Rhyme were sure that Joanna and Kemp were the only perps involved in the scheme but protocol insisted that every inch of a crime scene be rendered safe. She got the word that it was clear, and she radioed for the medics.

Soon the EMTs were in the room. Sachs performed triage, and

they tended to Kitt first, determining that he did not have a life-threatening amount of opiates in his system. That would have come later, after they'd staged the scene where he killed his father and then himself.

The medicos then tended to Joanna and her fiancé—the shattered face and, in his case, hand.

"You all right?" Sachs asked Averell Whittaker, who looked at her absently and nodded. He turned his attention back to his son and asked a medical tech, "You're sure my son'll be all right?" He was shouting, an aftereffect of the bang part of the grenades.

"Yessir. They just gave him enough to sedate him. He'll be fine."

"Kitt," Whittaker said and rested a hand on the young man's arm. His son turned his way groggily and gave no reaction.

Kemp said, "Look, Officer, please . . ."

Joanna glanced at her sniveling fiancé. "You shut the hell up. If you say one word . . ."

So witness intimidation would be another charge. Though that was the least of the woman's legal concerns.

A shadow in the doorway. And two other men entered the room, Lincoln Rhyme and Lyle Spencer.

Spencer saw the body of the woman personal protection guard. His face fell and he stepped to her, knelt down, taking her hand. He shook his head and stood. Spencer's angry eyes turned toward Joanna. Maybe Alicia and Spencer had been friends, or more, in addition to colleagues. He balled up his fist and started toward the Whittaker niece, who cowered away.

Sachs intercepted him. And touched his arm. "No," she said softly. "We'll get it done the right way."

He exhaled slowly and nodded.

Joanna cut an icy gaze toward Rhyme and then Sachs and asked, "How? How on earth?"

———————

"*Rhyme, I've got the results of that carpet sample in Kitt's apartment. You're going to want to see this.*"

He and Spencer look Sachs's way. She says, "Electrolytes: sodium, potassium, calcium, magnesium, bicarbonate, and phosphates, immunoglobulins, proteins, enzymes, mucins and nitrogenous products. It's saliva."

"*Whose? Kitt's?*"

Mel Cooper is operating the fast DNA analyzer. He holds up a hand. They have a sample of Kitt's DNA from his tooth- and hairbrushes, which she collected at his apartment.

"*Come on, come on.*" *Rhyme is impatient, though Cooper cannot will the equipment to speed up.*

Finally: "It's his."

Sachs says, "And one more thing. Blood. Very small trace in Kitt's apartment. Near the doorway. The stain you spotted, Rhyme."

Rhyme's pulse increases; he feels it in his temple. They're onto something here.

Another DNA test. The blood was Kitt's as well.

Spencer says, "Not enough quantity to suggest a lethal wound. Even a twenty-two'll leave more than that tiny stain."

Rhyme thinks for a minute. "Run a sample through the HA."

Mel Cooper turned on the hematology analyzer, a compact instrument the size of a bloated laptop. He runs the test and reads the results. "Mostly normal, but there're some unusual substances present, things you don't usually see in a normal blood analysis: creatine kinase, lactate dehydrogenase and myoglobin."

Rhyme says, "Kitt was hit with a stun gun. Those are muscle proteins released in cases of rhabdomyolysis. Skeletal muscle damage. That's how they subdued him. He fell and must've hit his head. The blood."

Spencer says, "Or maybe he bit his lip or his hand or arm to leave some trace."

Rhyme is nodding. "Yes, it's a possibility."

Sachs calls, "But who's 'they'?"

"Ah, the big question. Yes, yes, let's work with the premise that Kitt's being set up. He was kidnapped and the evidence was planted in his closet and file cabinets. By whom?" Rhyme then says slowly in a musing tone, staring at the whiteboard, "Let's look at the big picture. What's unexplained so far? Seawater, discovered only in Kitt's apartment. What does that tell us?"

No one answers, but it's a rhetorical inquiry anyway.

"Let's keep going. Another mystery ingredient. Fertilizer. Found in the Sandleman and in the Bechtel Buildings—when you found the candy wrapper, Sachs. No, no, no . . ." Rhyme is grimacing. "I don't think the Locksmith returned to the Bechtel Building at all. I think somebody else, the ultimate unsub here, returned to the building and dropped the wrapper on purpose. They kidnapped Kitt and planted the candy, the panties and other evidence in his apartment. But they inadvertently left things leading back to them. Fertilizer and seawater."

"They?" Sachs repeats.

Rhyme says, "If it's not Kitt, then—"

Spencer completes his thought, "—why would the Locksmith be leaving a coded newspaper page about Mary Whittaker's death?"

"Which has the effect of pointing the finger at Kitt," Sachs says. "And which was suggested by Joanna Whittaker."

Rhyme says, "Who has an oceangoing yacht and a greenhouse." He was recalling the articles he'd read online about the family. "And the wood polish we found; it's used on vessels as well as cars."

Spencer nods. "She raises orchids. I've been in her apartment in Battery Park City."

"And," Sachs says, "she'd have access to a whole library of past issues of the Daily Herald. She could get as many page threes of the February seventeenth issue as she wanted."

Spencer mutters, "She's going to kill Mr. Whittaker and Kitt. She'll inherit the company. Shit." He dials a number and listens. "Mr. Whittaker's not answering." He tries another call. After a moment his face grows stricken. "Alicia's not either."

Rhyme says, "That's our answer. Call Lon and get an ESU tac team together. Hurry. We're out of time."

Now, in Averell Whittaker's soaring apartment, Lincoln Rhyme responded to Joanna's question—how on earth?—by offering a droll look that said, Figure it out yourself . . . or don't.

Amelia Sachs—the officiating police officer present—now got to work. She walked up to Joanna and Kemp, who were sitting on the floor. The woman glared. "I want a chair."

It was as if Joanna hadn't even spoken. Sachs said, "We need to know the identity of the real Locksmith and where to find him."

"Why would I know that?" She looked aghast.

Sachs said evenly, "Because you hired him." She glanced at the knives stolen from the apartments of Annabelle Talese and Carrie Noelle, one of which was bloody; a plastic bag was around the handle. "And we can prove it. The knives won't have your prints on them but the bag will."

Silence.

"Tell us. And we can work something out with the DA."

Joanna Whittaker offered a sly smile. "I think it's time for the lawyer."

68

H ow's your arm?" Kitt asked his father.

Averell Whittaker looked at the limb. The fall, from Joanna's shove, hadn't done more than bruise the tissue. But it had taken the wind out of him, and the discoloration was impressive.

"Not bad," he said to his son. "And you're feeling . . . ?"

"Groggy. Still the headache. In my apartment Jo or Martin Tased me." He touched a scab on his head. "I fell. Then they injected me with something." His voice was a whisper. "My cousin. My own cousin."

They were in Whittaker's Sag Harbor getaway, a six-bedroom Tudor on Long Island Sound. The property was in the name of a trust. The press didn't know about it. The vultures were still staking out the high-rise on Park Avenue.

This house echoed with memories. He and Mary had built the place—the planning and construction occupied one of the happiest few years in their lives. The couple and Kitt had spent many a weekend here. Along with his brother, Lawrence, and dear Betty.

Joanna too.

Whittaker was staring out the window at the sparkles on the waves. Long Island Sound was a sloppy body of water, at least near the North Shore. Dun-colored and rocky and home to an infestation of horseshoe crabs, perhaps the most space-alien sea creature that ever existed.

"What was it like? Where they kept you?"

"It was their boat. Your old yacht. The one you gave Uncle Lawrence." He shrugged, suggesting what he'd endured wasn't that bad. But it would have been. Whittaker knew the conditions would have been nearly unbearable. He would have been chained or somehow restrained. And there'd been the cloud of impending death hanging over him.

The hopelessness he would have felt.

And betrayal.

Kitt and Joanna had never been particularly close—she hewed to her uncle's and father's society life, while he had no interest. But, my God, they'd shared dozens of holiday dinners. Spent family vacation time in Curaçao, Saint Martin, Guadalupe, Cap d'Antibes.

"Kitt. I made a mistake. A terrible mistake."

His son sipped his beer. His lips were parched, and Whittaker boiled with anger again at what his niece and her spineless fiancé had done.

"Your mother . . ."

He knew that Kitt had not engineered this terrible crime, but that didn't change the fact that Joanna's premise was true: Kitt had disappeared from the family because of that terrible day years ago, March 2, when Whittaker had sat in his office and, after agonizing negotiations, signed the purchase deal to buy the TV station chain and had not been in St. Theresa Hospital.

"Go on."

And he proceeded to confess about the acquisition. Then added, "I've only wanted to apologize and beg you to forgive me."

The young man seemed perplexed. "Because you weren't at Mother's bedside?"

Whittaker nodded and felt his eyes fill with tears.

"You *do* know that she lapsed into unconsciousness a couple of days before she passed. In fact, you were one of the last people to see her awake—that Saturday. You were there all night, holding her hand. The day she died, when I was there, she was asleep. The doctor said she'd never regain consciousness."

"My God, no. I didn't know that."

Kitt offered a pallid laugh. "And to be honest? I wouldn't've wanted you there anyway. What would we have had to talk about? Oh, Father, our lives went in such different directions. I never hated you, resented you. We were just entirely different people."

"I blamed myself. I neglected you. It was my fault you never had a career. I should have given you guidance."

"Never had a career?"

"Joanna said you jumped from job to job. Computers, drones, real estate, videography, oil and gas . . . One thing after another."

Now the laugh was hearty. "But I have a career and I have *you* to thank for it."

Averell Whittaker was frowning.

The handsome young man brushed his long hair from his forehead. "The truth, Father? I didn't respect what you and Uncle Lawrence did. The paper, the TV station? You weren't . . . helping people. I went in a different direction."

"What exactly do you do?"

"I'm CEO of a nonprofit I created. We use drones to look for environmental violations."

"I never heard about it."

"I use a different name. Mother's maiden name."

"What does it do?"

"There're rewards offered by the EPA and local environmental organizations. We create databases of violators and make it public on our servers. I studied all of those things Joanna mentioned, yes. Wasn't dabbling. They're part of the job."

"And it does well?"

"Not great, not by your standards. But we did about fifty million last year."

"My Lord," After a moment Whittaker frowned. "When you went missing, why didn't anyone from the company contact me? They'd know I'm your father."

"I spend most of my time in the field, running the drones. I'm gone for weeks at a time."

Kitt finished the beer and opened another. "Your articles and op-ed pages came down in favor of big oil and gas, anti-environmentalist. I didn't think you'd want to have anything to do with me . . . Hey . . ."

Whittaker had set down his wine and was hugging his son fiercely. After a moment the son reciprocated the embrace.

Kitt asked a question out of the blue: "Will you miss the paper and the TV station when they're gone?"

"Not at all. I can't wait to get the foundation started." He eyed his son closely and told him in detail what it would be doing. The young man seemed to approve.

Then Whittaker offered a coy, hopeful smile.

"What?"

Whittaker asked, "Well, I'm just thinking . . . How'd you like a slot on the board?"

A moment of consideration, then: "I would. I'd like that very much."

"Say, you hungry? Do you want some food? We can stay in. Better not to go out, or even order takeaway. Damn reporters. But Isla keeps the place pretty well stocked."

Whittaker walked into the kitchen and his son followed.

The father looked into the Sub-Zero, while the son watched, apparently amused, as if Whittaker had never gazed into a refrigerator before. Which was not far off the mark. "Omelette. It's really the only thing I can cook."

"That sounds good to me."

Whittaker opened a good Rhône, a Châteauneuf-du-Pape, House of the Pope, and poured two glasses of the spicy wine.

He began cracking eggs into a bowl and then coaxing out the few bits of shell that had gotten in. It was a tricky job. Kitt made toast, buttered the slices with a rasp of blade and put them on a serving plate.

Soon the shell-free eggs sizzled and spattered in the skillet, and Averell Whittaker's son walked to the buffet in the dining room to hunt for placemats and silverware for the table.

69

Defensive wounds.

Or, more accurately, the *lack* of defensive wounds.

There were only three knife slashes in the body of Alekos Gregorios—the man slashed to death in the backyard of his large Queens home.

Rhyme had earlier noted the wounds but, as he'd been asked only to analyze some trace evidence, hadn't paid much attention to them. Then Richard Beaufort had inadvertently ignited Rhyme's interest when he flashed his picture of the brag board.

The Locksmith was still at large, but once a mystery arose in an investigation, even one that was technically closed, Lincoln Rhyme could not let it go. He now gazed up at the whiteboard devoted to the case and considered the question.

Yes, one reason for the lack of defensive cuts *could* be that the killer had surprised him, as Rhyme had earlier speculated. But, after more thought, he asked himself: How could a stumbling, incoherent homeless man like Xavier get close enough to murder someone with three strokes of a knife and the victim not hold his hands up, fighting to grab the blade?

It was possible, certainly, but a more likely explanation was that Gregorios knew the killer, who was physically close to him, probably because they were having a conversation. Then, in a flash, out came the knife and the slaughter began.

Known to the victim.

Could be a friend, neighbor . . . or a family member.

Well, they had the name of one such person who'd seen the victim that day. His son. They'd had dinner at about six—at which time father had reported to son about the encounter with the homeless man.

Or, more accurately, the son had *told* the police that's what his father had said.

What if the man's son, whose first name was Yannis, had been lying, setting up the homeless man?

Had the son returned later, met his father in the garden and stabbed him? Then taken his wallet and dabbed his slacks with Miracle Sav medicine, a unique and therefore damning bit of evidence? And then planted the evidence in the homeless shelter, turning Michael Xavier into a fall guy for the killing?

Rhyme thought for a moment. "Mel?"

The detective glanced his way from the sterile portion of the lab.

"I need you to do something. It's a little . . . odd."

"Odder than conducting a postmortem on a fly?"

"Only a bit."

"Detective Tye Kelly?"

"That's right."

"Hey, this's Detective Mel Cooper. I'm out of the Queens lab."

"Okay."

"I worked with Lincoln Rhyme."

"What's the story about that, somebody at OnePP sidelining him? That sucks."

"Sure does. He did some work on the Gregarios case, right?"

"Yeah, he helped us close it."

"About that. I was looking over the file, just happened to see it, and I was having some doubts."

Kelly chuckled. "You're not sure about something Lincoln Rhyme concluded about a case? You really want to go there?"

They were on speaker and Cooper and Rhyme shared a glance. Cooper, it seemed, was struggling to keep a straight face.

"Hear me out." He recited what Rhyme had told him about the lack of defensive wounds and the theory that the son had set up the homeless man.

"But we checked out Yannis—that's the Greek version of John, by the way. I never knew that. Got him on security video nearby, getting out of his car around five thirty, walking toward his father's house, then walking back around seven and leaving."

Rhyme was thinking. He scrawled a note and pushed it in front of Cooper, who read and nodded.

"Detective," he said, "where did he park?"

A pause. Computer keys typed. "It was the Arbor Vale Convenience Mall, about a block away from his dad's house."

"His father had a driveway, didn't he?" Cooper was catching on. Rhyme hadn't needed to prompt.

"Yeah, he did, but the son said he wanted to stop into a grocery store and pick up something for dinner."

"Did he?"

"Yeah."

Rhyme wrote and Cooper delivered the lines.

"Seems a little odd he just left the car there and walked."

"I guess, maybe. One-way streets. Probably faster to hoof it."

Cooper read another of Rhyme's notes.

Kelly asked, "You there, Detective?"

"Yes. But you could also argue that he left it there to leave some proof of when he arrived and when he left. The video, you know."

"Give you that."

Another note.

"You have the whole night's video from the mall?"

"Yeah, we were looking for a homeless guy around the time of the killing, after what the son told us. But we didn't see anyone in the mall tape."

Rhyme jotted.

"Where was the camera?" Cooper asked.

"Across the street, pointed at the stores."

"Can you call it up?"

"Where's this going?"

Cooper improvised. "Just a few loose ends."

"All right." Kelly typed.

Rhyme wrote out his theory. Cooper shook his head and laughed.

"What's that?" Kelly asked.

"Buddy here just showed me a present he got his girlfriend." A chuckle. "Only I don't know whether it's more for her or for him."

"One of *those* presents, yeah. All right, I've got the video."

"Run it from a half hour before the killing to a half hour after. Scrub it. But look at what's in front of the camera. Look at what's reflected back toward it, in the windows of the vehicles driving past."

"Reflected," Kelly said absently. "Okay, I'm not seeing much, just the street at the base of the pole the security camera's mounted— Christ."

Again, the two men in Rhyme's town house glanced each other's way.

Cooper said, "Is it Yannis's car pulling up, and him getting out?"

"It fucking well is. I can see him in some bus window's reflections. Eight forty-eight. About ten minutes before his father died."

Cooper gave him Rhyme's explanation. "Yannis couldn't park in his father's driveway when he came back to kill him. Neighbors would see. He knew he could park on the street near the mall but wanted to be out of sight of the camera. The only place he could do that was directly underneath it.

"Later the son got into the shelter and planted the evidence implicating Xavier. I checked security and it's basically nonexistent. Anybody could walk in and out."

It had been Ron Pulaski who'd determined this.

"Damn. It's a whole new case. My partner and me'll jump on it . . ." There was some typing. "Okay, just got Yannis's DMV picture. We'll do some canvassing, check into his history with his father."

Cooper read what would be the final note. "You want to send me the full file, I'll take a look at the rest of the evidence. See if I can help shore up anything."

"Hell, yes." They heard some more typing. "Okay, it's on its way. Hey, I can't thank you enough. Clearing a case with the wrong suspect's worse than not clearing it at all." His voice drew conspiratorial. "Listen, Detective, I don't know how this thing with Lincoln Rhyme's going to fall out, but don't worry, I won't say a word you're the one second-guessing him."

"Kind of you, Detective Kelly. He can be pretty difficult."

"That's what I hear."

70

Something about his face.

Weaselly.

In his native language, he thought: *E keqe.*

Evil.

Trouble.

The doorman was watching the tall redhead stride from the lobby of Whittaker Tower—or the "Stronghold," which was how all the doormen around here thought of it. She walked through the police barricade set up to keep reporters back, though there weren't as many as on a typical day. The word had spread that Mr. Whittaker and his son had left town.

The sixty-five-year-old wore a long gray coat and matching hat. The epaulettes were a little too much, like a faded senior military commander on trial in the world court, but they'd come with the uniform, so there they were.

The Whittaker doorman, Frank, whom he saw about a hundred times a day, wore blue. Frank had joked about the Civil War. It took a minute but he'd gotten it. Their uniforms, blue and gray. He was from Kosovo, and he knew there was only one civil conflict of note: the one in which your family was killed.

The redhead, who'd just departed the Whittaker building, was on her phone as she walked north on Park Avenue, oblivious to the world.

Oblivious to the weaselly man, *e keqe*, who followed her.

The doorman thought "trouble" because of the way the weasel had looked around, and, head down, slipped from the shadows where, it seemed, he'd been waiting for her.

He was slim, in a dark jacket and jeans, a backpack slung over his shoulder.

Coincidence?

Maybe, maybe not. When she crossed the street at a light, so did he, though not at the intersection. He dodged through traffic and wove between plants in the divider between the north and south lanes.

When Redhead got to the other side of the street, she kept going north.

Weasel Man did too. The doorman noticed that his hand was in his pocket.

Was she in danger?

When she turned east on 82nd, so did he.

Maybe he should call 911.

And tell them what?

That a man in dark clothing was following a woman in dark clothing on the Upper East Side of New York? He could tell the dispatcher about the man's face. It too was dark. No, not a Black person. I mean, weaselly and evil.

The dispatcher would pause and ask if he could be more specific.

Ach, probably it was nothing, not worth a call, all that hassle.

Should he go and warn her himself? At this point it would mean a jog, and the ninety-kilo doorman certainly was not in the mood for that, not at this age, not with these bones.

Besides, he might lose his job if he did the good deed.

Fuck it.

Anyway, now he had to hold the door open for Mrs. Jankowski, who—even though her late husband owned a string of dental practices—tipped him five lousy dollars every Christmas.

The old *kurvë* . . .

Amelia Sachs continued along 82nd Street, cell pressed against her ear, noting how the buildings grew more modest with every block.

More deserted regarding passersby too.

Her nemesis—arthritis—had largely improved in recent years, but her mission now required her to walk briskly and she was feeling the pain in her left limb.

"No," she was saying into the phone. "They're not sure about the arraignment."

At the corner of York Avenue and 82nd, she turned north and continued walking, though somewhat more slowly.

She approached a warehouse she knew. It was here, last year, she'd nailed a human trafficker and rescued three young women he'd smuggled into the country from El Salvador for a sex ring.

She looked the place over. It was much the same, though in better shape than then. Apparently it had been bought or rented by a coffee bean supply company. The scent on the air told her this without her seeing any product.

The loading dock was recessed and as she passed, she turned inside quickly, dropped the phone into her jacket and lifted her switchblade knife from her right hip pocket. Flicked it open and, counting to three, stepped out fast, grabbing the man who had been following her from Whittaker Tower.

Sheldon Gibbons, the reporter, gasped.

She held the knife up and spun him around.

"What the hell?"

"Quiet!"

She put the knife away, ratcheted on cuffs and turned him back to face her.

Eyeing him closely, she said, "I'm curious. Did *you* decide to call yourself the Locksmith? Or was that Joanna Whittaker's idea?"

71

esus. I don't know what you're talking about."

Amelia Sachs frisked Gibbons and found only wallet, phone, keys and digital recorder.

She was explaining: "Something didn't seem quite right. You just happened to know I was a cop at Whittaker's building. And you just happened to be at Kitt's?"

"I do my research. I know all the cops that're media fodder. I don't mean that in a bad way. The press like you. Former model turns detective! Good material. Inspiring for the young girls out there." The words came rat-a-tat. "And at Kitt's? I have a police scanner. I heard the call."

This made some sense but she said, "I called Frontpage Media, the publisher of *InsideLook*. You don't work there. The number on your business card goes to a burner. They'd never heard of you."

"It's helpful to have a publication's label. I go undercover for my stories. Just like cops do. You're accusing me of being the Locksmith and you didn't even check my alibi."

"That'll be on the agenda."

"All right. The truth?"

Sachs wondered if her face tightened into a sardonic expression. Never heard *that* before.

"I was following you because I want to interview Averell Whittaker and his son. They're in hiding. Nobody at the company'll talk to me. The press department's shut me out. I thought you were going to see them. I'm writing an exposé about Joanna. She used to be the wicked witch of the media world when she worked for her father. Bullying employees, sources, playing politicians against each other."

Sachs kept an eye on his arms. If he were the Locksmith, this would be an easy escape. Distract her, slip the cuffs and swing, or turn and run, deciding to risk the chance of a Taser.

"And I've talked to employees at the charity she runs. She's the same way there—a Nazi. And how's this? One of the accounting people thinks she's cooking the books. Using contributions to fund some of her projects on the side. Probably that Verum thing she does."

"Give me a publisher's name."

"This is top secret. I'm only telling you be—"

"Publisher. Or jail."

"First Amendment."

Sachs said, "Publisher or jail."

The disgusted look was memorable. He then said, "Allen-Drews Publishing."

"Editor?"

Sighing, he gave the name.

"Number too."

She called and the man answered. She identified herself. "Sheldon Gibbons was at a crime scene and I'd like to confirm that he's under contract to publish a book with you about Joanna Whittaker."

"Well, that's right. Is something wrong?" the editor asked.

"No, I just needed to confirm that he had a valid reason to be at the scene."

"If it had to do with Joanna Whittaker, then yes."

"Thank you."

They disconnected.

"So, cuffs off?"

"Writing a book doesn't make you not-the-Locksmith. Give me an alibi for one of the intrusions." She gave him the dates and times of the Talese and the Noelle break-ins.

"Home, I'm sure. You can call my wife. We just had twins and I'm up with them a lot at night. And there's a doorman."

Sachs got the number and called. The conversation she had with the woman was pretty much what she'd expected. The wife confirmed his presence, with the duet of crying in the background lending credence. Sachs did most of the talking, largely reassuring the woman that her husband was not in any trouble or danger.

She disconnected. "Turn around."

Freed, he rubbed his wrists as she re-holstered the chrome cuffs and looked around. He smiled coyly. "So I'm guessing this isn't *too* far from Averell Whittaker's place, where he's hiding."

Sachs scoffed, flagging that his effort was a waste of time. "I only came this way, to the warehouse, so we could have this little chat."

"Can I interview you for my book?"

"No."

"Do you ever say, 'Yes'? Or, 'I'd be happy to help you out'?"

"Neither."

"Might raise your profile."

Considering that profile upping was the last thing she wanted to do—in light of the edict that Lincoln Rhyme was forbidden from investigating cases—she hit him with another negative.

"On deep background. No names. Can you tell me what Whittaker said about his niece trying to kill him?"

"Have a good day, Gibbons."

As he started away, a thought occurred. She said, "Wait."

He turned, his face wary, as if expecting to see the blade again.

"Have you been tailing Joanna and Martin Kemp?"

"That's right. Checking out their haunts, stores they go to, banks, lawyers, friends."

"In the past week, did either of them go to what looked like a warehouse or storeroom or workshop?"

"Actually, yeah."

"Where?"

"Lower East Side. One of the old tenement neighborhoods."

There wasn't much left of the ramshackle Manhattan. Hell's Kitchen in West Midtown was gone. Harlem was redeveloped. The railyards were now all underground, the surrounding residential and industrial clutter bulldozed away and the 'hoods turned into glitz. But there were still pockets of tattered buildings—one and two stories—south and east, where immigrants had settled in the late nineteenth and early twentieth centuries. Interesting, she reflected, this was one neighborhood that Kemp had *not* mentioned when asked about places Kitt was thinking of for a workshop.

"Who was there?"

"I didn't see. Joanna picked up a bag and dropped something off. I just saw the hand and then the door closed."

If it was the Locksmith's workshop, Joanna was probably picking up Annabelle's or Carrie's underwear and the knives to implicate Kitt.

"You have an address?"

Now he was coy. It was a what-can-you-do-for-*me* look. "If I had an exclusive or access to records, something . . ."

"Okay, I've got a good story for you, Gibbons."

"Yeah?" His eyes were eager.

"I'll even give you the headline: 'Reporter Does the Right Thing.'"

"In this business, you always have to give it a try." He shrugged. "Argyle Street, Lower East Side. I don't know the number but the building had a name. Something about baking supplies."

Well, that didn't end well.

I'm in my workshop in the Sebastiano building, I've called up a TV station on my computer. It's one of the traditional stations, not WMG, Whittaker's outlet. I suspect I wouldn't get an accurate account of the arrest of Joanna and her fiancé for attempting to murder her family members on *that* channel.

I'm packing up, suitcases, boxes. I won't be able to stay here much longer. Joanna will eventually sell me out in exchange for a reduced sentence. But I have a little time; she'll be a hard negotiator.

Glancing occasionally at the computer, I note that some of the unanswered questions that arose in apartment 2019 are now being explained: Joanna had planned the murders to gain control of the Whittaker Media empire. And the man she was setting up to be the Locksmith was none other than her own cousin, Kitteridge Whittaker, a handsome young man, with the face of a crusading politician.

Since he isn't in fact the perpetrator, that means, the anchor-woman says in anchor-speak, that the real Locksmith is still at large.

Which hardly needs to be said, but then I don't know the average IQ of the audience.

Yet the Shakespearean soap opera of the Whittaker family is of less interest to the viewing audience than the fact that Joanna is Verum.

This is taking the bulk of airtime.

There have already been incidents. Her supporters aren't happy she's been arrested. Arson, broken windows, graffiti.

I see a sign: *Free Verum now!*

One talking head speculates that she wanted control of her uncle's company because she hoped to use Whittaker's media outlets as a bullhorn in spreading her messages.

Another one offers that she grew disgusted by her capitalist upbringing and, like a true revolutionary, wanted to undermine the System, *"with a capital 'S.'"*

I actually laugh out loud. They have no idea that she whipped up Verum simply for the ego and the money.

A woman in an ugly knit hat and stained coat chants: *"Free her now! Free her now! We've said our prayers and we're prepared!"*

If I were truly God, and could moderate the content of humankind, I would delete this crone with a single keystroke.

The newscast ends with the comment that the police do not yet have any leads as to the identity of the Locksmith.

Back to work. Sadly I'm not going to get the full half million, but that's all right. The 200K plus my substantial savings and my inheritance is enough for a fresh start. A nice workshop/apartment—decked out with that new chair I've been looking forward to. We content moderators know a lot about the dark web. I can create a new identity for myself in a week.

And get down to doing what I was born to do.

72

The setup was this:

One sniper and her spotter, across the street from the Locksmith's suspected workshop, the old Sebastiano Bakery Supply building.

One surveillance team in a battered florist delivery van with eyes and ears on the place.

One four-person dynamic entry team south, one north, each a half block from the front door. They were inside, respectively, a plumbing repair truck and an unmarked but highly battered white van, not unlike the one that played a two-ton prop in Sachs's dramatic film debut earlier, directed by undercover cop Aaron Douglass.

And out of sight, ambulances and a squadron of uniforms. A fire truck too, given the Locksmith's attempt at destroying the evidence in the Sandleman Building.

Sachs spoke into her cell phone. "We're on location, Rhyme."

"Any sign of him?"

"Nothing. Windows're shuttered. Only one functioning door in and out, the front. The delivery entrance, in the back. It's been bolted shut. There'll be a small cellar with a coal chute. That door's been sealed too." She was looking over a photo from the Department of Buildings that showed the layout of the place. New York City records were very much as old as New York City. "Thinking if he spots us he could rabbit through adjoining basements, but he'd have to break through the walls—no adjoining doors. They're brick and sandstone. Anyway, we have eyes on the neighboring structures too."

Rhyme would normally have been on the radio, the frequency that was used for operations like this. But, of course, he was in NYPD purgatory. He'd have to find out about the operation after it was completed.

"You going in?"

"Yep. The north team."

He would know that that crew was going in first, and that Sachs, among the four, would be in the lead.

He wouldn't ask if she didn't want to leave the cowboy stuff to ESU, younger and most with military training. It would be like asking Rhyme if he was sure he wanted to spend another hour or two or three analyzing a smidgeon of trace that, somehow, might hold the key to identifying a perp.

"K. Let me know."

They disconnected.

Then Sachs, in helmet and full body armor, was out of the van, and with the three members of her team was moving low along the sidewalk to the front door of the baking supply company. The south team approached too and would go through the door after the north.

Using hand signals only, Sachs directed the fourth member of her team—the breacher—to the door, while the others covered him.

Unlike at the Whittaker apartment, they would here be using full-on C4 charges, on the hinges and on the three locks. They were formidable and new, certainly not the make and model that deterred burglars one hundred years ago.

The breacher approached silently and placed the sticky-backed charges beside each hinge and a larger one on the locks, then he backed away ten feet and hefted a battering ram in case the explosions did not completely knock down the door. Sachs nodded to the woman beside her—*Sanchez* stenciled on her tac vest—and they both front slung their Heckler & Koch MP5 assault rifles and pulled flash-bangs from their belts.

Speaking softly—the mikes were in low-volume-pickup mode—Sachs said, "Sniper?" She looked across the street and up, noting that the woman and her spotter were well hidden and the barrel of the Remington 700P .308 was not visible.

"In position, covering. No sign of movement."

"Roger. South team?"

They were only thirty feet away and rather than respond verbally, that team leader lifted a thumb.

Sachs felt her heart thud and she was filled with exhilaration. Two things brought her unlimited joy: driving on the edge, engine wailing, and the instant before a dynamic entry.

She gave the hand signal to all the troops to hunker down for the bang, then held up three fingers of her left hand. She tucked them away one by one. As the last curled into a fist, the breacher whispered, "Fire in the hole," and sent the signal to the plastic charges. Five simultaneous explosions shook the ground beneath them, as the door splintered and crashed inside. No ram would be necessary.

First Sachs, then Sanchez pulled the grenade pins and pitched them inside.

A few seconds later, when they detonated, Sachs and her trio, followed by the south team charged forward, muzzles swiveling up and down out of one another's way, as the tactical halogens affixed beneath the machine guns' muzzles swept the dim place. "Police, police, police!"

The officers fanned out in the large room, which appeared unoccupied.

There were some storage areas and a bathroom. Officers cleared them fast.

She looked around. There was no doubt it was the Locksmith's workshop. There had to be a hundred locks on the wall. Machinery too, and the key-making machine that she and Rhyme speculated he had. Books and papers. No computers, phones or tablets were visible, but they might be in drawers—or, she thought angrily, with him in a different location.

An apartment elsewhere, probably. There was a bed and a small kitchen but this didn't seem a full-time residence.

"Breach successful," she called into the radio. "Negative on suspects, main floor. Breaching cellar."

In the floor was a trapdoor. As she'd thought before, it would be an unlikely escape route for him, but maybe he had found one of the old tunnels that latticed this part of town, to move goods underground from one company to another. None were shown on the city maps that she'd examined but they often weren't.

The north team walked to the trapdoor. Sachs sighed. She hated clearing cellars.

"Away from the door. In case he rigged it."

The officers stepped back. Sachs gripped the rope used to lift the door and, moving as far away as she could, yanked the heavy, three-foot square of wood up.

No explosions, no gunshots.

She and Sanchez stepped forward, staring down into the darkness, illuminated by their tactical halogens. She saw only disintegrating concrete and brick. "Police! If anyone's down there, show yourself."

Nothing appeared but leisurely dust motes.

"Camera."

An ESU officer named Brill pulled from his belt the same model of camera that had been used in Whittaker's apartment. He fed the lens through the trapdoor opening and clicked the unit to night vision. A three-hundred-and-sixty-degree scan showed trash bags and boxes, stacks of wood, a few pieces of rusting machinery whose purpose she couldn't deduce.

"I count five instances of cover," Brill said. "Boxes and the trash west and north and east corners. And the coal bin in the back."

"Agreed."

Brill substituted his camera for his machine gun.

Pulling another flash-bang off her tactical belt, Sachs said, "I'm going down."

She glanced at Sanchez's belt. The woman front slung then nodded and lifted off a grenade as well.

"Two each, quadrant them."

If the Locksmith were below, he'd be hiding far away from the trapdoor. They'd fling the devices toward the corners of the cellar.

The woman nodded.

"One final chance. Show yourself!" When there was no response, Sachs tossed her first grenade then stepped back as Sanchez threw hers. As they were greeted with two loud cracks, they repeated the choreography, targeting the two remaining corners.

Sachs glanced down and drew her Glock, set her foot on the top rung of the stairs.

She stopped.

Jesus . . .

"Back, back!"

She clambered to the main floor, stumbling onto her side, and scrabbling away as a swirling cloud of flame shot from the opening and into the air, ten feet.

73

The garbage bags and boxes, Sachs realized, must have held more of the Locksmith's favorite substance: gasoline.

Just as she started down, she could smell the sweet aroma.

A trip wire, maybe on the door, would have started a timer, which he'd set to make sure that as many police as possible were inside before it activated a detonator to ignite the gas.

"Out, out!" She then transmitted into her radio, "We have fire. Need FD now."

She helped up Sanchez, who appeared to have broken or twisted her ankle when she fell escaping the explosive flames.

The orange and yellow tornado, accompanied by oily black smoke, roiled higher into the old structure.

Choking, Sachs helped Sanchez to the door, where another officer guided her toward the ambulance.

Sachs turned back, swinging her flashlight back and forth through the gathering flames and smoke, to make sure no one else was left inside. She didn't see anyone but counted heads outside; the entry teams were accounted for and there were no injuries other than Sanchez's.

Stepping back inside she examined the room—to the extent she could, given the smoke. The floor was solid oak and it would take some time to burn through it. She started toward the Locksmith's workbench, hoping for some—for *any*—evidence, thinking of the key trace that Lyle Spencer had snagged before that fire had destroyed the Sandleman Building.

She got halfway to the workstation before she began to feel lightheaded from the fumes.

Forgot about *that* little aspect of fires . . .

The oxygen thing.

She turned and stumbled through the door, sucking in masses of air and spitting out the smoke residue.

The firefighters arrived and began running hoses.

Just as well she left. Maybe the floor was holding, but the flames had risen through the walls and the entire main floor was now engulfed in a raging blaze. How much gas had he used? Gallons upon gallons.

The loss of clues to the man's identity was one consequence of the trap.

But it meant something else too. The Locksmith wouldn't have set it while he was still here. With the arrest of Joanna and Kemp, he'd know it was only a matter of time before they gave up his name in exchange for a plea deal.

Which meant that he'd undoubtedly bundled up his most important possessions, cleaned out his bank account and was presently a hundred miles from the city by now, and still on the run.

He had been as efficient at destroying evidence as he had been at avoiding leaving it at the scenes.

In the parlor of his town house, Lincoln Rhyme was looking at the photos Sachs had taken of the gutted Sebastiano Bakery Supply Company. He noted too that the neighboring structures were destroyed as well.

"Was it gasoline, like at the other site?"

"Yes," Sachs replied. She'd taken a lengthy shower, but the lavender scent from her shampoo was laced with the aroma of smoke from burnt wood.

"The building wasn't stable—the floors—but I could stand in the doorway and get some shots."

"All those are locks?" Rhyme nodded to the screen, noting the scores of scorched devices. "Quite a collection."

"You're thinking of the Watchmaker again."

He smiled briefly. He had been. The "nemesis" owned hundreds of timepieces.

"They're cut from the same cloth. Intelligent. Tacticians. Dark artists, you could say. And both obsessed with mechanical devices. Very retro."

"You're sounding poetic today."

His focus returned to the case. "And the reporter's alibi checks out? What's his name again?"

"Sheldon Gibbons. It does. Neighbors and his wife and—more important—phone records and security cams confirm it. Funny. He looked the sleaziest but turned out to be the most authentic journalist of the bunch. He's writing an exposé on Joanna."

"What's the rookie's status?"

"Finishing up soon."

Pulaski was walking the grid down at Joanna's apartment in Battery Park City and running her yacht too. They had no way of knowing when the Locksmith had been there last—a week or two, possibly. If he'd been there at all. There was little chance that the pair had committed to paper or bytes any identifying information about the Locksmith, and they would have communicated on burner phones. Rhyme had hoped for some trace evidence, at least.

This did not seem likely, though. Pulaski had reported it was obvious that an energetic cleaning crew had descended on the sumptuous living space not long ago. Whether this was for the purpose of eradicating any evidentiary connection between herself and the Locksmith, or simply Joanna's fastidious ways, the end result was the same.

In the sterile portion of the lab Mel Cooper was finishing up with the evidence collected at the apartment of Averell Whittaker, though Rhyme guessed there would be little helpful. The Locksmith himself would never have been to the abode.

And this was the case, Cooper reported.

Rhyme said, "Get on home. But make an appearance at the lab in Queens. Remember we're renegade."

Beaufort, Potter and Mayor Harrison still had a price on Rhyme's head and that of anyone working with him.

Cooper stepped out of the lab, and tossed out his gloves, cap and booties, then dropped the white cotton lab jacket into a wicker bin, for Thom to launder. He stepped into the first-floor bathroom, where he scrubbed up. Then, calling "Bye," he left via the back door.

A man's voice called from the lobby of the town house. "We're ready for you, Detective."

Rhyme called, "Go get him, Sachs."

She gave a brief laugh and walked into the front hallway of the town house.

Rhyme piloted his chair to the parlor doorway.

The film crew—three young men, in jeans and work shirts or T's—had set up a fancy video camera on a substantial tripod. One handed her a lapel mike and she pinned it to the front of her blouse.

A small monitor sat on a portable metal table. On this was being broadcast a press conference down at One Police Plaza. The point man was Commanding Officer Brett Evans—the supporter of Rhyme during the Buryak-acquittal incident. He was talking about the arrest of Joanna Whittaker and her fiancé, Martin Kemp, in the attempted murder of their uncle, as well as for the kidnapping of Kitt, whom they were going to frame for the death.

Sachs said to the lead cameraman, "You going to do the five, four, three thing with your fingers?"

The producer smiled. "You want me to?"

"Sure."

She took a deep breath. Amelia Sachs was a woman who had driven cars well over 150 miles an hour, who had been shot at, and on more than one occasion faced burial alive—her greatest fear—without a runaway pulse. And she'd been a fashion model for some of the biggest clothing and makeup companies in the world—but those assignments didn't involve speaking lines; she simply had to remain still and look sultry. Now, Rhyme thought she was nervous . . . and irritated with herself for feeling that way.

Rhyme smiled at her. She gave a faint laugh and turned back, to stare down the camera.

"Okay, coming up."

On the screen Evans was saying, "And we'd like to enlist the aid of everyone in the tri-state area to find this dangerous criminal. I've asked one of our detectives to give you a description of the Locksmith and some other information. If you see anyone who you think might be him, call nine one one immediately. And do not, I repeat, do not attempt to apprehend him on your own. Now to Detective Amelia Sachs, NYPD."

The monitor went silent, the red light came on, and the finger-counting engineer did his thing.

"Good evening." Sachs didn't have a script but didn't need one.

She stood beside a whiteboard on which Mel Cooper, who had fine handwriting, had penned the bullet-point descriptors of the Lock-smith. She recited them now. His sex, his build, his shoe size, his MO, his obsession with locks, his likely interest in lock-picking conventions, his connection to the Sebastiano Bakery Supply building on Argyle Street. He'd driven an Audi A6 recently, and he'd been known to visit certain locations—the sites of the recent intrusions and the Sandleman Building.

She added, "Now, we're making headway in the NYPD crime scene lab in Queens."

The improvised line was clever.

"We're analyzing some solid evidence we've just discovered. We expect a breakthrough soon, but evidence is only part of the solution in finding this man. We need witnesses. We need *you*." She nodded, and the little red eye on the camera went out.

She exhaled long.

"Good job." The cameraman lifted an eyebrow. "Hey, Detective, you ever get tired of the cop thing you might want to think about acting."

"I'll stick to policing. It's less stressful."

74

'm eating a Spartan meal in a modest coffee shop—a not unpleasant place filled with professionals bent over phones, tablets, computers; gabbing blue-collar workers; lovers who've passed the two- or three-month mark and no longer need fancy-night-out dates.

The lighting is green and cold, but not a soul cares.

A bowl of soup, Texas toast exuding butter. Soda. Caffeine free, of course.

I'm on a device too—my computer, reading the news about the death of my workshop. All gone, many of my beloved tools and locks and keys. I'm surprised they learned about it so soon. I have a feeling that it wasn't Joanna who gave them the address; it would be Lincoln and Amelia who somehow figured it out. (Oh, and sorry, Joanna—looks like you lost that bargaining chip.)

It's a shame that I had to booby-trap it (and a shame too that nobody was killed in the raid). But I had no choice. Time to take my money, my most important things and favorite lock-picking and other tools and flee.

But not quite yet.

I change screens and log on to Tammybird's channel once more.

Ah, the little thing is still with us. She's at her grandmother's house and is thanking everyone for their support. God too, which makes me smile, since He, of course, is me. She's going to get help. The comments continue to scroll.

Yay. Glad ur doing better!! LOL!!!

Happy for U. ♥

Loser.

U inspired me to go talk to somebody. ☺

Take your shirt off!

Who gives a shit, your more boring than unboxing vids.

Goodbye, Tam, I think. And go to yet another site. Now I'm watching a girl doing gymnastic maneuvers, which ten thousand other girls and young women execute daily and post on ViewNow, YouTube and the others.

I think of Dr. Patricia's happy assessment that I'm not beyond repair, since I have a girlfriend. Of course, the way she asked the question was: "Are you seeing anybody?" And I replied that I was. "Her name is Aleksandra."

What she didn't know was that, yes, I was indeed "seeing" somebody, but the verb "viewing" would be more accurate. I spent hours upon hours observing the young Russian woman's ViewNow channel. Aleksandra lives in a small suburb of Moscow and has never been to the United States. I have an intimate relationship with her, though it is one that she does not participate in. She doesn't even know I exist.

I remember that in the comments section of a makeup tutorial someone said that she looked like a gymnast, with her slim figure and bunned hair. She replied, "All Russian girls, when we are in youths, we are ballerinas or we are gymnasts. There are no exceptions to rule."

The girl I'm watching now, doing stretches, is talented, to be sure, though I wonder if she knows that the majority of the 7,435 views are by teenage boys and men, many middle-aged, who don't give a shit about the floor routines or her skill on the balance beam. I suspect she does not.

For myself, I'm not even watching Roonie Soames's contortions. I'm looking past her, confirming what I've learned about the apartment she shares with her mother, Taylor—the woman who surely remains troubled nightly about the question of who Ben Nelson really is and what did he want.

In particular I'm checking to see if she was concerned enough about the disappearance to change her security. I see she was not.

Hargrove Deadbolt and a knob pin and tumbler I could pick with two paper clips.

A simple alarm, no door bar.

Still no weapons—nearly always the rule in Manhattan (though there are the occasional hunters, and you might see Granddad's ancient WWII rifle, just as accurate and deadly as it was seventy-five years ago).

And since the last time I tuned in to the girl's videos, they have not bought a rottweiler or pit bull.

Smooth sailing for tonight's Visit.

Now, the girl is lecturing on hamstrings.

I wonder how devastated she'll be when she finds out that by her thoughtless postings, revealing to the world the vulnerabilities of the apartment, she'll be responsible for her mother's death? Roonie had already spilled to Ben Nelson that she'll be in Wilmington for gymnastics camp. I calculate this means she'll be gone by now. Leaving Taylor home alone tonight.

And if not . . . Oh, well.

I now memorize the layout of the apartment and click the computer to sleep. I finish the last scoops of soup—it's quite hearty and flavorful—and think about the fate of an innocent woman.

But then I correct myself.

Innocent?

Of course not. Oh, she did nothing to *deserve* what will happen, but neither does the gazelle who carelessly strays too far from the herd or doesn't act on the molecules of predator musk because those last few leaves are hard to resist. The idea of justice is singularly human and not a neat fit for every situation where one starts the day alive and ends it dead.

Ah, Taylor . . .

I feel the weight of the brass knife in my back pocket. Picture it hovering over flesh.

Picture it *within* flesh.

The check comes and I pay, and step into the New York City night, filled with the scent of exhaust, garlic from an Italian restaurant, the perfume on the necks of the female halves of couples walking by in date euphoria.

In a few minutes I'm at my car—not Kitt Whittaker's Audi, but my own more modest Toyota. In the backseat, I unzip a canvas bag and extract brown overalls. I tug them on and zip up. I walk around to the trunk and open it.

There's a carton, which looks like something a UPS man would deliver, and I slip into it an RF alarm-disabling device.

Down goes the trunk and, after a scan of the area, I walk several blocks to the subway and board a train. I mount earbuds, as if listening to music, but I'm not. I'm studying fellow passengers. Wondering about where they live, what are their apartments like, what do they and their partners look like and sound like when making dinner or making love.

I'm opening up their lives. Their secrets are mine . . .

We arrive at the station, and I step from the car onto the platform, into the salty, hot-rubber-scented air of the New York City subway.

And then to the surface.

A few blocks from the exit, I walk past the front door I will soon break into, eyeing it casually, looking for threats.

None.

All I see are people jogging, eating snacks, walking arm in arm, trudging, focused and self-protective.

No one notices me.

I'm a parcel deliveryman.

One of thousands in New York.

I'm invisible.

I lean against a substantial tree, pretending to make a phone call, until I decide that the threat to me is minimal.

Clutching the box, I climb to the door. Reaching into the carton, I press the switch on the RF transmitter, sending out its stream of radio waves to confound the alarm on the other side of the wood.

I pat my back pocket to make sure the brass knife is accessible. I then remove the two keys I made earlier.

I've seasoned them with graphite and they work perfectly in the locks.

I open the door, step inside.

A slow, deep breath . . . but the tense five seconds come and go; the radio jammer has worked its magic. The alarm remains silent as I ease the door shut.

There's no click this time. No risk of another 2019.

I take the knife from my pocket and open it, making sure that this act too remains completely silent.

75

Lincoln Rhyme was in an alien space.

His kitchen.

He had never cared much for cooking. He certainly didn't mind a good meal now and then, but to him food was largely fuel. If anything interested him, it was the chemistry of the process. Thom, an expert with whisk and blade and flame, had told him how yolks thicken and yeast inflates and oil and liquid—chemical enemies—become allies when headed for a salad.

He had suggested that his aide might want to write a book about the science of cooking. Thom had replied it was about a hundred years too late.

His phone hummed.

"Sachs."

"I'm downtown," she was saying through the speaker. "The war room. We've had over three hundred calls about my broadcast."

He wouldn't've expected that many.

"Anything useful?"

"Some possible spottings. Mostly people on Argyle Street, near the Sebastiano Company."

"And?"

"Still checking them out. We looked over the security videos around Joanna's apartment but if the Locksmith was ever there, he managed to avoid the cameras. There was a blind spot at the service entrance." She chuckled. "One caller said she knows the Locksmith's an alien. And I don't mean immigration-wise."

"They do come out of the woodwork."

She grew serious. "Have you heard about the Verum situation?"

"No. I'm in the dark, being a member of the Hidden."

"Seems like Joanna—well, her alter ego—has thousands of followers. They're not happy their beloved leader's in jail. Lot of online traffic, threats. Some riots. No kidding."

"This case's been one for the books, Sachs. When'll you be home?"

"Late. Two, three. Sooner if we get a lead and nail him."

"Optimist . . . 'Night."

He disconnected and looked around him.

The kitchen was paneled and windowed like any from a hundred and fifty years ago, but the many devices arrayed and installed here were state of the art—not unlike his parlor, forty feet away.

He noted oddly shaped knives and ladles and spatulas. There was a round wooden cylinder with inch and centimeter markings burnt into it. Ah, a rolling pin.

He was not here, however, to ponder the mysteries of turning flora and fauna into edibles. Whisky was his mission, a quite nice Glenmorangie, the eighteen-year-old version. He lifted down the bottle and wedged it between his legs, then sliced through the paper seal with a short, sharp knife. The cork stopper proved a bit more challenging but in thirty seconds it was out. He poured a glass and he didn't spill a drop.

He set the bottle back on the counter and took a small sip. Heavenly.

Driving via left ring finger, he turned the chair and motored into the hallway. He passed through the doorway into the dining room, a formal place with elaborate crown molding and a table that sat eight. The legs ended in lion paws gripping a ball—a flourish that Rhyme had always found ironic, since his own toes could grip nothing and probably never would. It was one of the many observations that had so pained him in the first months of his altered condition and that he now considered with amusement, if at all.

How perspectives change . . .

He and Amelia had had a very pleasant meal here just before the Buryak case and the Locksmith investigation roared to life.

With the chair moving nearly silently over the smooth oak floors, Rhyme steered into the hallway and then turned right through the open doorway of the larger of the two front parlors, the one that contained the lab.

There he braked to a stop and lowered the glass from which he was about to take a sip.

Wearing a deliveryman's brown uniform, a man of medium build, and with dark hair, stood with his arms crossed. He was looking at one of the whiteboards, the one that detailed evidence of the Alekos Gregorios murder case.

The intruder held a knife in his right hand. The pale-yellow color told Rhyme it was brass and it appeared homemade. He now guessed that the tiny filings of the metal Amelia had discovered at the scene came possibly not from making keys, but from sharpening the blade.

The man turned.

Lincoln Rhyme squinted as he stared at the man's face. He was rarely caught off guard, but he certainly was now.

Oh, he could hardly be surprised that the man in the overalls, who'd broken through his locks and security system so efficiently and quietly, was the Locksmith.

But what he would never have guessed was that the man's true identity—verified by a fast glimpse at the DMV picture on the board—was Yannis Gregorios, the man who had slashed his father to death in the backyard of the family's unpretentious mansion in a lovely neighborhood of Queens.

76

Before he said anything I was aware that Lincoln Rhyme had entered the room.

It's curious how this happens. Something about soundwaves maybe ricocheting and being absorbed differently when the dynamic form of a human being invades a space, all the more so when that person is in a complicated, motorized conveyance.

I tell him, "Don't bother to call anyone." I nod toward the RF box. "Radio frequency? It's jamming all the circuits. I turned it on when I heard you hang up with Amelia."

Lincoln's finger is in fact on a keypad. But the green light on my box means that the former cop and I are as isolated as one can be in Manhattan.

I turn back to the whiteboard on which he can see my picture and the picture of my father. His photo was taken by a crime scene technician and adequately captured the rictus of pain that preceded the peace of death.

So Lincoln considers me a suspect. I wonder why.

My picture is from the DMV. Not surprising that the police would have scoured the crime scene, my father's house, and discovered no suitable pictures of me. He had none.

Your son's a pervert . . .

"You didn't believe Xavier was the one?"

Unfazed, Rhyme said, "It wasn't my case so I didn't focus on it until I thought about the lack of defensive wounds. That somebody he knew might've done it. You'd been there earlier, maybe you came back. And were having a conversation with him. Then . . ." He nods at the knife.

I hear Joanna's voice:

Why did you want to kill me?

I needed to . . .

Like the kid posting the Los Zetas beheading, I had to have more and more and more . . .

Hence, my Visit to apartment 2019, the first time to use the knife.

And we saw how that turned out.

No. Absolutely not. You can't hurt a soul . . .

But the urge didn't leave.

And so I paid a visit to my father.

You need to talk to him about it. Tell him how the cellar affected you. It could be that he'll beg for forgiveness. You'll reconcile . . .

And that's just what I did. I met with him for dinner and talked about the imprisonment.

He said it made a man out of me.

I said, well, it certainly made me who I am.

I thanked him for dinner, left and returned a few hours later and, with three strokes, killed him.

He did beg, yes. Though for his life, not forgiveness.

Now, Lincoln studies me. It's an intense and chilling experience. The dark eyes probe. "I know you're good at what you do," he tells me and seems to mean it. "But here, how did you . . ."

Lincoln's voice fades and he gives a dour laugh with a glance at the front door. "The video that Amelia made! You got the make of the lock and picked it!"

"I'm good, yes, but I wouldn't have time to pick locks on Central Park West. I had keys to get in. I followed you down to that fire, on the lower west side. I was going to tap your assistant on the head and get images of the keys. He was lucky he left them in the ignition of the Sprinter. But I did need the video to see the type of alarm. A BRT-4200. That's a good one. I had to program three separate jamming codes. It's sophisticated." He nodded at the panel. "But as you can hear—or *can't* hear—it's not really sophisticated enough."

Lincoln closes his eyes briefly. "So *that's* how you got into the victims' apartments. Through their videos. Annabelle Talese was an influencer. Carrie Noelle ran her toy sales operation out of her apartment."

In his eyes there is a look that I choose to take as admiration.

"And it's how you met Joanna Whittaker," Lincoln says. "You watched her posts as Verum. That must have been tricky. She went to a lot of trouble to stay anonymous, I'd imagine."

I tell him, "The challenge." Then I click my tongue. "But I object to 'victim,' Lincoln. The posters are co-conspirators."

I share my theory of social media as a form of natural selection. "I'm just culling, eliminating the oblivious and stupid and weak."

Rhyme gives another look at the door.

"It's just you and me. If you're going to say your aide is back soon, I saw him leave a half hour ago. He got into his friend's car. They kissed. I know about Thom and his partner—there were articles about his loyal service to you online. So it's date night for them. And

Amelia's at headquarters. I heard her tell you. Anyway, I won't be long."

"Yannis. Do you go by that?"

"From my last name. Greg."

"Greg." His voice is analytical. Without a hint of anxiety. It occurs to me that someone in his condition faces death frequently. "Are there any other victims—sorry, but they *are* victims—other than your father?"

I think about how close I came with Carrie—the shower scene. My father's death had freed me, but Joanna had said no, and so I kept my knife in my pocket and left.

"No. Just him."

"And now you're going to kill me and leave town?"

While I would rather have made a Visit to Amelia Sachs's Brooklyn apartment—the image of her hair as hawk wings simply will not go away—it was Lincoln who had to go. Had I killed her first he would have done all he could to find me.

And when he's gone, then it will be time for my Visit with Taylor Soames.

I look Lincoln over closely. "We lock our cars, our homes, our offices, our money in banks. I know all about locks, every kind . . . But you're one that I've never come across before."

"Me?"

"A locked man. You're a locked man, Lincoln. And there's only one key to free you."

77

s that the murder weapon?" Lincoln asks.

"That's right."

"You just smeared some of his blood on the butcher knife and planted it in Xavier's locker at the shelter."

I nod, recalling sharpening my folding knife. It was that run-in with my father's ribs that required the satisfying whetstone.

Lincoln says, "Brass. Alloy of copper and zinc. Sometimes with some manganese, aluminum, arsenic.

"Chemically I've always found the metal quite interesting—it's a substitutional alloy. Some copper atoms are substituted for some of zinc. There's a symmetry to it I enjoy. But why brass? It's softer than bronze. That has a whole historic era named after it."

"Because," I tell him, "brass is the metal of keys." I scoff. "And, don't put it down, Lincoln. Brass *does* define a whole section of the orchestra."

Lincoln is shaking his head. "We found dried blood at the Locksmith's scenes. We dated it to about the time your father was stabbed to death. Never made the connection."

As if he's speaking to himself.

I move on.

"You've been banned from working for the NYPD. You're in your condition." I glance at the chair. "I'd think you'd welcome death. You've taught your wife and your protégés your skill. Passing on the torch. Do you have nerves in your neck?"

Lincoln says sourly, "I have nerves everywhere."

"You know what I mean."

"I have *sensation* in my neck. Nowhere below my shoulders."

"I don't want you to be in pain. So the jugular's out. But if I were to slice through the veins in your arms, you'd feel nothing?"

"Not true. I'd feel pretty pissed off."

How can I not smile? "You're a puzzle, Lincoln. Just like the best locks. Riddles and pin tumblers have a lot in common. You know Richard Feynman?"

"Of course. Physicist. One of the creators of the atom bomb."

"He loved locks. There wasn't much to do in Alamogordo when he was off the clock. He'd amuse himself by cracking the combination locks of the filing cabinets that held the nuclear weapons' secrets. Locks, puzzles . . ."

This has gone on for too long and now it's time to leave. I'm eager for my Visit with Taylor Soames and, perhaps, Roonie.

Stretch your hamstrings slowly and be sure to wear leg warmers . . .

I start toward him.

He tilts his head. "Before you do this. Please. Answer a question."

I pause.

"What would your idea of hell be?"

There's only one: being trapped forever in a place where I can't peer into private lives, can't slip into their bedrooms and bend close enough to feel their sleep heat radiate from their bodies. Can't cut open their secrets.

Can't cut open their bodies . . .

I do not answer him, of course.

But it seems I don't need to. I see in Lincoln Rhyme's face what might be a cast of perfect understanding. This is followed by the narrowest of narrowing eyes, which connote sorrow and regret.

And I realize to my utter shock, this look is conveying sympathy not for himself, but for *me*.

Oh, Christ, no!

The door to the second parlor, across the entryway, flies open and a half-dozen men and women, some in uniform, all with guns drawn, charge out. I'm not surprised to see Amelia in the front and I now understand what she said over the phone were lines that had been scripted to make me believe that she was downtown.

They are shouting, so loud I can feel the words in my chest, "Drop it, drop the weapon!" I'm so shocked that I'm frozen and incapable of moving, incapable of relaxing my grip on the knife.

Being trapped forever in a place where I can't peer into private lives . . .

I consider taking a step toward them.

And letting that be the end.

But they've done this before and, in the instant of my hesitation, they're on me.

78

W ell, if he isn't a people cop after all."

Rhyme cut a look to his former partner and grumbled, "Beg your pardon?"

Sellitto said, "Your interrogation. You got a confession about killing his father. And found out there were no other vics. Played a little of the old mind games. See, evidence *isn't* everything, Linc."

A shrug. "I figured as long as we had him, why not chat? Obviously he has father issues, so I thought I'd rile him up and see where it went. It's easy to get somebody to fess up when he's about to murder the confessee. But, for the record, evidence is a more *elegant* way to build a case and it always will be."

"Have to have the last word, don't you, Linc?" Sellitto was smiling.

"Uhm."

Yannis Gregorios sat in a chair, hands cuffed behind him. His eyes were constantly in motion.

Amelia Sachs did the Miranda thing, and asked, "Do you wish to waive your right to speak to an attorney before questioning?"

"No," Gregorios answered absently.

It hardly mattered; they had enough to put him away forever.

Rhyme noted that he was taking in doors and windows—well, specifically, locks and latches.

"Rookie?"

"Lincoln?" asked Ron Pulaski.

"Zip-tie his wrists."

"We've got the cuffs double locked. Nobody can get out of 'em."

Rhyme lowered his head and the man apparently came to understand that the prisoner they were soon to be taking downtown was nicknamed "the Locksmith."

"Oh, good point."

The young man slipped on the nylon restraints.

Gregorios's face revealed not the anger one might expect. His eyes were gazing at Rhyme as if the two were competitors in a champion chess match and Rhyme had just made the opening move in a game long anticipated.

The Watchmaker had once looked at him with an identical expression.

Two uniforms, a sturdy man and woman, arrived. "Transport to Central Booking."

Pulaski nodded at Gregorios and each of the patrol officers took an arm and led him to the door, Pulaski following.

"A moment?" Gregorios said. His escorts stopped. He looked back to Rhyme. "It seems we're now *both* locked men. I wonder who'll be free first."

He turned and the four vanished out the door.

To Gregorios, yes, Rhyme had expressed surprise as to how he'd breached his castle—and the other victims'.

In fact, though, his team had figured out the Locksmith's likely MO—Talese and Noelle had broadcast images of their dwellings, their security systems, their solitary lifestyles and such details as their tendency to take sleeping aids or indulging in a glass or two of wine before bed.

So Rhyme had proposed that Sachs broadcast a plea for help from the citizens in Rhyme's apartment, the camera angle wide enough to catch the locks and the alarm panel.

Would it work? They didn't know. But it was worth a try.

A surveillance team from NYPD Tech Services planted videos outside the town house and then Rhyme sent Thom off with his partner. Sellitto and Sachs had placed a tac team in the parlor.

The Locksmith had fallen for the bait.

Now, Sachs and Mel Cooper were packing up the evidence. The TV was on to a cable network's news channel and "Breaking Story" appeared. The anchorwoman reported, *"A suspect tentatively identified as the Locksmith has been arrested in Manhattan. Thirty-year-old Yannis Gregorios, a content moderator with ViewNow, has been charged with the series of break-ins that terrorized the city.*

"He was also charged with the murder of his father, Alekos Gregorios, stabbed to death last week.

"A source within the police department reported that the famous criminologist Lincoln Rhyme was part of the team that pursued the alleged killer. A former captain with the New York City Police, Rhyme is best known for capturing the Bone Collector, a serial kidnapper and killer who roamed the streets of New York years ago."

"Oh, shit," Sellitto muttered.

Rhyme grimaced. "I know, I know. Makes me mad too. They *always* get it wrong. A criminologist studies the sociology of crime and I can't think of anything more boring. I'm a *criminalist*."

"That's not what I frigging mean."

Rhyme realized that Sellitto, Cooper and Sachs had stopped their tasks and were staring his way.

And then it hit him.

Now everyone—including those in Police Plaza—would know he'd broken the prohibition on consulting.

"I don't see a problem," he said, feeling cheerful. "I *did* happen to catch the psycho, didn't I? Ten dollars says they'll forgive and forget. No, make it a hundred. Who's on?"

PART SIX

CRUCIFORM KEY

[MAY 29, 9 A.M.]

79

"Arrest him."

New York City Mayor Tony Harrison was standing at his office window, looking out at a wedge of the city, *his* city—a jurisdiction in which orders he gave and rules he set were to be carried out.

As clearly had not happened.

"Rhyme. I want him in jail. And I want his people fired. Sachs, Pulaski . . . All of them. Out. And no pensions. Can we do that?" Harrison noted that his sleeves were not rolled up in unison; some elbow showed on the starboard. He adjusted.

"I'd be careful with the pensions." This was from the large outdoorsman detective, Richard Beaufort, of his security team. He bore a striking resemblance to some actor whose name the mayor could not recall. Maybe a TV show cop. Or an FBI agent.

Beaufort said, "We have to handle it carefully. I mean, they *did* collar the Locksmith. And that Whittaker woman."

Abe Potter was present too. In contrast to the mayor's cultivated casual look, the aide was pristine in a three-piece suit, the sort you rarely saw.

The athletic mayor smoothed his lush pelt of graying hair, in a politician's 'do. "Have either of you seen Roland's statement?"

Edward Roland, his slick, billionaire opponent in the quest for the governor's mansion in Albany, had taken all of twenty minutes to issue a press release.

"No." From Beaufort.

Potter said, "I did. It's not good."

"What did he say?" Beaufort asked.

"He said that I can't control my own people. He called for me to step down. And he said the reason it took so long to stop the Locksmith was the breaches in the department. He cited those posts by Verum."

Potter observed, "Who was the psychotic niece of Averell Whittaker, and she's in jail for murder."

"The followers—and that's a lot of them—don't believe it. They're saying she was set up."

Harrison sat in the simple desk chair he'd used when he was a city councilman in Brooklyn. On his first day in the mayor's office he'd had the throne that the prior mayor had used removed and discarded. "Spin. We need to spin it. Okay, we'll make it clear that Rhyme didn't play any significant role in the investigation. That was misreported. And we'll say that what little assistance he gave—I repeat, *little* assistance—didn't contribute to finding the killer."

Potter cleared his throat. "Uhm, Tony, then why arrest Rhyme, if that was all he did?"

Harrison grimaced. Good point. He thought for a moment. "The security guard . . ."

"I'm sorry?" Beaufort rubbed his fingers and thumb together. The mayor noticed the I'm-not-sure-about-this gesture.

"Okay, Rhyme and his team commandeered the investigation. If it had been handled by the precinct and Detective Bureau, they would've closed the case earlier, and no one would have died."

Silence for a moment. Potter glanced from his boss to Beaufort, then back. "Well, I'm not law enforcement, but even I know that Rhyme and Amelia Sachs and the others close cases faster than any other team in the city."

"True," Beaufort said.

The mayor aligned sleeves once again. "You two may know that; the public doesn't."

The voting public.

"I take a firm stand. I acknowledge that they caught the Locksmith, but by running their own operation, in defiance of my orders, they set back the investigation and that *may* have resulted in the death of an innocent individual. But I'll be magnanimous about it. We'll let leak that I considered criminally negligent homicide against Rhyme but decided to go with obstruction of justice. It's a Class A misdemeanor, which means up to a year in jail. We need to find a judge who'll hit him with *some* time. Four, five months should be fine."

"Firing the others?" Potter wondered.

Harrison considered. "Too far. Suspension, no pay. Disregard of orders. Make it six months."

Beaufort stirred.

"Three months." Harrison received a nod from the detective in reply.

Potter said, "What about the disabled thing?"

"Detention can handle it." Harrison caught Beaufort's troubled face. "You and Al Rodriguez were fine spying on him, but you're not all right with this?"

Beaufort said, "The spying was for show. So the press—and the public—could see you were taking your order about consultants seriously. I never thought you'd actually want to collar him."

"It has to happen. Or I lose credibility. And Roland is all over me. We need to find a prosecutor to get on board."

Potter said, "O'Shaughnessy. He's young. He'll do anything we tell him."

Harrison said, "Call Rodriguez. Have him handle the bust. And arrange for Rhyme to come here. I don't want any raids on his town house."

"Yessir."

"No drama. He's in a wheelchair. Let's handle it with kid gloves."

"While we book him in the Tombs," Beaufort muttered.

"While we do just that," Harrison said, putting what he thought was just the right amount of whipcrack into his voice, not pleased with Beaufort's insubordination, tepid though it was.

Potter's phone hummed with a text. He read and frowned.

Harrison sighed. "Another broadside from Roland?"

"No, seems there's a disturbance on Broadway, Herald Square."

"What is it?"

"Demonstrators, protesters, about Verum. Nobody's sure yet. But Meyer's department store's burning."

He glanced at Beaufort. "Call Rodriguez. Have him take care of the Rhyme arrest." Then to Potter: "Call the chief and find out about this thing in Midtown." He scoffed and cast his gaze out upon the city. "Riot. Just what I need."

80

Alonzo Rodriguez slicked out his handlebar mustache, using the pocket mirror he carried for that purpose.

Fifty-two and somber and a cop blue to his heart, he had collared a respectable number of criminals in his days on the street. His arrest record was good and his arrest-to-conviction record exemplary. All of the perps he collared were guilty but many of them evoked some sympathy within Rodriguez. They were family men and women, they had fallen on hard times, they had children to support and the fact was the majority of them were in the slammer for non-violent drug offenses.

But the one thing that he couldn't stand and had no patience for was a law enforcer who'd broken the rules.

That offense should bring down the wrath of God.

His phone hummed. "Yes?"

His assistant said in her pleasant alto voice, "Lincoln Rhyme is here, sir. He's coming up with his aide."

"Yeah, okay." Rodriguez supposed he sounded gruff. No, he *knew* he sounded gruff. But try though he might, he could never deliver a single syllable that didn't have rough edges, like a piece of chipped shale.

He opened a bottom desk drawer and took from it a compact Glock 26. As a commander he hadn't carried a weapon on the job in several years. He kept it loaded, though not chambered. Glocks have light pulls. Now, he racked a round. Careful to keep his finger away from the trigger, he slipped the weapon into the holster, which he clipped to his belt.

Rodriguez rose and walked into the ante office. His assistant, a middle-aged woman with frothy brunette hair sprayed firmly into place, nodded. Her face was troubled. She wouldn't know what exactly was going on—her boss with a *weapon?*—but she would sense that the outcome wasn't going to be good.

In this, she was correct.

Down the hall, then into the elevator for a descent of several floors. He walked into Robbery. He approached a couple of detectives he knew. They were large men, one Anglo, one Black. They exchanged greetings.

"Need to borrow you guys for about fifteen. You free?"

With glances of curiosity toward each other, they said they were. One of them then noted the gun, and his expression made clear he had perhaps never seen a commander with a weapon affixed to his belt. "What's up, Al?"

"Gotta collar somebody. I just want backup."

"Well, sure. But only fifteen minutes? Where we going?"

"Not far."

81

had an office here," Lincoln Rhyme was telling Thom. "Back in the day."

They were on the twelfth floor of OnePP, in the hallway beside the elevators, one of which they'd just exited.

The NYPD, like many big governmental organizations, was forever renaming its offspring. Now the Crime Scene Unit was part of the Detective Bureau's Forensic Investigation Division. When Rhyme, a captain, ran the CSU, it was part of Investigation Resources.

He continued, "I didn't spend much time here. I was usually in the field or the lab."

Other differences between then and now: OnePP had been "the Big Building." The uniforms had been redesigned, and there were more women, more people of color. He inhaled. Ah, but the cleanser was the same. At least that was his olfactory recollection, though he allowed that it could easily be imagination.

He said to Thom, "Brutalist."

"What?" The aide was frowning.

"The style of the building. Architectural style."

"That's not real."

"No, it is. Concrete, angular, colorless. Ugly. Popular in the sixties and seventies."

"If I was the architect behind the movement," Thom said, "I'd hire a PR firm to come up with a better name."

The style was vastly different from the old headquarters at 240 Centre Street, which had housed the NYPD from 1909 to 1973. A more beautiful building was not to be found in Lower Manhattan. Victorian and rococo, sweeping archways and domes and spires. There was much marble and brass and beveled glass.

They continued down the hall to the office of Commanding Officer Brett Evans, the man who had volunteered to set Rhyme up with work in New Jersey and who had run interference for him with Potter and Beaufort.

Thom opened the door and they entered the ante office.

"You must be Mr. Rhyme," the personal assistant said. She was in her thirties, with quite dark skin and deep, black eyes. She wore a stylish lavender suit and Rhyme noted on the large desk two criminal law casebooks into which were wedged yellow pads, thick with scrawls. He wondered which law school she was attending at night.

"Ms. Williams," he said, noting the placard. "We're early."

She was completely unfazed that he was in a complicated wheelchair. "Commander Evans's on the phone. It should just be a minute or two."

It was just a moment later that Rhyme heard the door open once more and a voice said, "Lincoln."

He turned. Commander Al Rodriguez was accompanied by two large, unsmiling detectives. The jacket of one of the men was tugged back, perhaps so he could have easy access to his boxy gun. The gold shields looked Rhyme over and nodded. Rodriguez glanced at Thom. Rhyme couldn't remember if they'd been introduced. Maybe. He didn't bother to do so now.

"Sad day," Rodriguez said.

Rhyme was silent. There was no point in denying or validating the comment; Rhyme was interested in emotion only to the extent that blood at a crime scene contained increased testosterone and decreased cortisol, which suggested the bleeder had been angry or agitated, which might in turn allow a helpful inference about what had happened.

Other than that? Observations about feelings good or feelings bad were invariably a waste of time.

The personal assistant, Williams, appeared uncertain. "Commander Rodriguez. Commander Evans has a meeting with Mr. Rhyme in a few minutes. Is there something I can do for you?"

"I'm going to need you to step into the hall," he said firmly.

"I . . . why?"

"It's official business." He shot her a particular look and she gathered up mobile and purse and stepped out.

When the door closed Rodriguez said to Rhyme, "Let's get it over with."

The criminalist nodded.

They pushed into Evans's office—first Rodriguez, then the other detectives, then Rhyme, followed by Thom. The room was a large space on whose wood-paneled walls were hung photos and paintings of former NYPD brass.

Evans, as distinguished as ever, looked up, blinking in surprise. But the reaction faded quickly. A brief sigh. A tightening of his lips. He stood.

"You're not armed, are you, Brett?"

He shook his head.

Still, Rodriguez nodded at the detectives who stepped forward and frisked him. Rodriguez himself cuffed the commander.

"Brett Evans, you're under arrest for obstruction of justice, conspiracy, larceny, accepting bribes. There'll be other charges added later. Including homicides." Rodriguez gave him the Miranda warning.

Evans offered a soft laugh. "It's been so long since I've arrested anyone that I don't think I could do that without a prompt."

"You want to waive your right to an attorney?"

"I don't believe I will."

Rodriguez said to the detectives, "Central Booking. Lieutenant Sellitto'll be there. He's familiar with the charges."

"Sure, Al."

Evans was led out silently by the two big men.

Rodriguez pinched his handlebar mustache and said to Rhyme, "You ready to meet the mayor?"

He nodded. "This should be interesting."

82

In a dress shirt, with the sleeves rolled up, Mayor Tony Harrison rose and strode past the men in his office.

He gripped the door and seemed to debate slamming it. The panel was quite heavy, though, and it would not have been a particularly dramatic gesture. Besides, Rhyme sensed that he felt he should maintain some decorum.

Even under these circumstances.

Rhyme and Thom, along with Al Rodriguez and football-build Richard Beaufort, were in the spacious office, decked out with a museum's worth of New York historical memorabilia and offering quite the splendid view of the city, though a view that was a mere sliver of the urban sprawl that the man governed. Ironically one window faced north and in the far, far distance—invisible from here—was Albany, the place on which his sights and hopes were aimed.

Although Lincoln Rhyme had zero interest in politics, if he'd been forced to govern, he would have picked New York City in an instant over the state as a whole.

Harrison returned to his chair.

"Explain." The grating word was directed at Rodriguez. "*Brett Evans* arrested—and not him?" A look at Rhyme.

Rodriguez said, "A couple of weeks ago I asked Captain Rhyme to help me run a sting operation. It's been with full knowledge of the chief of department, the district attorney, and the department's general counsel."

"Sting? About what?"

"To get to the bottom of why there've been so many investigations and prosecutions compromised lately."

The mayor's eyes narrowed at this—the very incidents that his opponent for governor had been using as campaign fodder against him.

Beaufort sat and was silent, though he glanced toward Rhyme once or twice uncertainly.

Rodriguez continued, "I spent days looking over what went wrong, how stakeouts got made, how CIs had changes of heart—or ended up in the Gowanus Canal. I found dozens of incidents ruining investigations—incidents that just could not have happened unless somebody was tipping off suspects and defendants."

"Somebody inside . . ." Harrison muttered. "We had a mole."

Rodriguez nodded. "The only lead seemed to be that they were selling NYPD information to Viktor Buryak. So the DA had one of his prosecutors, John Sellars, bring a case against Buryak—for the murder of Leon Murphy."

"Which I threw," Rhyme said.

The mayor whispered, "You . . . you intentionally screwed up the case?"

"I did indeed."

Rodriguez added, "It was touch-and-go for a while. We weren't sure the jury would acquit Buryak but, thank God, they did. That put him back in play, on the street, with one big fear: that Lincoln—who's known, all respect, to have a bit of an ego—"

"Not a worry."

A faint smile appeared beneath the handlebar mustache. "A big fear that Lincoln would continue to go after him. We even made sure that Buryak heard that Lincoln was going to do anything he could to bring him down."

"How?"

"Oh, Buryak's people bugged the prosecution's briefing room in the courthouse. We thought it might happen and scanned it. Left the bugs in place long enough to deliver the message."

"The fuck."

Rhyme added, "We were sure Buryak would use the department mole to find out what I was up to."

Beaufort snapped, "So you were running an operation and didn't tell me or the mayor?"

Rhyme hated obvious questions and tended not to answer them.

But Rodriguez offered, "We didn't know where the leak was. Your office is copied on a lot of classified NYPD information. Somebody here could have been skimming it."

The mayor gave a laugh. "I was a suspect too."

Rhyme didn't point out the embarrassing fallacy that it hardly made sense for Harrison to deal in stolen info since screwing with investigations and prosecutions worked *against* his interest as a candidate.

Rodriguez answered more delicately. "Not you, sir, but you have a big infrastructure here. The leak could have come from anywhere." He continued, "The mole had to be pretty high up, someone with access to investigative information across all the divisions. That would include City Hall."

Beaufort asked, "How did you get to Brett Evans?"

"Just like what we hoped would happen: Buryak put one of his people on me to stop my supposed renegade investigation against him. Aaron Douglass."

Rodriguez explained, "He's a gold shield with the OC Task Force working undercover in Buryak's operation."

"Maybe he was legit but he was the only connection we had to Buryak, so Amelia and I made up a story about some drug drops at the Red Hook piers in Brooklyn."

Rodriguez said, "I put a team on Douglass. We ended up with this. Recorded at an outdoor café on the East Side. We got an undercover at a table next to Douglass and who shows up but Evans?" He put the transcript on the mayor's desk.

EVANS: *How's Buryak?*

DOUGLASS: *Thank Christ he doesn't watch the news. I told him I nailed that Sachs bitch downtown, ran over her. Then, the fuck, she shows up on TV talking about help us find the Locksmith.*

EVANS: *You could talk your way out of it.*

DOUGLASS: *Yeah, Viktor trusts me. More and more. Still.*

[Garbled noise.]

DOUGLASS: *Listen, I've got something good you can sell to Viktor. There's going to be a series of narc drops at the Red Hook piers. A lot. If you can get me details Viktor'll put it up at one of his auctions. He's got some customers'd pay large to know when a crime scene bus is taking the shipment to the Queens lab. Easy to knock over, especially if it's late at night.*

EVANS: *Excellent. I'll get on the horn with Narcotics now and get back to you . . . Aaron, let me ask you a question. You're walking a tightrope here. You haven't nailed Buryak yet. Isn't*

your captain getting impatient? Six months with nothing solid
against him. You have an endgame?
DOUGLASS: *I'm banking ten K a week. I hang in for another,*
maybe, five, six months, and then I'm out. Retiring.
EVANS: *And doing what?*
DOUGLASS: *Opening a chain of food trucks. Already got it planned.*
You can be my first customer. You get a discount.
[Laughter.]

The mayor pushed the document away. He muttered, "Jesus . . .
I never would have guessed Brett. He always seemed rock solid."

Rhyme said, "I was thinking I should've been more suspicious of
him too. There was something odd about him calling me up after I
was fired. Sure, I helped make his career, but that was years ago, and
we haven't talked much since. He was saying he'd get me a commercial job or a slot at the New Jersey State Police. But he was spying on
me, wanted to know what I was up to."

Harrison shook his head. His distinguished mane of silver hair
was at odds with his rolled-up shirtsleeves. Like now, his top collar
button was rarely fixed, his tie forever lopsided. "Looks like my firing you added a layer of complication."

Rhyme muttered, "To put it mildly."

Al Rodriguez said, "When I heard about your edict, sir, I called
Sally Willis and talked my way into overseeing the disciplinary effort. Had to run interference and make it look like Lincoln and his
team were toeing the line, while we went after the mole."

Then the mayor was looking out over the harbor. "The Murphy
murder. Did Buryak commit it?"

Rodriguez said, "No."

"What if the jury'd come back with a guilty verdict?"

"We have the real perp on ice—a safe house in Queens. A signed confession. Buryak wasn't at risk. And Sellars had some legitimate cause to bring the case: motive, means."

"We got our mole. What about Douglass?"

"He's disappeared. We're looking for him."

"And Buryak?" Harrison's face was grim. "Do you have him on tape?"

"No," Rodriguez said. "He's been as cautious as he's always been."

"So back to fucking square one with him."

"Well, about that . . ." Rhyme said absently and glanced at his phone.

83

Sitting in her Torino in a very pleasant portion of Queens, Amelia Sachs heard a crackle on her walkie-talkie.

"Detective Five Eight Eight Five, be advised, subject has been spotted in his car, heading toward home. Two blocks away. K."

"Five Eight Eight Five," she transmitted. "Is he alone? K."

"Affirmative. K."

Hell. She'd hoped to net two birds with one bust but this was the far more important avian and they couldn't wait any longer.

She dropped the Torino into gear and drove forward, then turned the corner and stopped. She was across the street from an elegant estate, nestled in some fine landscaping. She killed the engine.

"Five Eight Eight Five. I'm ten twenty-three. I have visual on subject's vehicle. Block and a half away. Get ready to move in. K."

She watched the white Mercedes sedan cruise smoothly toward her.

The four teams, in unmarkeds, responded they were ready.

She lifted the radio to her face, smelling the familiar pungent scent the devices off-gassed. "Five Eight Eight Five. He's at the intersection Holly and June. K."

Two minutes later the Mercedes pulled up to his front gate and Sachs saw his hand reach up to the visor and press the button on the remote to open the scrolly black metal gate.

Nothing happened. The receiver had been disabled by an NYPD tactical officer a half hour ago.

"Move in, move in, move in!" Sachs shouted, sprinting to the Mercedes. Her Glock was aimed at the driver's head. The other cars skidded up, one blocking him in. In just a few seconds, nine officers surrounded the Mercedes.

"Unlock the door!" she shouted.

The driver did.

"I want to see your hands at all times. You understand. At every second!"

And nodding, Viktor Buryak climbed out, arms raised. While the other officers covered her, Sachs frisked him.

As a beefy officer cuffed him, Buryak gave a wry laugh. "You're kidding me. Whatever Evans or anybody says, they're lying. You got no tapes, nothing. And what's all this goddamn SWAT shit for?"

Sachs didn't respond. She read him his rights on the charge of murder in the second degree.

In the office of Mayor Tony Harrison, Lincoln Rhyme disconnected the call from Amelia Sachs.

He nodded to Al Rodriguez, then said to him, the mayor and Beaufort, "Buryak's in custody and going to be transferred to Garner County on homicide charges."

Rhyme believed the mayor actually gasped.

Rodriguez said, "Buryak always kept himself at arm's length from anything that could implicate him. But for years we kept looking— and that included searching for any felonies or deaths within ten miles of Buryak's offices and homes—his mansion in Forest Hills and his vacation house in Garner County. Couple months ago, we found one, a contractor in Garner died in a car crash coming home from a job last year. It was written up as accidental but it was suspicious. It happened on a clear afternoon on a straightaway—and just three miles from Buryak's country house."

Rhyme said, "We got credit card receipts that showed that Buryak bought a couple thousand dollars' worth of building supplies around the time of the death. Just a theory: Had the contractor been working on his house and seen something incriminating? And had Buryak moved fast to eliminate the man and stage the accident?"

Rodriguez continued, "It all could have been a coincidence. But Amelia Sachs and Ron Pulaski drove up there and worked the scene. They found evidence linking Buryak to the worker's death."

"After all that time?"

Rhyme chose not to lecture the mayor about the skill of those two particular forensic scientists. He himself had been of some help too.

"We made him in March," Rodriguez continued, "and could've moved on him at any time, but we had to keep him in play to find our mole. Once we had Evans, it was okay to roll Buryak up."

"Jesus, Lord," Harrison said, shaking his head. Then he was gazing at Rhyme. "My apologies, Captain—the consulting situation. It was politics, of course. How I hate it."

Sometimes you hate it, Rhyme qualified silently.

"I'll cancel that goddamn ban right away. I'll call the commissioner and the chief of department." The mayor then sat back and tugged the loose tie from the left side of his collar to the right. He said to Rhyme, "And is there anything else I can do for you? Anything at all?"

After a long moment, Rhyme replied, "As a matter of fact, there might just be."

84

He'd had the lab to himself for the past hour, which was how he liked it.

Thom was in the kitchen, getting something ready for dinner, and Sachs was out buying wine and appetizers.

Tonight would be a celebration, he hoped.

He was finishing the report on the murder charge of Viktor Buryak. After Sachs and Pulaski had found evidence linking him to the same rock that contained the DNA of the contractor he'd killed, the local authorities executed a search warrant of the vacation home in Garner. The motive for the murder was what Rhyme had guessed. They found a room where Buryak was storing cash and thumb drives related to his business. It was a logical deduction that the contractor had stumbled upon the stash and was seen by Buryak. The mobster would have taken a hammer or blunt object to him and dragged him to the car then driven it to a deserted part of the state road and, with the dead man's foot on the gas, flicked the transmission into gear. After the crash, he'd then pulled the body out and struck it in the head with the telltale rock to make it seem that was the cause of death.

A small town, winding roads and more than a few accidents? The local authorities wouldn't think it anything untoward.

Rhyme put his digital signature on the report and sent it to Lon Sellitto, Amelia Sachs, the head of the NYPD's Organized Crime squad and prosecutor John Sellars, as well as the district attorney in Garner County.

On the TV high on the wall in the nonsterile section of the parlor, Rhyme noted the words:

NEWS ALERT . . .

You saw this frequently, but these words were in bright red, all caps.

The typography suggested it was not hype, but a significant event.

The chyron scrolled:

Riots and arson in three cities . . . one dead, dozens injured. Followers of Verum take to the streets.

He shut the TV off, hearing the bubbling of Sachs's Ford approaching. He'd have to tell her about these odd developments.

Glancing out the window, he saw the car skid to a stop—it seemed to be the only way she was capable of bringing vehicles to rest—directly in front of the building.

She shut the engine off but didn't climb out. She would be texting or reading a message. Maybe the report on the Buryak murder investigation he'd just sent.

It was then that he looked past her, across Central Park West, and noticed a man who seemed to be watching Sachs from behind a food truck selling Jamaican fare. He was eating a sandwich, wrapped in paper and foil.

He tossed out what remained of his sandwich and after wiping his mouth and fingers with a napkin pulled on sunglasses and a black beret.

No!

It was Aaron Douglass, Buryak's hit man.

Rhyme's temple was pulsing with blood from his accelerating heart and he struggled to remain calm as he ordered, "Call Sachs."

The phone's electronic voice replied, "Calling Sachs."

No ring; it went right to voice mail.

Christ!

Through the window, Rhyme saw that Douglass drew a gun from his belt and started across the street.

"Thom! Call nine one one. Gunman outside the town house!"

The aide appeared, phone in hand, not asking questions, dialing.

Rhyme called, "He's going for Amelia."

Thom started for the front door.

"Stop! You'll get shot too!"

The aide paused, talking to Dispatch, as Rhyme accelerated fast and slapped the automatic door opener. But before he could call out to her, Douglass stepped to the front of the car and fired a half-dozen rounds, point blank, through the windshield. The bullets easily penetrated the glass.

"No!" Rhyme cried.

Douglass turned and, as Rhyme reversed backward quickly, fired several shots his way. They were wide and hit the brownstone, digging out bits of shrapnel. One stung his cheek.

The gunman started toward Rhyme but then sirens were audible. He hesitated and sprinted south, out of sight.

A moment later Rhyme heard more shots. The police weren't that close yet. It couldn't be them. Douglass would be firing into the air to stop a vehicle and carjack it. Or perhaps simply to shoot a driver in cold blood, dump the body and steal the car.

His eyes turned back to the Torino.

Rhyme believed he could see an arm extended—perhaps beckoning for help or struggling to open the door or rising into the air as a last living gesture.

The limb remained extended for a moment and then dropped out of sight.

85

Wearing Tyvek overalls, the medical examiner was trudging forward slowly. He was not a young man, like most of the tour docs were.

If you wanted to rise to the top, the line ME work was seen generally as a stepping-stone to better medical careers—like assistant prosecutors aiming for Wall Street law firms. Rhyme knew Dr. Jonny Christen well. They'd worked together when Rhyme was a Crime Scene man and then head of the Crime Scene Unit. He and Christen would often arrive at a scene together—even when Rhyme was brass and had no reason to walk the grid, other than he loved to do so.

Christen was a legend in the ME's office. He'd officiated at the deaths of hundreds of celebrities, politicians and sports figures.

The deaths of cops too.

Which is what he was doing now.

He always seemed more respectful when examining the body of a fallen police officer than the others.

The rotund man with a white mustache now glanced down at the body that lay faceup on the sidewalk, the chest and face covered with a sheet. A shaft of sun happened to hit the gold shield on the belt and reflected outward, a sparkling starburst.

Rhyme nodded. He was looking at the bloodstained sheet. It was one that Amelia Sachs had picked out, dark gray, a color that pleased him, though you could make the argument that it wasn't a color at all, of course, but a blend of black and white. To be precise.

There was an argument to be made—Lincoln Rhyme knew this better than anybody—that the sheet might contaminate the crime scene. That was true in theory, but here, on this busy urban thorough-fare, there had been plenty of eyewitnesses and so forensics, while necessary, would be—in a very non-Rhyme linguistic construction—*less* necessary than under other circumstances.

Christen pulled up the sheet. "Three to the chest, one to the neck."

Footsteps behind him.

It was Ron Pulaski. "Lincoln, you okay?"

"Obviously I'm okay, Rookie. Don't contaminate the scene any more than it is."

Crime Scene evidence collection techs were already walking the grid.

The young officer stared at the body.

He was looking down when he heard the woman's voice. "How bad will it be?"

Rhyme turned to see Amelia Sachs walking up beside him. He answered her question with the phrase he'd just thought: "Pretty bad."

Aaron Douglass might have helped them put together hours of incriminating evidence against Viktor Buryak.

But Aaron Douglass was no more.

"No choice," she said, clearly troubled that Douglass had given her no option other than to kill him.

Returning on foot northbound on the sidewalk, Sachs had been carrying two bags of deli food. She'd witnessed Douglass fire the rounds into the Torino and at Rhyme, then run south, to where his car was parked. She'd dumped the groceries, drawn down and demanded that he drop his weapon.

He had chosen to engage—unwisely, given her handgun skills (second place isn't a blue ribbon, true, but it still means you put the slugs where they're supposed to be ninety-nine-point-nine percent of the time). Apparently his muzzle hadn't moved more than thirty degrees in her direction, before he received a tight group of rounds.

Rhyme wondered if he'd died curious about whom exactly he'd shot in the driver's seat of the Torino.

The answer to that question was: Lyle Spencer, the security chief of Whittaker Media Group.

It seemed that Spencer had quite the affection for sports cars, and Sachs had handed over the keys to him, saying, "There's a blue flasher in the glove compartment. Probably best to keep it under a hundred." She had then headed off on foot to the deli.

The lending of the car and the pedestrian grocery shopping mission were facts she had not shared with Rhyme until now—which explained his earlier panic.

Lyle Spencer, Rhyme was reflecting: the man who climbed a hundred-foot rope as if it were nothing to save Ron Pulaski's life.

The man who'd considered a swan dive from a broken window in the Sandleman Building.

The man who had been one hell of a cop but who risked it all, and lost, to try to save his daughter.

The man who now joined Rhyme and Sachs, hobbling slowly and wincing with each step.

"How are you?" Sachs asked him.

"Two ribs cracked and bruises that're the shape—and the color—of eggplants. Same size too. All right. Maybe I'm exaggerating."

It seemed that while Spencer's criminal past prohibited him from carrying weapons, he was never without PPE, personal protective equipment, when he was in the field. In this case a CoolMAX Level 3A vest.

"You'll have dinner with us." Sachs was righting the fallen groceries, the only casualty a bottle of Barolo Italian wine, whose shards she dropped into a trash receptacle.

She grimaced at the expensive loss.

"Love to but Mr. Whittaker called. He wants to see me. He's giving me a promotion." He glanced at his ruined shirt and jacket. "After a change of clothes."

"Promotion," Rhyme said slowly. He and Sachs exchanged glances, conspiratorial.

What came next fell within her bailiwick, so Rhyme remained silent and let her speak. "How'd you like a *de*-motion?"

"I'm sorry?"

"You caught the eye of some people in this case. Dep com level. They wouldn't mind if you signed on."

"Consultants are back in favor, hm? Well, honored, but you can guess what Mr. Whittaker pays me. I don't think that's in the city's budget."

"No, not consultant. True NYPD. You'd start at detective three. The demotion I mentioned was in terms of rank. You were detective first in Albany, right?"

He gave a hollow laugh. "Well, appreciate that. I really do. But the conviction, remember?"

Like most police departments, the NYPD did not allow felons to join their ranks.

Rhyme now navigated into the conversation. "You wouldn't be a felon with a pardon and an expungement of your record."

Spencer's face was still. "That only happens if there's a wrongful conviction. But mine wasn't. I did the crime, got collared. Anyway, even if the department wanted to, it can't issue pardons."

"But the governor can," Sachs said.

Spencer was frowning.

Rhyme told him, "And his handpicked candidate for Albany this coming November is Mayor Tony Harrison."

And is there anything else I can do for you? Anything at all . . .

"If you want it, we'll make it work," Rhyme continued his sales pitch.

The big man ran his hand through his short hair and Rhyme noted again the scar. And the tat on his bare arm. *T.S.* He inhaled deeply and was clearly considering the offer hard. Rhyme wondered if it were possible that his daughter somehow figured into the complex of thoughts surging within him now. Maybe he'd hoped she'd follow him onto the force.

He whispered, "Yes, I want it."

Smiling, Sachs said, "Good. Call Averell. Stay for dinner."

Spencer and Sachs returned to the town house; Rhyme had noticed Lon Sellitto pulling up in an unmarked vehicle and parking at the curb. A blue-and-white stopped just behind. He and two uniforms climbed out of their vehicles.

Sellitto looked over the crime scene at Douglass's body and at Sachs's Torino. Rhyme had called him to tell him about the shooting and that Sachs and Spencer were all right. Sellitto nodded to Rhyme then he and the others turned and crossed the street, walking up to the food truck Aaron Douglass had been using for cover.

What was this about? Long way for Sellitto and the others to come for grilled goat sandwiches.

Sellitto spoke to the vendor, who slumped and grimaced. He turned around and a uniform cuffed him and led him to the backseat of the blue-and-white. Sellitto joined Rhyme. "One of Buryak's plans was using food truck vendors as spies. Douglass ran them. We're rolling them up all over town."

The truck across the street had been there for the past few days. So Buryak's people had been surveilling him the whole time.

Sellitto nodded and said, "I gotta get downtown. You hear the latest?"

"What's that?"

"Check it out." He produced a phone and played a video of a news broadcaster. She was saying, "This clip was just posted on ViewNow and a number of other social networking platforms."

The scene cut to a video, depicting a pixelated figure in a dark, nondescript room. In a deep, electronically distorted voice, he or she said: *"Friends: Verum is a martyr in the fight against the Hidden. But I am here to pick up her cause. I am devoting myself to fighting for you— your lives and your liberty. The Hidden have to know that this is war.*

"Say your prayers and stay prepared!

"My name is Vindicta. Latin for 'revenge.' That's your sacred duty. How you pursue it is up to you."

Rhyme shook his head. So Joanna's nonsensical fiction persisted and apparently her offspring were taking it very much to heart. And the movement seemed to be growing.

He couldn't help but wonder too if the network's broadcasting the clip was itself flaming the fires. The constant battle of the press: Where was the line between informing and inciting?

Sellitto put the phone away. "We're all on alert. Somebody broke into the National Guard armory. Didn't get away with anything, but it was troubling enough." He gave a laugh. "And no, I checked, the Locksmith's still in custody."

Sellitto looked at Rhyme. "We might need you."

"I'll be here," he said.

Sellitto climbed into his car, started the engine and pulled into traffic.

On the sidewalk Rhyme swiveled his chair and looked over the street, noting the skill of the crime scene officers as they bagged shell casings, took photos and videos, made measurements of bullet angles and collected Locard's "dust." Other officers were canvassing passersby. Rhyme, Sachs and Spencer would be interviewed too, but no hurry on that.

Rhyme's eyes took in the swell of press and onlookers, moths drawn by the sharp glare of a crime scene: the astronaut-suited techs, the bus, the ambulance, the covered body, the bullet-hole-riddled windshield.

Some gazed with shock, some with fascination, some with glee subdued, some with glee unleashed.

And more than a few of them glanced at Rhyme too.

Immediately after the accident, so many years ago, he'd been aware that people tended to stare when they thought he wasn't looking, and to avoid him when they thought he was. At first this angered him; he wanted to shout, "I'm just as normal as you are!"

But over the years, Rhyme got over that. He learned that there was no such thing as normal. Who on earth had that perfect physical and mental incarnation that piloted them about flawlessly every minute of every day? Disabled is a continuum. We each have a spot on that vast bandwidth.

It's what we do with our unique frequency that counts.

Then he chided himself for lapsing into maudlin philosophy, however truly he believed those thoughts to be.

With his left ring finger, he turned the chair about and headed up the ramp to his town house, to join Amelia Sachs and their new friend.

ACKNOWLEDGMENTS

Novels are not one-person endeavors. Creating them and getting them into the hands and hearts of readers is a team effort and I am beyond lucky to have the best team in the world. My thanks to Sophie Baker, Felicity Blunt, Berit Böhm, Dominika Bojanowska, Penelope Burns, Annie Chen, Sophie Churcher, Francesca Cinelli, Isabel Coburn, Luisa Collichio, Jane Davis, Liz Dawson, Julie Reece Deaver, Danielle Dieterich, Jenna Dolan, Mira Droumeva, Jodi Fabbri, Cathy Gleason, Alice Gomer, Iven Held, Ashley Hewlett, Sally Kim, Hamish Macaskill, Cristina Marino, Ashley McClay, Emily Mlynek, Nishtha Patel, Seba Pezzani, Rosie Pierce, Abbie Salter, Roberto Santachiara, Deborah Schneider, Sarah Shea, Mark Tavani, Madelyn Warcholik, Claire Ward, Alexis Welby, Julia Wisdom, Sue and Jackie Yang. You're the best!